Library of
Davidson College

A

PAPER CITY,

BY

D. R. LOCKE,

(PETROLEUM V. NASBY,)

AUTHOR OF "SWINGING ROUND THE CIRKLE," "EKKOES FROM KENTUCKY,"
"MORALS OF ABOU BEN ADHEM," ETC.

THE GREGG PRESS
UPPER SADDLE RIVER, N.J.

First published in 1878 by Lee & Shepard
Republished in 1968 by
The Gregg Press
121 Pleasant Avenue
Upper Saddle River, New Jersey, U.S.A.

Library of Congress Catalog Card Number: 68 - 57539

828
L814p

69-3715

Printed in United States of America

AMERICAN NOVELS OF MUCKRAKING, PROPAGANDA, AND SOCIAL PROTEST

The United States has suffered quite a few spells of sickness, if one may judge by the long and varied procession of novels dealing with the ills of its society. As each generation has sought assurances for the social hope that springs eternal in a democracy, muckraking, propagandizing, and advocating reforms have been not only implicit in partisan politics but also germane to literary production. While it has been said that Americans are readier to believe in charlatans than in utopias, there remains a sneaking feeling that maybe Oscar Wilde was right when he remarked: "Progress is the realization of utopias." Some such moral—if indeed moral it be—may be derived from the Gregg series of "American Novels of Muckraking, Propaganda, and Social Protest."

One purpose underlying the selection of the titles in the series is to provide examples of socio-economic novels which are presently out of print but which are nevertheless important in showing the history of the genre, a topic so far treated by historians only sporadically. Most of these works can rarely be found in the original editions; and many were printed on paper which is beginning to shatter. The series should prove a boon to librarians and to scholars who work in the fields of literary history and the social sciences. Its usefulness as supplementary reading for college courses in American studies and social history speaks for itself.

In turning the pages of the novels we begin with the groping 1830's and the fabulous 40's—when, as Emerson put it, every man in New England was running around with a plan for reorganizing society in his vestpocket. And we end with the "Era of the Muckrakers"—when the long-existent fervor to remake the world nearer to the mind's desire became a contagious fever, and phrases were bandied about like "frenzied finance," "conspicuous consumption," "malefactors of great wealth," "how the other half lives" and "the shame of the cities." In this series we find artifacts from the days following the panic of 1837, when Horace Greeley devoted a regular column in his *Tribune* to the kind of "associationism" that overtook Brook Farm; and we come along to the period early in the present century when the "yellow" journalism of Hearst and Pulitzer reached full flower and young Sinclair

Lewis swept the floors of Helicon Hall, the socialist community supported by Upton Sinclair with the profits of *The Jungle.* That was the epoch when the young intellectuals stormed college halls to hear Jack London expound the principles of socialism. In between, we find specimens emanating from the Gilded Age, with the ensuing clamor against business combinations eventuating in the Sherman Anti-Trust Act of 1890, and the agricultural depression that aroused Midwestern farmers to "raise less corn and more hell" or to align themselves with the People's Party. Business panics in 1873 and 1893 stirred up the coals, young preachers discovered the social gospel, bewhiskered anarchists were the chief "reds," strikes became for the first time a matter of wide public concern, and the play based on *Uncle Tom's Cabin* was the best money-maker on the stage.

One of the features of the list is a careful selection of works concerned with the Negro. The earliest is *The Slave,* by the historian Richard Hildreth. It was not only the first fully developed antislavery novel, but a pattern-maker for the many subsequent tales presenting the chief character as a light-skinned mulatto. The Russians translated it in the 1950's. Another is Harriet Beecher Stowe's *Dred,* a sequel to *Uncle Tom's Cabin* and perhaps more cogent propaganda. The idea that the Negro is constitutionally unable to cope with American society is curiously set forth in *Liberia,* by Sarah J. Hale, a staunch Yankee best known for her verses about Mary and her little lamb. Mrs. Hale was propagandizing for solving the slavery problem by returning the Negroes to Africa. Presenting the Southern side, *Aunt Phillis's Cabin,* by Mary H. Eastman, has been chosen from the batch of novels which sought in vain to counter the effect of Mrs. Stowe's world-famed classic of protest. The blasting of Northern prejudice against the Negro after the Civil War is well illustrated in two works: Rebecca Harding Davis's *Waiting for the Verdict,* a title still apt a century after it first appeared, and Albion W. Tourgée's tract for the times *Pactolus Prime,* which vitriolically scores the essential prejudice of white against black and is, apparently, the first American novel dealing with the Negro problem with a setting in Washington, D. C.

Joaquin Miller's *Life Amongst the Modocs* deals with the mistreatment of Indians. Few in number but judiciously chosen for illustrative purposes are stories exposing the white slave traffic—

from the days when the Mann Act was legislated and city slums were being muckraked both in and out of fiction to a degree probably more thorough than is the case even today. Among the other problems considered in these stories are divorce, prisons, and the criminal code, political corruption, pacifism, states rights, the social responsibilities of the churches, the plight of the Jew and the Immigrant, and even medical frauds.

But the theme governing the largest single element in this collection is the business tycoon and the battle between the capitalist power elite and the working class. The range in the picturization of "the typical American figure," as Henry James declared the captain of industry to be, runs quite a gamut in the series, from the romantic treatment in *Sevenoaks,* by the first editor of *Scribner's Magazine,* to the excoriation of corporation machinations by avowed socialists not unacquainted with Karl Marx. The tycoons pilloried range from bankers, real estate promoters, mill owners, and railroad magnates to lumber barons. One might view the development of this theme in the amazing profusion of fictional examples as a symbol of the growing unrest precipitated in a traditionally agrarian society bewildered by its confrontation with huge industrial corporations and big cities. But possibly it proves no more than the homely wisdom distilled into the humorist's wisecrack: "We have met the enemy—and the enemy is us!"

PROFESSOR CLARENCE GOHDES
Duke University
Durham, North Carolina

September, 1968

DAVID ROSS LOCKE

David Ross Locke was born in Vestal, New York, in 1833, the son of Nathaniel Reed Locke, a Revolutionary War soldier, and Hester (Ross) Locke. At the age of ten, he was apprenticed as a printer's devil to the Cortland, New York, *Democrat,* where he remained until 1850. His apprenticeship finished, he worked as an itinerant printer, travelling in both the North and the South. It was during these years that he encountered and learned to detest the white trash whom he was to satirize ten years later in the "Nasby Letters." In 1852 he founded the Plymouth, Ohio, *Advertiser,* and married Martha Bodine. In 1856 he started the Bucyrus, Ohio, *Journal,* to which he contributed short stories. Two meetings with Abraham Lincoln in 1858 and 1859, and the beginning of the Secessionist movement projected the young radical newspaperman into a career of political journalism which was to make him the most famous pro-Northern propagandist of the Civil War and Reconstruction Eras. In 1861 Locke assumed the editorship of the Findlay, Ohio, *Jeffersonian,* and it was in this paper that the first "Nasby Letter" appeared. The letters were collected and published as a book in 1864. In 1865, Locke visited Lincoln in Washington, and then went to Toledo, Ohio, to become Editor of the *Blade,* which he later bought. He was Editor, for a short time, of the New York *Evening Mail.* Although offered political posts by both Lincoln and Grant, Locke's only political ambition was to become an alderman of the Third Ward of Toledo, a goal which he attained in 1886. He died of tuberculosis two years later.

Locke was a prolific writer. Not only did he publish newspaper articles and the immortal "Nasby Letters," but he wrote political pamphlets, essays, a narrative poem, and two very good novels. The "Nasby Letters" made him wealthy and famous, and are in print today in several editions.

"Petroleum Vesuvius Nasby, late pastor uv the Church of the New Dispensation, Chaplain to his Excellency the President, and p. m. at Confederate x roads, Kentucky," epitomized Locke's hatred of the ignorant, bigoted, anti-democratic, cowardly Southerners — the "Copperheads" who ranted about the necessity for Negro slavery and backed up their arguments with quotations torn from the Old Testament. These Letters were admired by his friend Lincoln, who said, a month before his assassination, "For the genius to write these things, I would gladly give up my office." And Grant called Locke "the fourth arm of the service" in the Civil War. The Letters were an immediate success with the Northern public, especially after the great political cartoonist Thomas Nast began to illustrate them.

In the "Nasby Letters," Locke utilized humorous devices such as misspellings, deformed grammar, *non sequiturs,* hyperbole, and fantastic juxtaposition of ideas, in order to caricature the warped intellectual processes of the country parson who "wrote" them. In his novels, which are equally bitter in their contempt for the baser elements of society, Locke adopts a more conventional, narrative literary style, that of the omniscient author. And his target is economic greed and mismanagement, instead of ignorance and racism.

In 1873 occurred one of the periodic "money panics" which shook the American economy of the nineteenth century. This time, the causes seemed to be uncontrolled speculation in railroad construction, and the general instability of the financial structure following the Civil War. The failure of the banking house of Jay Cooke made things worse, the New York Stock Exchange closed, and by 1877, approximately 18,000 businesses were bankrupt, as well as most of the railroads. Locke, in addition to his extensive knowledge of the grubbier side of politics, had studied the economic forces which brought about catastrophes such as the Panic of '73.

A Paper City, which appeared in 1879, was his commentary on this post-Civil War "boom or bust" situation. "New Canton, the meanest little town in the State of Illinois," is a community built on dreams, in which the citizen "lived in expectation of seeing. . .stately buildings upon his land, and of selling his ground for more per foot front, than it cost per acre." The town of "New Canton," with its vulgar, greedy, narrow inhabitants has reappeared many times in the American novel, reaching its apotheosis in Sinclair Lewis' "Zenith." But Locke is more interested in the analysis of a financial debacle than in attacking the Philistines. As a result, *A Paper City* has more to offer to the historian and the moralist than to the lover of literature or the bourgeois-hater. It is a coldly objective work by an author whose avowed purpose in everything he wrote was to expose and correct contemporary social, political, and monetary abuses; and who made Nasby say: "Wat posterity will say I don't know; neither do I care. It's this generashen I'm going for." Locke's writings exerted a tremendous influence upon those whom he hoped to reach, and are being gradually reprinted and studied today by those who wish to look at late nineteenth-century America through the eyes of one of its shrewdest and harshest critics.

Upper Saddle River, N. J.   F. C. S.
October, 1968

A WORD OR TWO.

THE wonderful growth of the Great West, a growth, which, in the short space of a man's life-time, converted vast praries and interminable forests into gardens, and the humblest hamlets into great and opulent cities, developed a spirit of speculation, which was, in some instances amusing, and, in others tragical.

All the cross-roads of the West expected to become Chicagos, and every man, owning one hundred and sixty acres of land, lived in expectation of seeing, before he should depart, stately buildings upon it, and of selling his ground for more per foot front, than it cost him per acre.

The following pages simply record the rise, progress and fall of one of the thousands of these "cities," and it has the merit, if no other, of being entirely free from exaggeration.

For many of the chapters of the book, I am indebted to the brilliant and facile pen of "Shirley Dare." The intelligent reader, and all readers are presumed to be intelligent, will have no difficulty in determining what part of the work is hers.

D. R. L.

CONTENTS.

CHAPTER I.
PAGE.
NEW CANTON AS IT WAS 9

CHAPTER II.
MORE ABOUT NEW CANTON 25

CHAPTER III.
THE GARDINER FAMILY AND SOME OTHERS . . 36

CHAPTER IV.
A CHANGE OF HEART 51

CHAPTER V.
NEW CANTON UNDER A CLOUD 61

CHAPTER VI.
JAMES GARDINER MAKES TROUBLE 74

CHAPTER VII.
Mrs. Burt's Husband's Wife 85

CHAPTER VIII.
A Wedding Council 101

CHAPTER IX.
A Public Meeting in New Canton . . . 118

CHAPTER X.
Tom Paddleford's Wedding 132

CHAPTER XI.
An Evening's Amusement in New Canton . . 155

CHAPTER XII.
The Ups and Downs of the City. — A Lawsuit . 171

CHAPTER XIII.
Eliphalet Butterfield's Daughter . . . 189

CHAPTER XIV.
James Gardiner makes an Effort to Reform . 203

CHAPTER XV.
New Canton in the Dumps 215

CHAPTER XVI.
A Chance Meeting 226

CONTENTS.

CHAPTER XVII.
Mr. Burt Displays Genius as a Financier . 233

CHAPTER XVIII.
The New of the Moon 246

CHAPTER XIX.
How New Canton Prospered 258

CHAPTER XX.
Flush Times in New Canton 264

CHAPTER XXI.
Playing at Love 273

CHAPTER XXII.
Mr. Burt Buys a Piano 287

CHAPTER XXIII.
The Conservatives begin to Believe . . . 301

CHAPTER XXIV.
High Scandal in New Canton 310

CHAPTER XXV.
New Canton Enters on a Higher Plane . . 325

CHAPTER XXVI.
The Cloud Bigger than a Man's Hand . . 340

CHAPTER XXVII.
EMELINE AND JIM 350

CHAPTER XXVIII.
ONE NAIL DRIVES ANOTHER OUT . . . 362

CHAPTER XXIX.
SOMETHING HAPPENS 373

CHAPTER XXX.
THE EFFECT ON NEW CANTON 377

CHAPTER XXXI.
THE TROUBLE THAT CAME UPON THE GARDINERS . 387

CHAPTER XXXII.
MORE FAILURES 395

CHAPTER XXXIII.
THE CONDITION OF THE PRINCIPAL FAMILIES . . 404

CHAPTER XXXIV.
WHAT MR. BURT FOUND IN CHICAGO. . . . 409

CHAPTER XXXV.
WHAT HAPPENED TO TOM PADDLEFORD . . . 416

CHAPTER XXXVI.
WHICH IS THE LAST 421

A PAPER CITY.

CHAPTER I.

NEW CANTON AS IT WAS IN ITS FIRST, SECOND, AND THIRD PERIODS.

NEW CANTON was originally the meanest little town in the state of Illinois, which puts New Canton very low in the scale of towns. At its beginning it had a post-office, a blacksmith's shop, a very small school-house, a Methodist chapel, and a dozen dwellings, set down in the mud and desolation of a wide prairie. It was the same for a dozen years. Wandering Israelites, of a misanthropic turn of mind, would, about three times a year, open a stock of ready-made clothing, and invite trade; but they invariably left the place as soon as they had gathered cash or credit enough to do business somewhere else. They always afterward spoke of New Canton with a sigh of regret for wasted time. About three times a year a sad-eyed photographer, thin of face and long of hair, who had failed everywhere else, would rent the upper story of the village store, and urge the people to "secure the shadow ere the substance fade," an invitation which only resulted in visitors to look, who all intended to have their "pictures taken" at some period more or less remote, but who never did. His stay was always short; and he generally walked to the next town, leaving his apparatus, as security for board, at the Eagle Hotel. The traveling dentist found his way thither at shorter intervals; but he generally followed the example of the photographer: and the lecturers on phrenology, who came regularly, always went away sadder and wiser men.

The landlord of the Eagle had a large and varied assortment of photographic, dental, and phrenological apparatus stored in the room behind his bar; for it was a melancholy fact, that those who left them in pledge never returned to redeem them; and it was his belief, that the unfortunate " artists," "professors," and " doctors " drowned themselves in Soggy Run, just out of the village. He felt that a short stay in New Canton by a stranger would lead to suicide, in the natural run of things.

"I don't blame 'em," was his remark. " New Canton don't take to picters, to science or teeth. I never know'd a dentist, a picter man, or a lectrer on phrenology to git out of here whole. They ginerally come in ridin' in the stage, all so gay; but they ginerally go away on foot. It's curious: people, not only in New Canton, but everywhere, are a-comin' in a-ridin', and a-goin' out on foot. I don't mind the dentists; their tools kin be used by the gunsmith, and I git suthin' out uv 'em. Photograph men an't bad; some day I shel be able to sell their cam'rers and kimikels, and my children kin play with 'em, anyway. But lectrers on phrenology! bah! w'at kin I do with a lot o' skulls? Not one on 'em ever had any clothes that I could levy onto."

And, thus saying, he would light another pipe, and

wonder, as he smoked, if New Canton would ever come to any thing.

It came to something, in the course of time. The prairie was rich; and immigrants from the Eastern States filled it up. A branch road was built from the Illinois Central to New Canton; and, trade centering there, it became a very decent, quiet village, of perhaps a thousand people, with churches, shops, saloons, and other modern conveniences.

At the time this history opens, New Canton was neither the insignificant prairie village nor the more substantial railroad town. Its sleepy quietude had gone; the sound of the hammer and saw was heard within its borders; busy and bustling men filled its streets; and its people dropped the word "village," in speaking of it, for the more satisfactory one of "city." Its appearance, however, hardly improved enough to justify the change; and it was made with some awkwardness.

The regulation building, for business and dwelling purposes, was a story-and-a-half frame house, gable end to the street, and, as a rule, unpainted. The few that had been painted looked worse than those that had not — healthy, natural ugliness being always preferable to decayed beauty. Beside the honest, weather-beaten walls, the patchy red and white of such as had been painted and peeled looked as though they had an attack of timber-measels, and never got over it.

The town had the whole prairie to grow over; and might have reached a hundred miles north and a hundred miles south without barrier; but, as if land was too dear to be wasted, lots were laid out as in the heart of a city, twenty by a hundred feet, giving room enough in front for a patch of red and white balsams, and behind for a clothes-line. The wood-pile, was invariably, in the back alley, which differed in no respect from the back alleys of other Western villages. A broken wagon stood at the entrance, convenient for the thin and piratical pig to pensively scratch against; its entire length was strewn with oyster and tomato cans, baking-powder tins, and broken dishes, left by the receding waves of the twice-yearly house-cleaning. Its precincts were sacred to that emblem of immortality — the cast-off hoop-skirt, the only article on the face of the earth utterly indestructible. Every housekeeper who had a broken or half-worn article, too good to throw away and too bad to steal, left it in the alley, sure of finding it should it ever be wanted. Wheelbarrows with broken wheels, old bedsteads, chairs mourning legs, burned-out stoves, cupboards that would not fit, — every thing that, from through carelessness or lack of use, demanded storage-room, was left in the alleys, to the weather, the pigs, and the boys.

In New Canton, to have a two-story house, with a garden and a currant border, was to be an aristocrat, especially if a man chose to further define his consequence by a picket-fence and gate-posts headed by two immense wooden balls. At the side of the lot would be a larger gate, — not that it was ever used, but as an assumption that it was necessary to admit the carriage of the owner. But few had carriages; but they liked the suggestion that in time they might have such taxable property.

There were few of these houses in New Canton; and, to enlist the sympathies of those who are interested only in the truly refined and elevated, it may be said now, with distinctness, that it is with the occupants of these two-story houses that this story has to do.

New Canton was the moon-ribbed, ill-fed ghost of a city — not a one-horse but a one-mule town, begotten by the lying promise of four spectral railroads, on the expectation of an impossible ship-canal. One speculator, with cheek of brass and tongue hung upon swivel; three speculators not so gifted, but equally unscrupulous, with just as little to lose; and one honest but deluded man, adopted the creature, and chattered men into the belief there was stuff in it for a lusty present and a vigorous future.

It had two newspapers, whose editors hated each other like pretty women, and who never agreed upon any thing but the prospects of New Canton; three churches, on very bad terms with each other, but on wonderfully pleasant relations with the world; four lawyers, each of whom spent the most of his time wondering how any man could entrust business with such knaves as the others; three physicians, each of whom in confidence assured everybody else that the others were quacks, and remarked, with solemn countenance, when the bell tolled for a death: "Mrs. Smith is gone at last, poor woman! I didn't think she would last so long. Borax" — or Blister, as the case might be — "was attending her. But she had a wonderful constitution. Time was when some qualification was necessary to practice medicine."

At this era in its history New Canton made a thriving show — upon paper. Railroads! Railroads were more numerous upon its map than common highways a year before. The "Great Central," the "Atlantic and Pacific," the "Midland," the "Consolidated Continental," each with its score of feeders, were all to cross at New Canton, making it the great railroad center of the United States. The map looked like a magnified spider-web, with New Canton for a fly-catcher in the center.

This map and the expectations on which it was based were the offspring of the active and intelligent mind of Mr. Charles Burt, a man of a type very common to the country during the last twenty-five years.

Mr. Burt settled as a dentist in New Canton. He came by accident, and stayed for a purpose. He intended at first to open an office, and "grow up with the country." He had known Mr. Gardiner, who did the small banking for the town: they were from the same Connecticut town, and had gone to school together. He did not open an office, however; but for several weeks wandered about the village, evidently carrying an idea, which in the course of time would see the light.

It came one morning — full-grown, adult. He got together, in Gardiner's bank, that estimable gentleman, Col. Peppernell, Capt. Peak, and 'Squire Sharp, and, in the phrase of American business men, "had a proposition to make to them."

The conduct of Mr. Burt was singular, before he reached his theme. Without giving any reason, he closed the blinds of the little back office, stuffed a paper wad in the key-hole, and carefully shut the door of the coat-closet, the others sitting in some wonderment.

"What under heavens 're you about?" asked Peppernell, his fish-eyes following these mysterious movements.

"Gentlemen, when one has a million of dollars to make, he don't care about showing everybody how it is done."

Sure that no one was listening, he unrolled a map of the state of Illinois on the table. With a pair of dividers, one point on New Canton, he described a circle with great solemnity.

"Gentlemen, this line shows a radius of one hundred miles from New Canton. I assert, and my action is based upon the assertion, that it is possible for New Canton to do the entire trade of not only that country, but of great areas in other directions."

He paused; and silence fell upon the company, as if they were considering this proposition.

"How are you going to do it?" asked Mr. Gardiner, as being the one, who, from his position as the financial head of New Canton, was the proper person to break silence.

"Soggy Run!" was the quick and decided answer.

"What about Soggy Run?" was the natural question of Mr. Gardiner.

"Dry six months in the year, frozen up rest of the time," was Peppernell's remark.

Mr. Burt took no notice of Peppernell, but proceeded to Mr. Gardiner's query:—

"Soggy Run, as you see, empties into the Catfish, twenty miles below here; Catfish empties into Eel Creek, twenty miles below that. There appears to be no connecting water between Eel Creek and the Illinois River, one hundred miles below, but I have no doubt that there is. If an exploration or survey fails to discover any such water, the building of a canal to connect the system of streams of which Soggy Run may be said to be the father with the Illinois River is not an impossibility in this day of enterprise and development. This done, you will see that the Soggy Run system mingles with the placid waters of the Illinois one hundred miles below Peoria, giving us just one hundred miles' advantage over that city. The idea is to improve Soggy Run — slack-water it, dam it here, dredge it there, turn Cow Run into it above this, so there'll be no want of water for any craft, from a stern-wheeler to the biggest side-wheeler that ever blew up on the Mississippi.

"What follows? All the produce of this vast territory must come here for shipment. This makes it a point, you see. All the railroads will have to come to this point, to get their share of the immense freight centering here. There is, probably, coal underlying this whole territory. With coal in exhaustless quantities and with our wonderful freight facilities, manufactures spring up, great mercantile interests center here, New Canton becomes next to Chicago in size and power, and every man wise enough to take advantage of it becomes a millionaire. I have made all the calculations. The work can be done for three millions of dollars — a mere bagatelle, considering the returns; and we will, if we are alive to our interests, put it through at once, gentlemen."

"How much money have you to invest?" queried Peppernell.

"Not a dollar!" was the prompt reply. "If I had three millions I shouldn't want to go into this — "

"None of us have a dollar," was Peppernell's answer.

"Of course, we haven't," was the cheerful reply of the philosophical Burt, as though the last obstacle in the way of their undertaking the project was removed. "If we had all the money we wanted, we'd see New Canton further. We don't go into enterprises because we have the money, but because we haven't. To carry out this particular great enterprise we don't need any money — that is, not much. Mr. Gardiner's name will give us credit, and credit is the same as money: for if people know we can pay they never want us to. With an array of respectable names, capitalists from abroad will furnish the means for the great system of internal improvements — and, by heavens! I never thought of it before — we can get an appropriation from Congress, if your member has sense enough to take stock in the enterprise and get inside with the railroad men so that his vote will tell. Money! All the money we want is enough to pay the cost of the incorporation of the company and maps. We can't get on without maps."

"But how are we to make money for ourselves out of all this?" queried Mr. Gardiner.

"My dear sir, we shall organize a land company. We shall buy up all the land, quietly, about this great center, at five dollars an acre. We shall lay it out in business lots, in manufacturing lots, in city-residence lots, and in suburban lots. That along Soggy Run will be laid out in levees. Then, with maps, pamphlets, and the papers, we will show the world what New Canton is to be, and —"

"Sell lots?" said Peppernell, inquiringly.

"Precisely so," was Burt's answer; "and whoever comes to buy will find that New Canton property has a value." (2)

The meeting dissolved without coming to any conclusion. Gardiner, Peak, and Sharp were disposed to laugh at Burt as an enthusiastic dreamer, a man of some ability, doubtless, but as for making a city of New Canton, that was more than Burt or any man belonging to New Canton was able to do.

Mr. Burt, however, took Peppernell aside that afternoon, and had a long conversation with him, leaving that worthy mightily convinced.

The next time the project was discussed among the four, Col. Peppernell looked wise. He had thought the matter over, and was considering it. It was well enough to laugh at Burt; but it would not do to set down every bold idea coming from original men as chimerical, just because we never happened to think of it. People laughed at Fulton's steamboat, and he believed it took a great deal of work to get an appropriation made for the telegraph.

Burt haunted his men in their offices, waylaid them in their houses, waited for them after church. In the most impossible places, no matter where they went, up started Burt, paper in hand, covered with figures.

It is justice to Mr. Burt to say that he was the farthest remove from any thing spread-eagle-like or Micaberish in manner. A patient, polite, keen-visaged man, equally considerate of others' self-respect and his own, who never made himself offensive in any way, never obtruded, never took too much time, but was pertinacious, agressive, interesting — he seldom failed to make himself acceptable, if not his schemes. If it had suited his game to play a loud, overbearing part, he, doubtless, would have proved equal to it; but business men like the treatment of gentlemen, and it suited Burt's physique and tastes to adopt it. His appearance was fitted to carry out the idea. His spare figure, always neatly dressed; his voice, moderate, gentle, and impressive, like his gestures, the most characteristic of which was a gentle, detaining pressure of two fingers on the listener's arm.

"Don't you see, Mr. Gardiner, twenty thousand acres of this land at five dollars — they will raise as soon as we want it, so we will put it at ten — is two hundred thousand dollars. Very good. Cut that land up into lots, seven to the acre — it's as well to be liberal, though you can get eight good lots out of an acre — and you have one hundred and forty thousand lots. Did you ever figure on the profit in this kind of thing? Suppose you sell those lots at the absurdly low price of one hundred dollars each. What have you got? One hundred and forty thousand lots at one hundred dollars each foots up the comfortable sum of fourteen millions of dollars — enough for all of us, I should say. But suppose we don't sell them all. The land will never be worth less than it is now. Suppose we sell half. Seven millions. But they will average more than a hundred apiece. They can't go less than three hundred, and they'll sell for that as fast as you can make the deeds for them. Forty-two millions. And the choice lots, the business property — a thousand dollars now, ten thousand ten years from now. Astor made his money in real estate. Real estate is the basis of every big fortune in America. Why, what do you suppose is the average value of arable land in England? Seven hundred dollars an acre! Mr. Gardiner, we sit here with our hands folded, with fortunes within our reach."

' But, Mr. Burt, to do all this will require capital."

' Not a dollar. We take contracts for the land, and sell the lots; start improvements — or say we're going to start 'em; people come in, and they bring the capital. Those who buy at a hundred will want to make them worth two hundred. They put money in Soggy Run and the railroads; and by that time we shall have capital — bonds, mortgages, and securities of all kinds. We help with the rest. Property goes up a hundred per cent, two hundred, five hundred, a thousand! It's clear enough."

"But why don't all towns do the same thing? There are other New Cantons."

"There are a great many New Cantons, Mr. Gardiner. But there isn't everywhere a set of far-seeing men who can see their opportunities and improve them."

And, after he was alone, he said to himself, "There are many New Cantons, but there is but one Burt."

With the others he was equally urgent, polite, and persistent.

"Talk of selling! What does a working-man have to pay for the lot in Chicago on which he builds his house? Five, six, seven, eight hundred dollars. Offer him one in New Canton for one hundred, and see how quickly he will come here, if we give him work to do. How will we give him the work? Easy enough. Start factories; encourage manufacturers to come to us; make business here. The bringing of business here sells the lots, and the settlement of the lots makes more business. Twenty thousand people support a theatre. A theatre employs fifty people. Those fifty people employ an extra tailor, an extra shoemaker, an extra printer. Then we shall have to have a drayman, and he will have to have a lot. New Canton will reach the dignity of a dray. All these people have to have lots. And we have the lots. We shall want water-works. We shall tax the city. We employ hundreds of working-men. They have to have lots. There have got to be lots for market-houses, churches, parsonages, colleges. All want lots. My dear sir, it's a dead sure thing. All that is needed is energy and promptness. Prompt is the word."

And, by dint of steady talk, and a suave persistency that waived taking No for an answer, with scraps of general information concerning the matter in hand which the others did not possess, he impressed the idea upon those he had marked, and led them away captive.

The New Canton Land Company, capital stock $200,000, was organized, with Peppernell, Sharp, Peak, Gardiner, and Burt, as directors, who immediately elected Col. Job Peppernell president; Thomas Gardiner, Esq., vice-president; and Chas. Burt, Esq., secretary and treasurer; these directors subscribing all the stock.

The company very promptly borrowed five hundred dollars of Mr. Gardiner; and with that modest sum got out maps and other printed matter. Col. Peppernell was so much interested in the project that he resigned his office of sheriff, in order to give his whole mind and time to the project, notwithstanding the fact that his salary had been enough to support him, and that his deputies were sufficient in number and anxious enough to hold their places to keep him full of liquor eighteen of the twenty-four hours.

Then the company bought up all the ground they could get on credit; or, rather, took contracts for all they could get. They were not particular about prices or terms, so that no money in hand was required. They made contracts by which they agreed to pay so much an acre for land within a stipulated time, the conveyances to be made by the seller, and mortgages to secure the back payments to be executed by the company, when the first payments were made.

They paid, or agreed to pay, ten, twenty, and thirty per cent more for land than its owners ever supposed it worth; and real estate went up in value to prices that a month before would have looked preposterous. Mr. Burt took all that was offered, and at any price.

When ordinary farming land reached fifty dollars an acre, the conservative Gardiner took alarm, and urged Burt to be cautious.

"Cautious, my dear sir! why, this is what we want, and is the bottom idea of the venture. What is land at fifty dollars an acre which we sell, when cut up into lots, at seven hundred? I am entirely willing to pay a hundred — as we pay it."

And he bought industriously till the land company had contracts for half the territory within five miles of the village. This accomplished, maps, gorgeously colored, were issued, accompanied by descriptive pamphlets. These maps and the pamphlets showed advantages appertaining to New Canton that the oldest resident had never dreamed of, and probably never would if it had not been for the efforts of these energetic gentlemen.

Mr. Gardiner found it much easier to get into a speculation with a man of the Burt kind than it was

NEW CANTON AS IT WAS.   23

to get out. Five hundred dollars once in, it was easy enough for Mr. Burt to checque another five hundred for other purposes, and, as he was the heaviest stockholder in the concern — that is, as he had one undivided quarter, in place of one-fifth — he was bound to stand by his investment, especially as it was simply a matter of advances, which would be repaid out of the first proceeds. And so, to build a building, and get out more maps, and send out agents, and employ surveyors, it was no time at all before Mr. Gardiner had ten thousand good honest dollars standing to his credit on the books of the company, all of which had been used in its business.

But he consoled himself with looking at the representations of the city, that his money had paid for, which on the maps covered an area of eight square miles. There were displayed on it beautiful squares, bordered with lofty trees, the avenues surrounding them filled with carriages of all kinds, from the modest pair to the ostentatious six-in-hand and the eccentric tandem. There were mechanics' institute halls, institutes of arts and sciences, fountains in full play, water-works, market-houses, engine-houses, city-halls, libraries, and all the buildings, public and private, for a city of half-a-million of people. In the pamphlet it was expressly stated, that, while the moral and educational facilities of the city had been looked after carefully, the more material aspects of civilized life had not been forgotten, as would be seen by the number of engine-houses on the map. No city in the country was better provided against fire, and it was right that it should be so. Of what use would be four universities, twelve churches, and four libraries, to the thoughtful student, if they were liable at any time to be licked up by the red-tongued destroyer? New Canton would be wise enough to profit by the misfortunes of her sister, Chicago, and make ample provision against such a disaster as that which would have killed any less enterprising and recuperative city.

On this same map — which, it is needless to say, was the work of the ingenious Mr. Burt — Soggy Run was shown as it was to be. There were long lines of levees, with steam-boats tied up, receiving and discharging freight from and to all parts of the civilized world. It was a stroke of his inventive genius to have packages of goods marked " Calcutta," of tea from China, and iron from Sweden rolling off from some boats, while others were represented as taking on cargoes of grain and manufactured articles, consigned to well-known and eminent merchants in those countries.

These maps and pamphlets distributed — they were, so to speak, the seed of the enterprise — Mr. Burt sat down calmly, and in confidence awaited his harvest.

CHAPTER II.

MORE ABOUT NEW CANTON.

THE maps and the pamphlets distributed, and the effect showing itself in the increased number of people that immediately came into the place with inquiries as to real estate, Mr. Burt became at once the most prominent man in the place. He was not only the inventor of the land company, but he was its motive power. Without him there would have been no land company; without him, it would not have survived its birth an hour.

And, as the land company was all there was of New Canton, its projector and promoter sprang into consequence. Strangers poured into the town, much to the profit of the publicans; and that class, as they counted their increased profits, blessed him unctuously. Those who had sold land at twice its value, took off their hats to him reverentially; and the old conservative element, while it did not go out of its way to do him honor, treated him with fair consideration.

His consequence was sudden, but it did not spoil him.

He was precisely fitted for the position; for " eminent respectability " was on every one of his features.

His face was eminently respectable; his figure was eminently respectable; his manner and his dress were eminently so. With all the rest, his habits were eminently respectable. He did not drink; he did not use tobacco in any form; his teeth were always white; his hands were always clean; his finger-nails always properly cared for; and a profane word had never been known to escape his lips. No man living knew better the importance and power of small virtues. By carefully practicing the minor virtues that are seen of men, one may safely indulge in all the larger vices. A patchwork quilt made of many pieces is a showy article.

The moment he was securely fixed in his position, as the financial magnate of the town, he put himself at the head of the Sunday school of the best — that is, the largest — church in New Canton. He was a zealous upholder of public and private morals; in brief, he was precisely the kind of a man that a savings-bank could well afford to pay a large salary to sit in the front window, and inspire confidence.

He always dressed in black. His coat was of black broadcloth, his vest was of black satin, both buttoned closely around him; and his pantaloons were black. His shoes, tied with a black ribbon, were always clean and well blacked. Not the shiny polish that his clerk affected; but a respectable, dull, clean, solvent polish; not enough to attract attention, but enough to look well. He was always clean shaved; Mr. Burt would no more have omitted shaving in the morning than he would have omitted prayers. He came to his office every morning as smug and as clean as if he had slept in silver paper the night before. He was always ready, never surprised, and never off his guard. Should his wife have had four children at once, it would not have astonished him — at least, so far as outward manifestation went. He would have looked as though he had always expected it, — as though it was a peculiarity of Mrs. B. to have four children at a time, and as though it was his mission to be the father of that number. And it is not unlikely, when the astonished nurse should ask how under heaven she was to provide linen for the unexpected three, that Mr. B. should tell her to look in the upper drawer of the bureau, and she would find it. He was the embodiment of coolness, readiness, and resource. When he died, he would require no ice to keep him till he was ready to bury.

Mr. Charles Burt had but one idea in life, and that was money. Born in the most abject poverty, he had an exaggerated idea of the value of money; and the getting-of-it was the sole object of his life. In every village of the United States, there is one family living in the outskirts, in the most miserable apology for a house that can be imagined, the boys of which — and there are always a good half-dozen of them — wear their father's old hats, and invariably appear with the flag of distress waving from behind. The mother is a hard-worked slattern, pale of face, and anxious; the father, a robust good-for-nothing, generally intelligent, but fearfully averse to continuous labor — that is, for himself, though always ready to do any thing for any one else, if it is not to be paid for. Always a politician, who can ever be counted upon to do any thing for his party; and always religous, with an insatiable zeal for his church, — in short, he is good for any thing except taking care of himself and those depending on him. He generally has a mild complaint of the hardness of the times in his mouth; but, as a rule, he sits down to his scant meal with cheerfulness, pondering, while eating it, how he can busy away the day with the least advantage to himself.

In this miserable family, there is always one boy who sees that the sons of the neighbors, who are better off, are treated better than he — that they have more consideration with the teacher and everybody else — that their whippings are less severe than those that fall upon his luckless back; and, very properly, he ascribes the difference to money. This boy determines to get money, and he always does it. He is a dentist, writing-master, singing-teacher, book-canvasser, or life-insurance agent; then a speculator in various ways. Finally, he gets into politics or financiering; and, being as industrious as an ant, acute as a ferret, having a strong motive and but one idea, he always succeeds.

Mr. Charles Burt was a very fair sample of this class.

Col. Seth Peppernell, the second director of the land company, was precisely the opposite of Mr. Burt. He was a loud, exaggerating, pompous talker, who bullied a man, if not into agreeing with him, at least into silence; and by this system succeeded in impressing a great many people with the idea that he was a strong character. If cornered, he could shake his fist — a very dirty one — under the nose of his antagonist, and swear him out of the field, unless he should happen to meet as great a bully as himself, which so far he had not done.

He had bullied his party into keeping him in office all his life, beginning on some supposed services rendered the Government in the Mexican War, where he got his title of colonel. It was ascertained, before he died, that his "services" were as an assistant in a sutler's establishment, and that the capital on which he established himself in New Canton came from goods that disappeared one night simultaneously with Peppernell. But, this not being known, the colonel talked of his company, and was as eloquent in matters of movements and charges and fortifications as a second Wellington. It was observed, however, when the soldiers were coming home from the South, during the last war, that he preserved a discreet silence about every thing military. When Col. Smith, of the 14th Illinois, tried to draw him out as to the difference between Scott's and Hardee's tactics, Peppernell dodged discussion by remarking, that systems had changed so entirely that he was not competent to give an opinion.

"Time was," he said, scowling furiously at the real colonel, whom he suspected of having a design against him, — "time was when I knew something of war; but, with these infernal long-range guns, with which you can pick off your man at a distance of three miles, war ain't what it used to be."

But Col. Peppernell was a very useful man in the land company, for all this.

His manner was that of a man of millions, and, to those who did not know him, was equal to a sworn statement of a fortune ending in six ciphers.

Mr. Thomas Gardiner, the vice-president of the land company, was a quiet banker, distinguished chiefly by a total unfitness for the business he was in, manifested chiefly by absolute honesty himself, and faith in the honesty of his fellow-men. He was an excellent man, of a kindly, trustful nature, who never could have got on in New Canton, only that the majority of the people, before the advent of the land company, were as honest as himself. He took their money, and paid small interest on deposits; loaned it to the people, at the regular rate of eighteen per cent. per annum; and so waxed rich. He made no losses; and his gains were considerable. He accepted the position of vice-president of the company; for he saw in it, not only profit to himself, but believed it would be useful to his fellow-citizens, which to him was quite as important a consideration.

Mr. Peak was a second-rate Burt; and 'Squire Sharp was the regular country justice of the peace.

Mr. Burt was cast to carry on the smooth, confidence part of the business, while Peppernell did the loud and aggressive. The others were merely figureheads, useful to refer to, and in the indorsement of the scheme, which their names gave it.

Smart offices were fitted up, the walls whereof were ornamented with highly-colored maps and plans of buildings; and there, from early morn till dewy eve, Burt and Peppernell, with the mild support of the other directors, sold lots to all comers.

It was as good as a play all day in the office.

Col. Peppernell, in the most aggravatingly impressive way, would place a pair of dividers on the map of the state, and triumphantly show, that, for a radius of two hundred miles, New Canton was not only the center, but the exact center. And, when a mild-mannered man from Boston ventured to remark, that the same thing could be done with any other point, — and a pair of dividers, — the Colonel would explosively remark, " What does a native uv narrer Noo England know of the expansiveness of the boundless West ? " which crushed the Bostonian so that he bought a block of lots at $25 a lot more than the Colonel intended to ask for them.

If Col. Peppernell believed in New Canton, what shall we say of the faith of the respectable Mr. Burt? It was less demonstrative, but more sublime. He held that the projected railroads must all be built, for New Canton was, in and of itself, the great pivotal fact of the Mississippi Valley; and he opposed the idea of the people of New Canton aiding these enterprises in any way, as the whole country, impelled by natural causes, had to come to New Canton. And, as it had to come, it would find its own way, never fear, without our going down into our own pockets. It was enough for us to do if we permitted them to come. And when those roads are finished, sir, and Soggy Run is slack-watered down a hundred miles or so, a mere nothing when the gigantic interests involved are considered, sir, New Canton will be the point of exchange, sir, for more territory than any city between the Atlantic and Mississippi.

And then Mr. Burt would heave a long sigh, and say it was a source of mortification to him that the town had not a more appropriate name.

" Canton in China, my dear sir," he would continue, in a silk-velvet voice — " it is true, is a vast aggregation of human beings; and, looking at the matter from the standpoint of population alone, the name is, perhaps, well enough. But, gracious heavens! sir, that is not all. New Canton is to be a great controlling city; which old Canton is not. It should have been named New London, sir — expressing at once population *and* power. And, by the way, that block of lots on the corner of 22d Street and Magnolia Avenue, sir, will prove an exceedingly good investment. I am so certain of it that I had reserved it for myself; but there has been so much complaint from European and Eastern capitalists, who have invested here — and I may say profitably — that the officers of the company were keeping all the choice lots for themselves — human nature in its best estate, as well as in real estate — ha! ha! — is selfish, you know — that at the last meeting of the board it was decided that we should relinquish all but a fixed number, and I was compelled — reluctantly, I admit — to give up the block. It is a most desirable block, sir, and whoever gets it may well be congratulated on his good fortune, sir."

And that block was sold. Whoever fell into the hands of the clear-starched Burt or the explosive Peppernell was lost.

There were other people in New Canton who will figure in this history, and who may as well be introduced here.

Mr. James Lewis was a retired trader, a man of capital, who made much every year lending his money to his neighbors at eighteen per cent. on undeniable security. Mr. Lewis was a spare, timid, nervous man, who had been in his early youth married by a robust, resolute woman of will, who managed her husband and household without the slightest regard to him who should have been its head. It had been a good thing for Mr. Lewis that he had married such a woman, for from well-to-do she had made him rich. It was she who made the purchase of the timber lot in the north tier, and who more than paid for it in ties when the branch was building. It was she who prevented his taking stock in the road; but bought choice lots, to sell at once, and double the money paid. She sat down on proposals for unsatisfactory loans, and could extinguish an undesirable applicant, before he asked, with a look. She had taken care to make the success of her wisdom so patent that her lord and master never forgot it. It was indispensable to her to control him; and it was a relief for him to be controlled. Her will was the law of the house; and its nominal head would as soon have put his hand in the fire as to have questioned one of her decrees.

In a period of relaxation from her graver duties, this Minerva condescended to add one to the census; and the world ought to have been obliged to her, for her daughter Mary, at the time we write, had reached the very pretty age of eighteen. She was a lovable girl, rather intelligent, very chatty and sweet; but very much under her mother's control — as who was not around her?

Then there was old Tom Paddleford, general merchant, who dealt in dry goods, groceries, hardware, boots, shoes, leather, millinery, wall-paper, drugs, medicines, and dye-stuffs, with "the highest price in cash for country produce;" a penny-splitting, flint-grinding old man, reputed rich, and who, with the help of Tom Paddleford, jr., his only son, did a very large and apparently thriving business. They lived in one of the best houses in the village; and their store, which was the satisfaction of the old man and the pride of the young one, was the staringest of the white frame buildings in the village.

Other people in the village, who followed the vocations common to such a place, hoped for the realization of the hopes of Messrs. Burt and Peppernell, but prudently kept aloof till they could see something tangible in them. Much to the dissatisfaction of these gentlemen, they did not at once bite at the hooks thrown out to them; but waited, in the most provoking way, for others to go ahead. The glowing prospectuses and the highly-colored maps unsettled them somewhat; and there was more leaning against hitching-posts and more talk of real estate than was good for business. And there was more discussion of the possibilities of railroads in a village that had been very glad to get the modest branch that connected it with the outside world; but they did not rush to avail themselves of the privilege of getting rich as fast as Col. Peppernell desired, and he cursed them, in his way, for a set of unappreciative idiots.

Mr. Burt, however, was not in such a hurry. "Our seed is sown — a part of it; but we must wait for our harvest. It will come," he said, quietly.

In the meantime, the two papers of the village were filled, week after week, with glowing accounts of improvements not only contemplated, but in such forward state of preparation as to make them certain. And when a transaction in real estate took place, the most was made of it; and, under the manipulation of Mr. Burt, their work was very well done, indeed.

From the " New Canton Sentinel."

" It is a fact beyond any question, that parties from

MORE ABOUT NEW CANTON.

Chicago, Cleveland, and Indianapolis — a combination of capitalists, representing millions — have purchased the Taylor Farm, at forty dollars an acre, on the usual payments. This would have been an enormous price for the land a year ago, but is now absurdly low. Mr. Taylor is an old man, who has not kept up in the march of events, and, when he was offered that sum for his land, innocently took it. It was cruel in the land-sharks to take such an advantage of an old man; but what will not such men do, in their eagerness for money? Our townsman, Mr. Chas. Burt, says the land to-day is not worth less than $200 per acre, and he has kindly undertaken to break the sale, and restore to Mr. Taylor and his grandchildren their inheritance. He looks upon the transaction as but little better than a fraud."

From the "Forum of the People."

"The land company has a force of men grading streets and planting trees on the old Mix Place, on the east side of the town. Mr. Burt tells us that lots in that addition are selling very rapidly at from $200 to $300. The future of New Canton is roseate."

In answers to correspondents: —

"L. M. — You can do no better with your means than to invest in New Canton real estate. Property that a year ago was dear at $10 an acre is now worth a thousand. The land company is liberal; its object being more to build up the city than to make immediate profits. Come and see for yourself."

CHAPTER III.

THE GARDINER FAMILY AND SOME OTHERS.

"OLD GARDINER," as he was respectfully styled in country fashion, being a well-preserved man over fifty, had one son, who was "Jim" Gardiner to every man, woman, and urchin; and, as only sons of bankers ought to be, was held the most desirable young man in the place. Like most desirable young men the world over, this popularity was owing to a figure near six feet high and straight as an Indian's; frank, pleasant face; handsome side-whiskers; and dark hair, of that thick wave which women admire on any sort of a man. For the rest, he was decently honest, sensitive on many points as a woman, and brave as a lion, when his sympathies or what he called his principles were enlisted — or set as a bulldog in his own way, whichever you chose to call it. In short, he had the usual virtues in the gristle common to young men.

Unfortunately, this paragon of all the feminine eyes of the village was the most indolent mortal that ever breathed.

He had studied law, and was in practice — that is to say, would have been if he had condescended to practice. He had an office, which was a convenient place to read novels, write verses, and smoke a huge meerschaum; and as good as any could have to keep his double-barreled fowling-piece, his ammunition and pointer. His fishing-tackle ornamented the space over the bookcase which contained his "library," and Ponto found under his desk the very best place to sleep undisturbed.

His father believed in him, was very fond of him, and, being wealthy, for New Canton, gave him a liberal allowance; and life, with him, was a lazy, delightful pastime, with no trouble of his own and just enough of other people's in it to keep him from rusting entirely.

He was as honest as the day is long — that is, he was as honest after business hours as he was during their continuance. He was afflicted with two demons, that prevented him from being very useful — one, his intolerable indolence; the other, a consuming passion for Mary Lewis; and the two kept him pretty effectually from work of any kind. When he was not lounging and smoking his meerschaum, or out gunning or fishing, he was certain to be with the girl; and, between the two, he managed, with great ingenuity, to get nothing done. The only thing he did show any perseverance in was in persuading the pretty Mary that it would be greatly to her advantage to marry him. Had he displayed the same energy in any other pursuit, he would have been a richer man than his father.

But who could blame him? The girl with whom this lazy young Apollo was in love was so exceedingly pretty! She was one of those full-figured, plump, rosy girls, with a clear red and white complexion, with great masses of fair brown hair, and with bright, soft, deep blue eyes — a girl made to be petted and waited on from church, and talked to in moonlight, and have presents of velvet albums and sets of jewelry made to her — the sugar candy of life, to be nibbled and tasted, and duly thanked for. She looked up to Jim Gardiner as all that was good and great in humanity, and loved him with all the intensity a little, amiable, confiding soul was capable of; and he loved her in the same way: and between them there was a great deal of time wasted that their parents thought — forgetting their younger days — might have been better employed.

He was coming home from the country college, where he graduated, the morning he met Mary Lewis on the cars, and fell in love with her. He was feeling every inch of his importance, from his fresh gray suit and bit of side-whisker to the diploma in his pocket, which he felt, through layers of clothing, in every fiber of his body. His first business was to take stock of all the pretty girls in the car, the only one of whom not positively uninteresting sat right before him in such a position that he could not get sight of her face. This he was anxious to do; for the back of her head offered such a charming study he longed to know if the face corresponded with it. Like all mannish young men, a girl could not be too soft and refined to please his fancy; and this one was delicacy itself. Neck and head were drawn with exquisite outline, the skin was fine, the ear was very pretty and thin, with a rose-blush; and there was something gentle in the very sweep of the hair, which, dressed high, showed a unique and bewitching charm in the finish of the neck-hair, which grew in a curl at the roots, shading off into soft brushmarks, which conveyed I don't know what of susceptibility and refinement in the character that wore it. The turn of the neck had something simple and caressing in it — that white, warm, girlish neck, which, with its silky whirls of hair, shaded like India-ink drawing, made the ardent imagination behind her long to bend and scrutinize it like a work of art. The face might prove disenchanting; and James waited anxiously to see it. It might not have suited a more practiced eye, which demanded romance and spirit to redeem it from tameness; but it was certainly a pretty girl's face, with a fresh, fine complexion, and rather small, dark blue eyes, which could droop pensively and irresistibly, but which, being well indulged, laughed a great deal of the time. All the pretty girl's attire, even to her parcels and satchel, were stylish, neat, and trim, so that the young man, who regarded himself as fastidious, was seized with the instant idea, that this was the very woman he was looking out for to make him happy or miserable. He devoted himself to getting views of her from every position, till the face, which had puzzled him with a fleeting likeness, suddenly flashed upon him as that of his old schoolmate, Mary Lewis, whom he left in long braids, and had not seen for four years. To claim acquaintance, in his most impressive manner, was the work of but few minutes; and the knowledge of so fair a neighbor made New Canton much more tolerable as a place of residence that he would otherwise have found it.

He had gone to the town school with Mary Lewis when she was a delicate, waspish little girl; but time had improved them both out of knowledge, and so when his father suggested a call on the Lewises, — his usual Sunday evening dissipation, — he obeyed with filial readiness. Miss Lewis was at evening church; but she got home before the visitors left, coming in in a charming summer bonnet, full of wild roses, which, as it was very becoming, she forgot to take off while the two gentlemen stayed. To show old acquaintances attention, she went out in the moonlight to pick some roses for them, in which quest James accompanied her, while Mr. Gardiner prudently stayed out of the dew, on the porch, finishing his topic with Mr. Lewis. The next night Mr. James's mother sent him over on an errand to Mrs. Lewis; and he stayed long enough to forget all about it. The next afternoon he came to see about something forgotten the evening before, just for a minute — of an hour and a half. The next day he did not go to the Lewises, but saw Mary at a friend's house; and, the next evening, they met, by appointment, with a musical friend; and he saw her home. He was very kind and useful to his mamma in those days, running errands to Mrs. Lewis's, till she laughingly declared she could invent no more excuses for him, and he must go on his own responsibility.

Three weeks of this was enough to bring the young folks to an excellent understanding; and for two years this happy state of things had not been allowed to languish. Miss Lewis had plenty of leisure, a pretty taste in dress, slim white hands, that showed to advantage on wool-work, and a graceful slipper; and, as she presented herself to her lover in picturesque surprises of toilet, with a manner that was a happy mixture of affection and coquetry, he was fond

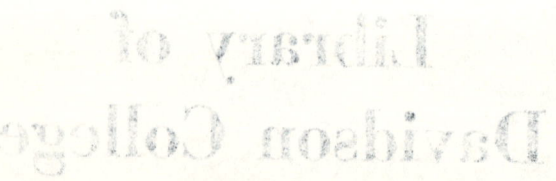

THE GARDINER FAMILY AND OTHERS. 41

enough to believe her seriously the only woman in the world worth knowing.

The elder Gardiner having furnished the money and credit for the land company, James was, of course, the attorney for that corporation. He managed to dodge the business connected with it with a skill born of long practice. Every day the old gentleman and Peppernell would come into his office, and find it vacant, with a notice posted on the book-case: "Back in a few minutes."

Peppernell would take up the young man's pipe, and finding it cold, would remark: "The rascal has been gone an hour. Where can we git holt of him? The papers must be drawn up immejit."

His father would sigh:—

"There isn't the slightest use hunting him. He's either gone fishing or off with that Lewis girl. He ain't gone fishing, for there is his tackle; and he ain't gone hunting, for his shot-gun is on the hooks. He's with the girl."

And then Peppernell would go to Jim's library, and, taking from thence an ingeniously constructed book — made of glass, covered with leather nearly enough like a law-book to deceive a clergyman, not a Baptist, with "Elements of American Law" in nice letters on the back —would take out the cork, and pour out a three-fingered drink, commenting on the degeneracy of the coming generation.

Picking up a loose scrap of paper from his desk: "Look at this! This is what your son idles away his time at, instid uv studyin' the law uv land contracts, or dispootid hoss warrantees, and other useful knollege for a lawyer. Lissen:—

'WATTS ADAPTED TO THE REQUIREMENTS OF MR. CHAS. BURT.

> " ' Blest be the man whose sole intent
> Is righteously to live.
> A pious heart and twelve per cent.
> Makes all that life can give.'

"The idee uv abusin' our secretary and treasurer this way! It's shameful! He's got the interest too low by six per cent! A pretty man of business!"

"James never did like Mr. Burt," the old gentleman would sigh; "but there is no use of waiting for him here."

"When I was a young man this kind uv a thing wouldn't hev done at all. I had to work, I did. There wan't no meershams for me to smoke and no gals for me to idle my time away onto. Ef I hedn't workt ez I did, and improoved w'at opportunities I hed, I never wood hev bin w'at I am. Hevens! Ef I'd only hed Jim Gardiner's opportoonities, I mite hev bin — "

And Peppernell, who had never done a day's work in his life, waved his hand impressively, leaving his auditor to imagine that, had he had opportunities, there was no pitch of earthly consequence to which he might not have reasonably aspired.

At the very time this discussion was taking place in Jim's office, that worthy was walking slowly in the grove in the outskirts of New Canton, with a young lady. They were walking very close together — with that peculiar closeness, that half-clinging manner, which betokened they had walked together a great deal.

Mary Lewis had put on a very becoming gown and bewitching hat, with blue ribbons, and walked in front of his office, where he could not but see her, knowing very well that he would follow her as soon as he could spring to his feet and throw on street-coat and hat. The little minx liked to do this. It pleased her to feel that she could control the movements of a strong fellow like Jim Gardiner. All women like such things, and the weaker they are the better they like them.

"When are we going to have something better than this seeing you by snatches, Mary," asked the young man, with a pleased expression on his countenance.

"Nonsense, Jim," was her reply. "You have asked me that question once a week for two years. I can't tell you. Possibly never. I may change my mind — there are a great many young men in New Canton. For instance, there is Sam Adams."

"A pleasant husband he'd make for you. He doesn't know as much as the mule he drives, and is meaner than the whisky he drinks. I'm not afraid of him?"

"Well, what do you say of Tom Paddleford?"

"He's the beastliest little beast in New Canton, and that is saying a great deal. He's bow-legged, sandy-haired, spiteful. If I didn't like you, and wanted to see you miserable all your life, I should work all sorts of ways to have you take Tom Paddleford. But you'd better make up your mind very soon. I feel in danger myself. Sarah Martin has been making eyes at me."

"Sarah Martin? Well!" The girl had a very sweet laugh. "She isn't old enough for you. She's thirty, if she's a day. She don't know which side of her bonnet's front or back, and she's as good-looking as she is bright. I am not afraid of poor, dear Sarah."

"Well, how about Nellie Davis? I can have her for the asking."

"So can anybody. She's been in that state for these ten years. She dresses like a fright, and she overruns her shoes. Besides, she writes poetry for the 'Sentinel.' I'm troubled about Nellie."

"I see, I'm as badly off for some one to play off against you as you are for some one to play off against me. Let's quit this kind of talk, and come to business. I want the day fixed, and have it over. We have been engaged three years; and if we are ever to be married we might as well have the good of it at once."

"I'll think it over Jim, and give you an answer —"

"To-morrow?"

"No — sometime."

By this time the young people were at the gate of the Lewis mansion, and James bethought himself that he had been absent from his office two hours, and left her. He knew there was business waiting, but that was not what troubled him. This was just about the time Dr. Perkins dropped in to play chess with him; and James had spent half the night studying a game that he was perfectly sure would vanquish him — which had been a problem up to this time.

James went to his office; and Mary went to her room, not in quite so pleasant a frame of mind as she parted from him. The allusion James had made to Tom Paddleford worried her. His description she knew was entirely correct, and there her trouble lay.

Mrs. Lewis had always favored the suit of James Gardiner. As she favored it, there was no necessity for any other parental interference. The elder Gardiner had amassed a large fortune, for New Canton, which James would inherit, being an only child; and, besides that, he was undeniably a young man of parts. True, he was addicted to pipes and novels, chess, and hunting and fishing, and had a wonderful aversion to labor; but time, she believed, would cure that.

He would some time go into politics, and, at least, attain the legitimate object of every lawyer's ambition — a judgeship. Should he go regularly into general politics, what could stand in the way of his going to Congress, and finally attaining the sublime position of governor of the state? He was a fine speaker and very popular. While Mrs. Lewis would have preferred that he would pay more attention to things material at the present time, still there was enough "out-come" to him, as she expressed it, to make him a very desirable son-in-law. She felt that she could ornament the Washington establishment of a congressional son-in-law with credit; for she was an exceedingly well-preserved woman, by no means ill-looking, and felt herself a match for that sphere or any other.

But, of late, she had, in the most unaccountable manner, changed her tone. She had given Mary very broad hints that she would be better pleased if the engagement with Gardiner were broken off. What the real reason was for this sudden change, Mary could not divine; and, when she insisted upon knowing the cause, the answer was any thing but satisfactory. Indeed, it was a long time before she got any reason at all, Mrs. Lewis being one of those infallible persons who cannot understand how any one can differ with them, and wonder why a reason is ever asked of them. She did finally condescend to give reasons; and, once started, they poured out in a flood. She found fault with his habits. She objected to his fowling-piece, to his fishing-tackle, to his chess, to his novel-reading, and to pretty much every thing about him. He had no energy; and, without energy, what was the use of his talent? After all, was he talented? What had he ever done to prove it? Had he shown any aptitude for the practice? Had he ever distinguished himself on the stump? How many cases had he allowed to go by default, because of neglect? She had a small opinion of a man who could do nothing for himself, but who depended on his father.

"But, ma, you knew all about that when you were urging me upon him before. He hasn't changed for the worse since we were first intimate," replied the pretty girl.

"Urged! Mary? Urged! What do you mean? Thank Heaven, the Lewises never had occasion to urge any one. Urge, indeed! Mary, I was at one time willing the young man should pay you attention, for I hoped he would reform. I hoped he would settle down, and acquire those habits without which no man has any right to think of taking a wife."

"But, ma, he can reform yet. He is young, and has a long life before him."

"Never, Mary, never. 'Just as the twig is bent, the tree's inclined.' He was bent, Mary, when he was a twig; and the tree has the wrong inclination. He is no man for you."

All this would have had no effect beyond annoyance upon the girl, had she been satisfied that there was nothing in it beyond a desire to keep her from Gardiner. If she could be let alone, she knew that time would conquer for her.

What alarmed the girl most was the frequent mention of Tom Paddleford, in contrast with the disfavored Gardiner. Whenever Mrs. Lewis got to dispraising Gardiner she invariably tagged in Paddleford as a possessor of all the virtues that poor Jim lacked.

It was this that disquieted poor Mary when the name of Paddleford came to her mind.

That she should object to Tom Paddleford was no wonder; for he was not precisely the manner of man to fill a woman's fancy. He was five feet six inches high, with a long body and short legs, answering all the purposes of legs except being ornamental — which was not necessary, for his body would have been a drawback to a good pair of legs. His head and feet took good care to be no better than the rest. When his feet were constructed, Nature had a six-foot man in mind, but had evidently changed in favor of a smaller pattern, and forgot to alter the feet. The legs were not only short, but bowed, which was a perpetual source of sorrow. He was the worry of the tailors of New Canton, always wanting pantaloons cut to appear straight; and he badgered them on this point almost to madness. Above those legs was a long body, on that a lean neck, and on that one of the meanest faces ever seen without a rope.

The description of the man begins at the feet, because it is always well to begin with the best of a subject.

He had a low forehead, a peaked nose, a thin, sensual mouth, cunning eyes, of no color, and stubborn hair, which only the wildest extravagance in hair-oil could keep in shape at all. A bristling moustache and a goatee were points in his appearance on which he felt the utmost complaisance. The beard was not handsome; but it was tolerable, for it hid a part of his face.

He had the appearance of a rat. His jaws, projecting like the point of a triangle, were armed with sharp-pointed teeth; and the struggling moustache, of which he was so proud, long, wiry and thin on the skin, helped the likeness.

His mind fitted his body. He was cruel to smaller vermin, timid in the presence of stronger beings, and could only be made to fight when crowded into a corner. He was stingy even in his vices; and, if a depraved appetite drove him to indulgence, his remorse at the expense more than balanced his pleasure. He once went to Chicago, and dissipated to the extent of a hundred dollars. When he got back to New Canton remorse set in — not for the dissipation, but for its cost. It gnawed at his vitals and tugged at his heart-strings. When he got home he deliberately charged that $100 to the accounts of a score of careless customers, who never examined the items in their bills, and spitefully added $25 to pay for lost time. That would have quieted the pangs of an ordinarily mean man, but it did not assuage his; for it vexed him to think that he might have charged the money all the same without having spent it at all.

He generally succeeded in getting what he wanted, but never by advancing squarely upon his desires. Rat-like, he would rather get at a cheese by crawling through a drain than walk straight to it; and, rat-like, he always ate his plunder from the under side, that no other might suspect his presence.

He was the dandy of the village. His tall hats were always glossy, his coats fitted him like the paper on the wall, his boots were painfully close to his feet, and in pantaloons he indulged in the wildest extravagance. While the cloth was new, and before it got broken to his unfortunate legs, they looked straight; consequently he had new pantaloons very often, whereat his papa, who was quite as penurious, would growl vehemently, to which the son would respond: —

"New pants make my legs look straight, and I will have 'em. Why didn't you have my legs straightened when I was a baby, and save me all this expense?"

"I thought of it, my son," sighed the old man; "but then, you see, it would have cost $25. S'pos'n' you'd 'a' died in infancy, it would have been wasted."

Tom Paddleford wanted to marry Mary Lewis. He admired the girl; he was desperately in love with the wealth of her father. And so, without a doubt of his success, he cast his little wicked eyes upon the lady. He made up his mind — not a very extensive operation — to marry her. Was not his father one of the richest, if not the richest, man in New Canton? In his estimation the mere matter of money settled the whole question. Barring his legs, which even his conceit could not straighten, he felt satisfied that he was rather a handsome young man, a delusion nursed by the score of girls in New Canton who, born and reared to the idea that their first business in life was to marry, would have gladly taken him had he been ten times the monkey he was. If they could hang upon and admire him, he could see no reason why any woman should not. (4)

Confident that all he had to do was to ask, he did ask, one day, and the girl laughed in his face.

Now Mary Lewis was not a cruel girl or a light one; and she felt, what every girl ought to feel, that, no matter how absurd it may be, any man's feeling deserves, at least, respect. But there was something so absurd in Tom Paddleford's proposing to marry her, that she could not but laugh. Then, repenting her levity, she told him kindly that it was impossible.

Tom tried to leave her under the impression that it was a matter of no consequence; but his effort was a failure. He looked at her out of his wicked little eyes in a way that she remembered many a year.

Jim Gardiner knew that Tom had proposed to her, and that she had rejected him; and many a laugh had they had over the matter. He had imitated Tom's manner and gone through the scene of his proposing to her a hundred times, in a most deliciously natural way, which amused them very much; but he did not know that Tom was more determined upon marrying her than ever. Neither did he know that Tom Paddleford had two mighty agencies working for him; namely, circumstances and Mrs. Lewis, or, rather, Mrs. Lewis impelled by circumstances.

CHAPTER IV.

A CHANGE OF HEART.

IT was not altogether well with the Gardiners. The New York correspondents of the banker of New Canton were the eminent firm of Slap, Dash, & Co.; and one day he had a balance in their hands of $20,000, which was nearly as much money as he was worth, though no one outside knew the fact.

Slap, Dash, & Co. were worth millions; but they wanted twice as much. Slap wanted a yacht. Dash had his eagle eye fixed upon a seat in the Senate; and it was likely to remain fixed there, without the help of a million or two of money. " Co.," whoever he was, wanted a variety of things that he did not have. To get their wishes, they made a bold stroke. They proposed first to " corner " all the cotton in the South, and, next, to control all the railroads of the country, judging correctly, that, if they had the roads, they could make them pay what they wanted; and, if they had all the cotton, they could levy tribute on every man who wore a shirt.

But this is a large country; and there are many Slaps, Dashes, & Cos., equally acute, and with as much money in their pockets. So Slap, Dash, & Co., after a most determined fight, went down; and, when their affairs were settled, it was found that they could not pay a cent on the dollar. Mrs. Slap was worth a million or two in her own right. Mrs. Dash consoled herself, after her husband's mortifying failure, with a villa at Newport and a small annual income of $40,000; and Mrs. "Co.'s" father, sternly reprehending the spirit of speculation which must always result in such disasters, with equal sternness refused to give up a dime of the half-million young "Co." had made over to him a month before the failure. The three went to Europe to avoid the harrowing sight of their distressed creditors.

Poor Gardiner lost his $20,000, as did a great many Gardiners in different parts of the country, all of whom cursed Slap, Dash, & Co. with a fervency proportioned to the amount of money they had in the firm. But cursing didn't bring any of the money out of the coffers of the firm; nor, so far as heard from, make its members sleep any less soundly.

The failure worried Gardiner; for, while he did not know himself exactly how he stood with the world, he feared he was in no condition to weather such a loss, if his depositors knew of it. But, thank Heaven! there was his interest in the land company, enough to make him independent, if all the rest should go. It comforted him to feel its affairs were in so good a shape. Lots were not selling rapidly; but Burt and Peppernell assured him that the railroads would surely be built; and he could see no reason why the speculation should not come out right, and leave him as well off as need be.

He went to Chicago one day with Peppernell, the object of the trip being to induce Chicago capitalists to take an interest in a new railroad project of Peppernell's devising, and came home comforted.

To see Peppernell in his room at the Grand Pacific, with Chicago men, was as good as a play. His wig was more than usually ferocious, his whiskers curled more fiercely than ever; and, in his blue swallow-tailed coat, just far enough out of the fashion, his ruffled shirt, and gold-headed cane, he looked the picture of a five-millionaire.

He was not here for money, gentlemen, not he! He had subscribed a half-million to the stock of the company himself; and he could easily put in money enough more to build the road: but he desired to have Chicago directly interested in it, and proposed it should reap some of the benefits of its construction. He wanted New Canton and Chicago knit together by iron bands. He wanted the present and prospective great cities of the world knit together indissolubly, to go hand-in-hand to the glorious future that awaited them.

"Are you related to the Peppernells, of Indianapolis?" asked Defrees, whose father, forty years ago, owned all North Chicago as a muskrat reservation, and who belonged to one of the first families.

"No, sir; not at all. The name is not the same, sir. The name of the head of that family is P*i*ppernell, sir; mine, P*e*ppernell. The similarity occasions me frequent inconveniences, sir; for I am very often mistaken for him, on that account. I presume that gentleman is a very excellent person; but it annoys me to be mistaken for him in a business way. Mr. Pippernell is not worth to exceed $250,000, if, indeed, he controls that amount of capital; and being mistaken for him once injured my credit, sir, at a time when I needed it all."

It did surprise Defrees to have this magnificent capitalist borrow $22 to pay his hotel bills; but he did it so magnificently that the lender could cherish no ill feeling when he forgot to return it. Twenty-two dollars was such a trifle to a man of millions! — how could he be expected to burden his mind with it?

Now it is not to be supposed Gardiner heard any part of this talk or was present at the discussions. Mr. Burt came with them to Chicago; and he managed to keep Mr. Gardiner away from the Grand Pacific till the meeting was over, much to his regret, as he said effusively. Peppernell did not care to have any one from New Canton by when he was dealing with outside capitalists. Still, Mr. Gardiner was impressed with the interest Chicago men took in the enterprise. In the corridors, he was introduced to Mr. Stone and Mr. Hawk, Chicago capitalists, who assured him there could be no earthly doubt of the success of the scheme; for Chicago could not afford to let it go by default. Gardiner went home thankful that he had put so much into the land company, and certain that his investments there would make good his losses in New York.

* * * * * * * *

Mr. and Mrs. Lewis were at tea. Mr. Lewis as meek as usual, and Mrs. Lewis, imposing as possible in a black alpaca, very full and glossy, white apron, with ruffles, and a cap of black lace over white, which was economical, as it would not show wear. Mr. Lewis spoke, between two bites of toast, —

"Gardiner wanted to borrow twelve thousand dollars of me to-day."

There was in his voice a peculiar inflection, which made Mrs. Lewis lift her eyebrows inquiringly.

"Did you lend it to him?"

"Well, no. I — we haven't got it, you know. But, while I was about it, I thought I would find out how he was really fixed. I found out."

Mr. Lewis chuckled a small, modest chuckle, the only approach to self-gratulation that Mrs. Lewis permitted in her presence.

"When I undertake a piece of work of this kind, I give my whole mind to it."

"A very small contribution, Mr. Lewis. You couldn't do less. Go on. What did you find?"

"He lost $20,000 with Slap, Dash, & Co.; all he is worth, unless the land company pans out as they expect. If it shouldn't — "

"Gardiner's gone, is he?" burst in the lady. "Very well, then Gardiner's gone. I know something about that land company. I know Peppernell, and I can figure up Burt; and I wouldn't give a *sou marquee* for what's going on."

"I know more than that," responded Mr. Lewis. "Most all the sales last week were bogus; and all the sales, for that matter, of the last four weeks were to men of straw, to keep up confidence. I shan't say nothing yet, but — oh! yes, old Tom let it leak out that all the money he had just now was depositors', and what he wanted of the $12,000 was to have it on hand, in case there should be any trouble, so he could weather it till he could realize from the company. I let no such man have money."

"But, Mr. Lewis, if this is so, it won't do to let our Mary marry Jim Gardiner. Goodness! Situated as we are."

"H-s-s-sh!" exclaimed Mr. Lewis, uneasily. "You never know who may be hearing of us."

"You show sense, for once," said Mrs. Lewis, lowering her voice. "Young Jim can't be any use if the old man goes, and it's a certainty he will. Tom Paddleford —"

The old man groaned.

"He's a rat; and it's a pity to give Mary to such a man."

"Rat or no rat," returned the lady, with some asperity, "he and his father are safe men, content with their business, and don't speculate. They are not in any land companies — or — North Alaska bonds."

Once more the old gentleman groaned.

"They own what they've got; and Tom isn't a bad young man. He might be handsomer, and he might know more; but he will always be able to take care of a wife."

"And her parents," sighed Lewis. "Very well. If it's got to be, it must; but I don't want to hear about it."

Mrs. Lewis had some motherly pangs at sacrificing her daughter to a man she knew to be unworthy of her; and she did not want to do it unless she was compelled. She set investigations on foot; and for a day or two her pump was in very active use, and what it brought was examined very carefully.

A few days after this conversation, Tom Paddleford was closeted with her for an hour or so; and when he left the house he cocked his hat with a jaunty

A CHANGE OF HEART. 57

air, and whistled cheerfully as he walked home, and, if an opportunity had presented itself that evening for doing a decent act, it is not impossible that he would have done it. None came in his way however, and he went to his grave with a record entirely consistent.

A few evenings after, James Gardiner, walking up to the Lewis house, saw Tom Paddleford emerge therefrom, with an expression of triumph on his face, and a peculiar look of satisfaction as he passed. James felt the presentiment of evil, and went swiftly to its fulfilment. Something unpleasant was to happen.

Mary or Mrs. Lewis had always received him at the door. The mother might have been thought more in love with him than the daughter; for she was always warmest in greeting, which was more than figuratively with open arms. She always spoke to him as "my dear James," and had been the most convenient mother imaginable. She knew with the nicest propriety how long to stay in the parlor with the lovers, and exactly when affairs in the rest of the house could not do without her; and knew how to go so that it would not appear as if she went on purpose. James had found the mother, in her way, hardly less delightful than the daughter.

To-night, he had hardly entered the house before he felt a change. He tried to put away the sickening suspicion that things were against him.

He was let into the hall by the little bound-girl, instead of happy sweetheart or courteous matron. The kerosene burned worse than usual, as if warning him of some dark fate that hung over him. The sitting-room had an air of unusual stiffness, with Mrs. Lewis knitting in one corner, and Mr. Lewis shielding himself behind the county newspaper, as if his prospects depended on his getting every line of it, advertisments and all. The place looked as cheerful as if the sheriff had put in an attachment that afternoon.

James wondered not to see his divinity in blue merino anywhere, and asked if Mary was in.

"She is," was the answer.

"Where is she?" was the next privileged question.

"She is in her room, and will not be down this evening," was the frigid response.

"Is she sick?" inquired the young man, anxiously.

"She is not very well," said the cool matron, intent upon her knitting. "In fact, she has been a good deal disturbed this afternoon."

Mr. Lewis at this moved his feet and tipped his chair in protest.

"But, Mrs. Lewis, can't I see her?" spoke James, warmly, wretched with the thought that his little idol was weeping, when he was so near to comfort her.

"I don't think it will do any good to see her," responded the Roman lady, sticking a knitting-needle she had just used into her hair, and going on busily as ever. "I think she had rather not see you."

James drew his breath as though a cold blast had struck him. Here was a welcome for an accepted lover. His hot blood could bear suspense no longer.

"Mr. Lewis, may I ask you what all this means?"

At the words, Mrs. Lewis's nose was elevated perceptibly, and something like a smile for an instant played over her features, like congealed lightning. Mr. Lewis, too nervous to bear the scene any longer, caught up his newspaper, without answering, and fled ignobly to the kitchen. His better half, not deigning to cast a look after her timid spouse, proceeded to deliver herself, with equal gravity and majesty, in the form memorial, which parents have used to quench the hopes of unwelcome lovers : —

"You have been coming here some time, Mr. Gardiner, and I don't know how far things have gone between you and Mary."

"Don't know!" groaned poor James.

"But I think you had better discontinue your visits; and, if there is any talk of an engagement between you, you will consider it at an end."

The words fell upon the young man's mind as cold and pitiless as ice-clods upon his bosom. He sat gazing at Mrs. Lewis with pale face and fierce eyes.

"Does Mary agree to this?"

"Mary is young, and not fit to decide for herself in such points. She will be guided in this, as in all other matters, by her moth — parents."

"Will you tell me the meaning of all this? Yesterday I was not objectionable to you as a son-in-law."

"I have nothing more to say about it, and it is not necessary to discuss the matter further," returned Mrs. Lewis, stonily. "I have my views, and shall abide by them."

"I can see her once more, I suppose?" asked the young man, determined not to get into a passion.

"Not at present. I don't think it would be best for Mary, and it certainly can do you no good."

Gardiner waited but one minute. His first impulse was to upset the kerosene lamp, walk over father and mother, rush up stairs to Mary's room, and carry her off by main strength, till he could compel her to an answer and find if she agreed to this summary dismissal; but he controlled himself, and left the house without another word.

As he passed out of the gate, he turned and looked beseechingly at a certain window. The white curtain was put aside, a hand waved a handkerchief, and behind the half-open casement he saw in the moon-light a form he knew too well. This consoling gleam told that Mary was true to him, and the trouble was none of her seeking. He went to his office in no good frame of mind, but feeling tolerably secure. He knew Mary loved him, and he fancied all the parents in the world could not keep them apart. Still, he did not know what was behind; and his dreams that night were as ugly as ever afflicted an imaginative young man very much in love, who found some large pebbles thrown into its smooth course.

CHAPTER V.

NEW CANTON UNDER A CLOUD, AND HOW IT PARTLY EMERGED FROM IT.

COL. PEPPERNELL, Captain Peak, and Esquire Sharp, of the great land company, were not in as pleasant a frame of mind as they might have been. New Canton was not pushing ahead as rapidly as they hoped. True, they had put nothing into it, and were in such position that they could lose nothing in the enterprise; for the most excellent reason, that they had nothing whatever to lose. But they had been talking millions for a month or two so glibly that each had come to consider himself a capitalist, and to look for the returns of vast amounts invested in the scheme. As the transactions were mostly among themselves, — like the two Yankee boys, who traded jack-knives all day with each other, and came out rich in the evening, — they had piled up a volume of property by selling each other land, which neither had paid for, and for which they had nothing to pay. Mr. Burt sold the Pelton tract, for which he had given notes for one thousand dollars to Col. Peppernell for ten thousand dollars, taking his notes in payment. Peppernell had sold it to Peak, also on time, for twenty thousand dollars, and justly considered himself a gainer of ten thousand dollars by the transaction, Peak's notes which he took being as good as his own. Peak sold to Sharp for thirty thousand, and there it stuck; and Sharp was considered as having the best bargain. If time was money, they were all rich; for "time" was the basis of all their transactions. These sales were always reported, that the public might get an idea of the anxiety of the land company managers for real estate.

Now and then, an outsider was caught, and induced to buy a portion on speculation; and good notes were taken worth something besides the security of the land. But these bites were too infrequent to suit the speculators.

"I want to see something besides this buying and selling among ourselves," was Peppernell's growl.

"I think it has gone on long enough," Captain Peak added. "It's time we had returns — something a man can take hold of."

"I think so, too," was the quick response of Esquire Sharp. "Something tangible."

And the three glared at Mr. Burt, as if he had been leading them to their ruin, and they had millions in his grasp to be worried about.

Mr. Burt smiled; and, the more they talked, the more he smiled.

"Gentlemen," he said, consolingly, "we are only at the beginning of our trouble. I don't see what you have to complain of. We owe for land, $200,000; but then we have the land, except what we have sold, and for that we've got the best of paper. Land we bought at ten dollars per acre we've sold for two hundred, and have interested a number of people with us, which must count in time. Time is the basis of our venture. Besides, we've anticipated our final success by each venturing something on his own hook. I have your notes for more thousands of dollars than I had cents when we began and I won't insult you by holding them worth a cent less than their face, secured as they are on New Canton real estate. You hold mine. The security is the same. It is our business to make this paper worth its face with the others."

"Just what I'd like to see," growled Peppernell, listening.

"The farmer sows and plows and hoes, — that is, he hoes out East; but not here, where Nature gives us enough soil not to have to rake it together with hoes, — and then reaps and threshes, before he gets his wheat. You want to gather before you have fairly sowed. Our enterprise is only two months old. There's a good deal to be done before we can harvest. The pamphlets are out, the maps are hung; but we've got to do more. We've got to put some actual money in ourselves, and have some sales that are not contracts, and not made among ourselves. In short, we have got to risk something."

"What way?" asked Peppernell.

"We've got to buy more land, and, what is more, pay for it, money down. We've got to make *bona fide* transactions. We've got to buy farms, and pay money for them, at good prices."

"I'll sell," spoke the three, in a breath.

"No, gentlemen; we can't buy of each other this time. It must be of outsiders; and the payments must be in good, clean, honest money, and the seller must have the cash to show for it. To catch pigeons, you have to spread ground-bait."

"Where are we to get the money?" asked Peppernell.

"Gardiner must furnish it. He has too much invested already to go back on us when we need to develop our plans. I'll see about getting it myself. I may mention what's encouraging — I heard from outside parties, that a man from Connecticut will be here Thursday — come on purpose to look at land in New Canton. If you will have patience, and not spoil every thing, we'll have this matter arranged in a way to get up confidence. If any of you have better plans to propose, I shall be most happy to hear them. I've carried the burden of this business so far; and, if any man wants to relieve me of it, I shall be very glad to have him, I can tell you."

Peppernell attempted to bluster, and find out details; but the quiet will of the really strong man was superior.

Thursday came, and with it the Connecticut man, who registered at the Grand Central, as "Mr. Thompson, of Meridan, Conn." His errand and importance being duly spread in the village, few of his motions were lost to the observing people; and, when he called at the office of the land company, to make inquiries about real estate, it happened there were plenty of men in, who pricked up their ears as they caught scraps of the conversation between Mr. Thompson, of Connecticut, and the Secretary.

To their surprise, and much to their chagrin, Mr. Thompson fought shy of the land company, in his transactions. He was not a fancy personage at all, — very plain-spoken and equally plain-dressed, one of those trading farmers, who, by holding tight every advantage they get in life, manage inevitably to amass money. He looked as if he knew how to make money and keep it, and how to invest it when he had his mind made up. His blue eye was cool and acute, his features weather-beaten and set, his manners utterly without polish, but decent, like his calf-skin shoes and blue-gray socks. As to his clothes, Fitz-Hugh indignantly observed to a bystander, "A suit like he wore never cost above twenty or twenty-five dollars in the world." In the course of coversation, before he left town, Mr. Thompson mentioned that they were his Sunday clothes, and he never owned any better. This left people a deep impression of his wealth, as it gave him the privilege of wearing such clothes as he had a mind to; but poor men of the Fitz-Hugh order, who never could pay for one suit before the next one wore out, called it thankless for good gifts not to make use of them to their fullest ability.

"If I didn't live something according to the station I was in," Fitz-Hugh said, talking it over before Wednesday-night prayer-meeting with a neighbor, "I should expect to have my means taken away from me," a remark which went to fix in people's minds the existing opinion, that Fitz-Hugh was capable of getting away with whatever portion fortune was pleased to send him, small or large.

Mr. Thompson stated confidentially to chance acquaintances at the hotel, that he did not like to do business with the land company, as it was interested, and he did not know how far it was to be depended on; but, as he was going to invest in Western land, after studying New Canton, he was satisfied, if he could get ground cheap enough, that it was the best thing he could do. He charmed Paddleford, Senior, by asking his advice. Merriman, on whom he called, was delighted with the man, and urged him to stay and settle in New Canton by all means. Merriman introduced him to Stokes and Bates and Luxton; and he got advice from all three.

By way of inducing Mr. Thompson to locate in New Canton, these men said more for the town than Burt or Peppernell would have done; and were so carried away by their zeal, that, without intending it, they found themselves in the land office, showing its maps and contemplated improvements as eloquently as if they all had stock in it.

Mr. Thompson was in no hurry to buy; but he privately told every one he had no more doubt of New Canton's future than he had of a Judgment Day. He was first attracted to it by studying the map of the state of Illinois, at home in Connecticut. It had a wonderfully promising geographical position, and, in the very nature of things, must grow into an immense inland city. It was as plain as day to any one who had ever made a study of the laws that govern the growth of cities. Every man who built a house or opened a farm within a hundred miles of New Canton contributed just that much to its growth; for his trade must inevitably come there some day. New Canton was already being talked of in the East; and "land lying around loose," as he expressed it, would not long be in the market.

Finally, he bought the Taylor place, the Adams place, and Gubbins's eighty acres, and paid a thousand dollars down on each, giving a mortgage for the balance, in four annual payments.

Then there was an excitement in town.

"What did he pay?" asked Paddleford, Senior, peering over the edge of his ledger and the desk railing.

"Hundred and fifty for Taylor's, two hundred for Adams's, and a hundred and twenty-five for Gubbins's," said Tom.

"Not per acre?"

"Yes, per acre. And, what's more, he paid a thousand apiece to each of 'em. There ain't no humbug about it. I saw 'em deposit the cash with Gardiner."

"What! so? Why, that land would have been dear six months ago at $20 an acre. The nearest's two miles out," was Paddleford's answer. And he went away sorrowful; for he could have had a million of acres at $1.25 an acre, if he had "struck in" ten years before, and had the million and a quarter of dollars to pay for it.

Mr. Thompson was asked why he bought so far out of town.

"Far out? Every foot of that land will be a long ways *in* town in three years. Don't pity me. I wish I had more to spend the same way."

The news reached Mr. Burt, and roused him mightily. He wanted to know why Adams, Gubbins, and Taylor hadn't offered the company their land before selling. They'd given bargains to a total stranger, when their own townsmen would have been glad to have taken it at the price, and possibly more. Peppernell denounced them for a set of idiots. The "Midland" had determined to locate its depots and shops out that way; and how Thompson became possessed of the facts was a mystery. He had taken them in nicely. The land company wanted the land, and was bound to have it, at some price or other. It was a necessity to them.

The "Sentinel" had an elaborate article on the sale, and laid great stress on the fact it was for cash, and good and lawful money had been paid for it, as if the inhabitants of New Canton had been in the habit of trading shark's teeth and red feathers in exchange for commodities. It was stated, in impressive italics, that the same land six months before would have been considered high at twenty dollars an acre; but that the price paid for it was not exorbitant, when the growth of New Canton and its certain progress was taken into account.

Gubbins, Adams, and Taylor began to feel as if they had been swindled; and, while in public they kept a good face, in private they doubted whether they had done wisely in selling so cheaply. They remembered the farmers in Chicago, who sold their land for one or two hundred dollars an acre, and, in ten years, saw it covered with fine buildings and worth more per square foot than they had got per acre. They came into town, and held long conversations with Burt; and there was much driving out and examining of plats and maps, and consultations of records and documents at the court-house.

A few days passed, and Peppernell called in the office of the land company.

"Thompson gone?"

"Yes."

"He paid cash for them farms?" asked Peppernell, inquiringly.

"Certainly; and the transaction gives confidence, which we want very much just now."

"I understand."

"It gives us capital to go on too. Thompson bought at what Gubbins, Adams, and Taylor considered at the time a big price. When they saw their mistake, they got sick. They wanted land again; and I sold Taylor the piece on the north line, Gubbins the piece next to it but one, and Adams one on the southeast corner; and they paid down the thousand dollars each they got from Thompson, and I took their notes with mortgage for the balance. I have their notes in the safe; and they have Thompson's notes, which are just as good as the land is. I hope he will pay them as they fall due. But the notes of our friends are perfectly good if the land don't sell for ten dollars. Besides, they paid more for the land I sold them than they got for their own, on account of its nearness to town; and they are all anxious to get more, before it's too high. We have good notes, which gives us something to go on. It wasn't very much of an operation, Colonel, but it'll do. The effect of the transaction will have a good influence. We had more inquiries yesterday and to-day than we've had for weeks; and there are a dozen good sales on the books now. It'll work, if we stick to it. By the way, Colonel, you want to lose that discouraged face of yours, and have Sharp and Peak look a little more as if they were worth a million. It would be a good thing if you could get a new buggy; — and, say, whitewash your front fence; and a new suit of clothes would help, for Peak. We must look prosperous. Whitewash your fence, and — spread whitewash over most every thing. We must look as solvent as we can, if we have to go in debt for it. People see the prosperity. They don't, thank Heaven, see where it comes from."

The advice was carried out to the letter. The four directors suddenly became pressed with business. Mr. Burt would not let them talk very much. He had no faith in any one's talk but his own; but they kept very hard at work. They drove furiously. They were taking strangers out to various parts of the town. They were riding long distances into the country, and returning in all sorts of mysterious ways; and Peppernell had a trick of driving down the main street, getting out in front of the Grand Central, and, stepping hastily into the office of the hotel, taking from his vest a map of the county, as if his life depended on tracing out roads and marking out certain tracts of land very carefully. What impressed people most, was, that, when on such occasions a friend would step up and in a familiar way ask him to "take suthin'," Peppernell would look up vacantly, and answer: "No, thank you. Haven't time. Hev you seen Timmins, of Whetstun Township, in to-day? No? It's lucky. He's probably at home." And he would drive franticly in the direction of Whetstone Township, as though his life depended on getting there in the shortest possible time.

"Well, I'll be d—d!" was the remark after he had gone. "It must be mighty important business 'd prevent old Pep taking a drink when he was asked. I've known him leave the court-house on a wink when he was sheriff, and he's now declinin' a spoken invite!"

From the New Canton "Forum of the People."

"WE were favored with a call from John R. Thompson, Esq., of Meriden, Connecticut, last week. Mr. Thompson came to New Canton on a tour of observation, for the purpose of making investments in real estate, if he should be convinced that the future of the city was as brilliant as supposed.

"Mr. Thompson is one of the heaviest capitalists in Meriden, and has operated very largely in Western real estate, preferring that form of investment to any other, as more certain, besides being immensely profitable.

"It is needless to say, that, after examining thoroughly, and making the most minute examination of our facilities, Mr. Thompson invested, as we stated last week. He purchased the 80 of John Taylor, the 120 of Daniel Gubbins, and the 160 of Thomas Adams, paying on an average for the three tracts $165 per acre. These lands would not have brought, six months ago, more than $20 per acre.

"Rapid as this advance has been, we assert that the land went cheaply; and that opinion is shared by the managers of the land company. We understand they contemplated the purchase of these pieces, on certain information that the 'Midland' intended to locate their depots in the vicinity; but Mr. Thompson purchased before they were aware that the gentlemen would sell. Mr. Burt acknowledged that the New Englander got ahead of him, and wrote last Monday, offering him a very handsome advance, which he promptly declined, saying that he would not sell at any price. 'If New Canton does what I expect it will do,' wrote Mr. Thompson, 'I have made a big thing. If it does not, I can stand it.'

"Messrs. Gubbins, Taylor, and Adams, feeling that they acted unwisely in parting with their real estate at this time, immediately repaired their error by purchasing other tracts, which are even more eligible and valuable.

"It is a fact which will be pleasing to the holders of real estate, that Mr. Thompson, whose investments have never failed to be profitable, was attracted to New Canton years ago by a study of the map of the state. He long since recognized the fact, that there must be at this point a great inland city; and his only regret is, that he did not come sooner. He intends to bring all his capital here; and this investment is the prelude to others of more importance.

"Mr. Thompson informed us that New Canton is already attracting a deal of attention in the money centers of the East; and another land company, made up of the strongest capitalists of the Nutmeg State, is not an improbable thing."

"THE block of lots on the corner of Elm and Locusts Streets was sold yesterday to parties from Worcester, Mass., for $167 each, one-fourth in hand, and the balance usual time. Five cottages will be commenced at once."

"THE projected improvements in the Fourth Ward are progressing as rapidly as the weather will permit. Col. Peppernell has purchased five hundred trees, in addition to the twenty already planted; and he will make that the most pleasant section of the city. The Colonel is at work indefatigably; and he is going about it in the right way. Would we had more Peppernells."

"PARTIES from Peoria were in the city yesterday, looking for a location to establish a manufactory of agricultural implements. They expressed themselves as delighted with our growing city, and returned to make final arrangements for removing their entire establishment. And so they come."

After all this, lots sold briskly; and the transactions were real. As hundreds of copies of the "Forum" were circulated gratuitously, containing these items, there were a large number of strangers in the town for awhile; and most of them purchased more or less, paying very small amounts down, and giving mortgages for the remainder.

The directors wore smiling faces. Mr. Gardiner, in particular, was pleased, as he had reason to be. Mr. Burt did not waste his time smiling; but he was a terror to the young man who mailed circulars in his office, and the town was pervaded with him. He wanted to keep up the effect his strategy had produced.

No one, not even Peppernell, knew that Mr. Thompson was Burt's brother-in-law, — that the money he paid for his land Burt borrowed of Mr. Gardiner, and repaid with the same money, received from those to whom Thompson paid it. No one saw the expression of relief on Mr. Burt's face when he took the money of Gubbins, Taylor, and Adams.

"It was a mighty close thing. What would have happened if I hadn't induced those idiots to buy, so that I could pay Gardiner? It was clever in Thompson to come and help me out."

CHAPTER VI.

JAMES GARDINER MAKES TROUBLE.

IT is not difficult for a young man to live cheerfully under the ban of his proposed mother-in-law, when he is sustained each morning by such an impetuous little note as this, from her daughter: —

"*Dear, dear, dear Jim:* Ma is determined that I shall marry Tom Paddleford, and quit you. She has worried me almost to death. But I never, never, never will give you up. I love you, and you only, and I will be true to you.
"Faithfully and forever,
"MARY.

"P. S. — I will always love you and be true to you. Ma shall not force me away from my dear Jim."

It may be remarked that Miss Lewis, the writer of this note, had cost her mamma and papa much thought and anxiety as to the proper school for their darling daughter. Considerable sums of money were spent to insure her graduating at the Mount Gilead Female College, from which she emerged with diploma, duly certified and ribboned, to expand her mind in writing such letters as the above. It may be taken as evidence of Mr. James Gardiner's deep and absorbing affection for her, that these notes seemed to him the most expressive in the world, and he could not conceive of a form of letter more satisfactory or beautiful.

As a rule, all love-letters ought to be burned within twenty-four hours of their receipt, lest they should fall into the hands of third parties, and straightway put them out of the idea of love and affection forever. A fond husband once showed a letter just received from his young wife, which he found too touchingly tender to keep from the world. In a burst of affection, the writer apostrophized him as her "hebenly pig," and signed herself his "ownie small white mice," symbols of much fond meaning, doubtless, to the parties, but not ravishing to the average friend.

The present fiat of Mrs. Lewis was inconvenient, because it forbade James the house, and the lovers had the trouble of finding other places to meet in ; but the little notes found on the office-desk were sufficiently reassuring for any man who only wanted to know that his love was true to him, and who held mothers and fathers cheap impediments in the way of young love. James felt himself master of the situation, and could smile superciliously at Tom Paddleford when he met him, and he returned with great courtesy the frosty bows of Mrs. Lewis, when fate ordained they met.

Thank Heaven, they did not live in feudal times, when parents had absolute control of the lives and persons of their daughters. Mary was of age ; and in good time what was to prevent her from putting on her bonnet, and walking out of the front door of the Lewis home, going with him quietly to the Rev. Mr. Latimer, and being united in the holy bonds of matrimony? Her papa could not order his cruel servitors to take her and confine her in the grated chamber of the northeast tower; neither could he seize Gardiner, and order his men-at-arms to bind the knave and hurl him into the deepest dungeon 'neath the castle-moat, for the reason that he had no men-at-arms, castle-moat, nor dungeon, unless a vegetable-cellar under the east wing of his house might be so used.

The main point was the truth of the girl herself and, as he got delightful epistles from her daily, and met her in the grove in long and sweet converse, he dismissed all fears, and regarded Tom Paddleford pityingly, as a man who would wake up some fine morning and find himself wofully deceived.

Still he could not help feeling disquieted when Mary told him that the little reptile came every night to the house, and her mother compelled her to see and entertain him till nearly eleven. She might plead headache, or earache, or any other excuse; but she had to sit and play and sing and talk with him; and it had gone so far that he had invited her to accompany him to a concert.

James kissed her for a brave little girl when she told him she refused, and, when her mother attempted to use her authority, rebelled, and there had been a terrible time about it.

"Ma told me I was an ungrateful girl, to fly in the face of my parents in that unnatural way. But I told her it was enough if I had to see him in the house, without going out with him, and making a show of myself to the whole town. We had words; and ma stormed and pa cried, and I was so angry you can't tell, but I wouldn't go. And pa and ma went out of the room and talked it over. I heard pa say it wouldn't do to crowd me too far at once, and ma sniffed, and they came back. And ma said that if I would be willful I might have my way; but I would be sorry for it. Tom came in the evening, and stayed half an hour later than he ever had, and begged me not to treat him so coldly, for he loved me; and he tried to take my hand, and — oh! Jim, I'm dreadfully miserable, and wish it was all over."

James folded her in his strong arms, in which she rested securely, feeling that there she was safe from all the Paddlefords in the world, supported and sustained by all the Lewis mothers that ever lived.

Assuring him that she would never marry Tom, never, and would be true to her dear James forever; and, after looking around in a frightened manner, to be sure no one had seen them together, she left him, and ran home like a frightened hare.

Despite this assurance, James was ill at ease. Their meetings grew less frequent, and she often failed in their appointments. He was always in the grove a full half-hour before her; and it is no small thing for a full-blooded, impatient man to wait for the woman he loves, when he has been looking at his watch every ten minutes, three hours before the time. When he had waited a half hour, walking up and down, to work off the impatience possessing him, he would curse all the world; and, after another half-hour, would go to his room and sulk the evening away, and wonder whether it wouldn't be better, after all, to cut the whole thing, and let Mary go.

But when the next time she came with eyes that showed weeping, and sprang to his side and clung there, and told with sobs, that ma kept so close a watch upon her that she couldn't possibly get away, and that wretch, Paddleford, came in earlier than usual, and she had to stay, and then broke down and cried as though her heart would break, Jim could but kiss her tenderly, and tell her that he would soon put an end to it all by carrying her off and making her his wife.

"What under Heaven has your mother against me?" he asked.

"I don't know, for I don't hear their talk. Ma don't talk to pa much. She don't need to talk to anybody."

"I understand. She is a whole family, all but a daughter, in herself. But haven't you any idea?"

"Once I heard ma say something about the land company, and once I heard something about some New York bank, and your father, but I don't know what it was about."

Gardiner looked grave at this. He knew what it meant; and how Mrs. Lewis had obtained the information puzzled him. But he dismissed the idea, as men do dangers not close upon them.

But when the little notes began to come infrequently and the appointments were kept rarely, and there was a confusion in her manner when she did meet him, which told she kept something back she dared not tell him, he began to feel his position unendurable. He begged her to tell him frankly all that was between them, but her only answer was a wringing of hands and floods of tears.

After a few such distracting passages he was not quite unprepared to receive this note, which came to him blotted and blurred, and he knew cost the poor girl a heartful of pain to write. As it came by the little bound-girl, direct from Mrs. Lewis, he knew whom he had to thank, though it was in Mary's handwriting : —

" *Dear, dear Jim :* It's all over. I can't hold out any longer. Ma has driven me to it. I can't tell you the reason, but I must marry Tom Paddleford, and that right away. Forgive me and forget me. You will know some day why I do it, and then you won't blame me. I shall always love you.
" In despair,
" Your Mary."

The next morning, when he met Tom Paddleford, that gentleman cocked his hat over his left ear — it had plenty of support — and winked such undisguised triumph that Gardiner only avoided knocking him down by crossing the street. Mrs. Lewis met him soon after, and assumed a aggravatingly pleasant air toward him! He could not strike her, nor was there any way in which he could express his regard for her. Old Lewis avoided him carefully. When likely to meet on the sidewalk, the old gentleman found it convenient to cross the street, even if the mud were ankle-deep; seeing which, Gardiner took a special delight in coming upon him where the mud was the thickest and the crossing all but impossible.

What vexed and worried him most was that he could not by any strategy see Mary. Either the dragon, her mother, kept too close a watch upon her, or the girl herself did not dare to meet him. Which was it? The truth was, the mother feared the influence she knew James had over her daughter, and

Mary herself was afraid to meet the man she had betrayed. She was sick at heart, and, having consented to breaking her troth, she wanted nothing to make the sacrifice demanded of her intolerable.

It was hardly possible, however, that trouble should not grow out of such exceedingly good cause. James Gardiner, smarting under the injustice done him, was in a state of mind that made him a very dangerous man. Had Mary died, he could have buried her and borne it; but to see the girl he loved, and who loved him, taken away and given to the last man in the world worthy so much sweetness, added gall to bitterness.

One afternoon, as he was walking toward his office, in the ugliest possible mood, he met Tom Paddleford in front of the Grand Central. As ill luck, which seemed to rule the day, had it, Tom had been for an hour at the bar of the hotel, filling himself with the whisky of the region, and was as reckless as he was ugly. As he left the group of stimulated men who had been with him, he saw Gardiner, and his little soul was filled with a delight that was almost a delirium. He could not restrain himself from showing off the triumph swelling his little soul to bursting. As Gardiner passed, he leered at him with an expression so malignantly small, of such devilish satisfaction that it shook all resolve and prudence out of Gardiner.

One well-directed blow from his nervous fist laid the fellow on the sidewalk, a rod from where he had been standing; and, before the bystanders could interfere, Gardiner had pulled him up and was bringing up all arrears of discipline from Tom's babyhood till now. One or two tried to interfere, but the only good

JAMES GARDINER MAKES TROUBLE. 81

they came in for was part of the neat and well-finished beating, and they wisely left him alone.

At last, tired and breathless, James dismissed his tormentor with one contemptuous kick, and left him, bruised and bleeding, on the ground. Turning to the crowd, he asked if any of Mr. Paddleford's friends were desirous of avenging his wrongs, and walked away.

He went to Esquire Sharp's office, and directed that worthy, if Mr. Paddleford should make a complaint of assault and battery against him, to plead guilty, and he would pay the fine. Then he went to his office, and locked himself in. The exercise and satisfaction made him feel better a few minutes; but, when he cooled down, he felt that it was no credit to thrash so small a brute as Paddleford, and that, while he had made Tom ridiculous, he had, in doing it, mortified himself.

It would require a better pen than mine to describe the effect of such extraordinary proceedings upon New Canton society. The standing of the parties, the unexpected assault, and its almost tragic ending gave the village something to talk over that was a first-class sensation. The first report circulated was that Tom had been set upon by Gardiner, and killed, Mrs. Paddleford had gone insane when she saw the dead body, and was now under the care of three physicians, and it took three men to hold her. This report was next morning contradicted: Tom was not quite dead, but his skull was fractured, and he could not live an hour. Surgeons had been sent for express to Chicago. The next news was that Jim Gardiner had gone to his office, after the deed, and deliberately cut his throat. Then that was contradicted. He had not really cut his throat, but was preparing to do it, and had the razor strapped and honed, but was prevented by Peppernell and his father, who came in the nick of time to save him.

But, when the cause of the assault became known, there were pickings for the teeth of the gossip-feeder. Mary Lewis had left Jim Gardiner and was going to marry Tom Paddleford, which was abundant cause for the terrible assault. What had she done that for? Because Mrs. Lewis found James had another wife in an adjoining county. Because he had committed a forgery and momentarily expected to be arrested. Because Mrs. Lewis had discovered this, and Mrs. Lewis had discovered that, and things yet unknown and too dreadful to be breathed.

Poor Mary did not escape. The trouble had begun when Gardiner found out she had another lover for two years; and Jim had thrown her on that account, and Paddleford had been trapped into taking her. But, as this rendering was hardly satisfactory, it was said that she had been indulging with a flirtation with Paddleford for a year, and that the night before the assault Jim had discovered them in a delicate position, but would not punish him then and there, because of the presence of a lady, but had warned him he would kill him the next time he met him, no matter when or where it might be. And the people said she must be an artful girl to manage the thing so nicely as to keep both Jim and Tom in the dark so long.

All this time Paddleford was at home, in bed, covered with vinegar and brown paper, a varied assortment of welts and bruises from head to foot, out of which he breathed threatening and curses, like a little demon, at James Gardiner and all that concerned him. He was equally indignant at Mary Lewis, as he would not have been in this awkward and ridiculous position but for her; and he swore great oaths that he would get even with Jim Gardiner yet. Not by meeting him in any way face to face — that he never thought of; but he lay in his bed and devised schemes for mean vengeance; and, to do him justice, never was a man better fitted for such work.

As for Gardiner, it was the end of all his hopes. Of course, he could never get near Mary Lewis again; and, to tell the truth, in a sick, despairing way, he had ceased to care. He resigned himself to his fate as best he could; and in a manful sort of way tried to accustom himself to the thought of seeing the girl he loved the wife of another man.

Mrs. Lewis acted in the premises very promptly. She announced, without more delay, the coming marriage of her daughter with Mr. Paddleford, and took vigorous measures to contradict the absurd rumors about her family. Mary had never been any thing more to Mr. Gardiner than a friend, which was to be expected, as both families were among the oldest in New Canton. She had engaged herself to Mr. Paddleford, as she had a right to do; and if Mr. Gardiner took offense at it he was exceeding all bounds. If he was in love with her daughter, he should have made it known before she had contracted herself to another. The whole affair was a mystery to her, as it was, she presumed to every one else. Mr. Paddleford was not seriously injured, she was happy to say, and would not have been at all had he been attacked in a manly way, as men of honor do such things. But what could he do? He was struck senseless before he had any opportunity to defend himself. Would further trouble grow out of it? She hoped not. She did not believe in brute force in a Christian land. She had exacted a promise from Mr. Paddleford that he would not have recourse to violence, but would treat his assailant with the silent contempt which his unmanly outrage deserved.

And her auditors all said "Certainly!" and "To be sure!" and "We knew it!" though every one of them knew that every word the good lady had uttered was false, and they knew that she knew it. But in New Canton, as elsewhere, much stress is laid upon that precept of morality which declares that truth is not to be spoken at all times, which some observe so carefully as to avoid speaking it at all.

Mrs. Lewis had many reasons for pushing the wedding with all possible dispatch, some of which she gave to the public and some she did not. She was a lady who knew just how much to say and just when to say it; and a preserve-jar with brandy paper and white of egg over the top was not more close about what seemed good to keep to herself.

CHAPTER VII.

MRS. BURT'S HUSBAND'S WIFE.

MARIA BOODY was a very pretty girl when Charles Burt married her, fifteen years before. A plump, full-fledged rustic beauty, with the fairest pink, white, and pearl compounded in her cheek; quantities of brown hair, warmed by the sun to a lovely shade; and large brown eyes, clear and exacting: her face was regular enough to be pretty, spite of its calculating, common-place expression. She was a good deal of a country belle, with the acres of the big Boody farm behind her, aided not less by the doors of the ample "butt'ry" at home, stored with rich pies and cake, ajar for youths on courting bent. Those deep, generous pies, puffy doughnuts with raisins in them, and "riz cake" played no despicable part in luring suitors for the eight Boody girls, with their thick hair, full busts, and slim waists, and capability for holding their own with a pretty tight grip. Burt, then, a promising and homeless youth, was one of the first flies lured by the sugar, and took to himself one of the daughters, thinking to found for himself such a home as she came from. For fifteen years Mate Boody had done up his shirts with wonderful precision, kept his house brightly clean, and stored his shelves with flaky pies and custards that rivaled her mother's, was generous at setting a table for his company, and managed to hold her end of the matrimonial contract with conscious precision, — a faithful, untroubled creature, with not two ideas outside her two lines of being a good housekeeper and a good dresser, and, as such, holding no mean place in the esteem of New Canton.

Time, however, which makes the prettiest faces carricature themselves, had played uncivil tricks with Mate's face and manners. Any household which finds its living in fried meats and rich gravies, and "never can sit down to table without pie," to use Mrs. Burt's formula, shares the attentions of bilious attacks and typhoid fever, neither of which are kind to hair, complexion, or figure. Hence the doctor was more essential to Mate Burt than her husband; and her support was drawn equally from the "butt'ry" and medicine-chest. She was given to "dull headaches" and "poor spells," when she took to her bed and sipped ginger-tea, and declared she never should want any thing but a nightgown to wear any more, and used up gallons of cologne, for which she had a *penchant*, as well as for all expensive and high-flavored scents. From these spells she always came out revived and cheerful, as if she enjoyed such seasons. But the time had passed when any one would think of calling her a pretty woman. Burt, whose natural bent was to find his own the best of every thing, used to mention her "graceful carriage" to his intimates, and call their attention to the "mingled cordiality and dignity with which she received his friends;" but even the partial husband did not venture beyond that. A ghastly woman, wearing curls, met his guests at his door; and the " mingled dignity " savored of stiffness and peremptoriness to strangers. But, as she said, in her good humor, she had had the use of her good looks, and that was enough.

The weather was warm for spring; and Mrs. Burt, in a loose wrapper, — in her own phrase, " looking domestic," and feeling, as she also said, " as if something would do her good," — had taken down her medicine-box, and was turning over its stores. With her sat a young woman, who held an anomalous position in the Burt household, as she was on a footing with the family, and certainly not a useless companion. In New Canton phrase, which hit the medium neatly, she was " keeping house for Mrs. Burt." That, in contradistinction to the term, " working out," implied both independence and responsibility, as well as actual service. Most people would have thought Mrs. Burt uncommonly favored in the choice of a housekeeper; for her companion was a bright and pretty young woman, who looked as if she had both a wit and a will of her own.

Mrs. Burt declared herself " all out of kelter," and said she must take something for the blood.

" What are you going to take? " asked Emeline, from her sewing.

" I don't know. I'll see what I've got," was the original answer, as Emeline's mistress sat down to sort over the contents of a tin box, which filled the room with the aroma of drugs and herbs, — pipsissiway and prickly-ash, rhubarb, jalap, and aloes, — making a running commentary on the unshapen papers, as she turned them over affectionately.

"Epsom salts. I don't like to take salts, if any thing else will do. They're so penetrating. I've known the taste to get into my system, and stay there a day or two. Mandrake pills I'm afraid of — a little too griping. Pulmonic bitters taste good. Emeline, don't you sometimes think there's something the matter with the lungs when a person feels all gone so? Or is it all stomach?"

"I should think something was gone. It might be the stomach, or it might be the dinner," was Emeline's answer.

"Iron and calisaya. I think I must go to taking that again. I have to leave off these tonics after I've taken them awhile. They're too strengthening. Just give me a spoon, Emeline. I'll take some while I'm about it, before I forget. If I had a cold nose, now, I'd know it was ague, and go right to taking quinine. I always feel as if I'd got hold of something sure when I get to quinine. Boneset. That's some of mother's. She always has a bed of it growing under the fence by the south-wall pasture. Calls it her herb-garden. What quarts of it I've taken in spring. Time of the March plowing, when the sun began to get hot, she used to call us in, and make us drink hot boneset all round, a good pint apiece, to clear the blood and get us in trim for the house-cleaning. We could just raise a dust off a clean floor, then! Powdered ants."

"I've heard Solomon recommended them," Emeline observed, at this juncture; "but I never knew how he meant they were to be taken. What's the dose? Can't you see your way clear to giving me some?"

Mrs. Burt was not sure whether she approved her

handmaid's levity with her sacred herbs, and it was with repressing gravity she explained: "They're blistering, like Spanish flies. I had them on my chest, my bad turn, last May. It was this growing weather;—dreadful opening to the pores, you know;—and I slept with my window open, took an awful cold, and threatened lung fever. Aunt Maria had been complaining of ants all the spring. They were just overrunning her. When she heard I was taken on my chest, she said she knew just what them ants were sent for; and she scooped a handful, and mashed 'em up on a plantain-leaf, and came over with it on her hand, and clapped it on my lungs; and it drew beautifully, just like Croton oil. Ever take Croton oil, Emeline?"

"That's something I've always thought I should rather give than take," said the girl, demurely, turning a delicate fell.

"Fond of giving folks something smart, aren't you?" said Mrs. Burt, in one of her tart moments, while Emeline busied herself with her sewing, as if she had not heard. "There's dill and catnip and pennyroyal. Isn't pennyroyal good for something in spring? I always thought it must be of great use some way, if we only knew what, there's so much of it. Mother Doble's Extract. Oh! here's what I was so set after all the while. I couldn't contrive what had become of it. It's excellent for summer, as any thing I've got a hint of. Keeps the pores open, and keeps one state of health so satisfactory."

"You aren't like Mis' Payne, down by the creek. She says she always enjoys poor health; but it's the dosing and worrying to get well takes the most out of her," said Emeline.

"Mrs. Payne is a very respectable woman," said Mrs. Burt, with dignity; "and I don't believe in her making such frivolous speeches. I'm not one who believes in dosing all the time; but I do think if people would pay more attention to their health it would be for their advantage. Daylight Pills. When must I have taken them? If my memory preserves me, it must have been after New Year. I always take a big dose about Thanksgiving; and I don't feel necessitated to pay any particular attention to what I eat, like some folks. I can't bear to see 'em sit down to a good meal of victuals, and they 'can't eat this,' and the other 'don't agree' with them, showing disrespect to the person that asked them. I'm no great eater, and none of my family was, though my father never was the man to sit down to a poor meal in his own house. Now, after eating fat turkey and sparerib with sage, at Thanksgiving, I always have a rising in my throat (I suppose the bile swims on top of the stomach, till it's disposed of); and I just take four or five pills, and feel as clear-headed — seems as if I could see daylight right through me. That's what they're named for, I suppose — Daylight Pills. Then I can eat buckwheat-cakes and sausage with anybody, till house-cleaning time, without being obliged to call in a doctor for my liver, as most do. Brandreth's are more searching. I like to take a dose of them after Thanksgiving time, and again at Christmas; but I don't like to use them quite so common as to lose the effect. I prefer the Daylights for ordinary; they're such a mild, genteel pill. Perhaps others wouldn't advise taking medicine so promiscuous; but I say, why shouldn't they take it while they're well, and get the effect of it, and not wait to lay by and have to give their whole attention to it? There's most always some hidden matter with them, that the medicine is sure to search out; and I think it's a good thing to take something ahead."

"I guess I'll take something ahead, then, for a bilious fever; for I should mortally hate to have to stop for one by and by," said Emeline.

"Here's what I shall have to give you if you ever get any thing on the nerves — lady-slipper. I wake up in the night, with my nerves all giggetting and upset, feeling just as if I'd got a call to die before morning; and Mr. Burt, he wakes up and reaches right over to the bureau for the mixture and the cup and spoon, and counts the drops, and I go off to sleep just as comfortable. When I go to bed, I have every thing ready I want in the night — the camphor and lady-slipper, and the mustard for hot drafts, and some vinegar and flour, and a rag to spread it on, and a cup and spoon, and an alcohol-lamp to heat it by, and knife to spread it with, — I don't neglect a single thing, — and the hot-drops if I need 'em, and an extra blanket to lay over the bed if it turns cool in the night, and my double gown in case of fire. I believe in being prepared. Don't the Bible say, ' Be ye also ready'?"

"That's a good verse to follow," said Emeline, this time wickedly. "I try to be always prepared, especially if it's any thing in the shape of good luck."

"How you do run off the track," said Mrs. Burt, impatiently, taking up the conversation. "But I don't have to doctor as I used to. When I was first married, I had no health at all; and, the first two years, the doctor's bills run up to three hundred dollars. I saw 'twas going to take the profits off; and I got Gunn's 'Domestic Medicine,' and I studied it. There's more in taking care of yourself than folks give in to. The first thing in the morning, when I wake up, I take a peristaltic lozenge in my mouth, to get the acid out of my stomach, and a swallow of iron and strychnia after breakfast. All that ever I could find do any good before eating was to chew a piece of salt codfish 'fore breakfast, to give an appetite; or, in hot weather, a dose of tanzy bitters. When I was doing my own work, I kept the pitcher of herb tea in the cupboard, where I could drink a sip handy; and I wear red flannel winter and summer, 'count of that neuralgia I thought was coming on the winter Mr. Burt was so near losing his property."

"I didn't know that could happen to such well-off folks as you," said Emeline, interested.

"Oh! I won't pretend to say that some folks would have held it any great of a loss; but he had some mortgages at twelve per cent., and, come to find out, there was a claim never been settled, against the estate; and the equity court gave judgment against the holder, and made our mortgage only a second one. I declare, Mr. Burt didn't see his way to making a cent out of it, and 'twas much as ever if he got the principal back again; and I was so worked up I didn't sleep a wink for a week, and didn't get over it for a month. It was all of eight hundred dollars Mr. Burt had left him by an old uncle he never expected to get a cent from; and he'd salted it down for me, in case any thing ever happened."

"It was pretty hard to have all you had put in danger so," said Emeline, sympathizingly.

"Oh! 'twasn't to say all't we had. I don't suppose it'd made any considerable difference; but it was losing money, don't you see? It'd been a thousand dollars in another year, compound interest; but we had to take six per cent. to get any thing, and the mortgage was lifted at the sale. It seems as if people had a grudge against allowing those that have money to make any thing by it. I wanted to settle it by law; but Mr. Burt said that it wasn't worth throwing good money after bad. Well, as I was saying, when you interrupted me, lying awake nights and having that loss on my nerves, upset me, so I had my face bound up most of the time. Now I wear flannel, and keep a little bunch of sweet balm next my skin, and I don't feel it any more."

To say that Mrs. Charles Burt was a strong-minded woman would be a faint expression. Her strength of character showed itself, not in shrieking after privileges, which she would not know what to do with if she had them, or in craving for knowledge that would be of no use to her if she got it; but in keeping a firm hold over her feelings and those of everybody else, — in getting what she wanted, quietly and irresistibly; and doing favors for her friends, for which she exacted full credit and return. Mrs. Burt did not scold, or turn things. She just gave them a push, when they worked her way, where she wanted, and brought no arguments to bear save her own irreproachable performance of duty and the absolute impossibility of ignoring her claims. She was calm, — when money was out of the question, — bright, even, and rather a witty woman in her way; at least, she had the reputation of being the bright one of the family. In her inmost soul she did think highly of Charles Burt as her husband, and as secretly held the belief that the best of the world was always to be found in the Boody family and such males as had the advantage to be connected with them by marriage. On the faculty and wit of her sisters-in-law she reserved her opinion.

Though her person had not the charms which made her attractive in youth, it developed others, not always found in a lady of forty odd. She wore a pad of hops on her waist; and to her inner vestment the year round clung a faint odor of poultices and herbs, as it would to a garret-rafter. Whoever was fond of the odor of musk lozenges, or the pungent oil of spearmint, or the dreaded bitter of picra and rhubarb, would find attraction in her presence, but hardly otherwise. She would take chicken-broth for the colic, or Croton oil for any other dissipation of the interior organs, with equal indifference. Health was her great object, she said; and she sedulously studied to build up her tabernacle of the flesh. The young druggist never failed to send her word of any new medicines he might receive; and she had shown a ready spirit in trying, at his recommendation, Eucalyptus and Vinegar Bitters, Tarrant's Seltzer, and Winchester's Hypophosphites, Nichol's Bark and Iron, somebody else's steel, port wine, and beef-tea, with "liquid lightning," fever-and-ague pads, patent shoulder-braces, and magnetic soles. She used medicines without prejudice. If an alterative wouldn't do, an astringent would. Castor oil, jalap, senna, podophyllin, and dandelion-root stood for the same thing in her dispensatory; and, if she couldn't get calomel, she took as contentedly a double portion of cream of tartar.

The drugs and herbs duly disappeared before tea-time, but not the obnoxious odors, which remained to dismay Mr. Burt's overkeen senses. "You've been having an herb-bee, I should think," he observed, mildly, on opening the door.

"The things hadn't been looked over in the medicine-closet since last fall; and I do hate to see medicines go to waste when they cost so much."

Which was all so proper that no fault was to be found with it.

"Seems to me the house might be aired a little more before we sit down to supper," Mr. Burt ventured to say.

"Certainly. Emeline, put up the window. Did you ask Bateman if that tonic phosphate had come yet?"

"No, I forgot it. Things went wretchedly to-day at the office. People won't buy, and you can't make 'em."

"Why, the paper said you sold several lots this week," said his wife.

"Humph!" was the gracious answer to this observation. Mr. Burt did not confide his business affairs to his wife, any more than a great many other good husbands do; and she was just as wise as other people outside of the land company.

"It's a pity Chicago people with money won't come in and buy," said Emeline, thoughtfully, as she served the canned peaches.

"What interest have you in it?" asked Mrs. Burt, looking at her coldly, but with natural surprise.

"They say there's going to be a town library as soon as they can afford it," said the discreet young woman; " and I should like to take books out just as soon as convenient. Can't you hire somebody to start the bidding, as they do at auctions," she said, glancing mischievously at Mr. Burt.

Mrs. Burt observed, in a negative tone, that " New Canton had more important business than getting a library for young folks to take novels out of," which Emeline heard with indifference.

" Find me somebody to start the bidding, Emeline, and half a dozen men who believe in New Canton as you do, and you'll make my fortune and yours, too," said Mr. Burt, carelessly throwing half a glance toward her side of the table, at which he sat, in the fashion of prudent Canton husbands, with a shoulder turned to any woman except his own wife.

" Faith comes by hearing," said the pretty housekeeper, lightly. " If one Canton man hears his neighbor has bought a lot, he will buy one, if he mortgages his house to do it. What one does the rest do. You haven't lived in New Canton long enough to find that out," she concluded, demurely.

" Maria, you always have an idea worth listening to," said her husband, turning deferentially to that lady, and putting the nicest slice of hot toast for her plate.

Mrs. Burt's manner showed that she had considered her husband and handmaid had been allowed sufficiently to indulge in topics of their own choosing. She turned to the former with an air of renewing rational conversation.

" Caroline Spencer is back from Chicago."

No response to this news.

" She brought back Miss Caddie Kinsley, her friend,

from Wabash Avenue!" impressively, to call attention to the important announcement. " She belongs to the very best society there. Carrie has invited her friends to call to meet Miss Kinsley expressly on Thursday, so that she will not feel obliged to see those who come on any other day."

" Confound Carrie Spencer for aping high airs. I suppose you intend to trot out, then, in your silver-plated harness." Mr. Burt had this playful mode of alluding to his wife's best toilet.

" Of course!" with dignity and a fashionable air, happily suiting the topic. " I shouldn't think of hurting dear Carrie's feelings by not going; and it wouldn't do to refuse Mrs. Spencer."

" Well, I suppose you women must have that sort of thing," said Mr. Burt. " I wish, though, I could see any hope of things getting along faster in business. If Condit could only be got to take that plot for a factory, you could have the rooms furnished just as you want them. Isn't sister Laura coming, as we expected? We could put her in the best chamber."

" She will have to bring her husband's sister with her; and I'm not going to stir up the best chamber for any such company. Delia Vance never has been used to any thing; and I won't have her spattering my wall-tidy and lopping down on the Marseilles you gave twelve dollars for."

" Laura won't like it; she is dreadfully sensitive if any of William's folks are slighted."

" I don't care. I'm not going to fix up my best things and have them used for folks there is no inducement to treat so."

" Have it your own way. I don't see but the

Vance girl is nice enough for anybody's best room. The Vances always had things very neat and tasty when I was there."

"Yes; but they had no more idea of style than you could put in one eye. Laura says the Vance girls would just as soon be caught in a calico dress afternoons as not. She had all she could do the last time Delia was staying with her to make her put on her black alpaca. The girl said she didn't see that a clean calico wasn't as good as an alpaca, any day. To have no more feeling for dress than that shows a dreadful common way of looking at things."

"Gardiner came round with a long face to-day. Was afraid he couldn't lift that paper for us next week, if he didn't hear better news from New York. I suppose I shall have to go up to Chicago and shin round for some money next week among those fellows; and they're harder to deal with than rocks."

"Isn't there any way to interest the Chicago men in New Canton, so that —"

There was an interest in Emeline's tone that sounded pleasantly to the overworked man. But the harsh voice of Mrs. Burt interrupted her in the middle of her sentence.

"Did he say whether Mrs. Gardiner was home from Chicago yet?" said Mrs. Burt. "I want to get the pattern of her *polonaise* — she is always so obliging about any such thing; and she always brings home some new idea. I declare, I think she is the only woman in town who has the least notion of what style is."

"You will want your new flannel shirts, won't you, if you go to town?" asked Emeline's soft voice.

"You took such a cold the last time, in the lake winds. I can hurry them up before you go."

Mr. Burt, with all expression banished from his face, was looking at his wife, with her spotless ruffles, the gold chain about her skinny neck, the chatter in her lips, and made absent answer, as he took up his paper. He was wondering if this was all the sympathy a man was to expect from a wife. She served him well in practical matters, but somehow he wanted more than this. What, he could not say; and she would have called it foolish if he had said it. Or, if she petted him with those fingers that were used to hold things in so firm a grip, he felt as if it would not suit him; and the voice of the hired servant in their house fell pleasantly on his ear. There was something of human kindness and warmth in her tones, clear from the trivial interest and self-seeking he had been treated to all his life from other women. If Mate only had known how to give him the kindness he craved like a schoolboy just then!

Fifteen years, he recollected, he had walked with this woman without a heart — a woman who could say pretty, silly things, and call him darling in the same tone in which she asked for more of that dumpling. As other wives did when they felt it part of their matrimonial policy to be tender, with an eye on the main chance, she could give him kisses that felt as if his lips had been touched with flannel; of all which just then he felt mortally tired.

"I guess I'll run across the road, and sit awhile with Mrs. Beers," said his wife. "Mr. Burt is so wrapped up in his newspaper, and he never was much of a hand to talk, anyhow."

And with her mind full of *polonaises*, the Spencers, the Vances, and similar matters of importance, she left her husband with the housekeeper.

Not much of a hand to talk? She should have heard him talk to Emeline. For Emeline talked to him of matters in which his soul was wrapped; and, if she was not well-informed, she, at least, felt an interest in them, and sympathized with the man who was carrying such a load and carrying it alone.

When Mrs. Burt came back, she wondered if they had been sitting in dead silence all the evening as she found them.

CHAPTER VIII.

A WEDDING COUNCIL.

"A MAN isn't married but once in his life," said the bridegroom-expectant, as his mother-in-law desired his opinion on the form with which his nuptials should be celebrated.

"Not rightly speaking, he isn't," said that bland being, more intent on diplomacy than correctness. "If ever he wants things to suit him, it's then. And, if you have any preference for a private wedding, to be more exclusive about the invitations, and have Mary more to yourself from the first, why, we would fall in with the idea willingly."

"A private wedding is well enough when people are going to cut a swell away from home," said Mr. Paddleford. "But I don't see that young folks with our prospects need to get married behind the door. A private wedding's the right thing when a fellow expects to put all his money on a showy trip, and shine at the big hotels. But I don't see the need. A fellow comes home feeling poor for a month afterward!" said this veteran, who talked as if he had been married a dozen times. "I don't want to begin like that. It isn't in my way. But, if Mary feels as if it is the proper thing to have a trip, why, I'm agreeable."

"Then you'd prefer more of a demonstration?" asked Mrs. Lewis, finding her efforts to avoid giving a large party confronted by the dread of giving offense to her prospective son-in-law.

"I'm for having a good time," said Mr. Tom. "But I don't want to take the responsibility on me. You know how a man likes to have his friends treated at his wedding; and I'd rather you'd carry out your own ideas. A man don't feel called on to interfere in such a matter. The next party we give, Mrs. Lewis, things will be different," he ended, with a smile, meant to be engaging.

"Suppose you speak to Mary about it, and you can arrange it to suit yourselves," suggested Mrs. Lewis, as a last hope.

"If Mary wants a trip, you'd have no hesitation in letting me know," said Tom, with a pre-engaged air. "I wasn't thinking of seeing her this morning: it would keep me too long. And I don't want her to get tired of me, while she might lose me, you know," with another of those smiles that would be charming if they were only entirely different. "I'll leave the matter to you; and I guess Tom Paddleford's wedding won't be the slowest one ever seen, neither. Good-morning." And the young man went down the steps jauntily, with a sense of having put his mother-in-law on her mettle and checkmated her evident wish to get out of giving him a party. Going to beat him out of his wedding party, and the only time he was likely to get married and have a wedding in his life!

This consultation took place within a few days after the note had been sent which quenched James Gardiner's hopes and bound Mary Lewis to the man she

A WEDDING COUNCIL.

detested. When it ended, the mother went in search of her daughter; and was rewarded by finding her in her own room, upstairs, white, and drenched with tears, and apparently sodden with crying.

"Mary, don't look so downcast," said Mrs. Lewis, with real concern at the sadness of her daughter, now that she was sure of her own way. "Your mother has seen more of life than you have, and knows what will make you happiest in the end. And she is sure you have chosen wisely."

"Chosen!" thought Mary.

"You have the man half the girls in town are wild to get for a husband; and he is dead in love with you."

This consoling idea made Mary's flesh creep.

"You fancy you have a preference for another man; but you don't know how soon that wears off. As far as love is concerned, one man is as good as another a year after a woman marries him. The best husband is the one who can keep you best. Mr. Paddleford can give you any thing you want; and, if you know how to keep up your influence with him, you can make him do any thing. I'm going to give you a wedding that will be something to think of all your life. I never had any wedding, to speak of. My mother died three weeks before I was married; and I wanted the wedding put off a year, but your father wouldn't hear of it. He said that I needed his care then, if I ever did; and, though it wasn't what I intended, I didn't feel like disputing any thing, and I let him have his own way that time."

"It was the last time," thought Mary. "Mother, if you care a thing for me, have it just as plain as you can. I sha'n't care for any thing. I wish I could marry Tom Paddleford and be dead before he laid a hand on me. I do."

"Mary, I am ashamed of you! As good as married to a man who worships you, and you talk in that sinful manner. I wouldn't have your father hear you for the world. What reason have you to abuse Mr. Paddleford? He isn't to blame for your having a first attachment and its being unfortunate. It isn't every man loves a woman so he would come near her after he knew of a prior engagement. And you may thank your mother for bringing you up, or there wouldn't be any second choice for you to put on airs about. Most girls take the first man who offers, and are thankful to get him. Your mother knows what's best for you, my child."

This said, Mrs. Lewis took out a genteel Russia-leather portfolio, with ornate gilt lock, drew out a mother-of-pearl pen, that looked as if it was designed only for very elegant correspondence indeed, and began writing with the serious brow of a secretary of state. Mary stole off to her own room, to fall down on her bed, cover her face with her hands, and think.

She had signed herself away. She refused to take it so, just yet. Something might — it would, surely — happen to prevent this horrible, unnatural thing she had been crowded into.

Mrs. Tom Paddleford! She shuddered at the word. Instead of living care free, a happy, girlish life, it meant staying at home all day, and receiving Tom Paddleford at dinner, and riding out with him in his spruce phaeton, in one of her wedding dresses, as she saw other young brides doing, very sober and still, and not as if it were the most agreeable performance they were submitting to. She remembered how one young married man had made fun for his friends by describing how he and his bride made out together. " Ju and I have the best times ever was," he would say, in an impartial way. " We haven't had but three fights a week yet." This when they were married a fortnight, and just back from their wedding tour.

It would be pleasant to have tiffs with some one you were fond of, so that you could afford to differ and make it up. There would be something sweet in making allowance for the little rough tempers and foibles which, she thought, made life more tender for having to forgive. But if she were bound and delivered to Tom Paddleford! She shrank and shivered at the thought. She could never call this new man she was to love, honor, and obey, " Tom." He would always be " Mr. Paddleford " to her, just as other loveless wives called their husbands Mr. Brown or Mr. Doolittle. She supposed he would be fond of her. It was understood that he was madly in love with her; and she, in a blind, cold way, was willing to take the benefit of his passion. She would let him be good in all sorts of ways to her, while she endured to be loved and worshipped in return. She was willing he should devote himself entirely to her; while all the return she was to make was to endure him. Such is the just and equal division which girls are willing to accept in life.

Between these thoughts would come the face of James Gardiner, pale with suffering, as she had seen it last. But she dwelt upon it no longer. The honor of a delicate girl rose between her and the old love;

and she shrank from the one thing that could disturb her peace. She would forget James till she could look upon him like any other acquaintance. Her thoughts turned to the coming days; and she wondered if she belonged to Mr. Thomas Paddleford now, and how soon he would be privileged to put his arm around her waist, and call her by her Christian name, and mention her as " my wife."

Well, she thought she could endure it. Very many, indeed, most of her respectable lady acquaintances, told her that they did not love their husbands when they married them. They accepted those gentlemen to please their families, or because they were pointed out as good matches; and they were now contented, and ready to tell every girl that she did not know what happiness was till she was married safely. After all, it was only one of the necessities of life, like being sick, and meeting accidents, and dying. Oh! if it was only all over, the last bed, and death —

" Mary!" called her mother from her room. " What is Mrs. File's first name?"

" Frances. Why, what are you writing to her about? I didn't know you and she ever wrote."

" She's one of the best people in this town; and I'm going to have her here, if I have to leave out a dozen others."

" Why, mother; what are you about?" asked Mary, turning red, and feeling as if called to life by unpleasant cold water.

" Making out the list of invitations to your wedding. I suppose you know they must be out two weeks, and there's barely time to send them round."

Mary put both her hands to her face, with a shock

which surprised herself. She did not know that she could feel so deeply. She lay there, with hands over her eyes, counting the throbs of pain, like the pulses of a wound that had just begun an aching never to end.

Then it was really true, and she was going to be married, and there was no help. Her mother was writing the invitations. That little thing brought her fate nearer than any thing yet had done.

At this moment a light breathing and a solid step was heard on the stairs; a white sunbonnet, under which shone a pair of knowing black eyes, was put in at the door, a neighborly voice cried, " I thought I could find you. Why, you're serious as an inquiry meeting. Haven't got into the wrong house, have I?"

"Mary Farrell!" cried Mrs. Lewis, in genuine relief, "you're one of the scarce folks that never come but they're wanted. I was missing something, and I believe, on my soul, it was you."

"That's a relief to my mind. Some of my neighbors are so little account I'm driven to make myself an infliction on the rest."

"If you had waited ten minutes more I should have sent for you," said Mrs. Lewis. "It isn't everybody I can speak to as I can to you, Mary."

Mary Farrell was a jolly, capable spinster, who lived with her mother next to the Lewises, and had, by summers and winters of faithful, shrewd neighboring, deservedly won the trust from Mrs. Lewis which she withheld from her own daughter and spouse. What would be mischief told to Mr. Lewis or Mary, with their romantic notions and inconsiderate way of speaking, was entirely safe with Mary Farrell. So there was a path across in Miss Farrell's yard, and a gate in the fence, through which confidential embassies went back and forth at any hour of the day. In token of perfect amity, the ladies lent each other their preserving-kettles and their cut glass for company; and Mary Farrell thought no more of appearing bonnetless on an errand at Mrs. Lewis's door than she did at her own.

"I have the greatest respect for Mary Farrell's judgment," Mrs. Lewis once said to her husband, as she tied her nightcap strings. "She always agrees with me."

"Folks talk about Mrs. Lewis being set in her way," Mary Farrell said in the early days of their acquaintance. "She thinks every thing of her way, and I think every thing of mine, so we're of a mind on that subject." And on these grounds the alliance stood and flourished.

"I suppose you know we're going to have a wedding," was Mrs. Lewis's first formal announcement of the fact.

"Yes; and, as I haven't heard of you or Mr. Lewis getting a divorce lately, it must be Mary's."

"I declare, Mary Farrell," owned the woman of faculty, "if I didn't have your head to look to, as well as my own, I would hardly try to get up a wedding."

"That's not singular," said the spinster, briskly. "You haven't lost a daughter before. What I want to know about the match, before I give my consent, is whether you're going to marry her off, or a son-in-law on?"

"I guess Mr. Lewis and I will require a son-in-law

A WEDDING COUNCIL. 109

who can take care of himself. He can't settle in our spare room the rest of his life."

"The young man can give security as to that," said Mary Farrell, rubbing her nose delicately with her forefinger. "Well, I'll go right home for my apron, and come back ready to work. I haven't helped at a wedding for so long I've forgotten the taste of wedding cake. So bring on your raisins. People are never lawfully married unless they seed just so many raisins. It's the meanest work in creation, and I never hear of a wedding that I don't expect to be sent for to do it."

"Never mind stoning raisins just yet. What I want now is ideas. I'd like to do what's proper for people in our position, and I don't want this to be any common chocolate-cake wedding, but a nice, quiet affair, such as won't look strange to our friends from Chicago. I want to do all that is expected from me, Mary; and you must consider with me."

"Spring is the most inconsiderate time for getting up a wedding," observed Mary Farrell, briskly. "There's no choice but ham and eggs; and ham and eggs aren't just the things for a wedding. I don't doubt most folks would enjoy 'em more if they told their own minds."

"There are people who haven't any more taste," remarked Mrs. Lewis, pensively. "When Bishop Findlay was here two years ago, Mr. Lewis brought him to dine; and I had a ham boiled in port wine on purpose for him, and such ducks as you never saw, and frogs' legs with a new sauce, I went into the kitchen to make, myself, though I've brought the girl up myself, and she can do most dishes better than I pretend to, not having my hand in. You know the clergy are generally men who understand good living. But if that man didn't make his dinner off some lake trout and a potato. He never *saw* any of the nice things I had taken so much pains to get for him ; and I told Mr. Lewis, afterwards, ' Don't you *ever* bring that man to dinner again.' The Bishop was so taken up with some convention business that morning, it was as much as ever he knew what he had on his plate. I don't know as I would want to see a minister think very much about his eating, but I do like to see him set an example in matters of taste."

" The looks are the great thing about a wedding supper," said practical Mary Farrell. " Silver and frosting and flowers, and love, I suppose, fills in."

" I shall have plenty of salads and jellies. It is so much handsomer to set out plenty of relishes than sweets and cakes. All you ever get at a New Canton wedding is a plate of ice-cream and a piece of cake."

" I'll try that ' Macedonian ' in the church cook-book I brought home from Chicago last winter. I've been reading it; and I'm just spoiling to try my hand at some of the things," said Miss Farrell, who reads receipts as a composer reads music.

" Three dozen orange jellies," said Mrs. Lewis, loftily, making up her bill of fare : " as many calve's-foot, with wine, twenty *m'rangs*, and four dozen custards. People know what they are and aren't afraid to eat them. But they're so afraid of showing their ignorance of *m'rangs* and chocolate *éclairs* by handling them, they'd rather go without."

" I can make the turnip and beet-root flowers for the cold meats," said Mary. " Brother Spence's wife showed me how to do them for her companies. Will you have chocolate?"

"I don't just know whether it would be the thing," declared Mrs. Lewis, with gravity befitting the question. "I've never heard of it, except at lunch. Have you? Mrs. Pliny Smith has it at her afternoons, I know. They didn't have it when Mrs. Senator Williams gave her parties."

"I was at Mrs. Wallace Swayne's for an evening, with Spence's wife," said Mary, with a touch of pride at being able to throw light on a question of elegance. "She had five urns on the sideboard — hot water and coffee, and black and green tea, and chocolate—and a big glass pitcher for the claret, and it did look so rich and particular."

"That's what I like to see," said Mrs. Lewis. "Some people hit on such handsome notions every time. I don't want to be using other people's ways all the time, any more than their towels and spoons."

"She had hot soup, too, handed round in cups; and it was beautiful," hazarded Miss Farrell, with an eye to see how the notion took.

"I sha'n't undertake to have *bouillon*," said Mrs. Lewis, judicially. "People are not advanced enough for that here in Canton. I never should hear the last of having soup for supper."

"Shall I send out to the Branch after some eggs for you?" asked Mary, a trifle disappointed. She did want to try the effect of handing around *bouillon* in china cups, and seeing the young ladies who read the magazines recognize it.

"A hundred dozen if you please. Brandy and lady cake, and jelly rolls. Gold and silver cake are going out. All the girls have got to making them for their parties. I'm sick of marble-cake and chocolate cake. The first thing a girl learns of cooking, nowadays, is to make chocolate cake. I'm going to have some of that real old-fashioned black cake. I haven't made any since Mr. Vinton left the church."

"Are you going to have the cake in high or low dishes?" said Mary, bringing Mrs. Lewis back to the matter in hand.

"I want to have it all in baskets," said Mrs. Lewis, while Mary Farrell looked awe, at the idea of such brilliance.

"I have two baskets, and I can write for Hannah's; and, if you'll lend me yours — I want them to go in pairs. There is Mrs. Burt's, I know she would lend me; for she borrowed mine last New Year, when she had the family. I'm going to ask her to let her girl help wait on the tables; and I'll get two from the hotel."

Just as Miss Farrell was leaving the room, a genteel wheezing was heard on the stairs; and, with the free-and-easy manners of New Canton, a lady walked in, without knocking. It was one of the privileges of belonging to good society in that delightful town that one must allow all one's friends to walk into house and bedroom without ceremony. The visitor in this case proved to be Mrs. Burt, with a knitted hood thrown over her head and a large house-shawl in which she was wont to parade the neighborhood informally.

A look, not overpleasant, shot between Mrs. Lewis and Mary Farrell. But the two ladies smoothed their faces out politely by the time Mrs. Burt's pink hood was inside the door.

A WEDDING COUNCIL.   113

"Good-morning, Mrs. Lewis," she said, with the affability of a duchess. "I hope you are as well as you look this morning. Miss Farrell, how is your mother? I haven't been able to get in to see her since the protracted meeting. She was afraid then she was going to have a felon on her right finger. I inquired after her three or four times; but nobody seemed able to tell how she got on."

"We drove it off," said Mary Farrell, "with hot carrot poultices. I guess, after all, it was nothing more than she had caught cold in her finger."

"Ah! that's fortunate," sighed Mrs. Burt, who always put on a languishing style in company, a compound of elegance and Christian condescension. "I was going to tell you mashed cranberries are good for felon. We had it in our family several times, and I always found mashed cranberries afford the greatest relief."

Mrs. Lewis skillfully introduced a diversion.

"Mrs. Burt, I am going to tell you our news first one. You're not to say an old neighbor, though you have made yourself one of us; so it seems as if we had known you all your lives," began the lady of the house, while Mrs. Burt sat properly uncomprehending till the precise moment of announcement.

"We, of course, expect to part with Mary sooner or later. A mother makes up her mind to it in the course of nature," said Mrs. Lewis, with a sigh. "My daughter is to be married to Mr. Paddleford; and I hope we shall see you and Mr. Burt at the wedding."

The news was received with becoming gravity and interest. Mrs. Burt made her congratulations, not quite able to help saying that she expected to hear another name for the gentleman.   (8)

"Yes," Mrs. Lewis said, quietly. Mary's name had been coupled with other gentlemen; but Mrs. Burt knew what all that amounted to. The wedding was to be in about three weeks. The gentleman, being the son of one of our old townspeople, and Mary not going to leave town to find a home, she found no good reason for opposing the wishes of the young people. They had always known each other, as old Mr. Paddleford had been, like herself and Mr. Lewis, one of the first settlers in New Canton. She (Mrs. Lewis) knew all about the young man, and approved his habits, as a steady, self-respecting young business man; and she felt that her daughter would be spared many of the trials which beset young people who began life on small means. She felt that a hard life in youth always left its traces.

Mrs. Burt was glad to hear the young man was so well off. He had a pretty fortune to call his own, and, with good investments — she trusted he had the foresight to make investments in property, as business had its risks — he might continue so. She was glad that he could give his wife a good home, to begin with. It was what she always had been used to herself.

She had never had the care of a daughter; but, if she had, she should feel it a great responsibility to find her a good husband, with high principles, liberal and public-spirited, and, above all things, good constitution. Mr. Burt had the soundest health. Never was sick a day, unless he was taken down with bilious fever or something unavoidable. He never had those sick turns, up and down, that some men had, and made it so trying for their wives to take care of them.

She was sure she and Mr. Burt would take great pleasure in being at the wedding. Mr. Burt would make a point of being there, though his business lately called him so much away. Would the wedding be a large one?

Well, Mr. Lewis naturally wished most of his friends about him on such an occasion.

Mrs. Burt was sure it would be no common wedding. To say nothing of its being an only child, and Mrs. Lewis wouldn't expect to be called on to give another wedding soon, it would be natural for Mr. Lewis, one of the best-off men in the town, to make a show of being liberal on such an occasion. Times were altering in New Canton, and people expected more from each other. A great deal had been done and was doing for the town; and it was quite proper to take on more polish and pay more attention to style than they had been doing. The advance in the value of property and the increase in the wealth of the city carried with it responsibilities. The man whose property had advanced two hundred or two thousand — she had forgotten which — per cent. (what per cent. is she didn't know, but it was something Mr. Burt talked a great deal about) ought not to live as he did before the per cent. came. The railroads would bring in city ways. "Well, we shall all expect to enjoy ourselves here as we don't do anywhere else. Give my sweet love to Mary. She is a very precious child, Mrs. Lewis. It is well she gets a husband so much to your mind, and one that's well able to take care of her. Mr. Paddleford has the good luck to have his way already made for him, and he can give your daughter a home, such as she's been used to.

But, how long I'm staying. I just came in to borrow the pattern of your gored wrapper. Mr. Burt says, 'Why don't you wear your dresses and have the good of them?' There are so few places it's worth while to dress for, we're really quite obliged to you for giving us a chance. Miss Farrell, I do wish you would run in oftener, and let me know how your mother is. It is so seldom I can get round to see her. Good-morning."

And, with a grandiloquent air, marching very erect, Mrs. Burt took herself off. The ladies left behind were too old not to know better than to smile at each other the minute a guest was gone; for re-entrances might prove awkward. In this case, Mrs. Burt had only got half-way down-stairs, when she bethought herself, and appeared again at the chamber door, and peered through, on tip-toe. "If there is any thing that I could spare to convenience you, Mrs. Lewis, I should be too happy, and would do so with the greatest of pleasure. Any thing like cake-pans or trays? Or sha'n't I send you over something to take? Mary ought to take something strengthening, and commence right away — say taraxacum, or bark and iron, or colocynth; and you, as her mother, would be the better for some lady-slipper or most any thing. Mr. Lewis — I have known the fathers of the bride to need something supporting on such occasions — he can have any thing I have. Mr. Burt is so high-strung, if he had a daughter he was going to give away, I'm sure I should have to do something to keep him up to himself."

The silence that followed Mrs. Burt's departure was more marked than words could have been. At last Mrs. Lewis said, " Her mother was part Irish!" which was held by the thorough-bred Yankee women to comprehend all that was demanded of reprobation and excuse.

After this there was no hope for poor Mary. She had consented; her mother, Mary Farrell, and Mrs. Burt had sat in council on the case ; and her doom was sealed. It was impossible that she should not marry Thomas Paddleford.

CHAPTER IX.

A PUBLIC MEETING IN NEW CANTON.

MR. BURT was a quiet man, but not a idle one- Sleeping, he dreamed of New Canton, and waking, he carried it. As what the heart is full of the mouth must speak, it followed, that, whoever was in Mr. Burt's company for a longer or shorter time, left with a perceptible infusion of land company in his thoughts. The steps of Burt left behind them a scattering of slim and pertinent pamphlets, the burden of which was the natural advantages of the city and the certainty of its glorious future. These cunning leaflets had, rumor said, been found even in the pews of the church, that, in the event of a specially dry sermon, the uninterested might surreptitiously refresh their minds with a skip from the gloomy prospect of a hereafter to brighter promise close at hand.

The land company was a fixed fact. The investments of Thompson, of Connecticut, had given an impetus to business; and the money made by the prompt sale of the notes of Taylor, Gubbins & Adams had enabled the managers to spread its fame still further.

But this was only the beginning of Mr. Burt's ambitions. He wanted to sell a hundred lots where he was selling one; and he wanted prices to go up a thousand per cent. He was ungrateful enough to be dissatisfied with his support. Peak, Peppernell, and Sharp were well enough; but their names did not carry weight. Gardiner was excellent; but he was tired of harping on the strength of one man, and here James Gardiner's hand came in, and his hardly disguised opposition almost neutralized the effect of his father's endorsement. That clear-headed young man held his judgment in suspension on the matter of the land company's deserts; and the breadth and exceeding liberality of its schemes furnished him with a subject for his satire, that he made full use of. His meditations on the business principles of the company one day took poetic form, which found a wide circulation on the streets of New Canton, being handed, in strict confidence, about from one vest pocket to another of about fifty citizens, in the course of one forenoon.

" WATTS FOR TO-DAY.

"[*Respectfully dedicated to Mr. Charles Burt, of the New Canton Land Company.*]

" Oh ! blest be he whose only plan
Is righteousness to get ;
Who sweetly skins his fellow man,
And ne'er lets up, you bet! "

On reading it, every man would say it was too bad of James Gardiner, and he ought not to make fun of serious business matters and such a respectable man as Mr. Burt. And each man would immediately read it over again, and insist on taking a copy of the lines to show the next person he met. Mr. Burt could see that the hits at him were well relished, and a shrewd distrust was working in the community against him.

He was sure, that, for the present, he held his place, not by popularity or personal good liking, but by virtue of the closest and best management.

This did not suit at all; and he determined not to put up with it any longer. He wanted the reputable men in town with him; and he wanted the weight of their names. They did not take ground against him; for they were willing enough that their acres should be turned into city property, if Mr. Burt or anybody else could do it, without costing them any thing; but they were waiting to see what there was in the idea. If it proved a success, there was time enough to step in, and share the credit of the enterprise : if it was a failure, there would be an excellent chance to demonstrate their wisdom by having kept out of it. Like the storied hunter, they aimed to kill if it was a deer, and miss if it was a calf.

Much of the shrewdness in the world is meanness, doing business under the firm name of prudence and conservatism.

Mr. Burt meant that these good citizens should endorse the land company. He knew better than to approach them directly. They would have sheered off at the mention of the land company, as from a ghost ten days old. Instead, he found much to say of the town — its needs and capabilities. He thought its principal streets ought to be lighted, the sidewalks improved, the school-grounds fenced and trees planted, and the approaches to the town improved. There was no need to plunge into expense; but the walks certainly ought to be rebuilt, or, if that was too expensive, the planks might, at least, be turned, and newly spiked, so that a woman could walk without having her dress torn off.

The seed did not fall upon stony ground. Only the day before Mrs. Paddleford had torn her dress upon an ugly spike-head, which the decayed plank had left bare, and Mr. Paddleford had been vexed thereat. The skirt was ruined; and he made a mental calculation that fourteen yards of double-extra-rolled French poplin, at one-dollar and a half a yard, and three yards of silk, at one seventy-five a yard, was more than his share of the tax for repaving the entire town, to say nothing of the insurance against accidents of the kind in the future. Mr. Paddleford agreed with Mr. Burt, that the sidewalks should be relaid.

Mr. M'Tavish, the head teacher, approved the idea of improving the school-grounds. He desired to have grounds and buildings to point to with pride, so that strangers could see that New Canton was interested in something besides mere money-getting.

Other citizens, especially those who were in the habit of staying out late at night, agreed that the streets should be lighted, and the town brushed up to outward signs and tokens of its prosperity. By suggesting what he knew each desired, and letting them do the talking after he had started them, Mr. Burt succeeded in awakening a general movement in the direction he wanted.

Mr. Paddleford wished to be informed as to the best method of getting at the matter.

"Clearly, by carrying out your suggestion of a public meeting," was Mr. Burt's answer. (Paddleford was as innocent of making a suggestion as he was of murder.) "There is no use, as you observed, of two men attempting to carry out so comprehensive a scheme of improvements as you have suggested; for they will not be able to do it. Unity of action is what we want. Suppose you draft a call for a meeting."

Mr. Paddleford agreed that it was the thing to do, took a pen, and spread out a sheet of foolscap, carefully selecting one too soiled to be fit for a business letter. And then there was an awkward pause.

"Suppose, Mr. Paddleford, you commence it, 'The citizens of New Canton —'"

"I was about writing it," said Paddleford.

— " desiring to improve the condition of the city, are requested to meet at the town-hall."

" It had better be at the town-hall, had it?"

Mr. Burt answered in the affirmative, and went on dictating the call from first to last. When it was finished, he took it up and read it.

" Mr. Paddleford, you have a marvelous faculty for clear, terse statement. This is precisely what I wanted. It is admirable. Now, Mr. Paddleford, I would suggest — doubtless you intended to do it — that you get the signatures of the best citizens to the call, and have it out in posters, as well as the papers. Good-morning. You will bring about good results. This action should have been taken before."

"Smart man, that Burt," said Paddleford to himself, as the secretary vanished.

" The old idiot will get every name in the village," he said to himself, " if I don't appear in it."

The call, issued with the name of every prominent citizen on it, was an innocent-looking document, with no reference to land companies, but merely desiring the citizens to meet to take counsel as to the present condition of the village, and to devise measures to improve its condition.

The evening came; and the hall was filled. Those who never paid any taxes were there in force; for they wanted improvements they did not have to pay for: and those who did pay taxes were there, to oppose or urge, as interest dictated.

Mr. Burt was there, quiet and modest; but his quick eyes took in every thing. Just as Mr. Paddleford was rising, Mr. Burt, a second in advance, nominated James Lewis, Esq., for chairman. It was carried. Mr. Lewis took the chair on the platform, and, with the regulation cough, asked the meeting its further pleasure. The watchful Burt immediately nominated Mr. Thomas Paddleford and seventeen other reputable citizens, who had fought shy of the land company, for vice-presidents; and they all filed up on the platform, constituting the ornamental part thereof. The editors of the " Forum " and " Sentinel " were made secretaries, which was the regular thing, and the meeting proceeded to business.

Mr. Burt was called for, in a voice that sounded wonderfully like Col. Peppernell's in the first or early evening stage of intoxication. Mr. Burt took the floor, without eagerness or hesitation.

Being comparatively a stranger in New Canton, Mr. Burt felt a delicacy in appearing before so large a gathering of the best men of the city; and his only apology was the deep interest he took in the prosperity of the place of his adoption. New Canton was to him wife, child, every thing, —

(Feminine voice from the audience, *sotto voce*, " Oh! Charles!")

— and every thing that concerned its growth and welfare interested him beyond his power of expression. He believed in New Canton. Years before he had ever filled his lungs with the pure air that swept over the prairies —

Mr. Paddleford. " Them sidewalks on Main Street."

— or his foot had ever planted itself upon its teeming soil, he had noticed its position with reference to the trade of an immense area of territory, and felt convinced that there was to be some day, and that day not far in the distance, a great city, a controlling city, a powerful city. He had brought with him some maps, which he would show the citizens present, that they might understand his enthusiasm and the solid ground upon which it rested. Here —

Mr. Lewis (fidgeting in his seat). " The lighting of the streets."

— here flows Soggy Run, and there the Illinois River. Could any thing be clearer? With railroads running from Chicago, southward, bearing enough to the west; with railroads running across the middle of this great state from east to west, and bearing enough to the north, all crossing at New Canton (and where else, he would ask, could they cross?), what could prevent New Canton from becoming the most important inland city in the West? And, then, with coal underlying the entire section, — and he believed it did underlie the whole section; at least, he should assume that it did underlie the whole section, for no man had ever shown him that it did *not* underlie the whole section, — with cotton south of us, with iron in the Lake Superior region north of us, and in Ohio and Pennsyl-

A PUBLIC MEETING IN NEW CANTON. 125

vania east of us, and south of us in Tennessee (with reference to iron, what city stood better geographically?), what could stop the —

Mr. M'Tavish. " In respect to the matter of planting trees — "

— growth of the city, or prevent it from marching steadily forward to a station among the proudest of the cities of the country? Its commerce would make it; its coal would make it; the nearness of iron would make it; its geographical position would make it. Here were four elements, either of which were sufficient. Add them together, it was more than great — it was gigantic.

Only one thing had dampened his ardor or made him pause in the work he had set for himself in developing this great idea; and that was the apathy said to exist in the minds of the leading citizens of the place toward the great enterprise. But the large number present to-night, representing the wealth and influence of New Canton, and the cordiality with which they, by their presence, had endorsed the efforts of himself and his associates, gave him fresh courage. In union there is strength. With united action we can go forward. Without it, New Canton will remain as it is. Now that every leading citizen of New Canton had given the land company his right hand, and bid it God speed in its work, he could go confidently on, and without misgivings. Thank Heaven! there was union at last.

Col. Peppernell and the friends of the land company applauded vociferously, as did that vast number who, not having a dollar to make or lose, in any event, always applaud; and the example aroused something over the half of the meeting. Mr. Burt sat down very well satisfied with his success.

Mr. Paddleford, Mr. Lewis, and Mr. M'Tavish made an effort to get the floor; but Col. Peppernell was called for, and responded with suspicious promptness. Up to this time New Canton had not deserved to be any thing but a little dirty prairie village, as it had been, before some men who could see an inch ahead of their noses perceived its natural advantages, and took hold of it with the determination to make something of it. Now he felt its future assured. When the best citizens (the men of weight in the town) came to the front, as they had to-night, and showed by their presence a desire to hold up the hands of the land company, and to endorse it, and give it the weight of their names, the powerful influence that such names always carried, he felt no doubt of glorious success. He was encouraged beyond his feeble powers of expression, and should resume his labors in the morning with new zeal and redoubled ardor. All that his friend (he was proud to call him his friend) had said of the advantages of New Canton he endorsed. His townsmen would remember, that, years before, when the village consisted only of a dozen houses, he had prophesied the same thing. And, if his hopes had not been realized before, it was because the people, those most deeply interested, had not taken hold of the matter as they should have done. Thank Heaven! this apathy no longer existed. And, with the impetus this meeting would give the town, it would go forward to the destiny that Nature intended for it. When he looked at Chicago, and saw what the uncontrolled spirit, the unfettered work of free Western minds, which were as broad as their prairies and as strong as their winds, could do, — when he saw the summits of grandeur that the unconquerable American mind could accomplish, when relieved from the narrowness of Eastern education and the dwarfing experience of old countries, which had run in ruts for centuries, — spirit which had room to develop and soar, — he felt that there was nothing that New Canton could not aspire to. New Canton was now what Chicago was twenty years ago; and what Chicago is New Canton can be in twenty years. And now that the solid men had come to the front, and taken upon their shoulders a part of the burden which he and his coadjutors had been carrying for months, there was no more doubt of the onward progress of the town than there was of the onward progress of the country at large. He was willing now to give himself entirely to the work.

Mr. Paddleford, getting the floor at last, suggested that something had been said in the call — or, rather, it had been discussed by citizens — about the condition of the sidewalks, and he hoped —

Mr. Burt hoped Mr. Paddleford would excuse him: sidewalks, important in and of themselves, should not monopolize the time that could be devoted to more weighty matters. He should like to hear from Mr. Simmons.

Peppernell was astonished at this call; for he did not know that Simmons had a private interest with Burt in several speculations which hinged upon the success of the land company. No one knew it; and, consequently, Mr. Simmons's endorsement of the scheme, coming from one supposed to be disinterested, carried weight.

Mr. Simmons said he had, too, had a belief in New Canton, which amounted to a faith. He believed that it was destined to be the first among the inland cities of the country. While he did not believe that the hopes of the gentlemen who had preceded him would be fully realized, he still believed that New Canton had a future. And, feeling that, for what had been done and what was to be done, the city was indebted to the enterprise of a few public-spirited gentlemen, who had organized the land company, and made what of notoriety the town had obtained, he had prepared a series of resolutions, which he would offer. Mr. Simmons, in good resolution voice, read : —

"*Whereas*, The citizens of New Canton have faith in the future of the city, and are desirous of doing every thing honorable to promote its progress and realize expectations that they believe are well-grounded; and, —

" *Whereas*, Several citizens have associated themselves as a land company, for the development of what we believe to be the unparalleled resources of the location ; therefore, be it —

" *Resolved*, That we most thoroughly endorse the work of the New Canton Land Company, of which our esteemed fellow-townsman, Col. Seth Peppernell, is president, and our equally well-esteemed fellow-townsman, Mr. Charles Burt, is secretary and treasurer.

" *Resolved*, That we unhesitatingly commend the land company as worthy of confidence, and assure all having business with it of the integrity, probity, and single-heartedness of its managers, believing that they are acting for the good of the city, first, last, and all the time.

" *Resolved*, That we unhesitatingly affirm our confidence in the land company and its managers, and endorse them fully in all respects."

Mr. Burt would offer, as an addition to these resotions, the following : —

"*Resolved*, That it is the duty of the city, through its constituted officers, to at once devise a system of lighting the streets, of laying sidewalks, and of improving the school-grounds; for, without these improvements, the work of the land company, in developing the interests of the town, will, to some extent, be rendered nugatory."

Capt. Peak moved the adoption of the resolutions. Some of the old settlers, who were not in the land company, were opposed to the wholesale endorsements contained in them; but, whenever one of them rose, Mr. Burt or Col. Peppernell was on his feet just before them, with remarks; and, before the citizens knew exactly what they were about, the resolutions were put and carried without a dissenting voice, and the meeting adjourned.

On their way home, Paddleford remarked to Lewis, —

"Did you go to the hall to-night to endorse that blasted land company?"

"No; but we did it, though. You didn't vote agin them resolutions, did you?"

"How could I? There was Burt and Col. Peppernell and the rest of them all there; and I didn't get a chance to say a word till the meeting adjourned."

"Smart man, Burt," said Lewis, quietly.

There was considerable side-talk about it the next morning. But, as the meeting had resolved, and as not one present would admit that he had been led into it against his will, there was a very general acquiescence in the action; and the land company stood many degrees higher than it had.

The "Sentinel" and the "Forum" blazed with it. The head-lines were of the largest type the offices possessed; and there was the most extravagant expenditure of capital letters and exclamation points. "New Canton Aroused!" "The People in Council!" "The Best Men of the City Unqualifiedly Endorse the Land Company!" "Stirring Resolutions!" and so on.

In their accounts of the meeting, they were careful to state that the meeting called to endorse the land company was presided over by James Lewis, Esq.; and every one of the eighteen vice-presidents were named in full; and the resolutions were condemned as altogether too tame for the expression of the feeling of the audience. They assumed, that, now the land company could depend upon the co-operation of the solid men of the town, every one might know, from the endorsement that it had received, that it was not the speculation of a few men, but that the whole town was enlisted in it, with a solidity that could not be questioned. There would be no holding back, no delay. When such men as Lewis, Paddleford, M'Tavish, Simmons, and a long list, embracing all of wealth and respectability in the town, endorsed the land company, who could question either as to its aims or its responsibilty?

Mr. Burt went home in good humor, and Peppernell was radiant.

"Colonel," said Mr. Burt, the next morning, as they looked over the papers, "the meeting will result in great good. I was charmed with the readiness with which the leading citizens supported us, and the cordiality of their support. It cheered my very soul to see them on the platform ; and the attention they gave us when speaking was truly encouraging. Now that we have this endorsement, the people ought to have more money."

"You mean *we* ought to have more money," said Peppernell.

"No: the people. If it was only flush times! If money was floating about, so that everybody had money that they didn't know what to do with! Heavens! What couldn't we do if the people only had something to do with! — if money (I wouldn't care a straw what kind) was only plenty here! If we only had a bank, and could issue — "

Mr. Burt stopped very short. He had an idea, which he would get into shape before making it known.

CHAPTER X.

TOM PADDLEFORD'S WEDDING.

TOM PADDLEFORD always said, that, if he couldn't be married in style, he wouldn't be married at all. His ideas on this subject, as well as on the perfections of the lady to share this rite, were so emphatic that his most intimate friends were of the opinion he would have to dispense with the ceremony altogether, as some of his better-informed brethren are in the habit of doing. But it is given to few mortals to see their dearest wishes gratified as literally as Mr. Paddleford's were. The lady he was to marry had his favorite points of style. She wore a number two slipper; and, to use her future husband's phrase, "she held herself together well," assisted by a sixteen-inch corset, and " dressed as if she knew her business." Mr. Tom's bride was suitably perfect. What shall be said of Mr. Tom's wedding?

It was curious; but everybody who spoke of the event invariably called it Tom Paddleford's wedding, as if that sufficient and pervasive young man meant to take the whole share and glory of it to himself.

In general, strict propriety demands that a bridegroom should be the last person to know any thing of the preparations for his nuptials; and he is on his honor to ignore such hints of them as fall in his way. But Mr. Tom was not to be bound by any conventionalities but those drilled into him by Chicago commercial men. Mrs. Lewis, a mother-in-law holding lightly points of etiquette which did not come through her oracle, the Chicago sister-in-law, was not aware of the responsibility put upon her by modern high breeding. She would have disliked it in this case, as depriving her of most zealous and efficient help in her arrangements. Mary Lewis would do nothing, decide nothing for her own wedding. Tom and her mother managed the invitations, chose the supper, and Tom, with his own hands, aided to arrange the parlors the afternoon before the bridal. As Mrs. Lewis and Tom took a last look at their work, about half-past five, before going to dress for the evening, the result seemed not unworthy the pains bestowed upon it.

Like many country houses, the Lewis mansion, apparently spacious without, was cut up in contracted rooms within. But, if the parlors were not as large as expected, there was no limit to their showiness. The first thing one was conscious of, on entering, was a glare of light wall, in contrast to a carpet of dark, high colors, which took precedence of every thing in the room. Mrs. Lewis took pride in her parlor carpet,— none of your cheap tapestries anybody could buy who had a carpet at all, but a "body Brussels," of substantial price and vigorous pattern and color. A visitor, whose mind was narrowed by notions of taste, complained that the carpet in question always made her think of hell-fire, its black ground, with lurid scrolls of red, having a fire-and-smoke effect that recalled popular images of torment. But the robust imagination of Mrs. Lewis was above such weakness. She liked a carpet that gave her " something to study on ; " and the blood-red arabesques of her beloved Brussels held such roses and blue tulips as you could not cover with your foot, or make out in a day. Further, the double parlors owned the dignity of a full-length pier-glass, with marble slab and flourishing gilt brackets, and a mantel mirror of the same lavish blazonry, both bought at a hotel auction in Chicago, after the war. The newness of the walnut and gilt window cornices was rather out of keeping with the bygone splendor of the mirrors. But the eyes of New Canton guests did not suffer from such discrepancies. Curtains of Nottingham lace, very stiff, very blue, and very chilly, without the aid of chintz or damask, veiled the long windows ; and the furniture of striped green reps was bright and new as a coffin dealer's stock. The piano, bought with an eye to four round corners and the largest, scrolliest legs in Chicago, set across a corner — the prevailing idea among New Canton young ladies of giving a room an artistic air; and the walls further reflected the " taste and refinement " of its owners by life-size crayon photographs of Mr. and Mrs. Lewis — the lady in a spread of lace-shawl, with cameo ear-drops and necklace, which was the envy of all female friends who did not know these properties were borrowed from her sister in Chicago, the wife of a grain speculator, who bought his wife ornaments as a safe investment, which the law could not levy on. There was a smaller picture of Mary, apparently habited in a lace shawl, from which her bare shoulders rose like the moon from a cloud ; her hair let down her back and her eyes uplifted, in the style most affected by photographers. A chromo of Lake George balanced one of Niagara, beside of a fruit piece, bought by Mr. Lewis at the county fair, to give struggling home talent a lift. A portrait of Mr. Lincoln, uglier than it was necessary to make that thrice-martyred man, opposed a diploma won by Mr. Lewis's Cochin China fowls at the same fair; and any vacant space was filled by an assortment of mottoes, in gay illuminated colors, such as " What is home without a mother? " highly suited to any house where Mrs. Lewis held that relation, and texts of the most affeeling sort, such as " Jesus wept," or " We all do fade as a leaf," cheerfully adapted to the thoughts and feelings of the usual visitor. The back parlor gave the place of honor to Mary's drawing of her old home, which people recognized the moment they were told what it was. A crayon head of the " Water-Witch," by the same fair artist — the hair hardly rooted to the head, and looking as if the nymph's teeth hurt her — showed great room for promise, as a stray *connoisseur* ventured to say. Nor were small feminine elegancies wanting to give rooms a homelike charm — such as velvet-photograph stands, woolly as to the velvet, and, as to the gilding, thin, or hanging bead-baskets filled with artificial flowers. The usual bay-window grew red geraniums, callas, and orange flowers, which women cultivate because they give the best show and smell for the trouble, and are to a house-garden like a white calf among house-pets. Mary's piano showed the correct assortment of music—the last high-pitched song of Millard's, some pretty jingling waltzes, which sounded as if played with the forefinger by the fair performer, and sentimental pieces, like the " Maiden's

Prayer," "Streamlet's Murmur," or " Spilling Spray," in company with the " Golden Lute," the "Nickel Censer," or whatever metallic fancy in names had then taken the place of the " Carmina Sacra," and " Mendelssohn Collection," with their honest harmonies. A small table held the family Bible, in turkey leather and gilt edges, presented to Mary's father and mother on their marriage, and which looked as if it had never been opened since; Mary's album of her girl friends and lovers; and a slim, brilliantly gilt volume, with the menacing inscription " Autographs," to fill which Mary had sweetly badgered authors and statesmen, and so far succeeded that she felt her collection would be complete if she could get Victor Hugo's and Talmage's. A Turkish chair, with large red roses done on a black stripe, was the work of Mrs. Lewis, in the elegant leisure of summer visits; while sawed and pressed carving in brackets, wall-pockets, frames, and puzzles abounded, till the parlors wore an air between a furnishing-shop and a church fair. Mrs. Lewis and Mary belonged to the school of women who dread to see a room look bare, if it has room to put a newspaper down, or a yard of wall for the eye to rest upon.

But for Tom Paddleford to have a wedding just like anybody else's would be worse than having none at all; and his genius must show itself worthy the occasion. Rumors were rife of further splendors waiting in the Lewis mansion. The afternoon train from Chicago brought hampers, addressed to the bridegroom, exhaling undisguised sweetness; and it was rumored that the ambitious young man meant to have flowers at his wedding — flowers in March — flowers by the bush'l-basketf'l.

In his visits to Chicago, Tom had made a point of going to all the fashionable weddings and funerals at the churches; and his friends, the drummers of business houses he dealt with, kept him kindly informed of the most brilliant ceremonies, and were good natured in securing seats for him when the church was open to the public. What appealed to Mr. Paddleford's sensibilities most on such occasions was what he was never heard to mention save as "the floral display." Roses and lilies would have stood a poor chance of Mr. Tom's acquaintance on their native soil; but, combined with florist's skill, in harps, anchors, ships, crowns, and such natural and graceful forms as flowers lend themselves to when well wired and packed on frames, his soul was carried captive by them. His heart was set on introducing such a "floral display" at his nuptials, and he went so far as to drop in at a florist's and inquire the cost of the pageant; but the answer was such as to quench all thoughts of shining by a city florist's aid, and he left the shop in a state of burning indignation at the greed of fashionable purveyors.

But, when the time came that Tom wanted flowers for his wedding, fortune befriended him. One of Tom's Chicago friends was the wife of an army officer killed two months before by the Indians; and, when his body was recovered, the officer in command had no more discretion than to forward it, putting Mrs. McCullom to the expense of a funeral, just as she had spent every thing on her mourning, in the assurance that there were no burial costs to come in. Tom, in town the day before his wedding, could not resist going to condole with her, and talk about his own prospects. McCullom was even then at the depot, in his pine box; and his widow must disturb her well-settled grief by giving him a funeral. It would not do to give him a shabby one, either; for his folks would be there, and she had money coming from them, and flowers came so expensive this time of year.

Tom steadied the exultant throbs of his heart as well as he could, and gravely proposed, not selling the flowers — no, indeed; but, if a friend of his, who had lost a child, said Tom (inventing as he went), and been disappointed in getting the flowers wanted, could have the use of her flowers afterward, without injury to Mrs. McCullom's feelings, there might be an arrangement made, relieving her of part of the bill. He wouldn't dare to mention such a thing; but he happened to know just how both parties were situated. He would take it on himself to arrange, so that neither party need appear in the matter.

The McCullom saw her point, and made a faint show of reluctance, the end of which was, early morning obsequies for the lieutenant, and prompt dispatch of his flowers, packed in wet cotton, to Mr. Tom Paddleford. The flowers really were a credit to the widow's taste; and she had the florist's bill sent to Tom, writing him that his friends could pay what they felt like, and she would make up the rest. Tom paid the bill, but never a dollar did he get from the McCullom. But this is dipping into history too deeply.

"You — your friends will break up the pieces, won't they?" Mrs. McCullom said to him, before he left. "I shouldn't like to run the chance of any one's recognizing the flowers" — a movement of pure decency on her part which deserves to be recorded. Tom promised, of course; but, when he came to unpack the flowers, he was so taken with the beauty of the designs and their appropriateness, as he found it, that he tossed his promise over his shoulder. Accordingly, in Mrs. Lewis's parlors, brilliant with swinging lamps of kerosene, the mirrors reflected the flower-pieces, in their whiteness, like ornamental specimens from a stone-cutter's yard; and their fragrance was dying on the air. The slab before the pier-glass was graced by a Bible in white hyacinths, with the words "loved and lost" in deep purple heliotrope, an inscription much commented on by the guests, as elegantly expressing the feelings of a father and mother giving up their only daughter; while the bridal pair stood up between a huge cross of black ivy leaves, chosen by the McCullom because ivy made such a show for the money, and a tall cross of tuberoses, surmounted by a crown of violets, taken to set forth the expectant cross and crown of married life.

"There never was any thing like it in this region," Mrs. Clements, who went out by the day in approved families, declared that evening, to Mrs. Fitzhugh, the cobbler's wife. "The table-cloths came down to the ground, so they had to pin 'em up at the corners; and Miss Lewis must ha' borrowed all the best glass out'n the store, for there was nigh on to two dozen tall deeshes, with fancy fruit and jels. And," lowering her voice to suit the impressiveness of her news, "she's got real silver on the table — six cake-baskets, and three tall branches with nuts and confectionery! It goes beyond any thing New Canton ever saw before. I expect everybody of them that has money will have to be laying in silver now; for there won't none of 'em allow the rest to get ahead of her."

"I reckon we've paid as much as thirty or forty dollars on that silver, then," said Mrs. Fitzhugh, a brown, sallow, waspish-looking woman, who had several children too many, and lived in a state of chronic discontent with the world. "A man who lends money at eighteen per cent. to poor folks, and has nothing to do but sit and wait for it to grow, can afford to give his wife what she takes a notion to. If other folks got paid in proportion to their labor, other folks might have silver at their weddings too. Luella Adelia, get along into the house this minit. How often have I told you not to run out in the sun without a bunnit. You'll need all the little good looks you have; for your father can't afford to get no silver for you to get married with."

"Well, I don't know," was the soothing response of the Clements, who had been all day helping for the wedding, "Miss Lewis is a good neighbor as I'd ask to have if I want a using of baking powder; and she isn't above coming into my house, with her apron over her head, Mondays, to borrow my bluing-bag, more'n if she hadn't an account at the store and no questions asked for this or that. I was up-stairs, to see the bride in her wedding-dress, which she was trying on; and she gave me word to come over in the evening and have a peep at the company, and there would be some cake saved for me. 'I want everybody to get all the comfort they can out of my wedding,' says she. But she did look pretty as an image. Brides always do look well — that veil softens their complexion so. I should think they'd hate to put it off, and come out like other mortals. I don't see how Mary can ever come down to planning what she'll have for dinner and what will take the spots out of her husband's clothes, after she's been training round in that veil and gown and flowers. Tom Paddleford will make life serious for her, though, fast enough. He's got an angel for a wife; and it's mostly them that needs angels gets 'em."

It does not come easily to human nature to wholly approve a neighbor's doings; and it is by this truism that Mrs. Lewis would have consoled herself for the opinions held in common with Mrs. Clements by some of her better acquaintance. These opinions were not hinted merely, even within the walls of her own house and on the very night of the wedding.

"I never knew Mrs. Lewis looking better than she does to-night," said one of two brightly-dressed young matrons, who had subsided on the chintz lounge in the sitting-room, while the gayeties of the evening went on about them.

"I suppose you and I'd feel satisfied if we were marrying a daughter off as well as she thinks she has," was the answer.

"Mine are all boys," said the first; "and I've often wished one of 'em was a girl. But it wouldn't be to marry her to that Paddleford young one. I always thought he was dreadfully inferior."

"She's got new parlor curtains," said the other, deeming it prudent to change the subject. "I know, for she lent the others for the church tableaux at Christmas. I was on the committee, and came over to help take them down, and they were on her parlor windows then."

That is the way our neighbors keep the run of details in our households of which we ourselves are hardly conscious.

"That was the time James Gardiner and Mary acted in the 'Spirit of '76,'" whispered the incautious neighbor. "This wasn't the wedding we expected to attend then."

"It isn't the thing to say in her own house," said Prudence. "To my mind, Jim Gardiner was worth twenty like Tom Paddleford; and, if I'm not mistaken, Mrs. Lewis will find out she hasn't done such a smart thing by her daughter, after all."

"Who is that girl in the lavender dress, with crape *ruches?*"

"She's Mrs. Burt's housekeeper; came over to see to things, and take the care of Mrs. Lewis. Did you ever see a party go off better? Mrs. Lewis says the girl saw to every thing — set the tables, and got the dressing-rooms ready. Mrs. Burt said there wouldn't have been glass enough to go round, if Emeline hadn't sent out for a dozen and a half extra."

"I never should take her for a housekeeper. There isn't a prettier woman in the room."

"I couldn't see her looks, for her manners. You don't mean that's old Butterfield's daughter, out by the Youatt Bluff? He stole her, then; for I'll declare she's none of his."

"Hush! She's behind us. Do you suppose she heard?" asked the neighbors, with distress, as the gliding figure came near them.

"She don't give no sign. Peppernell's coming this way. I wonder what he'll have to unfold."

The Colonel, gorgeous in blue swallow-tailed coat

and white vest, had been trying to assist everybody to a pleasant evening, and now thought it time to take some enjoyment on his own account. Not to the matrons on the sofa were his attentions directed. He hated women with stuck-up notions, he said; and, as his ideas of stuck-up women included all who objected to miscellaneous swearing and a generally unbraced and shirt-sleeved style of manners, his acquaintance was not coveted by the ladies of New Canton. His steps were apparently directed to the side-table near which sat Emeline, the spread of her pure and silky skirts, graceful, though of most modest material and fashion, her hands crossed in superb indolence, her eyelids down, resting with an air that would not have shamed a *débutante* of Mount Gilead College. A sense of respect had come with her invitation to the wedding; and she felt self-poised, and acted so.

Burt, whom nothing escaped, saw the change with some wonder. The young lady in the long dress of pale lavender mohair, soft and sheeny in its folds, made with a surprising attention to style, and worn with an uprightness and smoothness of carriage that distinguished itself among the awkward, giggling girls of the crowd, looked and moved at least the equal of every creature about her. The man of discrimination, used to wider society than poor Burt, would have recognized her at once for what she was — material for a high-bred lady, one of Nature's most gracious molds; for she has many and varying ones. Burt had natural taste enough to approve the change from the demure maiden his household had known; and he watched quietly to see what might come of it. He saw Peppernell draw near, ostensibly for a glass of water; and his eye sparkled with malicious mischief.

"I think I shall venture to claim acquaintance," the Colonel said, with a fascinating grin of the kind apt to go with blue beetle-winged coat and brass buttons. "We have met often enough" (he had seen her at Mr. Burt's) ; "and I am sure I have had the pleasure of seeing you before you came to town."

"I live at Mrs. Burt's," was the answer, given without the least hesitation ; "and my father is Mr. Butterfield, who lives out by the Youatt Bluff."

Two listeners on the lounge heard it with reddening ears.

"The bride is looking sweetly to-night," was the Colonel's next observation. "I approve the custom of countries where the women wear a veil all the time — most women. There are faces which I would be sorry to see hidden," with a bow which made his words a neatly turned compliment enough. "We are favored to-night with beauty adorned and unadorned — that is, not much," said the Colonel, lamely and embarrassed, finding his idea had not altogether the right sound. "I can't spare all my admiration for the front rooms, you see," — where the bridal party was then conspicuous.

"Much obliged," said the unmoved beauty ; "but you had better keep such pretty speeches for the front rooms, Colonel. They know better what to do with them."

"I shall be pleased to do so," said the ready beau, "if you will allow me to escort you there, where you belong," bending his arm with alacrity.

But it did not suit Emeline's book to attract notice

in the ill-flavored escort of Peppernell. Neither did she mean to offend the doughty Colonel's self-love, as a girl of less tact would have done. She laid the tips of her fingers on the blue coat-sleeve, took half a turn round the back rooms, and, before the Colonel knew how, he was talking with one of the Lewis cousins, while Emeline escaped. Burt saw the manœuvre, and smiled grimly at Peppernell's discomfiture. He marked his approval of the girl's cleverness by sending her more acceptable attentions than those she had so adroitly disposed of. Not in any open fashion. That would have been gross tactics for Burt. He sauntered up to a knot of young men who were eyeing the ladies, after the manner of home-bred youth; and it hardly needed the financier's temperate judgment, that any gentleman would show his taste in paying civilities to Miss Butterfield, to draw them one after another to her side. What one man admires, another man is sure to find good; and the pale lavender dress and the pretty wearer had no reason to complain that her evening was a dull one. It would have done old Hannah Butterfield good to see her beautiful child watched and admired, in a modest way, as she was this evening. Burt glanced at her occasionally, with a quiet satisfaction under his impassive air. He knew his work, and was pleased with it.

Later in the evening, the bride drew Emeline to her side; and, as the two stood together alone — one, a pale, shimmering figure, with face as white as her dress, with the glowing, dark-eyed, opening lovliness by her side, Emeline, looking up, caught Burt's gaze, from a distance, which changed to a smile as he met her's, — a smile so frank and kind as changed the whole character of his face. It seemed to bid her have confidence in herself, and be happy. It was a tribute so direct and sincere, that never afterward did Emeline doubt she had a friend in her polished, undemonstrative, taciturn employer. This unexpected kindness was all that was wanting to turn her evening into unalloyed pleasure.

But she had been working very hard all day; and, toward midnight, fatigue began to tell even on her young strength. She stole to a window in the entry; and the soft light of a young moon, just large enough to make the darkness delicious, made it tempting to rest. The next minute, a bevy of rustling young ladies invaded her retreat, which was next the dressing-room.

"Make haste," cried one, who had the first chance with her powder-puff at the glass. "They are going to have a waltz next; and I want to dance with Tom Paddleford."

"Wait, can't you?" cried another. "My pannier is all to one side. That last turn. I knew it."

"I always draw mine so close that it can't slip," said another young lady, who quietly kept the glass to herself.

"Yes, and wears every thing so tight she can hardly breathe," whispered another. And the gay besiegers fled, with freshly adjusted toilets, appearing below flushed and complacent.

"How sweet it looks in the moonshine," said one who lingered, looking over Emeline's shoulder. "It's so warm in these rooms. Let's go out, and walk a minute. It's lovely out."

They borrowed a shawl apiece from the dressing-room, and stole out unseen. The night was a mild one for March, with the scents of fresh leaf and sprouting grass in the air. The girls strolled down the deep Lewis grounds, back of which were vacant lots, where the turf was green and soft as velvet and the white-oaks threw long shadows. They lingered in the welcome spell of the moonlight; and the younger one, with the ready friendliness of girls, stole her arm round Emeline's waist, who thrilled at the touch with sudden pleasure. It was new for her to be on familiar terms even with her own sex. She had been kept at a distance from all whom she would have liked, and had held herself studiously apart from those near her own level, who would have sought her.

"The Colonel is taken with you to-night," said the girl, laughingly. "I hope you will be good to him, and console him. He has the best eye for a pretty face you ever saw."

"He has no need to come my way, then," said Emeline, disdainfully.

"Come, now. Do you want to get somebody to tell you that you are the handsomest women at the wedding to-night? Everybody is noticing you. If I just had your good looks, there isn't a man in Canton that I would not have, if I wanted him."

"Are they to be had so easy? Won't you give me some lessons?"

"A woman with such looks as you have don't need much teaching. But I won't say any more. If you don't know what you are, the men will teach you fast enough. You keep the Colonel on a string, and don't let him once get too near you, or you may be sorry for it. Other girls have been. But you can stay and smell dew as long as you want to. I'm going in."

Emeline lingered a moment alone with the secret that had been revealed to her by common lips. She was beautiful, then, and very beautiful, by this girl's account. Was it true, and could she trust what such a gossip said? She would try her gift, sometime, when the right man came.

As she rested, concealed by a screen of thorny locusts, she heard a tread turn off from the street to the footpath which led past the end of the grounds — footsteps weary and dogged, like those of some laboring man going from his work. They stopped just by the hedge where she stood, half dreading to be accosted by some loiterer. Moments passed; and she heard a whisper so full of passion that she thrilled with involuntary pity — "Oh! Mary." And the slow, weary tread turned away, like feet dragging themselves from a beloved grave. Who was the loiterer, and what did that sigh mean, the irrepressible, ingenuous utterance of sorrow? Emeline had heard of this being a forced wedding — of a wronged lover and a false bride. Had she herself been called to receive the last sigh of a faithful heart grieving over its priceless hopes? If some one had been so true to her, would she allow it to sigh so? Such thoughts, half formed, came through the head of the girl, who stood bareheaded under the faint March stars, while the wind that blew up from the valley seemed to bring hopes and promise of love and all she longed for most.

Games and dances followed each other gayly. Tom Paddleford was with his chosen friends in a little room off the supper-room, whence issued sounds of clinking glasses, loud talk, and uproarious laughter. The bride left the dance; but no one misses her, who, with joyless eye and pallid cheek, has contributed less than any one to the merriment of the evening. The veil and white dress have been taken off by careful hands, folded, and laid away; the wreath and gloves placed in their perfumed boxes; and her mother and eldest bridesmaid have left the room. Shouts of laughter from the room just below indicates that her solitude will not soon be disturbed. For the first time that day, she feels free, and draws a few breaths of such freedom as will henceforth only be left her when alone. She feels calm, numb, like hunted creatures in the grasp of the destroyer. She goes to the window, veiled by the darkness, and looks out at the silvery beauty of the first spring moon. She forgets the moment, in the delicate shadowy peace that is abroad. A passing form lingers under the trees by the walk — an idler, attracted by the lights and sound within.

Unhappy love has nothing to blind its vision. The watcher, drawn by a strange, indefinable impulse, had left his solitary musings to see what he might of a wedding that should have been his own. He knew the window of the girl's chamber, and, from the shadow of the trees, traced the white, slight figure between the parted curtains, perfectly. The same numb calmness fell upon him, too, at the sight. He could not have told what made him gaze at it, as at a coffined face, delayed too long from the grave which claimed it. A reviving pang warned him that the waking from his trance was near; and, with one eloquent gesture, he flung his last kiss to the silent phantom figure, and hurried away.

From the "Forum of the People."

(The editor and his family were invited to the wedding; and Mr. Paddleford advertised in the "Forum.")

"BEAUTY AND FASHION!

"THE SOCIAL EVENT OF THE SEASON!

"WEDDING IN HIGH LIFE!

"THE NUPTIALS OF THOS. PADDLEFORD, JR., AND MISS MARY LEWIS. — ADORNMENT OF THE HOME OF THE BRIDE'S PARENTS. — THE BRILLIANT THRONG PRESENT. — THE CEREMONY. — THE BRIDAL PRESENTS.

" Wednesday evening the most brilliant gathering that ever graced New Canton assembled to do honor to the occasion of the marriage of Thomas Paddleford, Jr., Esq., son of our old and highly esteemed townsman, Thomas Paddleford, Sr., and Mary, daughter of James Lewis, an equally old and well-known citizen.

" The families represented in this most auspicious event are among the most prominent of the city; and the occasion was one which caused too great a flutter in the high social circles of New Canton to be passed without extended comment.

" While neither of the contracting parties was born here, they passed their earlier childhood in New Canton, and may be said to have resided here all their lives, except the time spent abroad in gaining the education and training, which, combined with mental endowments of no ordinary kind, has fitted them to adorn any sphere to which they may be called.

" It would require a more graphic pen than ours to describe the splendor of the Lewis mansion on this occasion. The well-known taste of Mrs. Lewis, the almost prodigal liberality of the father of the bridegroom, and the exquisite taste of the bride, combined, made the scene one of unparalleled magnificence, which will remain long in the memory of those present. We may be pardoned for saying that we thought we detected in the floral display the keen sense of the beautiful which has always distinguished the bridegroom, and which every lady within miles of the city has had occasion, for many years, to employ in her personal adornment.

"The ample rooms of the Lewis mansion were filled with the *crême de la crême* of New Canton; and many of the *élite* from Peoria and Chicago honored the nuptials with their presence.

"At precisely nine o'clock the bridal party were ushered into the grand parlors. The subdued strains of the 'Wedding March,' rendered in the most faultless style by the talented organist of the First Church, Miss Ganson (the elegant piano that has so long graced the Lewis mansion was never better employed), floated through the air, and filled the rooms with a flood of melody. They took their position under an immense floral arch; and the Rev. Mr. Latimer, D. D., of the Presbyterian Church, stepped forward, and, in a ceremony remarkable for its good taste, pronounced the happy words that united two fond hearts according to the beautiful formula of his church, and two loving souls were united indissolubly.

"The lovely bride was arrayed in a heavy white silk dress, low corsage, demi-train, the sides looped up with orange flowers, and profusely trimmed with Valenciennes lace. Her brow was surmounted with a wreath of exquisite orange blossoms, from which issued the gauzy bridal-veil, which floated gracefully to the floor. She attracted the attention of all, and presented a picture the like of which Raphael might have given half his life to have reproduced. The groom appeared in the conventional black full-dress coat, faultless pantaloons, and white gloves and tie.

"The ladies present vied with each other in the magnificence of their toilets. It was the remark of gentlemen from Chicago, that never in that city had they ever seen gathered together more elegantly attired ladies or more *distingué* cavaliers.

"After the ceremony, the happy pair received the congratulations of their many friends, who all united in wishing them the most perfect happiness, and that their life might flow on as peacefully as course of babbling brooks through summer meadows, with no clouds to ever cover their happy sky.

"The old veteran, Col. Peppernell, excited much amusement by comparing the appearance of the mansion, in its dazzling splendor, with the first wedding he attended in New Canton. The flowers then were gathered from the prairie, the bride was arrayed in calico and wore a smart white apron, and the groom sported on the occasion his best suit of Kentucky jeans. 'There were no crosses of flowers from Chicago,' said the Colonel; 'no table groanin' with all the luxuries of the season; no silks and satins and velvets; no floors covered with cloth for dancing; but there was a log cabin, one room and a big fire at the end of it; and the refreshments were pumpkin pies and venison and hard cider — no champagne in them days. And the wedding presents — there was no silver cake-baskets and things; but we all chipped in and made up a purse for the couple to get 'em something to go to housekeepin'. I performed the ceremony, as a justice of the peace; and I gave 'em my fee (which was not a twenty-dollar gold piece) and a half-dollar besides. But we danced as long and were as jolly as we shall be to-night. Earthly grandeur counts but for little.'

"It is a bold flight of the imagination and one can scarcely conceive of such a thing; but, if our hopes are realized, the wedding of ten years hence will excel this in grandeur as far as this excelled the humble scene so graphically described by the distinguished director of the land company.

"The bridal presents — composed of many useful and ornamental articles, vertu and *bric-a-bràc* — were rich and elegant in the extreme, and excited the admiration of all. The following is a partial list of them. Want of space precludes a full enumeration:

"REV. MR. LATIMER and WIFE: book-mark, with Bible, embroidered in two colors.

"MR. CHAS. BURT: deed of lot in Fourth Addition to New Canton.

"MRS. CHAS. BURT: silver cake-basket.

"THOS. PADDLEFORD, SENIOR, father of the bridegroom: ten lots in Second Addition to New Canton, deeded directly to the bride.

"MRS. THOS. PADDLEFORD, mother of the bridegroom: set of solid silver spoons and richly plated knives.

"COL. SETH PEPPERNELL: to bride and bridegroom each a lot in Third Addition to New Canton.

"SQUIRE SHARP: lot in North Addition.

"CAPT. PEAK: lot in North Addition.

"MRS. CAPT. PEAK: silver cake-basket.

"MRS. SQUIRE SHARP: solid silver napkin-ring.

"MRS. COL. PEPPERNELL: silver cake-basket.

"MRS. ABSOLOM THOMPSON: silver cake-basket.

"MRS. J. G. ROBINSON: silver napkin-ring.

"MR. and MRS. PETTENGILL: silver cake-basket.

"MRS. PETER TORRENCE: elegant carved wooden salad-fork and spoon.

"MR. and MRS. SAM'L MARSH: silver cake-baskets.

"MR. and MRS. PETTIGREW and DAUGHTERS: pair of solid silver napkin-rings.

"MR. and MRS. SHUBAEL SANDERS: pair vases.

"MR. and MRS. NAT. HAUGHTON: silver cake-basket.

"There were other presents equally valuable, from almost every family in the city, who took this method of testifying their respect for the happy pair."

From the " Sentinel."

(The Paddlefords did not advertise in the "Sentinel," and the editor was not invited.)

"Thos. Paddleford, of the firm of Paddleford &

Son, was married, Wednesday night, to Miss Mary A. Lewis. A very respectable company, in point of numbers, was present."

The next morning Tom Paddleford gazed at the presents, so ostentatiously displayed, and tried very hard to preserve a smiling exterior. But it was a failure. He turned away with disgust so plainly depicted on his features as to be visible to any one.

"Fifteen cake-baskets and thirty-one napkin-rings, and all of them plated except ma's, and that I have to pay for. Popham, the jeweler, had a big stock on hand, and closed 'em out cheap. We deal in the same goods, but nobody bought 'em of us. Bah!"

CHAPTER XI.

AN EVENING'S AMUSEMENT IN NEW CANTON.

JAMES GARDINER had always promised himself, that, when a clergyman should pronounce him "man" to some one else's daughter, he would begin being good, in the sense that the world has it. On the altar of Hymen he would sacrifice all his vices, and all his foibles should evaporate in the rose-colored cloud above it. All young men swear this, just as on the second of January, their heads aching with the wine taken at calls, they swear off drinking. On the third, when they feel better, they fix the date of their quitting ; and, that they may have time to strengthen for their effort, they prudently make it the next New Year.

When he became the head of a family, James would bury his meerschaum, give away his fowling-piece and fishing-tackle, burn his cards, read novels sparingly, and settle down to law. He would revive his ambition ; he would attend to business ; he would speculate ; he would attend caucuses, and get into the legislature, and finally into Congress ; in short, he would follow the paths of a legitimate American ambition, and, possibly, die in a senatorial chair.

But the stern edict of the Lewis *père* — that is to

say, of the Lewis *mère* — and the fatal weakness of Mary killed this out of him. His love was gone ; and he did not care what became of what life left him. She had been the very light in his sky ; and when it faded out he would no longer lift his eyes in that direction. But in the other? Hell is easier to find than Heaven; for its doors are never closed, and it never puts out its guiding-lights. A man can always take refuge there, as Gardiner discovered ; and he turned his face that way with the only determination that had ever characterized him.

"He had a weakness for that girl, and it has run into recklessness," said his friends. "He will get over it in a month." But they were mistaken.

He did not get into his bad habits by degrees, as men generally do. He made a business of them. His office was the headquarters of the wildest young men in town ; and the games of poker played there nightly made Peppernell's hair stand on end, when he heard of the way the boys were going on. It must be confessed that James's idleness, his easy way of taking life, and most of his former associates, made the way to recklessness very smooth to him. His amusements had on occasion been as high-flavored as those of most young men born with money ; and he had cultivated games of chance and skill to such purpose that he could give points to the oldest hand in the village. He seldom slept ; or, if he did sleep, no one could tell when. The little glass bottle had given way to a demijohn, which was never allowed to get empty ; and it came to the point that he was to be seen at Pilkin's doggery at all times when he had not something worse to do. He would leave the office with his hangers-on, after daylight, and, with bloodshot eyes and matted hair, go into the bar-rooms and "billiard-parlors," to get stimulated for the day's work. Then woe to the man who crossed his humor; for he was strong as a lion and ferocious as a bear.

Yet, in losing the preciseness of respectability, he was no less handsome. His fiery, reckless air was fit to take the imagination of an impressible girl, if she believed (and what woman does not?) herself strong enough to hold the handsome animal in check. The loosely-tied, high-colored handkerchief about his neck fitted his style better than the plain black bow of his careful days; and the prompt recklessness of his actions was more taking than his careless, lounging manners before. He never stopped to think. It pleased him to indulge every impulse; and he troubled himself as little with forethought as with repentance.

He was sitting one evening like the French fashion of the *boulevards*, with other loafers, before Pilkin's saloon. James prided himself on his democracy nowadays, and professed not to be above seeing good in any company. He found a vast fund of worldly wisdom in Slack Williams's not overclean and carving-knife observations on human nature, in general, and all property-holders in town who paid tax on more than twenty-five cents' worth of estate, in particular. He found an appetite for the scraps of songs, satiric and beastly, which that worthy could troll out, in a voice that had been worth better matter. James made the excuse to himself that he never listened to such things unless he was in liquor. But he took care to be in that state most of the time. When he woke up in the morning, he could not remember much of the evening before, but a general suggestion of foulness, as if he had slept in a night-hawk's nest; and his head ached too badly to leave much attention for his distracted morals. There was no getting over the ache without a stiff dose of alcohol, now turned medicine. All the noons of his past, of love and hope, tormented him, till he would have flown to the breast of Hecate for relief; and at night there was nothing to do but go through the same routine of chaff, cards, and whisky, now taken as refreshment, and thus turned the endless chain till next morning.

On this evening in particular the fun was low; and one of the oldest of the set rose with a laugh, declaring that he could find more fun at home, in a tone that intimated satire could no further go than to suggest any thing attractive with one's family. The rest waxed sulkier at his desertion, till one of them, spying a woman coming down Pilkin's side of the walk, which women were usually shy of, prepared for sport. The light was uncertain; and he sprawled over the narrow walk so that his foot unavoidably caught her skirt, as she hurried past. She stumbled and nearly fell. The ruffian uttered a coarse laugh, volunteering the excuse that he " wasn't used to being carried away by strange women so sudden," and advised her to " turn her pretty face to account, though it wasn't so ketchen, after all."

He lacked teeth and voice for further insult, by reason of finding the one knocked down his throat and the other clean out of it, while he fell prostrate under the uplifted arm of James Gardiner.

The impulse of citizens under the chivalry of rum is to hit first and ask what the matter is afterward.

And this inquiry was hissed out with poor Jim's head between Sandy Beverstock's arms, in a grip in which thought was fragmentary. For it was Sandy's friend who was lying prostrate; and he had been stricken down for doing what Sandy would have done, had it occurred to him. It is usually the chivalric young fellow who knocks everybody out of his boots, and only comes off with scratches enough for his girl to cry over; but the writer, not being largely educated in polite fiction, can only describe things as they fall under the eye in common life. There the biggest fellow with most skill invariably comes off best. Now Sandy, being a larger man and more skilled in encounters of the sort, and less under the influence of liquor, and having, moreover, the sympathy and support of the assembled crowd, was proceeding to punish the chivalrous James severely, when there was a rush that parted them.

"What's all this about?" asked Peppernell, on his way to the Continental for his game at cards. "Jim, what is Sandy pounding you for?"

"He's a white-livered dog, and so is every one who stands by him. He insulted a lady, and I struck him for it."

"Who was the lady?" not unnaturally inquired Col. Peppernell.

Not one of them could tell, till a timid loafer, in the background, whose acquaintance was more extensive than the rest, tendered the information that it was old Butterfield's girl.

The loafers only remembered the girl in her early days, coupled with her father's notorious disregard of appearances and decencies; and the word was received with screams of derisive laughter, which put the crowd in good humor directly. — " Old Butterfield's girl, down by the swamp ! " — " Butterfield's girl, that hitches up the horses ! " — " Seen her digging taters, barefoot, frosty mornings ! " — " Father no better than a hoss-thief ! " and so on.

"My young friend's gallantry does him honor," said Col. Peppernell, drawing James's arm through his.

"Burt's handsome housekeeper," he said, not careful how the crowd heard him. "Your spirit does you the more credit, shown in defense of a servant-girl. She's handsome enough for a man to skin himself for."

James had a memory of dark eyes which flashed up into his, as he sprang against the rough, Sandy; but the fact of the matter was he would have fought for Peppernell's Durham heifer, or Pilkin's cat, if opportunity had offered that night. His nerves were overstrung, and wanted some excitement to restore them to their tension. He felt a little awkward at finding that his gallantry had been expended on a girl who had been a chambermaid in a hotel, and was now a housekeeper, and a pretty one enough to make him the subject of the sly jokes of the crowd. If it had been Miss Clymer, for instance, the lady librarian of the village, or Grace Gibson, who sang in the choir, he would have shone with becoming spirit; but to fight for a "pot-walloper," as he put it to himself, put his prowess outside the pale of polite approval. There was nothing further for it but to spread his shirt-collar open further, call his democracy to his aid, and declare that he would as soon help a kitchen-girl as the best lady in town, and he wasn't going to see any woman put upon by any miserable wretch whose mother hadn't taught him to behave himself when ladies were about.

Despite the fact that the man he knocked down and Sandy Beverstock were in the saloon, he walked boldly in, and ordered drinks for them all, and stayed there, perfectly willing that they should assault him again, if they chose to. Peppernell had, however, quieted the party; and no further unpleasantness grew out of it, though Sandy came up, rather ostentatiously, once or twice, and glared at him. But, when he saw Jim's determined manner, and realized, that, if he "tackled" him, he would have to take him alone, and it would be an expensive victory, he contended himself with glaring at him in the ferocious way of ruffians when tolerably certain that they will have to make the attack.

The woman in question, as soon as she could recover her footing, started on a frightened walk, that never slackened till she found herself on the high road leading out of town. As she paused by the bank, in the friendly dusk and starlight, she found that tears wet her cheek. It was characteristic of the girl that she sat down in a sheltered nook, and cried her shaken quiet back, then set off, with interior calmness, over her long, lonesome road. A mile and a half brought her to a low house, half buried in trees. Her step was waited for by a tall, thin woman; and a boy, in rough jacket and barefoot, sprang at her, in company with a pet dog. Which was most glad to meet her, it was hard to tell.

"You were out watching for me?" asked the girl of the mother. (11)

"To see if you were coming to-night," was the answer, with slight habitual repression. "We could see you coming up the bend, in this moonlight, if you were coming at all."

The bend was nearly a mile away.

"Father's gone to Lexington, and said he shouldn't be home till late," was the boy's first speech, made as if it was a piece of news which removed the only bar to entire freedom and privilege.

"Come in," cried Emeline, her joyous self again, leading the way, under the leaning orchard boughs, to the house. "You dear little tow-head! How I do love to see you again! Ring, you beautiful, black-coated fellow, are you glad to see me?"— catching the boy, and then the dog, and smothering them with kisses, which both returned with fervor. She had them both in her arms at once, where the boy stayed, while the dog set off on a chase round the room, giving a short bark at intervals, as if to relieve his feelings. "Mother, put yourself where I can look at you," said the girl, looking up, her warm cheek flushed with kisses. "How nice the place looks! I should know father was away, or you never would have got so much cleaning done. Where did you get these flowers?" springing up to the rude mantle, where a tumbler held the first and freshest spring tribute — willow catkins, yellow and perfumy, with blossoms of the birch and red sprays of blossom-like leafage, that shed faint incense through the room.

"Tom went for them, when he got done plowing. He would have been disappointed if you hadn't come to see them."

"They're for my pretty sister," said the boy, who

looked almost a child by reason of his small stature and innocent face. "And, oh, Em!" with profound mystery, going to the closet, bringing a crown of willow blossoms, and dropping it lightly on her head. "I saw those; and they looked like you; and I climbed for them. Yes," putting his head on one side a little, and marking the effect, "they're the right thing; I'm satisfied."

This opinion, pronounced with great gravity, was enough to upset an ordinary mortal; but these women had not been trained to laugh. They smiled contentedly, and with deep affection, at the boy; and Emeline began opening several packages with which she had loaded herself.

"Tom, I suppose you think I've forgotten you, because I always do," — a sisterly fiction. "Here are all the pieces of pie and cake I had for my share after the wedding; and there's enough to make a little boy stop growing, if he eats enough of them. There is one with a little white rose in the frosting, and one with a sugar dove; and some fruit-cake I advise you to keep till it's blue-moldy, and then throw away without eating it. It's all nightmare and indigestion — don't you see how black it is? Here it goes!" popping a piece into his mouth, in conclusion to the harangue.

"O-o-oh!" danced the boy, cutting capers noiselessly. "With white sugar on, Em! Oh! don't they look pretty? Mother, I didn't think it would be a feast when Em came home. Let me have the white plate to put them on, — the white plate, mother, — and see how it seems to eat real white and nice, like people. I can't do any thing but look at it now; but

I *shall* think so much of myself when I get to eating that cake." And Tom, in his ecstasy, balanced himself on the edge of the table, with hands spread out, but quietly, his whole face lighted up in adoration of the cake, which shone white and beautiful to his eyes as crumbs from a fairy feast.

When he had eyed it long enough, he took off all the least temping portions, and laid them on the table, then took the plate, silently traveled round the stove, and put it in his mother's lap, without a word.

"I couldn't eat it without she did," was his matter-of-course explanation. Em's eyes shone a little at the sight.

"Tom, going to church to-morrow?"

"Why, no," with a injured look. "What do you ask such a fool question for, when you know I haven't got any boots?"

"His father made him put a piece of old oilcloth inside his shoes, where they are broken, to wear wet days, when he had to be out plowing; and that's all he's got till after taxes are paid."

"Do you think these would fit you, Tom?" cried Emeline, holding out a pair, shining as boy's boots never shone before. "It's a pair Mrs. Burt told me to throw away, when we cleaned house. I got them mended down town, and they look neat as new. I went after them to-night, down to the other end of the street; and that's what made me so late. Job Fitzhugh gave 'em a good blacking for me. I'll get you a new pair, Tom, when I come to it; but I want to get mother fixed out a little, and the house."

"Was the wedding a large one?" asked the mother, as if the question was out of pure civility. Emeline threw herself down on the lounge, luxuriously; and her eyes sparkled as she prepared to tell her mother, her only confidant, the evening's triumphs and pleasures. Old Hannah Butterfield sat at ease in the big rocking-chair, with mild pride and pleasure softening the immovable expression of her face. The boy, curled on the floor at the sister's feet, looked up in her face, admiring, wrapped up in what she had to tell.

"Everybody was stiff enough for awhile. The gentlemen stood by themselves, and the girls waved their fans at them; but they didn't come. The old ladies had time to ask after everybody in their families, from the grandmothers to the last baby. The girls got the bride dressed half an hour after the time for the ceremony; and the last thing, a yard of trimming, ripped off, and had to be basted on again: and Miss Peak came for me to do it; for she was dressed, and all the rest of the bridesmaids were dressed, and they couldn't kneel down to get at the flounce. So I had the best chance to see what their dresses were. Miss Lewis was as white as if she was faint, anyhow; but the bridesmaids put a little powder on, to make her look interesting, they said. Norman Peak came up, and said they must hurry; for everybody was waiting, and the minister had to go four miles to see a sick woman after the ceremony. Miss Lewis said they might as well go, and have it over with; and the way she swept off showed she was her mother's own child, for all her delicate looks. Mother, what is there sounds so sweet to a woman as the swish, swish of a white silk dress? Talk about the winds in the trees! I'd rather hear silk a thousand times; for it tells about happy things and lovely things, — people without care, being admired and making love.

"Then Mr. Latimer performed the ceremony: he was short with his good advice; and he dwelt on the mutual-forbearance part, as if he thought it would be called for. All the folks needed something to revive them after the suspense; and nothing was to be thought of, after the congratulations, but supper. And wasn't the bride-cake complimented?

"Tom, can't you give me an opinion on it by this time?"

"How did you enjoy it?" asked the mother, wrapped up in her bright, lovely daughter, with no ear for any fortunes but hers.

"Well, my dress fit like a bad character; and that was more than several better ones there did. I squandered a dollar in crape *ruches*, they look so frosty and soft; and then three yards of velvet ribbon to tie round my neck, as the young ladies wear it. Mother, two weeks' wages gone in finery for that wedding!"

"Well, it's time you thought of yourself," remarked Hannah, as if she were stating the most matter-of-fact idea in the world. "You've put all your year's earnings on this rack-a-bones of a place and on us, and got nothing but a thank-you for it; and that's all you're likely to get. It did me good to know you were going to spend that money on something that would please nobody but yourself."

"There has been something done, and money never went better," said Emeline, looking up with a little pardonable complacence. The place showed a fostering hand that had carefully tended taste and convenience. Sundry furnishings were to be seen, which, in that country, were only found in better houses. It looked oddly, in that log house, with rough-cast walls and the small, sunken windows which no carpenter could ever make straight, to see, instead of the traditional green-paper shades of the region, white spring blinds, as stainless and well-fitted as the pride of a New York housekeeper at her parlor windows. A curtained corner cupboard showed a glimpse of a neat set of white ware; — not china, but the best of its kind; — and the home-made lounge, covered with glazed calico, was inviting enough for a lady's chamber, with its frills and pillows. A low, walnut rocker and a carefully kept Shaker arm-chair, the most comfortable things in the way of seats, kept company with a pretty and substantial work-table; nor was there wanting a good paper and book for leisure hours.

Emeline lay a moment, taking in these things, the sight of which, earned by months of toil, was fresh pleasure every time she looked at them; but the moments of Saturday evening's visit once a fortnight were precious, and there was more to be told.

"You couldn't go to the wedding, so I've brought part of it to you, mother," the girl said, seizing one of her unopened bundles, with which she fled to her own little room. Agitated sounds were heard there for a few minutes, — fewer than ever lady who reads these lines takes to dress, — and there was silence. Turning their heads, the woman and the boy saw a picture lovely enough to fill a panel in a king's cabinet. Emeline stood there, in her party dress, the pale lavender, made like the princess robe of our time, which shows the lines of a full figure so deliciously, the feathery willow blossoms lying in a golden crown upon the silken waves of her hair, and her arms clasped before her with that exquisite turn of the arms which no woman without the instinct of grace ever attains. It was a girl's masquerade, got up for home, — for eyes that seldom rested on any thing but poor and common objects; and a sweet picture she was for their delight. The hair rippled away from her wide forehead in the old Greek fashion; her cheeks were burning, with the wind and the walk, through the creamy dusk of her face; and her eyes shone like stars with gladness and affection, as she stood there, drinking in the admiration of those dear ones, for it was passionately sweet to her. The whole world lived for her in those two — the gaunt woman and the barefooted boy, who gazed at her with all the longing of a barren life gratified in that moment. Old Hannah Butterfield drew her breath softly, to think she had mothered so fair a thing, and forced herself back to her usual repression.

"The Lord be good to you, with those looks, Emeline," was all she said.

The young beauty, in her delicate dress and golden willow crown, threw her arms about her mother at this, and held her, looking into her face with such ardor as, in their children's eyes, compensates mothers for all their pangs and the struggle of afterlife. The mother and brother sat by in happy content. The wedding had come to them in their own beautiful girl, with her soft dress and every leaf and ornament she had worn before, and the white and spicy fragments of the feast she spread before them. The spirit of fun in her came out in the freedom of home. She rehearsed Peppernell's speeches, and made the humors of the evening live for them — how Mrs. Lewis's older sister, whose husband was worth a quarter of a million, took off her white gloves at supper, and folded them in a piece of brown paper, and putting them in her pocket; and little Mrs. Mole capered about her husband, protesting she felt like flirting dreadfully, but couldn't find anybody to flirt with her; and Miss Cleve preferred to sit close in a corner all the evening, and "study human nature," as she said, forgetting that she was human and might afford a study to others in turn. Emeline swam, floated, shone before them for ten mortal minutes — the loveliest Emeline that ever bewitched in a three-shilling gown.

In this warm and peaceful hour, the sounds of wheels in the lane were heard; and fun and comfort fled, like lights and laughter from a fairy-ring. Emeline hurried to her own room, and tore off the dress; Tom was up the stairs and in bed before the wagon was stopped; and Mrs. Butterfield lighted a lantern, and went to help put up the horses, as was her wont, to save the tired little fellow, who else would have had all to do. Her presence was acknowledged without a word. The new-comer watered and fed his team, and stalked into the house in solemn silence.

"What ye up for, burning kerosene this time o' night?" was the first speech. "Oil's most gone. I could have put the horses, if you'd left the lantern; or you might have called Tom up."

To this the prudent wife made no answer; and the man ate his supper of bread and milk in a surly silence.

"Tom planted those potatoes?" he asked, as he set down his bowl. And this was all he had to say at home-coming. Shortly after, he turned heavily into bed.

Emeline lay looking out through a crack in the roof, that many a time had let in heaven and starbeams to her pillow, and let her thoughts go free. The fright on the street came back to her. The coarse grasp, at which her heart bounded as the ruffian caught and set her on her feet, the insulting words, and the one reeling moment, in which she looked up, to see a flushed, handsome face blazing between her and her tormentor, before she fled down the street. But, short as the moment was, it was one of those which might last longer than her life. Soft, unvisited, delicate, her nature needed but to come under the glow of that handsome, generous ardor to receive the impression forever. It was with a child's joy she thought of the bold, kind, daring face that had come to her help; and, glad that such strong, quick, generous creatures live for the protection of those weaker than themselves, she fell asleep.

CHAPTER XII.

THE UPS AND DOWNS OF THE CITY. — A LAWSUIT.

TO write the history of New Canton is to write of changes rapid as the shifts of a pantomime.

"It may take years," Burt would say, "or it may come sooner; but fortune must come. It was by no chance that Chicago is where it is. It was no chance that made London the financial center of the world, or New York the metropolis of America. And the same laws that made them will make New Canton. I may never see it; but my children will — that is, if I had children."

Thus saying, he would resume his business in a clean-shaven, serene way, with the look of a man who had made a discovery of inestimable value to humanity.

Mr. Gardiner was nervous about the land company. His loss in New York was not generally known; but it had crippled him seriously. He had advanced heavily to the land company; and he had not enough coming in from his deposits to meet the demands made upon him, without borrowing, and was impatient to realize something from the company.

The demands on his capital were larger than ever before. Lewis, who had formerly been ready to play the Good Samaritan to the financially wounded, at eighteen per cent. on undeniable security, suddenly began to pass by on the other side. Paddleford, who had always been ready to loan, utterly refused all applicants; and those who had formerly depended upon him, came to Gardiner. He did not dare to refuse responsible people, for it would have shown weakness; and he had no resource but borrowing, unless he could realize. From sheer necessity, he became as zealous on the merits of New Canton as Burt himself, and vastly more effective.

There grew up in the minds of some people, grave doubts as to whether New Canton was, after all, the exact center of the globe; and those who had bought began cautiously offering to sell. Buyers became more cautious and slower of movement; and there was a lowering of tone when the town was under discussion. The flow of money and obligations into the land office was checked; and there settled down a gloom, for which no one could give a reason. Lot-owners began to ask troublesome questions — why the railroads were not commenced; why the improvement of Soggy Run was not begun; why the turnpikes, which were to bring trade into New Canton, had no existence save on paper; and men began to scowl at the elegantly colored maps in the land company's office. Several hundred lots had been sold, and prices had gone steadily up; but the advance had stopped, and, while nominally as high as ever, there were no actual transactions. People were frightened. They wanted to see something of the golden wave that was to wash through that section like an inundation of the Nile, leaving its rich deposits on every man's property. They wanted to hear the shrieks of the locomotives that had been promised them; they wanted to see steamboats puffing and snorting on Soggy Run; and they wanted to see some movement made toward the long rows of massive warehouses and palatial residences that the eloquent and florid Peppernell had described to their willing ears so long.

"Something must be done," growled Peppernell, in his gruffest way, to Burt, as they sat in the office, one night, later than usual. "Something must be done, and that right away. Jobley is going about swearing that the scheme is a fraud, and that there ain't a-goin' to be no railroad nor no nothin' else, and that the thing, from first to last, is a scheme to sell out the people for the benefit of the land company; and blast me if they don't more than half believe him. If it wasn't for old Gardiner, they'd bust us in a week."

"New Canton can't afford to be 'busted,' as you term it," replied Burt. "No, indeed! Never fear. We are not to be busted. Wait, my dear sir; wait. A new light will dawn on New Canton, and confidence in her future will be restored. The faith that I have in its destiny is grounded on—"

"Bother that stuff!" growled Peppernell. "It's all well enough for the street; but in here—"

Burt laughed a soft, pleasant laugh, and laid his hand on the Colonel's coat-sleeve, soothingly.

"Colonel, I never forget New Canton, even in my own house. I talk it to Mrs. Burt. Have patience and faith. Faith is every thing. It will come out right. We shall realize all that we hoped for, Colonel."

While the town was in this state of betwixt and betweenity, undecided as to whether it should turn its back upon its greatness and settle back into the little village of ante-Burt times, a new excitement rose, which swallowed up other topics, as Aaron's serpent swallowed up the rest. It appeared that, some weeks before, a gentleman, or one whose clothes would entitle him to that distinction in New Canton, got off the cars, and took rooms at the Grand Central, registering as John F. Price, Chicago, Ill. He was a rough and gruff sort of man, was Price; and the people did not know exactly what to make of him. In the afternoon of the first day, he had John, the hostler of the Grand Central, drive him out.

He rode all over the village and extended his excursion a long way into the country. He had John stop at various points, and asked questions: —

" Who owns that block, John ? "

" The land company, sir."

" Hum-m! " was Mr. Price's soliloquy. " Burt knows its value as well as I do. No chance for a speculation there."

Then he asked about the ownership of various other pieces of ground, and made great use of a note-book, in which he made divers and sundry entries, being very particular to pump John in a sly way about the circumstances of the owners — as, for instance, whether they were sufficiently pressed for money to be compelled to part with real estate, and as to whether ready money was a desirable thing in New Canton in real estate transactions.

It was after dark when he got back to the hotel; but, late as it was, every inquiry he had made and every remark, whether in soliloquy or otherwise, was faithfully repeated by John to the crowd about the hotel; and long before they retired to their several couches every man knew all about it.

The next morning Col. Peppernell, acting for the land company, had an interview with Mr. Price. Not a private one, by any means; for they sat in the reading-room of the Grand Central, and were in earnest conversation half a day. The casual listener heard enough of their conversation to learn that it was about real estate, that Price was anxious to buy, and Peppernell equally anxious to sell; but that, as is always the case, the seller asked too much and the buyer did not offer enough. They finally rose and shook hands, Mr. Price remarking : —

"No need of any papers, is there? It's all understood."

"None, sir; none. My word is as good as my bond." Which it was — just about.

"The Busbey Farm and the block at the head of Elm Street; four thousand in hand, and the balance in one, two, and three years."

"That is it; and you shall have the deed when you make the first payment."

The gentlemen parted, Mr. Price returning to Chicago.

In about a week Price appeared one morning, approaching every man who had outlying property, with very large offers. The very liberality of his offers defeated his purpose. People grew suspicious of the man, and nobody wanted to sell. It was a peculiarity of New Canton that, as soon as a man came to buy, no one would part with their real estate at any price.

New Canton grew very conservative; and its people put such prices on their ground that Mr. Price sneeringly observed that they must each of them believe that he had a gold mine under it. They were afraid to sell, for fear there would be an advance that would make them repent their imprudence. Every man became suddenly afraid he would lose the fortune hoped for when he made his investment.

Mr. Price was fain to content himself with what he had already purchased of the land company; and he walked to the office of that corporation and demanded his deed, expressing himself ready to make the first payment, according to the verbal agreement with Peppernell, its president.

To his intense disgust and dire displeasure, both Mr. Burt and Col. Peppernell refused to make any deed and utterly ignored the transaction.

"Do you pretend to deny," roared the choleric Price, in the presence of half a dozen sitting there, " that you sold me that land?"

"From Col. Peppernell I learn," said Mr. Burt, coolly, " that there was some talk with you about land, and that a price was named for the Busbey Farm and the lots at the head of Elm Street. But there were no papers drawn nor was the transaction completed. Subsequent events have made that especial property much more valuable, and we decline to sell. You should have closed on the spot, Mr. Price. Two weeks is a long time to wait, as property is here now."

"Then you won't give my deed and take my money?"

"Not at that price. Decidedly not."

Col. Peppernell echoed "Not at that price;" and the gentlemen interchanged epithets the reverse of complimentary. Mr. Price gave it as his opinion that the land company was a swindle; and the two managers informed Mr. Price that he was nothing but a land-shark, who was trying to take advantage of honest men.

"Honest men!" exclaimed Price. "To sell land and then go back on your word."

Then the usual proceedings were taken. Mr. Price consulted Mr. Perkins, one of the four lawyers of the town, who assured him that he had a clear case against the company; and, authorized by Mr. Price, Mr. Perkins called upon Col. Peppernell, in his capacity as attorney, and demanded a deed of the property, the alternative being an action at law.

Threatened with a lawsuit, Col. Peppernell became active. Long experience in and about courts made the prospect of a legal struggle pleasant to him. As the first step, he consulted Mr. James Gardiner, the company's attorney. Now, any other citizen of New Canton — that is, any reputable citizen — would have gone directly to Mr. Gardiner's office, that being the place where attorneys are supposed to be during business hours, except when "professionally engaged." But not so Col. Peppernell. He knew that when he had gone thither he would be rewarded by finding on the door, written in a good clerkly hand, the legend "Back in a few minutes," dust and finger-marks showing that it had been there a week. Peppernell would not go through the empty form of looking at the office. He went straight to Pilkin's, and walked through the bar-room into a private room at the back, where he found Mr. Gardiner playing seven-up with three other choice spirits, around a greasy table, with a great deal of not over choice spirits inside them.

Col. Peppernell told Mr. Gardiner he had a piece of important business on his hands, which he desired him to look after, and suggested that they go to the office to talk the matter over.

"A party is trying to swindle the land company," said Peppernell.

"Do they know you and Burt?" asked James, without looking up. "Six and six, and my deal."

Col. Peppernell did not relish the insinuation that anybody attempting a swindle should know better than to engage such experts as himself and Burt; but he affected not to notice it.

"Come, Jim," was the Colonel's answer. "I can't wait all day!"

"In five minutes, Colonel. Don't you see, we are six and six, and it's my deal? It is a principle with me never to neglect pleasure for business. You can take up business any time, but a pleasure lost is lost forever. You may say that you may drink another time, but, alas! you can never drink the drink you didn't drink. John, another whisky, hot. Be a little more economical of water than you were the last time. It's wicked to waste water, this dry season. If you would use more whisky and less water, how much labor you would save at the pump? In a few minutes, Colonel. John, bring Col. Peppernell a very stiff whisky, plain. As a mere matter of form, you may ask him what he will have."

The game ended, the whisky swallowed, the pair left the saloon, and went to Gardiner's office, where instructions were given and taken; and Gardiner, promising to look the matter up with all due diligence, went immediately back to Pilkin's where cards, and whisky not drowned in water, employed him till his usual hour in the night.

Law was not the slow thing in New Canton that it is in larger places. There were no crowded dockets to be cleared off; and, as both parties seemed anxious to have the matter decided, there were no vexatious delays. The county court was in session; and Mr. Price was only detained a few days till the case came on. Mr. Perkins was always ready and never more eager for a fee; and, for the other side, Gardiner, feeling the responsibility that rested upon him, as his good old father was interested in the suit, let liquor alone several hours, and went into the case finally in decent condition.

A lawsuit is to the Western American what a bull-fight is to a Spaniard, or an opera to a Frenchman. The struggle of matadore and bull is represented by the pettifogger and the witness; and it affords as exciting amusement. Any lawsuit in New Canton, in which a sum so prodigious as four thousand dollars was involved, would draw a throng; but this case excited especial interest. The value of land interested every landholder within range of the operations of the land company, beside a great many who did not own lands and never expected to.

For days it had been the topic of conversation in blacksmith shop, grocery, and at cross-roads. It displaced the deaths, marriages, and "vandoos," and even the state of the country — topic always dear to the man who has no stake whatever in it — was compelled to give way to the "Great Land Case."

Public opinion was divided. "If I was in Burt's place," said Dubbly, the blacksmith, as he turned a horseshoe, "I should give the Chicago man the deed and take his money. A bargain is a bargain, and common fairness — "

"Yes," was the reply of Farmer Whipple. "But there's another side to it. Peppernell says there was no sale; and, besides, if there was, suppose Price concealed facts that had a bearin' onto the value of the property. Why, Price was down here after my farm; and, if I hadn't been warned, he'd 'a' got it for a hundred and fifty an acre."

And Whipple, whose land was dear at ten dollars, shuddered at the narrow escape he had made.

"There ought to be no law for these speculators," was his closing remark; "and I'm glad Burt is fightin' 'em."

Whipple, whose twenty acres afforded his family potatoes, in good seasons, had been afraid of these land-sharks ever since the offer and rejection of four thousand dollars for the Busbey Farm, and lay awake nights, racking his brain as to the best and safest way of investing money. It troubled him. Stocks? Stocks went up and down. Business? He didn't understand business. Worried as to what he should do with his wealth, he hunted through his pantaloons to find a quarter of a dollar, and rode into town and went incontinently to Pilkin's to spend it, talking over the land-case.

The town was even more excited than the country, being more directly interested. Cobblers left their benches, and blacksmiths their forges; and they did it with perfect safety, for they knew no one would come near them that day. Pilkin and his kind were the only ones who could reasonably be expected to do any business when so exciting a case was pending.

Before daybreak, people were pouring into town, in all sorts of vehicles and upon all sorts of beasts. There were teams — mere reminiscenses of horses — harnessed side by side, to give each something to lean on, to keep them on their feet. There were wagons so patched and mended that hardly a stick of the original was visible; and, the poorer the horse and the frailer the wagon, the more men and women were riding behind them.

The court-house in New Canton was a barn-like structure, devised, to show, by actual experiment, how much ugliness and discomfort could be put into one building. The excited people had tried in vain to get some idea from the presiding judge on the merits of the case. When approached on the subject, he replied that it was a very important case, and it was not proper to express any opinion till the evidence had been heard and the case was before the court in a purely legal way.

"But, Judge, can a man take property before — "

"My friend," the Judge replied, with great gravity, "you will know all about the law in this case, when you have heard my charge to the jury."

The court-room was crowded to overflowing. Indeed, not half the throng could get into it. Those who, not possessing land enough to be buried in, were, as they always are, first on the ground, and secured the best seats. They felt they had a right to them. They had left potatoes undug, corn in the field, and stock uncared for, and their wives had left household duties, to be present at the trial of the land-case; and they were not going to be defrauded out of their pleasure. Mr. Perkins was a master hand with timid witnesses; and Gardiner had given promise, in his few appearances, of having mettle in him.

At the outset, Mr. Perkins, in the most formal manner and in the most ostentatious way, counted out four thousand dollars, and, in open court, tendered them to the defendants, for the land, specifying, with great exactness, what land it was.

"Gracious Heavens!" exclaimed a hundred farmers, in the suppressed tones appropriate to such places. "Four thousand dollars for that Busbey Farm! It could have been bought for five hundred a year ago."

"There ain't no doubt about it," whispered another to his neighbor. "There's the money, and it's good money."

"This same spekilator wanted to get my place — a hundred acres — for two thousand! I was too smart for him. He didn't take *me* in."

Public opinion was against Mr. Price; for every man who owned an acre of ground would have believed that he was taking an undue advantage if he had offered ten times the sum for it.

Witnesses were examined, — Mr. Gardiner being prompted by Mr. Burt, — in the course of which it was made public that Mr. Price's anxiety to possess the land arose from information that the operations of the Midland Company were a sure thing, and that negotiations by the company made other railroads a certainty, and the Soggy Run improvements were to be forthwith commenced, with more to the same purpose.

There wasn't the slightest occasion for argument, nor for any charge to the jury; but Mr. Perkins would no more have permitted the case to go the jury without addressing them than he would have declined his fee. And a good two-hours' plea he made, which was quoted in the "Forum" as a model of forensic eloquence. He hurled at the heads of the unfortunate jurymen all the land-law that had ever been made; he went into the question of agreements, the effect of verbal agreements — where they held and where they did not; and he was severe upon the bad faith of the land company, as a man might reasonably be expected to be who had been mortified at the promotion of a young practitioner to the place he was entitled to. After instructing the jury that the eyes of the civilized world were upon them, that the question at issue involved the entire framework of society, and that, if they brought a verdict against his client, there was an end of every thing like comity, and chaos might be properly said to have come again, he closed.

Gardiner contented himself with showing that it was necessary for the plaintiff to establish a sale; which was impossible, as he did not pretend that any of the formalities necessary to the transfer of land had been observed; and the case went to the Judge. His honor charged the jury — but why detail his charge? During the progress of the trial, he had been calculating his chances for re-election, and knew as much about the matter as he did of the Schleswig-Holstein question. But he said, with an appearance of profound wisdom, that, if the evidence had been so and so, they must find so and so; but, if it had been otherwise, they would have to find otherwise, which sapient conclusion impressed people with a sense of judicial fairness they had not expected.

As the jury owned real estate in New Canton, and were, therefore, unprejudiced, they brought in a verdict for the defendants without leaving their seats; which every man of them would have done, no matter what the evidence. Mr. Price was disgusted, and made threats of appealing the case where he could have justice done; but, before leaving the court-room, he approached Mr. Burt and offered him two thousand dollars more than he had originally bought the ground for, saying that he had rather submit to the swindle than bother any more with law. This Mr. Burt declined, and defied him to do his worst.

"I know what that land is worth, Mr. Price," was Mr. Burt's answer, with a knowing inclination of the head; "and I don't propose to give it away."

"He won't take six thousand dollars, cash, for the Busbey place!" echoed the crowd. "And in good money!"

Mr. Price now threw off all reserve. He wanted real estate; he had money to pay for it, and he intended to have it. He should get that which he had bought of the land company, if there was any justice in the land. Holders of ground became more and more averse to selling, and Price increased his offers exactly in proportion to their unwillingness. The people were puzzled. Should they sell and realize? They could make an exceedingly good thing by doing it. But, then, suppose the roads should be built — and this man evidently was acting upon information. The tender of four thousand dollars was an indication not to be disregarded.

Mr. Burt, when appealed to for advice, was very reticent.

"Gentlemen," said he, "you all know my opinion of New Canton. My hopes and expectations may be realized, and may not. New Canton may become the great city. I hope it will, or I may be mistaken in my calculations. But, while I will not advise you, I can say what I shall do, in a very few words. We sell, because we have to sell; but, were I otherwise circumstanced, I would rather buy than sell. I don't know this man. He may be a wild speculator, who believes it safe to invest anywhere in lands, at present prices; or he may be a shrewd man, who has studied natural advantages and sees something in the future of New Canton. I don't know. Every one of you must act on his own judgment and do what he thinks best."

Mr. Burt refused to talk further; but went calmly on with his business, with a half-smile of pity for the poor people who could not see through so transparent an operation as this Chicago shark was trying to make.

That afternoon, an old farmer, whose land Mr. Price was trying to buy, received this note:—

"FRIEND ELKINS:—

"Price is on the inside of the great Midland Road. He is here trying to buy up every thing in the way of real estate that he can get contracts for. Burn this as soon as you have read it, and say nothing about it to any one.
"BURT."

"The thief! Trying to swindle us!" said Elkins to himself; and he mounted his horse, and rode furiously over to his brother-in-law, to save him from this wolf. The brother-in-law, in turn, told a friend of his; and by nightfall it was half over the county.

The result was, that Mr. Price found it difficult to get New Canton real estate at any price. He had secured several refusals before his position and purposes became known; but he could no more have got another inch than he could have bought the Capitol at Washington. Owners laughed in his face; and he was chopfallen when he found that his purpose was known. He offered some very large prices for a very large amount of real estate, and wasn't at all particular where it was located.

The next day saw increased activity in the real estate market. The few who had rashly sold to the scheming Chicagoans were pitied, and those who had held on were congratulated. People were justly indignant that the directors of the roads should take advantage of their knowledge of affairs to swindle poor farmers out of their property, and did not hesitate to say so.

Burt told them that it was only natural; and Peppernell swore great oaths that it was precisely what he would have done, if he had the point that Price and Hawkins had.

"You bring it upon yourselves," was the Colonel's indignant commentary. "You go about growlin' like bears with sore heads because we can't do everything in a minit; and you invite these fellows to come and gobble you. They are at the centers of information — they know all about it; and, when they see people impatient, and they know there ain't no reason for it, they come in and take advantage of the feelin'. If any of you have any property to sell, come to me with it. You might as well give a townsman a chance as a stranger."

The "Sentinel" next week had a long and humorous article describing the attempts of a Chicago real-estate sharp to get the advantage of the people of New Canton, and how the attempt was foiled by the shrewdness and public spirit of Mr. Burt. It described the lawsuit, laying stress upon the $4,000 episode, and went on to mention what prices had been offered and refused. It congratulated the citizens upon the improved prospects of the town, which resulted in a great influx of people, who actually bought of the land company, for cash.

All this was encouraging to Gardiner. The land company was his only hope. Never since its beginning had the speculation showed such vitality as since the advent of Mr. Price. He consulted his son as to the propriety of selling part of his interest, to replace the money he had lost in New York.

"I doubt if you can sell," was the discouraging reply of the young man.

"Why not? Didn't Price offer $4,000 for the Busbey Farm?"

"Price testified too readily; and Burt — Burt is a smart man — prompted every question I put to him, and they all went to establish the soundness of the land company and the desirability of New Canton real estate. Price was a very willing witness. Don't take too much stock in these men or what they do."

"James, you seem to intimate something like collusion between Burt and this man. If it was true, it would make them out dishonest men," said old Gardiner, in his simple integrity, as if he had named the most utter impossibility in the world.

James looked at his father with a blending of reverence and compassion.

"Then there's nothing more to be said," he remarked briskly; and he went out feeling detailed to keep close watch the proceedings of the land company, and Mr. Charles Burt in particular.

CHAPTER XIII.

ELIPHALET BUTTERFIELD'S DAUGHTER.

EMELINE. At the soft, out-of-fashion name, the image of an ardent, gracious woman rises as a face grows out of the breath on a mirror. Berries, fair flowers, the breath of hayfields, warm evening flushes — have their counterparts for men in the beauty of women. But the charm of Emeline Butterfield was off the common order. It had the spice of talent — not the common feminine instinct, like that of moles, which certainly see a great deal further in the dark than we do, but the quick, working intelligence, which makes a plain face better than the wealthiest beauty, and which, added to beauty, makes it next to divine. In favor, Emeline was more than a warm, dark rose, all deep blush and perfume; or a wild red crabtree blossom, delicate in its subtle, tea-like odor; or a raspberry, all redness and *aroma*, — than any frailer flower or berry, brighter in color and uncertain in sweetness. She had been a handsome creature when, in the early days of New Canton, she rode into town on her father's load of wood, her bare feet hanging below her gown, showing a leg and foot as straight and fine and true as ever was turned. At the time this story begins, she had long since learned to keep her pretty foot hidden in as neat a shoe and white a stocking as could be seen in New Canton, and was not unaware of a few of her good points. Her figure, low and luxurious at sight, was lithe as a whip, and carried with such ease and spring that every man in town turned his head to look after her, and was itself capital enough for any woman to set up for charming. Her face, in all its tints, tended to depth, so that the purple-dark eyes, the glow of her cheek, — like a cleft pomegranate, — and the redder lip, even to the tendril masses of dusky hair, were shades of the same richness. She was a woman made for the bliss of some warm, clinging heart, with a soul as joyous as her face was sweet and her mind acute. Yet she was the daughter of the poorest man in the county, and the most miserable.

Emeline Butterfield was the daughter of a small farmer, as poor as a man could be owning eighty acres of Illinois land. His horses were the roughest the county ever mourned over, and his wagon the poorest that ever came to New Canton loaded with wood. Wood was the only thing he came to market with; for it was a crop that grew without human interference. He was not to blame for the wood that grew on his place. If he had been responsible, his luck would have killed it. If he had to plant it, the seed would have been too late to sprout; and if, by some mistake, he had planted it early, there would have been late frosts that year. Fortunately for such farmers, wood grows and takes care of itself: all they have to do is to wait till they get hungry or cold, and go out and cut down fuel, — something which everybody wants, — and sell it. Wood-lots are made for shiftless men among the poor, as sinecures are among the better classes, as they are called. But for wood-lots, Eliphalet Butterfield would have lost heart and hope.

Emeline made her first appearance in New Canton riding on a load of the meanest wood her father ever brought to town. It was the meanest, not because he was dishonest, but because it was the nearest, and he could get at it with least trouble. It was all swamp elm and fallen wood and limbs; but what of that? There was no meal in the house, and no molasses; and the family had to have both. Emeline, with notions of her own, rode behind the rough, burr-stuck horses, whose harness was tied up with ropes, on a wagon repaired so many times the maker never could have recognized his own work. The world was before her, the town more to her than Paris to the provincial French; and she meant to make her point there.

Out on the farm, in the poor cabin where she had been born, the girl had dreamed of better things. Born with that sharpness which belongs to all the daughters of poverty who have wits at all, she had read enough to know that there was something in the world better than the life she led. She rode through New Canton, saw the painted houses and the women with shoes and stockings on; and she vowed, that, some day, she would wear a dress that came down to her feet, and shoes and stockings. So she walked into New Canton one day, in a Shaker bonnet, with a gingham cape over her shoulders, and opened her way.

She was too bashful and too desperate, at her first attempt, to go to people's houses and ask for a place; for she fancied her manners were against her, and she did not want to be noticed till she could do herself justice. She walked into the hotel, offered her strong, willing, and quick arms there for service, and was engaged at higher wages than she dreamed of getting — three dollars and a half a week. She did not mean to stay there long; and, indeed, her position there soon became intolerable, for the notice her looks attracted. A good woman advised her to find a less conspicuous place, wisely judging that her beauty might some day bring her good fortune, with which a long engagement as chambermaid at a village tavern would interfere. Her next step was to the village dressmaker's shop, where, in three months, she learned all that was to be taught her; for she was, like every really clever woman ever born into the world, fond of and ready with the needle. At the tavern and the shop, she learned the ways of village folk, and earned a few becoming clothes; then, hearing that Mrs. Burt wanted somebody to take a sort of housekeeper's place, she applied for the position, and got it, making what seemed to Mrs. Burt the very reasonable stipulation that she should sit at the table and be one of the family, in consideration of doing all the work of the house and taking all the care off her invalid's shoulders.

This was Emeline's first real step upward. She felt instinctively, that, to be a hotel girl or a milliner's apprentice, would keep her among low-rate people, while, as Mrs. Burt's companion and independent housekeeper, she would hold a place among the best, even if every stroke of the work was done with her own hands. At least, she would be among pleasanter people; and refinement, however partial, drew her toward it like the sun.

Mrs. Burt thought herself favored among women the month Emeline Butterfield came to her house. She saw at a glance where the house needed cleaning, the walls whitening, and the beds and clothes wanted airing and looking over. She put the house through a course of purification beyond any thing ever dreamed of in Mrs. Burt's philosophy; and she came of a race of good housekeepers. But Emeline unconsciously illustrated the difference between conventional housewifery and housekeeping for the love of it. She rinsed windows and frames in as fair water as if they were china for the table. No trace of smear escaped her, no shade lay on the lily whiteness of the walls and sheets and linen she superintended. She mended and refreshed *con amore*, because she liked to see things look nice around her; and she felt as if her mistress's house was her own, only there was no such word in New Canton as mistress.

It seemed as if all the faculty Eliphalet Butterfield lacked had been restored to his child. She was a born manager. She cut down the expenses of the Burt household a third in the first four weeks, and, getting hold of a cook-book, surprised the family with an alteration in the bill of fare, which for two generations had been unaltered in the Burt family. They had, for breakfast, fried steak, with potatoes warmed over, and coffee; the dinner was boiled meat, or steak again, with the variety, in cold weather, of spare-rib, turkey, and buckwheat cakes; and the tablecloth was spread three times a day the year round for precisely the same viands. But Emeline's soul aspired to muffins and pop-overs and fritters and waffles for breakfast. Other housekeepers demanded the best of every thing given them, and then condescended to exert their skill in triumphs of the culinary art. But it was Emeline who could take second-rate flour, and yeast not first-rate, and watch and work and tend it into bread of incredible sweetness and lightness. The bakers do it every day. Why shouldn't she? And the flavor of her company cake and the delights of her pies — let me forbear to make my readers envious with them, seeing that plain cooking is a lost and dishonored art, and our women are all learning to make *remoulades* and *salmis* and game soups, and making them, for the most part, very vilely.

Still, though the girl was giving satisfaction and keeping house as if her whole soul was in it, she had another aim, which was the secret of her content. Her mistress knew, when the work was done afternoons, that her clever hired girl got a book from Mr. Burt's library, and sat down to read it with as much relish as she herself ever felt over a pet dress, or having a neighbor come to tea. She did not know that she had any thing against this queer streak of taste. Emeline did her work well, and gave good satisfaction to her and Mr. Burt. Mr. Burt was very particular about his shirts; but he had never been so well suited when she'd done them herself. It kept Emeline at home to her hand, if she wanted any thing; and it wasn't as if she wanted to go gadding as soon as her work was done. Dear! how much trouble she had had with girls who went down town every afternoon, when dinner was over, and left her to wait on the door, and, as like as not, make the fire for tea herself, before one of them showed again. She wondered that Emeline should have such an odd streak, being very gay and quick and noways wanting in other respects; but then everybody had not the balance, the respectable common sense and freedom from all eccentricity or uncommonness in their make-up that belonged to the Boody family. With these thoughts floating hazily in her mind, Mrs. Burt would sort her pieces for silk patchwork in silence, feeling very benevolent that she did not disturb Emeline by calling her to keep her company.

Mrs. Burt was not aware what intentions Emeline carried around with her kneading of bread and sweeping of carpets. What does any woman know or care to know of the hopes nursed between her kitchen floor and attic? Mrs. Burt's help meant to be as well-mannered and well-taught as any woman in Canton or outside of it, her ambition in this respect growing more extended as she came to compare village society with that she found in books. When she read, with a memory that held like a letter-clip, all the books she found about the house, — annuals, stray magazines, Mr. Burt's old school-books on composition and rhetoric and philosophy, — it was with a desperate meaning some day to be good enough and bright enough to be not unworthy the company in her favorite circles, where she had calling acquaintance with Lucy Snow, and Fleda, in "Queechy," and Marian Harland's people of gentle manners and hard lots. She shut herself up in the attic to hunt up places that she read about, in the old geography, and wrote out passages that she liked on bits of the white wrapping-paper that came round bottles from the druggists. Mrs. Burt unconsciously took good care that her stock of this should not be wanting.

The Chicago and county newspapers were searched and read, treasuring every hint she found there — a rule of etiquette from a society letter or a gleam of taste from the criticism in a chance editorial — thin teaching; but there are minds which you cannot tell one thing without making them wiser by half a dozen. If Emeline had a predilection, secretly confessed, it was for the elegant village society pictured by New England lady writers as peculiar to their part of the country, where the old ladies wear beautiful zephyr shawls and silver curls, and the pretty girls are always piquant, and everybody is interesting and devoted and high-minded, with principles and toilets and manners all off the same piece of perfection, except that their conversation runs to transcendental slang. Emeline fancied, that, if she could mingle with these people, she might catch their manners, and they would understand her. Poor little girl! she did not know how her *gaucherie* would have cooled their sympathies, so that she might as well have tried to live outside a world of glass as with them. They would not have flouted, they would have ignored her. To such people, it would have seemed rather bad taste in her, or in Nature, or both, for Eliphalet Butterfield's daughter to have such unnecessary beauty. If she had been merely interesting, they might have tolerated it; but for a Mrs. Burt's hired girl, in a vulgar, money-making town, to have beauty and brightness was absurd. New Canton was not far behind cultivated society in its inaccessibility. It might not be so much when you got into it; but it could show the world that it was as hard to get into as the best.

Emeline did not know that she was unknown or

ignored. Her days flew by on happy wings, keeping her house spotless and in order, hoarding her hours for study and spending evenings at home, where she was now able to go with something to make the old house glad. It might be only a new cover for the lounge, or spice and raisins for the pantry, — 'twas earned by her own hands, and brought with such free-heartedness and pride that the quenched faces there began to catch some of her own light and look forward with her hope. They might not always be " Eliphalet Butterfield's folks " — looked down on as the lowest of the neighborhood. With this strong, eager, brave girl to the fore, with her looks to open her way and her sense to follow it, — with the improvements everywhere taking place in their village world, what might be possible, even for them?

Her mother, seeing the girl's beauty improve month by month, was not without thought that Emeline might make her own good fortune and theirs by a shorter way than that to which she had set herself. But then came the certainty that her chance was closed by being Eliphalet Butterfield's daughter — of a poor and, what really signified more in that natural society, slack family. What man would venture to marry into such a degraded family, where the children were brought up to know less of the world than their low-down neighbors? Some one, not belonging to New Canton, might come and carry her away; and the unselfish mother found heart to wish that he might, for Emeline's sake, though it would be taking the very light out of her own life. But Emeline was worthy such a mother; for, had such a fortune been offered her, on condition of forsaking home, it would have had no temptation. The love of kindred and ambition for them drank up all other views; and, though she dreamed of love and having some one to cherish her, as other girls do, they were the haziest of dreams as distant as they were enchanting, and set down by her as impossible, unless she found a man who would marry her and help her family. She knew little enough of the world to believe that such a thing might be, only she did not think such men grew in New Canton.

Yet she might have found such had she known her power; for the girl was very fair, with such a plenishing as Nature sometimes delights in giving a poor girl, and for which she stints the dowries of a hundred better born. In after years, she was elegant in face and manner, as became her beauty; but slight and fret had left a sullen trace on her features and a sharpness in the eyes, born of tantalizing wants and desires long denied. Still, though given over to wearing cheap suits and the thinnest of ribbons, she was a presentable creature; and the instinct of a woman taught her the simplicity that best set off her luxuriant, glowing style. Already the girl was remarked in meeting, Sundays, for her dark dress unrelieved save by the collar of white, and a white silk tie at the throat, her modest, rough-straw hat, with black velvet folded closely about it, a sprig of ivy berries for sole trimming, so different from the bright, staring blues and garnets that prevailed in New Canton; but interest in her dropped on finding that it was Mrs. Burt's housekeeper and 'Liphalet Butterfield's girl, down on Soggy Run. Some of the men could not avoid imprudent expressions in her favor, and were rated by their womenfolk; but, as Emeline kept her eyes religiously to herself, the harm was not mutual. Already women's brows were beginning to cloud at the mention of her name coupled with enthusiastic comments. The main treason, in that town of sallow, angular, dispirited women, was to be an incarnation of health and joyousness, like this girl; and her intelligence and nice proprieties, even her reserved gait, were held as putting on airs, uncalled for in old Butterfield's daughter.

In that town of a practical turn of mind, her looks were hardly as much to her good as the fact that she was a born manager.

She showed this by the way she had put her hand to the old homestead. —

"There's no place like home"

always had a bitter sound to Emeline. The song sounded like a sarcasm and a jeer to her for years; for a place run down season after season, a dispirited mother, and brother too young to help things, and a father, who, without being idle or dissipated, contrived to make his family about as miserable as if he had been both, were all that home had to offer her. The unsightly farm was shut up in the heart of the woods; and they lived away from everybody, losing even the habits of the unsophisticated life about them.

The road past the mill, on the edge of the village, struck across the open to a spur of the wood southwest. There, a lane led amomg tempting shade and wild vines, nobody could see whither. Through the green, rose the smoke of a low house, not far from the main road; but wild trees and orchard were so thick about it as to hide the house in summer, and in winter their stems formed a screen for the homely building. The front yard was overgrown, the back and side of the road littered with all the rubbish that gathers on a badly kept farm; the fences were patched and propped, and the stables ruinous. Yet it had not lost all charm; for Nature had done her kindly best, hiding the old plows and harrows in grass knee-deep, and had set the fences thick with sprouting poplar and wild-cherry, and showed old Butterfield that she could and would counteract his unthrift and hate of every thing that was not laborious and unbecoming.

He could have spoiled life for anybody; and he had conscientiously tried to make it a burden to his family for twenty years.

He had been an ambitious and young farmer when he married one of the shyest and handsomest girls of one of the best families in the district. Ill luck came to him overquick and fast; and, when he was glad to leave New York and settle in Illinois, where land was cheap and manners primitive, he deliberately settled into hatred of the ways of his better neighbors, and centered his aims on getting a living by hard work, which he managed to make twice as hard as the curse left it. His temper was soured; and he managed to be as little respected as if he had been a thief instead of being an honest man. He went looking like a ruffian and a horse-thief, and shambled and skulked as if he was one, till he gave himself a bad name by the very economy meant to make things better. It had been Emeline's grief at home that they could never "have things like other people;" and she had put her hand to the old place at the earliest moment. Eliphalet Butterfield had always forbidden such nonsense as the planting of vines to hide the old house, they rotted the walls so. The first use Emeline made of her freedom, on coming of age, was to stipulate that she was to be let alone in such improvements as she chose to make about the place, on penalty of refusing to contribute her earnings to the family support. Eliphalet, who had a great respect for a dollar and a half at any time, had made a great show of refusing, but finally had given way.

The result showed that he had better have given it to her a good deal sooner.

A good-for-nothing husband and father could not prevent the sun from shining or the rain from falling or seeds from obeying the kindly impulses of Nature and germinating, nor could he rob the soil of its qualities; and, as Emeline had the sun, the rain, the seeds, and soil, and, as she had got sufficient control to have the use of these free gifts, — it was well for her that they were free, — he could not prevent her from having some vines clambering about the windows in front of the house, hiding, with their wealth of green, the hideous brown of decayed wood, and giving the room inside another and a better look. Nor could he prevent her from laying out beds, and filling them with rich mold, in which she planted the flowers she loved, and watched and tended them, finding delight, not only in the flowers, but in the humanizing work of caring for them.

And, to his great disgust, — for he wanted both the children in the potato-patch at the time, — aided and abetted by Tom, who was somewhat less afraid of his father, she cleaned out the brush that, for years, had dammed the little run, and made an unsightly swamp in the very front of the grounds about the house, and so directed the flow of the water that the little rivulet, released from the degrading bondage of the brush, became a very pretty stream, and was an ornament instead of a blotch upon the landscape.

And so one thing after another she did, till the Butterfield house, cheap and miserable as it was, became a very pretty place, and all, as Butterfield himself was constrained to admit, without costing a cent. And her ambition soared to higher things. She was not without hopes that the turn of things in New Canton might benefit her father's place in some way; and her shrewd brain spent many hours over the prospect.

CHAPTER XIV.

JAMES GARDINER MAKES AN EFFORT TO REFORM.

THE lawsuit between Price and the land company ended at four P. M. Had it continued late enough in the night, the counsel for the defendants might have gone to bed sober, providing that the grasping Pilkin had not kept his place open in anticipation of said counsel's coming. But, going to the jury at half-past three, and the jury not taking a minute to consider their verdict, it left him the weary hours from four onward, with the worst company in the world — himself.

The truly good man is entitled to a great deal more credit than he gets. If there is in him a weak spot, ever so small, evil finds it. Opportunity is always against the man who is striving to do better. Chances for good are rare; but who ever was good for want of opportunity to be bad? Rum-mills are open from Monday morning to Sunday night. Churches manage to keep open twelve hours in the week. Vice has a tremendous advantage over virtue. We climb to goodness; we slide to the bad.

He had been sober for twenty-four hours, and the enforced abstinence told on him. His mind, relieved from other matters, went straight to Mary Lewis, now Mary Paddleford ; and, to get away from her, he went to Pilkin's. There he took revenge for the self-denial of the day. He surprised his boon companions by the frequency of his potations, and delighted Pilkin by including every man who came in in his invitations to drink. Every loafer in town was there in half an hour; and James Gardiner, talking with all and paying for all, inaugurated the wildest debauch New Canton had ever seen. It kept up till late in the night, and ended no one knew how. The next morning, Gardiner found himself in bed, with his clothes on, torn and horribly soiled, and with a headache that was the tortures of a dozen combined. There floated through his mind an indistinct recollection of Sandy Beverstock, — of allusions to "'Liph' Butterfield's daughter,"—of broken chairs and glass-ware, and a general free fight, with a dozen men attempting to hold him, — of prostrate, bleeding men, upset tables, and cards strewed over the floor, yells of murder, and a general pandemonium.

He awoke feeling like several different persons, each more cranky than the other. Waking with the song of birds and the flush of morning, to feel as fresh and eager as the new day, is like being created anew. But, to wake with a head red hot and a throat husky with vile reminders, with youth and nerves gone, and in their stead the shaking hand and weary spirit of eld, is the nearest foretaste of Hell.

James turned from the light, as if he loathed being face to face with it again. "Eleven o'clock," he said, taking his watch from his vest. " What's the use of giving a man days to waste like this?"

He dressed, went down street to his office, and

locked himself in. He had not breakfasted; for he could not eat, but supplied the place of food with potations, which gave the brain and nerves a new cut, and spurred them to take up their work again. He hated the idea of meeting a single face; and he drew the blind down, and sat down by the table, laying his face on his arms.

He was sick to death of himself and the life he led. The low converse of the last night's company rang itself over in his ears, till he thought he was going mad. He wished he was dead. Everybody was dead. The world had nothing pleasant about it; people had nothing worth caring about in them; if he was sicker of one than another, he did not know which it was. A decent, orderly life had no charms for him. Was it not the decent, orderly, and respectable who had broken faith with him and ruined his life? He hated the good and all their ways. What were they but thin-blooded, selfish policy-jobbers? He hated equally the low, selfish hounds among whom he found himself. He hated old Keyser, who cheated at cards, and was too sly to be caught at it, and stole and cheated in business the same way; he hated young Starkey, who had taken a waiter-girl out of the Grand Central, and kept her in red ribbons across the river; he hated Carpenter, the broken-up lawyer, who had an affair with a married woman in Chicago, and could not help talking about it in his cups. He was tired of the talk men had together — lively and spicy they called it, though sometimes they lapsed into silence, worn out with their own ribaldry. And that cruel, miserable girl, and her still more cruel mother, had sent him to this; and they, with all the straight-walking, respectable matrons in town, were feeling a great deal too good to speak to him or have any thing to do with him. "Old prudes and harridans," Mr. James profanely called them, to himself, as if they did not do things every day, under their saintly cloaks, that he would put his hand in the fire rather than do — backbite and grieve and ruin innocent people in their way, with no more compunction than they killed flies. He despised and loathed them all.

He could not go on as he was doing. The disgust of the life would kill him. He meant to leave it off — not to join the company of the Lewises and Burts, the elect of the town, but because he hated the roughs and sinners as much as he did the Pharisees who prided themselves on their behaving. It would be a cold, weary life, with no heart in it; but he would have such company as he wanted, or he would have none at all. He promised himself the sorry satisfaction of showing New Canton folks that he could be as orderly and diligent as any penny-scraper in town; and, when they were looking up to him as a model of punctuality and a man who met every claim upon him, he would snub the puny souls, and show his immeasurable scorn of their petty ways and precepts.

Few have made such resolves with less heart in the work than James Gardiner. When he told himself he would enjoy the privilege of cutting Pilkin's set, he was not sure that the ill-favored movement toward better things would not yield to the dullness of the next evening alone, and he be driven to that unsavory company for want of better. He did not care any thing in particular about being good. If he had a choice, it was to be just as wicked and reckless in another way. Only it must be in some way that did not disgust his taste. He did not want to be good, but to be clean.

The first thing he did was to send for a woman to clean his office, with orders to have it dry and in order by three o'clock. The next, was to go home and take a hot bath, in which he scrubbed himself, as if moral defilement was a skin secretion, to be rid of by soap and polishing with a rough towel. Then he carefully endued himself in a fresh tweed suit, and flung his gay neckerchief into a drawer. (Starkey's Bill had praised it the other day.) He hesitated about submitting to a prim cravat and collar, and, as it was warm weather, compromised for a low collar, fastened by a gilt button. This done, and flattering himself that he did not look too much reformed, he went to his office, locked the door, and set the windows open, with the sweet air drawing through the half-opened shutters. In passing through his mother's garden, as he left the house, he had cut a great bunch of roses, hoping they would yield him some sort of pleasure; and the office wore a very tidy air.

Then he sat down to be good, and, the truth must be told, with poor encouragement. The office was too damp to be comfortable, and the bareness and loneliness weighed down James's spirit. Barren, cold, and dismal the future rolled before him, a procession of such interminable dull hours as this, the charnel chill of which struck to his soul. He would win honors, and know a great many people, not one of whom would interest him. All that he cared for had been lost by the falseness of one white-throated, slim-waisted girl, whose picture floated ever before him, its sensitive hair wound about her delicate head and curling in large rings about that sweet neck he had so often kissed. Is there any thing in this world that can so disgust and weary one as the remembrance of kisses given to one no longer loved? She had smiled at him with such beguiling sweetness in her glance; her fingers twined round his arm so clinging and impulsive; she knew how to call him such dear names; she met him with such pretty eagerness, and had rested in his arms so confidingly and happy when he gathered her to him!

The thought of those old sweet hours sent him mad again. He hated all bright, loving, lovely things, in his despair. The flowers mocked him. What was he, a cheated lover, doing with roses, as if he might be happy in their blush and perfume? He sprang up savagely, tore open the blind, and flung the roses into the street, as if he meant to throw away all hope and trust and desire with them.

A girl was coming down the plank walk, and James went back hot and affronted in his anger. What did he care who saw what he did? New Canton might call him crazy, if it chose, as it called him lost and dissipated. But his afternoon was no longer a passive dullness. He drew the blind again, and took a book, musing how many years he must sit down to that table in that methodical fashion, with as little relish as he felt. Carpenter tried the door-knob, and went away, without suspicion that the occupant could be within and not feel disposed for his company. Five minutes after, Starkey strolled along, and, finding the door locked, put his head in at the window, and interviewed his friend from that position.

"Less go down t' the place, Jim."

"What place?" without lifting his head from the book he was studying.

"Presbyterian Church, o' course. Where else?"— with a burst of laughter.

"Don't want to," said Jim, doggedly, digging into his book as if it had absorbing interest for him.

"Aren't you going down to Pilkin's?" asked Starkey, in open wonder. "It was too lively last night; but we'll have a nice genteel game to-night, and not let those rough fellows in. Take Pilk's little room. See?"

"Can't go," responded James, briefly.

"Oh, pshaw! Now that won't do. What are we going to do without you? You're not going back on us?"

"I'm not going, I tell you," said James, with decided emphasis. "A fellow hasn't got to go to that blasted hole unless he wants to, has he? Don't you see I'm busy?" And James turned his back and squared his shoulders in a way which cut off all chance for conversation.

Half an hour after, along came Carpenter again, curious to see what sort of a change was working in James's mood. Gardiner spied him coming down street, and, by way of friendly salutation, slammed down his window. Carpenter knocked twice, thrice,— waited,— tried a fourth time, and waited again. He knew the tenant of the office was within; and he wanted to see how long the siege would hold out. While he was standing on the step, a foot from the sidewalk, Peppernell strolled along.

"What y' standing there for?" was that worthy's

salutation, taking airs of being James's next friend. "Last place to look for Gardiner."

"He's inside," said Carpenter, in an undertone. "I saw him shut the window a minute ago."

But not for Peppernell or Carpenter or Hewitt or Pilkin himself was James to be badgered out of his den that afternoon. He locked the door, and went home to supper, deranging the family habits by this unlooked-for regularity. He took care to hinder anybody from raising expectations of him, being as surly and unsocial as ever, and, when the meal was over, disappeared to his office again.

For a week, the haunts that had known Gardiner knew him no more. This sudden defection was the subject of much curiosity in the circle of which he had been a favorite. His manner when he met any of the gang was still more open to criticism. If he saw any of them coming, he made no secret of turning short corners, and would cross the street anywhere to avoid them. His answers were of the briefest, and not the most civil. For a bow, he turned his head away from the person speaking to him; and a mumble or a growl did service as a response to greetings. When invited to join the old party, at Pilkin's, his answer invariably was, "Busy." Not one of them had ever been able to get into his office since the day of James's reform house-cleaning; and when they met, unavoidably, his freezing and unaffected indifference was more than those sensitive souls could stand. Questioned by the boldest as to the change and accused of wanting good feeling for his friends, he listened in solemn silence till the complaint wound up, with an astonished "be hanged!" which had the effect of leaving the questioner feeling small and sentimental. To the next appeal he vouchsafed the consoling reply: "Can't a fellow wait for company till he wants it? *I'm sick of gab!*" This course of conduct reduced that uncertain quantity known as his popularity, but it rid him of harpies. He was even set on a higher plane at Pilkin's, as a man whom it was no longer prudent to slap on the shoulders or ask personal questlons.

Peppernell — who, as a self-appointed minister of police, kept an eye on his fellow-citizens — was much exercised to know what James did with himself, as he was no longer to be found at Pilkin's or Dutch Sam's, over the river. Two or three nights' watching and cautious reconnoitering through the blinds put it beyond question that he spent them in study at his office. When papers were to be drawn, James was on hand; and the statutes were as much at home on his table as the " Three Guardsmen " or " Locksley Hall." He volunteered his counsel in a short case, soon after, and carried it through before Squire Sharp, with such choice of vituperation and utter disregard of probabilities as carried away both judge and jury, and brought in a verdict for his astonished client.

When the man, a mended and faded specimen, with bleached hair, came to pay his fee, James chucked it in his face again, and told him to take it home to his wife. " Don't let me hear of your spending any thing at Pilkin's, though," he said, sharply. " As sure as you do, I'll put the other side up to points, and have the case tried over; and I won't take it next time. Go home, and mend your fence; and save your politeness till you get there. Your wife hasn't heard a pleasant word out of your mouth three years come January, old of the moon. Get!"

This speech was repeated, and, strange to say, approved of generally.

But the barren midnights, the weary dawns, and wakings to a life out of which all pleasure had slipped were more like the record of some woeful girl's first blighting than the experiences of a young, strong man.

He could not work always; and there was nothing in the world to which he could turn that yielded relief. He could keep his mind on play for awhile; but cards and chess pall when played steadily six evenings in a week with the same partners, before one is forty. Novels had lost their sovereign charm; and the only solace he found, when tired studying the dryest chapters of law, was to take up his Shakespeare, and find in those living pages words vivid enough to draw his mind away from its own griefs or some echo that gave them voice. And, letting the book fall, he would brood till, with the long sigh that ended every day, he would rouse himself and go to bed.

His reform left him as entirely alone as if he were in the middle of the Great Sahara. He needed a friend who could fill the void left by Mary Lewis's desertion; but where could he find any companionship of the sort he craved? Not among the men of his acquaintance; for he loathed the low set with whom he had identified himself, and those who were sufficiently respectable were too stupid to be desirable company. He could not help thinking what a relief it would be to find some woman who wouldn't bore him, who was, at least, friendly to him, and had enough in her to save him from getting tired of her. But such a woman would be a white crow in New Canton.

In turning, he glanced out of the open window, and met a face and a look that filled him with a momentary sensation that he had actually found the comrade to take his mind from his loneliness. It was a woman's face that looked into his, speaking, against its will, in a slyly eloquent way — a gaze prolonged a moment, unconsciously, as though the giver of it waited recognition. There was neither admiration in the look nor actual invitation, but that blending of both best expressed as recognition. In law phrase, it was a case of Nature *vs.* Prudence, in which Nature always wins.

The girl passed on; but not so her face or the look, which remained with him.

James Gardiner thought for a moment, and, rising, went to the window, and gazed after the vanishing form of the girl.

It was the woman at whose feet, a week before, the roses he threw out of his window had fallen, and who had given him the glance of pity, which he still remembered.

"What a splendid step she has, with that figure! It's old Butterfield's girl, Burt's housekeeper, the one I pounded Bill Thompson for, the night Sandy and I got into that row at Pilkin's. That square look at me meant the girl wants to be grateful. Be as grateas you please, young woman." And he turned to his books, feeling less lonely than he did before the "Butterfield girl" passed his window.

"I wish I could get interested in somebody again,"

he mused that night, as the west wind waved his window-curtain gently, keeping idle time to his thoughts. "Men are rough. If there're nice, they think too much of themselves. I wish I could find some girl who would bear thinking about. I wouldn't care what sort of an attraction it was, if it would only give me something I didn't actually despise to feel friendly to. I wish to Heaven I could fall in love. That's past hoping for. O Mary!"

CHAPTER XV.

NEW CANTON IN THE DUMPS.

SIMON said "Thumbs down," in the land game, and New Canton was down.

People who had put money into the speculation, on the magnificent promises of Peppernell and Burt, were anxious to find their treasures growing, and, child-like, were pulling up their beans to see if they were beginning to sprout. Silsbee had bought six lots in the North Addition, as an investment; but old Orr died unexpectedly, and his heirs wanted to sell that corner which jutted into Silsbee's farm, and upon which he kept an Ahab's eye ever since he settled in the country. It kept coming into Silsbee's head what an uncommonly nice piece of business it would be to sell two of those lots at a large advance, and make the coveted piece of grass-land his own. Amos Pritchard's youngest daughter was going to be married, and her father would find it handy to sell a lot for her portion, and save taking in the comfortable, tidy mortgage where his odd money was lying. Levi Parmalee had put his wife's money into lots, instead of paying off the mortgage on his place, intending to sell at the first rise, and clear his house with the profits, leaving the investment clear. But the mortgage was coming due, and the lots were not selling. Fitzhugh, whose wife could not bear not to see him doing as other men did, had made a payment on a poor little lot, which he would be very glad to sell just now for enough to pay his grocery bill for a year.

Thompson, of Connecticut, was not named; and even Burt did not find it prudent to recall the memory of that eminent financier. Price had faded out of mind, save of a few who remembered him long enough to say, with the exceedingly shrewd expression which showed how much they would like to know the truth of what they guessed, that " Burt played that pretty well, didn't he? "

Hap Chapman gave it as his opinion, apropos of land company matters, that an empty barrel looked as full as a full one, provided you don't peek into the bung-hole, intimating that he had looked into the land company's barrel, and it didn't swash any when he rolled it.

There were no thousands of Irishmen on the ground, with picks and shovels; no railroad-building machinery appeared; and no Chinamen made the streets yellow. Mr. Burt held, that, in building the railroads, Chinese labor should be employed. " There is a prejudice against them," said he, " because they work cheap. That is what recommends them to me. I am laboring to develop the wealth of this region, and I want the cheapest labor. They are heathen, it is true; but what better is a Catholic Irishman? We may convert the Chinese to Christianity, and they may carry back the Gospel to their benighted countrymen. Cheap labor and cheap missionary enterprise! When godliness is gain, I believe in serving ourselves as well as others."

NEW CANTON IN THE DUMPS. 217

Mr. Burt went so far as to mention to his church a project of organizing a movement upon the Chinese, when they came, that as many as possible might be gathered into the fold.

But neither heathen Chinaman nor Catholic Irishman appeared, and the railroads were not.

Mr. Burt and Col. Peppernell tried all sorts of expedients to restore confidence; but in vain. They went to Chicago, and returned with the statement that work on the roads would begin within ten days; but the news was received with a cool incredulity that drove Peppernell mad and worried the cooler Burt. When Col. Peppernell opened a letter at the post-office, and, with an expression of relief, exclaimed, "There, the picks, shovels, and wheelbarrows have been bought, and it is going on now, sure!" there was a smile from all who heard it.

A series of articles from Burt, on the cheapness of Chinese labor, and detailing the experience of the Central Pacific, excited no attention, even though the "Forum" gave them the best place in the paper.

The more people would not listen to him, the more he dinned into their ears. He was a man of singular pertinacity, and the word fail had never been in his dictionary. The mails groaned with his circulars and maps, and the two newspapers of the town were filled with the most encouraging statements of its prospects.

Col. Peppernell showed the editor of the "Forum" the letter from Chicago mentioning the purchase of material for the new road; and the "Forum" announced the cheering intelligence under great headlines, and assured its hosts of readers (it had a circulation of nearly two hundred) that the time for doubt or uncertainty had gone by ; the clouds that had hung so long upon the mountain's brow had been swept away by the breath of enterprise. Of the completion of the Midland there could be no longer any earthly doubt; and the other roads must follow, as a matter of course. The " Forum " went on : —

" Within a year the Midland will be finished, and the C. & C., A. & P., and the G. C. C., will be well under way. The long-hoped-for improvement of Soggy Run will have become an accomplished fact, and what then ? With fleet locomotives, with breath of flame, and muscles of iron, speeding across our fertile plains — with scores of steamers, from the palatial side-wheeler to the diminutive but still useful dinkie, covering the bosom of Soggy Run, bearing the commerce of the world to our marts — what may we not hope for New Canton? We do not say it will become the first city of the continent, for we desire to always speak within bounds. We had rather understate than overestimate ; but it will certainly rival the proudest cities of the Union. We can see the shadow ; the solid substance is not far behind."

In its answers to correspondents, the " Sentinel " had these : —

" A. B. — A dinkie is a small stern-wheel boat, used largely on the Ohio. You will see many of them on Soggy Run, when the improvement is completed; for they will run up in shoals from the Ohio and its tributaries. The lots you mention are very cheap."

" PUBLICOLA. — Lots in New Canton are remarkably cheap, considering the prospects of the city. What is $40 per foot front, now that the completion of the Midland is assured, for lots on Pennsylvania Avenue ? "

"Marcus. — There is sand fit for glass-making in abundance two hundred miles south of New Canton. The completion of the Midland will bring that sand, and soda from the East, and limestone from Ohio, to our very doors, as well as coal from Pennsylvania. There is no better point for the manufacture of glass in the Union."

"X. Y. — New Canton will, of course, be a cotton manufacturing center. With the improvement of Soggy Run, we shall be very close to cotton; and the Midland will bring us fuel from Pennsylvania, at a very low rate. The same may be said of tobacco, and, for that matter, of every thing else. The iron of Tennessee and the coal of Pennsylvania will meet here. New Canton must be an immense manufacturing center."

The elder Gardiner was growing very uneasy over his prospects. The work Mr. Burt was doing required considerable money; and he was advancing it, though every dollar was a drop of blood. He sought James, as he always did in trouble, and cautiously asked his advice.

"I should get out of it as quickly as possible," was the son's ready answer. "Burt is a scheming speculator, and Peppernell is as mean a man — "

"Not mean, Jim; not exactly that. I have known Peppernell a great many years; and, while he is not altogether what a man ought to be, he is a very kind one, and there is a great deal of good under his roughness."

"There ought to be, for he never lets any of it out."

"I don't think you ought to say so, my son. Only this morning he came to the bank with a case of distress, in a way that did him credit. A poor widow in the second ward had not a mouthful to eat, and no clothing for her children; and her landlord, a grasping, avaricious, unfeeling man, threatened to turn her out before noon. Peppernell said it was a shame that a poor family should be turned out to perish in New Canton, and proposed that we make up the amount amongst us; and we did. Peppernell went out with the money to pay her rent, and said he was glad to feel that we had made one poor creature happy. A man can't be bad who has such a heart for the sufferings of others."

" What widow was it?"

" McGinnis, down by the railroad."

The irreverent James burst into a peal of laughter, which was long continued.

" What in the name of manners are you laughing at?" asked his astonished father.

"Father," replied Jim, between his guffaws, "this is the best I ever heard. How much did you make up?"

" About thirty dollars."

" Mrs. McGinnis is the Colonel's tenant. She lives in one of his shanties; and that thirty dollars will pay arrearages and rent for a quarter in advance; and the Colonel himself is the avaricious landlord. This is too good."

It was well enough for James to advise his father to get out; but getting out was not so easy a matter. He could not get out with the money he had advanced, nor could he get out of the obligations he had assumed. What was worse, he felt, that, to save what he had already invested, he might be compelled to invest more; and so, depending upon the genius and activity of Burt, he did all he could. He waited.

The air of universal distrust and disatisfaction weighed down even the iron-willed Burt. He could bear ill tongues while his works showed such results as he was looking for; but, skillfully as he might toil, no cheering sign appeared to lift his soul. He was disheartened, though he fought manfully not to show it; — who was there to show his depression to? — but he called up his endurance to stand by his venture to the last. He had staked all he had on the success of his plans, and would never give up as long as there was a chance of winning. If they failed, what was there worth living for, anyhow? He said to himself, that there must be a way out of all this trouble, if it would only come to him. Other men who speculated had these deep waters to go through; and he might as well die trying to pull through. There must be some way, he repeated; and he spent midnights and dawns and noons and evenings, Sundays and weekdays, planning, calculating, and studying the board anew, waiting, and keeping a calm face by force of habit, though in an agony of suspense that took savor from his food and drove sleep from his eyes.

He went home one night ready to give up. He had labored all day, as he labored every day, with all the energy he possessed, and with the usual result — nothing. He had not sold a foot of ground that day, or that fortnight; and he could rouse no one to sufficient interest to lend a hand in any of his schemes. His townsmen he had talked with not only refused to do any thing, but he had been suffered to overhear remarks which would scratch the skin of a more callous financier. What galled him most was, that Gardiner, Senior, in whom he trusted and hoped, as the prop of his undertakings, had come into the office two or three times that day with the air of a man who had something of a disagreeable nature to say, and went out as if he had not the heart to say it. Paddleford, Lewis, and men of their stamp, looked at him in the peculiar fashion with which safe men regard speculators of whom it is prudent to predict any thing damaging and immoral. The smaller men who had been induced to invest their earnings in lots, mustered courage to walk boldly into the office, and demand something definite about the enterprise on which they had staked their money, and were not to be overawed by high looks or bluffed by non-committal answers. As Burt had very little encouraging to say, and, as they did not believe a word he said, they went away refusing to be comforted.

Burt went home tired — that was nothing new; but he had the worse fatigue of discouragement. It was so evident that the tranquil man was distressed, that Mrs. Burt bustled round for a good strong dose of colocynth, and, failing to get him to accept that, was fain to urge upon him podophyllin, which would be sure to do him good, because it was fresh, and how lucky she thought of it. Emeline, who divined at the first look that he was troubled, kept the silence she knew most grateful to him; but could not forbear a glance or two, as she went about laying the supper, to which she gave more than usual care. The spotless cloth, fresh from its ironed folds, some nice pieces of china, a delicate loaf of cake and a tempting glass dish of purple grape jelly against one of amber honey, coffee which announced its *aroma*, and some fragrant browned birds appearing at last, made a meal in which a troubled man might find comfort without knowing it. The brightness, the sparkle, the savor of the table, the clear light, shed consolation over Burt; and he showed it by dropping into talk as he ate.

"Things wrong at the office?" his wife began.

"Wrong!" Burt replied, savagely. "They could not be worse. Stagnation is no word for it. It's death."

"Aren't you selling lots?" asked Emeline, quietly.

"Not a lot to-day, and only two in a week. It is terrible. I don't like to give up this thing, but, if it doesn't improve, I shall."

"Everybody would be glad enough to buy if they only had the money to pay," said Emeline.

"Precisely. They haven't any money. There isn't any money here in this dull hole, except in the hands of a dozen men; and they take precious good care that it shan't do anybody else any good. People outside won't take hold till they see that our own citizens have some sort of faith in the matter; and so it drags. I wish I had never gone into the thing."

"Why don't you make money?" said Emeline, innocently.

"Perhaps you can tell me how to make something out of nothing."

"I thought banks made money. They always have enough, and are always taking it in, and never seem to pay much out."

"Emeline, what nonsense you are talking," said Mrs. Burt. "Give me another biscuit. What do you know about banks and money and such things? All that *I* know about money is, that it is very hard to get, and very nice to have when you want it."

"But if we had a bank?" asked Mr. Burt, not heeding his wife's interruption.

"If I were a man, I would have a bank, and make money plenty for the poor people, keeping the biggest share for myself," said Emeline, mischieviously.

"Emeline," said Burt, lightly, "the land company could afford to pay you a salary to tell all you know and all you don't know," — a doubtful compliment to which she made a pretty mouth, glad she could divert the moody man even by making him laugh at her.

"There was the fisherman," she said, "who found a magic mill, that ground out whatever he wanted it to — food and clothes and things. It always seemed to me a bank was like that mill. It made money for a man just as he wanted it to. Mr. Burt, how do banks make money? Is it just by printing the bills? What's to hinder their having as much as they choose to?"

"Emeline, were you just three years old yesterday?" asked Mr. Burt, with an indulgent tone, which took the edge off his words. "This is what happens when young women talk finance. We old folks have to sit back and learn wisdom."

Mrs. Burt thought it was time for her to interfere.

"Emeline," she said, emphatically, "when you or I can teach Mr. Burt any thing, it will be when we have both lost all the good looks we're so proud of," which was the most biting satire that could be uttered without entire breach of the peace. Mr. Burt ate very slowly; and, when Mrs. Burt made a remark, he paid no more attention to it than if that worthy lady had been discussing a new pill. Hastily drawing his meal to a conclusion, he went to his room, and locked himself in.

"That slip of a girl has struck the very idea that has been in my mind for months," he said to himself. "If Peppernell was a better man — a man with more character — why can't I get hold of the right men?"

He sat down at his table, and covered sheets of paper with figures, which occupation kept him till late in the night.

CHAPTER XVI.

A CHANCE MEETING.

ALL the long spring days, Emeline loved the walk along the wood-road afternoons, home, when Mrs. Burt was away, and the Burt household slept in peace, — when the side door was locked, and the key hung up in the porch, where Mr. Burt could find it, if he came home early. After the mill was reached, and the long road that lay in sunshine, she was her own mistress, and fancy free. Her face, with the moist, dark masses of feathery curls, that hung about her cheeks in the old, lovely fashion that might have belonged in an old French court; and her figure, of middle height, as supple as it was round and firm, charmed even the eyes of the old women, who took their cob pipes out of their mouths to look after her with "There goes the likeliest gal I've seen these twenty year. Women ain't put up that way nowadays."

One day she went homeward, firm-stepping over the short turf, her hands full of flowering-currant and bits of sweetbrier and woodvine, that grew wild by the ruins of a burnt farmhouse. In her sun-hat of coarse white straw, woven by her own fingers, with a full pink rose, just plucked, behind her ear, she was a maiden image of the May. It was a piece of neighborly civility in those parts for any one to offer a ride to a woman on foot; and Mr. James Gardiner, driving past, out of careless good nature, drew up beside her. As she took a seat, he caught the first glimpse of her face, which the hat had hidden from his eye, and it fixed his gaze, for an instant, involuntarily. He had offered a seat in his wagon to a young person in a calico gown and Quaker hat, who, on closer sight, upturned to him a face like a velvet-petaled rose.

"A woman, and a handsome one," was James's first thought. "I'll take good care to let her alone." And this young fellow, once the most gallant of his sex, lapsed into utter silence, keeping strictly to his own affair of driving, and really wrapped in his own thoughts. The girl at his side did not resent this in the least, but sat decorously away from him as far as the limits of the carriage would allow, looking straight ahead, studying, in fact, how to make the trimmings for her mother's dress. And so the finest young man and woman in the county rode side by side through that spring-lighted region, while happy winds about them played; and neither thought or talked of love. Unnatural conjunction, for which Mrs. Tom Paddleford, deeply exercised that afternoon about the way her husband's shirts were turned out of the week's wash, was responsible.

Nothing could have proved so much to James's taste as a woman who could sit beside him without making talk. This pretty young lady did not seem to be thinking of him or herself at all, as he stole a cold glance her way; and he had relaxed so far as to think of speaking to her, when they came to a little green lane leading to a house hidden in the boughs of orchard trees. "This is my way," she said. "I'll thank you to stop here." And, before he could get down to help her out, she alighted, and vanished, with thanks brief and sincere. His eyes went, with a touch of curiosity, after the neat, composed figure, as she went over the grass in smooth, rolling fashion. A man of the world would have been impressed with Emeline at a glance; but your country youth, engrossed with his own merits, is somewhat obtuse to the charms of Nature or woman, unless duly presented and certified to. If James had heard Miss Butterfield spoken of as a pretty girl, with elegant manners, and been told that she came of a very good family, he, with all the rest of New Canton young men, would have stood outside the church, Sundays, to see her, and have shown no little ingenuity in devices for making her acquaintance. As it was, in a calico dress, with no pretention, walking over muddy roads, he found her pretty, but not worth a second thought from the lover of Mary Lewis. A sick heart dreads nothing so much as being tempted to repeat the experiment of loving, which has already cost it so dear. There is an insult to its virgin fidelity in the idea of receiving a new image to the place of the lost, which it mourns so piteously. It is a poor, thin-blooded passion which seeks distraction from its mourning, and can lift its eyes from a dead love to the face of a new one, without protest.

James drove home in the warm, long sunset, to find his father in a state of mind, for want of some papers the delinquent Burt had failed to send over before closing his office. The dutiful son turned his horse, and drove to Burt's, fully minded to collar and convey him down-town again, and stand over him till he unlocked and delivered papers which ought to have been in hand by noon. In the dusk of the house he could not see who opened the door.

"Mr. Burt is not at home," said a voice singularly free from those nasal whines, which the women of New Canton considered ornaments of speech. "He left word, if anybody called, I was to let him know. Will you wait?"

James followed the unknown into the sitting-room, deliciously cool and fresh with sweetbrier and flowering-currant. On the table was a white basket of mended socks, a newspaper scrap and bit of brier thrust among them, woman fashion. The room was trim, the lamp waiting to be lighted, and an open book lay on the window-seat. A child loitering by the fence was despatched for Mr. Burt; and the young woman seated herself, not without a glance at the book; for the visitor had cut short her precious hour for reading.

"I think I'll go out and take a look at Burt's place," was James's remark, as he turned his back unceremoniously, and went out to the cabbage-beds and tulip-borders. Emeline made a little face behind his back. "You can't be civil to me now," she said to herself; "but sometime I may be worth even your talking to."

The young fellow out in the garden was no phenomenon because he did not feel called on to be pleasant to Em Butterfield. He saw, and said to himself, that she was handsome; but he did not care for that style, or any style, for that matter. He was not after women. The only charms in the world for him were delicate, rose-tinted features, with pale hair in large, coiling fashion; and a figure light and gentle, with a clinging grace, that looked as if it wanted to lean on something. But the only woman of that sort for him had gone. He hated the sight of any thing like her, because he loved her so; and he despised all other women for not being like her.

But cabbages and tomatoes would not last long; and he came back with his ugly, contemptuous look on his face. Emeline was reading at the window, and did not disturb herself.

"You must have an interesting book to keep you in such an evening," he said, not over politely, the red light drifting after him through the open door.

"It is," she said, shyly, lifting the volume so that he could read the title.

"'An Arctic Boat Journey.' Good summer reading. Keeps ideas cool. I thought young women preferred novels."

"So I do, unless I can get the real thing, like this."

"The real thing? I don't catch your meaning."

"The interest we want in every thing and find in adventures — our own and other people's."

"Such as what? I'd like to know what you find in your book to make life interesting."

"Isn't it pleasant, here in the sunshine and the flowers, to read about the dead, cold night at the North, 'the hills covered with snows and the valleys filled with drift"' (quoting from the page), "'peaks of snow inland, peaks of ice out at sea, and the stillness?'" She spoke under the spell of the description, and her voice fell, as if she felt the awe of the inviolable silence.

"Stillness except when you could hear the ice go off, with a crack like a cannon," he said, falling into her mood.

She looked at him, delighted at being understood; and their eyes met in the glance of an interest too genuine for blush or droop of eyelid.

"People up there must feel as if they were in another world — in the moon."

"Aren't you fanciful?" James said, rather coldly, checking this flow of talk, perversely.

"No!" — with spirit. "Thinking isn't fancy any more than floating in a boat is rowing. And, if it was, is it wrong to fancy?"

"In a world where you can't be sure of fact, you'd better not risk any thing on fancy," he said, gravely and bitterly.

It sounded pitiful to Emeline that any one should look up in such a hopeful world, and utter such intolerable unbelief.

She remembered the man's trouble, heard from New Canton gossips; and she was silent with excess of pity. She was too unused to find any turn of words to express it indirectly; but, as Gardiner half turned to see why she did not answer, he caught the glance of gentle, compassionate eyes, as they turned, fearful to offend by sympathy.

"You must like Jean Ingelow's 'Off the Skelligs,' then, if you're so fond of Northern scenes," he said, going back to the book. "I can't think any thing happier than the life she draws — in a yacht over the green and yellow waters of melted icebergs, the light and air and the islands all strange, and flocks of white wild-fowl sitting in armies on the rocks to see the ship, as a curious spectacle. You never read it? My mother has it, and I dare say will send it over for Mrs. Burt and you to read," — as if that lady ever opened any thing further than the leaves of her Sunday newspaper, and as if he was not well aware of the fact. But, disguise it ungraciously as he would, when Burt came up the walk the moment of recognition and freshness for both was over. Gardiner carried away vague, piercing scents of sweetbrier, and the pleasant sweep of a woman's tresses from a low, pointed brow; eyes eager and untrained, with something tender and alive looking through them; a voice rapid and varied in its notes. What had she been saying? He would hear her voice once more, perhaps know its owner further. Here endeth the first lesson.

CHAPTER XVII.

MR. BURT DISPLAYS GENIUS AS A FINANCIER.

IT is no small matter for two or three men to take a bubble from a wash-hand basin, and blow it up to the size of a church. It was no small matter for the directors of the land company to get the people of New Canton to believe that they were rolling in wealth when they couldn't pay their bills. Fitzhugh, the cobbler, when congratulated by Burt upon the holding of lots which would make him a rich man, thought that perhaps, by and by, he might be rich; but he would like to get something comfortable out of it now. Rich as he was, he had not been able to exchange his short black pipe for a fragrant Havana; and he yet depended for his potations upon the invitations of reckless men in the saloons, who were far enough gone to ask " the whole house up." They might all be rich; but it was too far in the future to suit their notions. "A square meal on the table," quoth one of the grumblers, " is better than roast turkey after one has starved to death." — " What do I care for lots worth ten thousand dollars when all I need is a burying-lot?" was the remark of another. " I'd rather have a new pair of boots to-day."

Peak and Sharp wished many a time, that they had

not put their names to an enterprise that made them unpopular with their neighbors; but Burt and Peppernell kept them to their work. The four were in consultation at the office, when a new move came under consideration.

"It won't do," said Capt. Peak.

"I quite agree with Capt. Peak," said Esq. Sharp.

"Gentlemen, it will do!" was the reply of Col. Peppernell. "To develop the resources of this glorious country, especially this particular part of it, we must have capital. Without capital, gentlemen, of course we can do nothing. We want to sell lots. The boy waiting at a woodchuck hole was asked if he 'spected to catch that woodchuck. 'Catch it! catch it! Thunder! I've got to catch it! The preacher's coming to-morrow, and we're out of meat.' We've got to catch our woodchuck, for we're out of meat. What is the use of waitin' on our woodchuck till doomsday? He must be coaxed out of his hole, and we'll have him, first time. We must lay out streets, put up buildings; we must show there's life 'n' energy 'n' every thing in the way of progress in New Canton. To do this we must have money. We can't grade streets 'thout money; we can't plant trees — not so much as locust thinnings or swamp-sycamore — 'thout money. Have we the money? If you've got any, it's more than I have."

The two smiled in a ghastly way, as if the farcical idea needed no further answer, while Mr. Burt, pleased at the Colonel's oratory, rubbed his hands softly, and smiled deprecatingly, as though not to have money was an especial grace and something to be proud of.

"Very well," continued the Colonel, "if we have not the money, how are we to get it? From Gardiner? We have all he can spare; and, even with a savings-bank, we shall need all that we can get out of him hereafter. From whom, then? From them who're to git the benefit — New Canton people. They share in the profits, and ought to 'sist us, particularly as it won't cost them any thing. Gentlemen, you are asses to object."

"My worthy friend, Peppernell," broke in Mr. Burt, with his blandest smile and his most effective touch on the arm of Capt. Peak, "expresses clearly, though I admit with some warmth, my views on this important matter. This savings-bank is a scheme to which I have given much thought, and I am satisfied it is our only hope. The citizen does not buy, he does not display that eagerness to possess himself of New Canton real estate that I wished and hoped; and he must be impelled, not by dragging him, but by holding a turnip before his nose. Very good. We start a savings-bank in connection with the land company."

"Where is the capital to come from?"

"My dear sir, you are not usually obtuse; but you astonish me in this. The depositors furnish the capital. We shall want a safe and a set of books and a few thousand certificates; but I hope the credit of the New Canton Land Company is sufficient for that. Once in operation, and confidence established, — confidence is the main point, — the people pour in their money, and we pay interest on it. We shall not limit the benefits of this institution, to the rich. The humble possessor of a five-cent piece will be, proportionately, as welcome in front of our counter, as a depositor, as the princely possessor of a hundred dollars. We issue our certificates, promising to pay on demand; and — "

"But, when they send them in for payment," asked Capt. Peak, "what will you do if you have used up the money?"

"We shall only use a portion of it in that way. We shall keep a reserve on hand for those who desire to have their certificates cashed; and there will be no trouble on that head. But, my dear sir, procuring capital for our own uses is the smallest part of the profits of the plan. What New Canton needs, as my friend Peppernell would have remarked if he had given his mind to this branch of the subject, is money."

"If they furnish money to deposit, and we give them certificates they can call in any time, how do we increase capital?" growled Capt. Peak, impatiently.

"My dear sir, there is a vast amount of capital here — millions — locked up for want of something to move it. New Canton needs a tonic; its financial system needs stimulating. Our land has cost us ten dollars an acre. It really represents, as we believe, $1,000 an acre; and, if money were plenty enough, it would bring that immediately. It is our duty to enrich the city, by making it worth that; and it is worth that as soon as people will pay that for it. We issue our certificates, — we buy horses with them, — we pay more than any one else will pay in any other money, — we pay say $100 for a horse that we sell for $50, — we are getting rich."

MR. BURT DISPLAYS GENIUS.

"How! Haven't we lost $50?"

"Not if we take up that certificate by selling a lot for $100 that cost us exactly fifty cents. When enough of our certificates are in circulation, and every man has his pocket full of them, they will buy lots; trade will revive; men will speculate, for they will have something to speculate with. When we pay $100 for a $50 horse, we have conferred a benefit on New Canton; for we have doubled its capital. If the man is to be honored, who makes two spears of grass grow where one grew before, what applause shall we give him who makes two dollars exist where there wasn't any before? Our certificates will be convertible. We will permit the holders to convert them into lots as quickly as they please; and they will be especially pleased to do so, if they see any thing in the shape of bank-bills in the transaction."

Capt. Peak and Esq. Sharp saw the point, and yielded assent.

"Thank you, gentlemen; and, when a thing is to be done, it can't be done too quickly. The building we are in will do. No: appearances are every thing; we will put up a new one. It will be inexpensive; but it shall be so constructed as to inspire confidence. It shall be painted, and the ceilings inside frescoed. We will have, for the purpose of inspiring confidence in the minds of the populace, the board-room in front; and" — here he paused, and surveyed Col. Peppernell's flaming face — "no; on second thought, we will have the board-room in the rear and the cashier's office in front. I will sit there, and inspire confidence. I will send the papers off to-night, for the incorporation; and we'll get to work immediately."

This accomplished, the next point was organization. Mr. Burt desired very much that Mr. Gardiner should join them in the enterprise, and be president of the new bank ; but he had sounded that gentleman, who had declined to do any thing, on the score that it might possibly injure his own business. Mr. Burt did not press the matter; for he had reasons of his own for not desiring trouble to befall Mr. Gardiner's bank just then. So Burt, Peppernell, Peak, Sharp, and an outside man, Simmons, who was supposed to be responsible, made up the directory, with Peppernell as president and Burt as secretary and treasurer.

" It is a strong combination," said Mr. Burt ; " and results will come from it. Simmons is a man whose voice should have weight in any financial institution."

The papers were sent off the very next mail, and the buildings were planned and contracted for immediately.

The moment the papers of incorporation arrived, Mr. Burt ordered a book of certificates of deposit printed, and was particular about them. He had them printed in three colors, with the vignette of a dog guarding a safe, on the left end, and the legend, " Savings-bank of New Canton," prominently and handsomely displayed, with appropriate and proper places for the signatures of the president and secretary and treasurer of the company.

He was very particular about having the certificates done in three colors ; and he lamented that he could not have the vignette of the dog and safe printed in three colors also. " If that dog was printed in three colors, with the expression of absolute watchfulness there is in his face, no man could see it and refuse to take a certificate. If his judgment said No, the expression of the dog and the colors would dazzle him."

As the book was handed in, he remarked to his fellow directors : " There isn't a sounder looking certificate than that in the State of Illinois. Mr. Gibson," — to the printer, — " I congratulate you on your skill. You have hit the happy medium — richness without vulgarity, solvency without pretentiousness. Your bill ? Very good. The man who would refuse to accept one these certificates — in three colors — has no confidence in the future of the country."

While saying this, he was filling out one of the documents, which read : —

" This certifies, that R. C. Gibson, Esq., has deposited, in the Savings-bank of New Canton, thirteen dollars, on which interest, at the rate of ten per cent. per annum, will be paid, if allowed to remain for six months.

" JAS. SIMMONS, *Pres't*.
" CHARLES BURT, *Sec'y and Treas*."

This he handed to Gibson, asking him to receipt his bill.

" What's this ? " asked Gibson, somewhat astonished.

" You have deposited with us thirteen dollars — not absolute money, but paper, ink, labor, and skill, which represents money. Any time you desire to draw your deposit, present it at this counter, and it will be paid to you, in any other kind of money you desire. But you won't want to draw it. It is money — better than any other kind ; for, while it is as safe as any, it is earning interest, which other kinds do not. You will be able to use it in your business. Pay it to your grocer; he will pay it to his shoemaker; the shoemaker will pay it to his tanner; his tanner, if he is a dissolute man, — which, in the interest of morality and virtue, let us hope he is not, — will pay to the bar he poisons his body and ruins his mind at; the whisky-seller will pay it to his distiller; the distiller will pay it to the farmer, for the corn he uses in his nefarious pursuit; and the farmer will pay his yearly contribution to his church with it: and so it will go on one unceasing, never-ending round of doing good, with a train of blessings following it at every step. Possibly, it may come back to us for lots, and, if so, we shall unhesitatingly take it. We may be doing the community an injury by receiving it and retiring it, because by just that amount we are contracting the circulating medium on which it is doing business; but we are all selfish. Every man must take care of himself; and land companies are no exception to the general rule; for land companies are only aggregations of men for a specific purpose."

Stunned and dazzled by this flow of oratory, the meek Gibson took it, and went his way; and the directors were delighted, for they had each expected to be called upon to contribute his share to pay for the book.

Mr. Burt went to the office of the "Forum," and had a long interview with the incorruptible editor of that paper. He reminded him, that, so far, all the printing for the company had been done in his office, and that henceforth the most of it would be, — that such an enterprise would double the population of the town, in no time, and would bring no end of business to the place, all of which would make newspaper property worth its weight in gold; and how could a newspaper serve itself better than to build up its own patronage? And Mr. Burt left the incorruptible with contracts for half a dozen lots, on various streets.

"My dear sir," he remarked, at parting, "when the land company and the savings-bank are accepted as facts and regarded as they should be, those lots will be worth $1,000 each. You can help yourself to $10,000 by helping these two enterprises. Good-morning. I don't want to influence you, but I am working for the general good."

From the "New Canton Forum."

"We are happy to announce, that the savings-bank inaugurated a week since by Messrs. Burt, Peppernell, Sharp, Peak, and Simmons is now in successful operation, and is receiving deposits and issuing certificates. Such an institution has long been needed in the town; indeed, in our present condition of rapid development, it is an absolute necessity. The directors (the same gentlemen who compose the land company) have determined to manage it in the interest of the city, rather than their own, and, to that end, will pay the highest rate of interest possible; — namely, ten per cent.; — and, that its benefits may be as widely diffused as possible, the humble laborer, with his ten cents, will be as welcome as the richest owner of New Canton real estate. The names of the directors are the best guaranty of its management on the best business principles; and people do not need to be assured that the interests of depositors will not suffer for want of sagacity and fair dealing. The safe arrived yesterday. It is the largest ever brought to New Canton, and marks an era in the growth of our city. The open doors are beautifully ornamented with the vignette on the bank's certificates, — which were printed at the "Forum" office, — a dog guarding a safe. The deposits the first day were over two thousand dollars; and the office was kept open till after eight last night to accommodate those who could not come earlier. Mr. Burt says he will keep it open till midnight rather than any should be disappointed. Such men are a credit to any city; they make cities."

When the bill for lumber, stone, plastering, shingling, painting, and finishing the building came in, they were all paid the same way; and people accepted them in payment unhesitatingly. So, in getting the bank started, an amount of its paper got into circulation, enough to get people used to the sight of it and accustomed to handling it.

Once in possession of the means of paying for labor and material, Mr. Burt was not idle. Streets through the various plats were graded at once, trees planted by the thousand, and excavations were commenced immediately, for a score or more of buildings, in various parts of the city.

The uses for money increased; but Mr. Burt was equal to the emergency. He issued certificates sparingly; that is, he exacted full money value for every one of them; but they went out. "When writing one's name will do for money," was his remark, "why shouldn't New Canton have all the capital it needs? It is arduous labor; but, in view of the necessities of the town, I will do it if I die at my post."

The next thing was to get others to build. There were people living in rented houses, who wanted, as all men do, to own their own property; and Mr. Burt made the way easy for them. He would sell them a lot at $150, they paying down say fifty dollars, and giving a mortgage for the balance. Then, he would advance them money;—that is, his money, which, as it was current in New Canton, was as good as any other; — enough for them to put up a dwelling, generally enough to finish rooms to live in, taking a mortgage for the whole at ten per cent., with clauses in the mortgages which enabled the land company and the savings-bank to keep a saving hold on the property and do with it as they pleased.

The effect was miraculous. The poor of the town made haste to obtain homes on such easy and certain terms. Mr. Burt prepared elaborate tables, showing that the saving of ten cents a day would do so much, and a saving of twenty cents a day would do so much, and that, with the help of the credit of the land company and the savings-bank, there was no trouble about building homes at all. He demonstrated, that the workingman could get him a home by cutting off his pipe, by cutting off his glass of beer, by cutting off a meal a day; and by doing any one of a thousand things which men never did nor never will do to the end of time. Beyond all, it was demonstrated that the land company and savings-bank had just one mission, and that was to save the laboring man from the cancer — rent. But he omitted to mention, that, while avoiding the Scylla of rent, they went bumping on the equally fatal Charybdis of interest,—an omission which public benefactors often make.

Not only the people of New Canton were firm converts to the theory, that something could be made out of nothing, but they came in from neighboring towns and from other counties to try the experiment. Long rows of cottages were built or begun; mechanics came to town, and settled; operators started business; and the wonderful growth of New Canton filled the air from Chicago to the Mississippi.

Farmers got an advanced price for their products, taking pay in certificates, which they held "as good as any money;" Burt and Peppernell starting a warehouse for the purchase of the same, and did an immense business. Merchants took the certificates for goods, exacting an additional profit, which was willingly paid; for prosperity breeds carelessness.

The corporators were troubled, and were frequently in counsel. That is, Peppernell, Peak, and Sharp were troubled; Burt, never.

"How long can we stand it?" was Peppernell's first question at these conferences.

"Stand it till they get to buying lots freely, and money, actual money, comes in from abroad. The pot don't boil enough yet; for there isn't enough of our certificates in circulation."

"How much money have we in the safe?"

"About fourteen dollars."

"How much of our paper is out?"

"Only forty-three thousand dollars. But never fear. I can always get five or ten thousand from Gardiner, for the use of the land company; for he likes this new activity, and is pushing it on. We shall have a good day Monday for deposits; and we shall get returns Tuesday from the last shipment of wheat to Chicago. You must turn off what horses and cattle you have on hand, at whatever you can get for them, and see that you are not paid in our money. Peppernell, the last sale you made you were compelled to take some of the very certificates you gave for the stock. That won't do."

The pot was boiling, nevertheless, but not as fast as the industrious Burt desired. He was busy pouring oil under it; for no pot could boil too fast for him.

New Canton was at last growing, and citizens and strangers could see evidences of it. Did a man doubt, he was shown the long rows of cottages. The stranger was shown first, the maps; he was taken to Soggy Run, and shown where the levees were to be; and then he was triumphantly shown the buildings actually finished and the score that were in process of erection. Who could doubt all these evidences? And, when, after an examination of the real, he was brought back to the ideal, and was left in company with the maps and pamphlets, if he did not invest, he was set down as worse than an infidel.

Mr. Burt got another idea, which he improved at once. Within a week, the papers published in the money-lending portions of the East contained advertisements of " Chas. Burt, agent for negotiating loans on Illinois real estate ;" and he gave as his reference the " Savings-bank of New Canton." Who could refuse to entrust money in his hands, with so respectable a reference? Mr. Burt did a very nice business in placing loans for Eastern investors.

CHAPTER XVIII.

THE NEW OF THE MOON.

IT is regretted that the course of events compels me to introduce Mr. Burt under the prosaic conditions of a bilious attack. He came home from Chicago frequently with one of these disorders, which Mrs. Burt attributed to the deleterious character of hotel cooking and the want of plain home fare. Burt's sypathizing friends gathered round him to alleviate the tedium of these attacks. Peppernell came over to heave Johnsonian English, with occasional slips into slang. Old Gardiner sent over the religious weeklies for him, which Mrs. Burt read aloud, yawning over the editorials and shying at hard names, till it was found that Emeline could get through the papers without getting a headache or allowing the housekeeping to suffer, in her magical administration.

It was the third day of the attack. Mrs. Burt did not deem it prudent to let her husband out of her sight just yet; and he was submitting to a day of house-petting with a meekness which was an example to all spouses similarly situated.

The odor of boneset tea was banished from the room; and, unknown to Mrs. Burt, the window was down at the top all of three inches, letting the sweet spring air wander gently around the room, instead of the close smell which she considered the proper thing for a sick-room. A nice hand betrayed itself in the raising of a curtain to let in a half-light, — in the array of a table covered with work and newspapers, presided over by a vase of roses, dark red and rich, which lent their odor and grace to the room. Burt lay on the lounge, the only sign of illness about him a slight pallor from staying indoors three days, and a plaster of vinegar and brown paper on his forehead, which Mrs. Burt made haste to apply for symptoms of nervous headache on her offering to read from the county paper. Emeline, finding this a frequent prescription in the household, had won largely on Mrs. Burt's esteem and Burt's gratitude by inventing an aromatic vinegar for medical use, fragant with herbs and oils, which lessened the infliction. Emeline had taken up her task of reading for the day; while Mrs. Burt, in her white invalid shawl, crocheted pink and white wools. A pretty domestic scene it made, as Peppernell remarked, on his way down-town.

"If I haven't a good mind to take off my frills, and give out for sick, and be petted myself. Would, if I could get such coddling. My folks never would indulge *me* that way. They'd send for Borax first thing, and he'd pour a dose of quinine down, and have mustard plaster where it would tell the most, and lay me up for a fortnight, with the Masons coming to watch — ugh! And it would take all I could earn for another six months to pay the bill. But you, with your devoted wife to attend you, instead of hireling medical aid, and the resources of our charming — hem!" (as a glance from Burt's warning eye put the Colonel off the track an instant) — " charming season to make your illness tolerable, it has its compensations. Bless me!" said the Colonel, relapsing into calm sincerity, " if I wouldn't stand being pilled and blistered for the sake of gettin' such tendin'."

" Gardiner was going to send over some papers, wasn't he?" asked Mrs. Burt, in a half-hour or so. " James said last night he would bring them over for you, and his mother's ' Review ' for me. How much that boy has improved. He's growing such a thoughtful young man, so kind to his friends; just like you used to be, Charles, before we were married."

The amiable Burt did not look flattered by the reminiscence. " Likely as not he'll forget all about it. Nice enough young man, but feather-headed."

Speak of the sun and it shines. A ringing foot came down the plank-walk to the gate.

" Coming again," thought the young housekeeper, as she heard it. " He was here Monday, and yesterday evening, and now to-day again. I shall see his face, and have a bright word. How nice to have anybody like to come so often."

Burt took a little side observation of Emeline, as the tall figure came up the walk but her eyes were on her sewing, and neither smile nor blush rose on her face as Mrs. Burt motioned her to the door when the bell rang. Astute Burt, how came you to feel so satisfied that the girl had heard those footsteps half a square away, and that her firm lips and steady eyes concealed content that needed neither smile nor sign? She put down her sewing, and moved away with her usual promptness; but the entry found time enough for her face to bloom into warm, frank pleasure before she opened the door, and met a glance as kind and unconstrained.

"Are we able to see visitors this morning?" he asked, with mock gravity and concern.

"Only on errands of necessity and mercy," was the answer sent, with a face as grave as his own, and eyes of solemn mischief.

"Then I may rush in where my betters fear to tread. Is there boneset to-day?"

"Another step and you will know all about it, without asking. It is double strength to-day."

"Unkind!" he said, under his breath, following her to the sitting-room, "when you knew I was coming. Couldn't you get it out of the way, for once? People say you have things pretty much after your own notion in this house."

He expected she would take this as a tribute, but she looked no pleasure at it. They were at the door of the sitting-room; and there was but time for her to "justify" her face, as printers would say, and put on the unmoved look with which she met all events.

"She might have been a second or two sooner," Burt thought, on his lounge, and turned his head to see the two enter — twin youth, strength and beauty.

He was tall and fresh as a young ash; the girl who came after him, full of warm bloom as a maple flowering in April, and lissome as the young cat stretching velvet paws by the lily-beds in the sunshine. He wore the air of negligent style that became him; his rough morning-coat setting loosely on his fine figure, with fine white cuffs, and heavy gold buttons at the wrists of his shapely and well-kept hands.

She was purely neat and homely in her brown print

dress, sweet with the lithe form it held, the white collar and scarlet bow against the creamy throat, and dark waving hair, put back with most evident intention to get it out of the way, but all the more becoming for that.

Burt was getting better fast? Yes. Would look at the papers when he could get the letters off his hands, which he must have written first. Thanks! He would not be obliged to trespass on Mr. Gardiner's kind offer to write for him. Mrs. Burt would do all that was necessary.

"Anxious to get me out of the house," thought James, nettled by finding his overtures treated so coolly. But a glance from eyes of infinite mischief, out of Burt's range, confirmed his inclination to stay without encouragement; and he proceeded to make himself agreeable.

Never did invited visitor prove more agreeable to his host than James Gardiner then. He inquired with enthusiasm for the latest news, and, finding Mrs. Burt meagerly furnished, he proceeded to manufacture, guess, and rehearse the most extraordinary gossip ever unrolled in one short hour. Mr. and Mrs. Fitzhugh were not as loving as they might be, everybody was aware; owing to lofty views on the part of the lady, and a chronic inability to make a living on that of her husband. This was not such an uncommon grievance among New Canton matrons as to arouse much interest when alluded to. But, when James made out that Mrs. Fitzhugh was meditating a divorce, and had written to her sister-in-law asking advice; and it was certain that a separation, at least, would have been a fixed fact long ago, if it had not been for the children; and that Mrs. Fitzhugh had her views on Peppernell, if she was free when his wife died,— here was matter to secure the narrator joyful entrance to any hearth in New Canton.

James, finding these figments well received by both his auditors in chief,— Burt forgetting even the satirical version of Watts, in his amusement at such lively scandal,— let his imagination loose. He knew every thing. He hinted at clandestine correspondence between the leading soprano in church and a young Chicago business man. He knew that Miss Ashton and the Deacon were going to be married, and that Miss Ashton was going to wear white silk, with a demi-train, and lace-veil, and that she had written to Florida for real orange blossoms. Oscar Hewitt, who had run away from his father two years before, was doing well in Omaha, and was going to set up for himself, and come back and marry Katy Rice. He told of Mrs. Sam Livingston's going off in the middle of a snowy night last winter, to her father's, when Sam came home late, and could give no good account of himself, which, as it was an unlooked-for piece of scandal, made him as welcome as any piece of humanity on which Mrs. Burt had set her eyes for six weeks. His news was conveyed in a masterly style, without effort or hurry, not gabbled or poured forth, like those injudicious gossips who shell out all they have to tell and are thrown away as husks immediately. Mrs. Burt was soothed and edified by the recital. As a finishing stroke, his invention giving out, James next besought Mrs. Burt to draw near while he pointed out the devices which struck his taste favorably in a fashion paper, and was soon delivering an animated lecture on dress.

"Why can't women always wear something pretty, like this?" said the courtier, taking up a corner of the lady's white Shetland shawl between finger and thumb. "They haven't the taste to choose it," he added, with ardor.

The effect on Mrs. Burt was judicious; and as a mark of favor, she soon after invited James out to take a walk in the garden to see Mr. Burt's flourishing cauliflowers and give the family name of a new striped bug that had appeared on the cucumbers. Their way took them through the kitchen, sunny, and sweet, where Emeline was getting up dinner. The morning saw the audacious James familiar with the Burt lettuce, border, flower-beds, and grape-vines, playing the attentive gallant to Mrs. Burt, drawing her shawl about her shoulders, holding the tomato-vines back from her dress, and going so far as to gather a spray of morning-glories, and offer them for her bosom, a *devoir* to which she responded by plucking for his buttonhole next to the prettiest rosebud on her bushes. She might want the very best one herself, or somebody of more consequence. Mrs. Burt was thrifty even in rosebuds.

It was compensation for a walk through a kitchen-garden with a woman who wore curls and prosed, to catch the sight of a drooping dark head, rich with scarlet in lips and cheeks, against a window-screen of blue and white morning-glory. James felt, for once, that he should like to put that lovely play of color on canvas, and found chance to loiter near the window, while Mrs. Burt was hunting a plant to send his mother.

"Were you looking for any thing last night, when

you took your walks abroad, or only waiting for it to come to you?"

She looked puzzled at this style of questioning.

"You were going down the Creek Road, dawdling along, half by moonlight, half by the light on the water, as leisurely as if you had got done with this life and was waiting for the next."

"I was done with this world for one night," she said, with an undertone of mockery, catching his tone. "The last stitch was taken, and there wasn't a straw out of place about the house. I could have gone to Heaven, and nobody would have missed me."

"You should choose company on your walks. Or do you find yourself such excellent company it spoils you for any other?"

"I'm not particular. We like change, you know, if it isn't for the better. Thank you for the hint. I'll borrow Mrs. Strong's Archie the next time I go after Moses to whitewash. That was what I was dawdling after down the river-road."

"Do you often go for Black Moses of an evening?"

"I go for him of an evening when I do go, because we're all of more of a color then, you see, and the difference don't hurt his feelings. But, as a rule, we only whitewash spring and fall."

"Ah! Then I needn't expect to find you going that way again for five months? May I ask where you take your walks the rest of the time?"

"Where I'm least likely to meet anybody," she said, demurely, rising to put the fruit to stew she had been picking.

The next moment Mrs. Burt's skirt swept the late dew off the border where the young man stood.

"Thanks! Mrs. Gardiner will be delighted to have the lemon balm. Mrs. Burt, how can you have the heart to keep a fellow away from his office so long? What if I should have lost my only client while I was here? Let me bring you the 'Bazaar' next week, and I will ask my mother for the pattern you spoke of. Delighted to be of use, madam. Take care of Mr. Burt, and don't let him get to business too soon. No, I don't think anybody can quite do what he is doing, but we will try to worry along without him. If there is any thing I can do for him, — looking over papers or looking into matters, — I should be too glad. Good-morning. Good-morning, Miss Butterfield," lifting his hat to Emeline with a profound deference, half put on, to astonish Mrs. Burt.

The lissome girl smiled at him, as much at her ease as if she had been a duchess — a smile that followed him in his thoughts.

"That girl is handsome as a witch," he mused, as he went down the street to his office. "Pity she hasn't a better show for herself. A man might make much of such a woman;" and he wondered to himself again over the clear red and white of her face, and the finish of her hands, spite of the work she did. Man-like, he wondered how it would seem some time to hold those hands and feel the softness of her hair. "Confound it!" he said to himself, "there's no comfort seeing her with those old folks about, ready to take things up if a fellow says a word to her. It would be nice to have her where a fellow could look at her, and draw her out. There's spice in her, and sweetness too. I'm after the spice. That's all I want of any woman now. Wonder if his wife will report that parting speech of mine to Burt correctly. I'd give her a box of rouge, if she would. She needs it. What fun it would be to get up a flirtation with the old girl, just to make Burt mad." It was with such inventions the young dog pleased his fancy in moments of grim humor.

Life could still hold interest for him, and the knowledge bore the double sweetness to him that sensation does to one who deemed himself paralyzed for life. He did not mean to love; but this clean, blissful creature brought the same pleasure as a flower or shell or vine, — any thing natural and complete, as God made it. Old men turned in the street, and looked after her, as if she brought their youth to them; and old women, in her bright smile, saw their own vanished charms live again. James Gardiner was beginning to find in her presence the charm and support of affection — that life of the heart, that love without love.

He owned as much to himself, without reserve. She was the prettiest woman in the county, let them say what they would; and any man might feel honored by being with her. His father's son could go with a poorer girl than Emeline, if he chose to amuse himself so; and he swore to himself that nobody should look a cross look, while it suited his lordly pleasure to admire the girl. So he abandoned himself to the pleasure of following sweet Emeline.

He changed his route of going home, to go by the Burt house, two squares out of his way, for the sake of catching sight of her. The exercise was good, anyhow. It was heavenly, balmy weather; and, if it did him good merely to see the roof that sheltered her, was there so much pleasant coming to him that he should deny himself this indulgence? He was holding himself aloof from his fellows; and this new attraction — mild, delicate, and mystical as the light of the young May moon — was shedding rest on his hot and weary nature. Is it strange that his lonely twilights began to be lonely no longer, but that the face which charmed him should seem to fill all pleasant positions in life.

When the pipe was lighted in his solitary room, the visions which it brought no longer had power to torment. Instead, they were of a gracious, smiling face, with dark tresses, and warm, tender bloom, — a woman's face, with sleeping devotion and a world of loyalty in its enchanting eyes. He saw Emeline, — an elegant, bewitching creature, even in her simple gown, cool and pure and winning as she always met him; and his fancy took wide liberties in dreaming of her. Sometimes they were reading together, and she looked up in his face with that pleased, sudden look at a new thought, as if she expected to read the same pleasure in his eyes; or she was floating about him, her lips wreathed in mischief, her eyes bright with roguery, as he had seen her in her lawless moods; or she was opposite, with her changing, irresistible face, a mute, yet most absorbing companion. He was in that mood where all that a man asks of a woman is to look at her and be blest with the influence of her beauty. Could he have worked Browning's magnetic spell, he would, and brought her dreaming to his room; in reality, he would have been content to sit with his pipe in his lips, and gaze at her the evening through. He had just been through a sore and scorching trial, to a true nature; — and, with all its foibles and faults, his was essentially an upright one; — and it had left him, as fevers or accidents do, with the passionless calm and gravity of convalescence. But it was every thing to be thankful for to find something his mind could dwell on, and relieve it from the bad dreams which nearly worked its ruin. He nursed the fascinating influence; he fed upon it, never asking what it would grow to or where it would take him. He was in fancy wandering through spring-lighted aisles of wood, with Emeline by his side, her eager face upturned to his, her falling hair making a cloud behind it — walking in sacred, blameless companionship. At eve she was sitting in the porch in the dusk, smoothing his hot head, that ached so. When he drew his books toward him to study, it was with a fancy that she was sitting beside him, watching his movements with her serious, bright, friendly face.

Life has no reality to compare with the sweetness of such dreams.

CHAPTER XIX.

HOW NEW CANTON PROSPERED.

THE prosperity of New Canton was a fixed fact. Every man had in his pocket a decent load of savings-bank certificates, and every man took them as pay for what he had to sell. Burt and Peppernell were in the market for every thing of value, and they got into a habit of paying good prices. Was it a horse that Patterson brought to town? Before the days of the savings-bank, the animal would not have brought forty dollars; but it was nothing now to pay a hundred for him, and Patterson was always sorry that he did not ask twice the sum.

Was it a house that Brown, Jones, or Smith had to sell? Before the bank days, it would have hung a long time at $1,000 ; but now they thought nothing of asking $5,000, and got it. Then they invariably turned round, and paid the same rates for lots on which to build a house twice as large as the one vacated.

It was a delightful time for the dames and daughters of the aspiring city. Calico went out, and cashmere took its place. Cane-seat chairs, once good enough for parlors, found their way to the kitchen. The rag carpets, once the pride of their hearts, were hidden away up-stairs, and in their place Brussels, in all sorts of colors, were put upon their floors; and shaky furniture, in striped and green reps, took the place. The paper shades were contemptuously torn down, and Nottingham, or, as the housewives delighted to term it, "real lace," was put up; and many a family, that a year before had been glad to find something to eat with steel knives and two-pronged forks, rose to the grandeur of silver-plated knives and forks. But it vexed the women to see their liege lords continue to eat with their knives, in the same old, comfortable way.

How could Thompson refuse his wife these luxuries, when the house they lived in had risen in value five hundred per cent.? How could he help it, when the little out-lot where, in the old Arcadian days, he pastured his cow, and was content to cobble shoes for a living, was now down on the map as a part of the fourth ward of the city, exactly on the line of the Great Midland, waiting to be purchased by that company for their machine-shops, and would cut up into seven lots to the acre, which would bring five hundred dollars apiece, at the very least.

The fact that Thompson had paid five hundred dollars an acre for that ground, and given a mortgage not only on the ground itself, but on his own homestead, did not affright his soul; for what was fifteen hundred dollars' indebtedness. Three acres made twenty-one lots. Twenty-one lots, at five hundred dollars each, ten thousand five hundred dollars; besides his house, at $5,000! Fifteen hundred dollars! Pooh! A mere nothing!

Josiah Mason quit shoemaking, and went to "operating" in real estate. He bought ground, putting a second mortgage on his house and what he already owned, and brought into the vortex some brothers he had in Connecticut, who, seeing fortunes to be made, came, and put their good money into New Canton lots.

Mason became something of a public character, and spent a great deal of his time around the bar-room of the Continental, where his remark to "put it on the slate" was taken by the obsequious bar-keeper as readily as though he had been a government collector.

Then came greater improvements. The old hotels were not ambitious enough for the city, and a joint stock company was organized to build a mammoth hotel. A company of contractors from a neighboring village, impressed with the glorious future of New Canton, took the contract to build it, and took seventy-five per cent. of the price in town property, which the citizens subscribed with reckless prodigality. Burt, Peppernell, and Sharp were the committee who valued it; and lots on Sixty-third Street, Magnolia Avenue, Park Avenue, and other outlying streets were put in at enormous prices. Up went the hotel — a tremendous four-story structure, with "all the modern appliances." It was a gorgeously uncomfortable place, and nearly frightened the country couples to death, who came there for their honeymoons, with its upholstery and its bills. But it answered its purpose. The contractors distributed some ready money in town, and citizens had the stock among their assets.

New blocks of buildings were begun in every direction. "Commercial Row," on Tenth Street, was half a mile from the rest of the town; but it was confidently expected by the foreigners who built it, that, before it was completed, it would be imperatively demanded by the wants of the growing town, especially as it was on the line of the Grand Trunk.

Men, who, a year before, scarcely knew where their next bag of flour was coming from, now blossomed out as property-owners and capitalists. Those who had nothing to sell, and no money, were making it very fast in buying; and there was a " growing heat " of universal prosperity over the heads of the fortunate citizens.

How was it with Burt and Peppernell in this shower of gold; that is, of paper promises for gold? Mr. Burt would remark: " Sansom, you ought to build a new house. You have made too much money to live in that rickety old concern. It might have been well enough ten years ago; but it's out of place in this time of prosperity. Did I do wrong when I advised you to buy that block on Fifty-ninth Street? Eh? But you sold too quickly. No? Well; you did hedge on Forty-eighth. But, seriously, I believed that Fifty-ninth was the better 'spec' of the two. You were shrewder than I was. Good-day."

Col. Peppernell met the citizens, as was proper.

" Timson, you fool, you have blundered into a good thing. I told you to buy that whole square, no matter what the figures were. You bought a third of it, and see where it is now! Worth ten times what you paid, and going up ten per cent. a day. None of you had faith in the power of expansion of the country,— no faith in that destiny, which I, old as I am, will live to see fulfilled. The expansive West hez a people that kin see its past, comprehend its present, and hev faith in its fucher. The country and its people wuz made for each other. Timson, I see you drivin' a hoss to-day that I fancied. Ef yoo want a lot in the last addishen to the tenth ward, I'm your man. I hate to part with the lot, but I fancied that hoss."

And Timson got the lot, and Peppernell the horse.

But these worthies did not confine themselves to horses and such movable property. The prudent Peppernell secured an excellent farm of a thousand acres, out of the "city" a little way, and erected an exceedingly comfortable dwelling, with conveniences to match. He imported fine stock from Ohio and Vermont; and his house was furnished as nicely as any gentleman farmer could wish. He had other property safely invested; but certain wise men noticed, that it was all of a character that could not be affected by the rise or fall of New Canton real estate. It would have been good in any county, and it was all in his wife's name.

Burt did not invest in real estate. But he made frequent visits to Chicago; and it was discovered by Tom Paddleford, that he made investments there in bank and other stock, convertible any minute into money. Burt never mentioned these matters in New Canton; and, when the story got about, he denied it. All the investments he had made in Chicago were in the regular course of a large and extensive business. His permanent investments had been made in New Canton.

Sharp and Peak imitated the astute Peppernell; and Gardiner contented himself with lending all of them money, and getting such pieces of choice real estate as he could. He was entirely satisfied.

Col. Peppernell was passing the bank one day, and noticed that the painters were putting a new coat of color on the front of the building.

"Deuce take it, Burt! What is the use of all this extravagance?" was his irate question. "Ain't we loaded heavily enough without going to this expense?"

"My dear sir," said Burt, taking him quietly by the arm, " it only costs a hundred dollars, — payable in our certificates, — and it looks solvent. I am going to have the front office of the bank and all the rooms of the land company kalsomined to-morrow. And I believe I'll put up a glass partition on the counter, the next day. Only sound institutions can indulge in comforts."

CHAPTER XX.

FLUSH TIMES IN NEW CANTON.

COL. PEPPERNELL remarked, "The pot's a-b'ilin'!" The ambition of the directory had been attained, and the town was crazy. It was a miniature Wall Street before Black Friday. It was Pithole immediately after an enormous strike. It was, in short, as perfect a financial pandemonium as the Devil, who invented greed, would wish to see.

The storekeepers — merchants now — had never brought on so many fine goods in all their lives. Silks, satins, and even velvets were becoming common in New Canton; and nobody thought any thing of it. Mrs. Philips, the milliner — alas! there were three milliners, where one, who had been compelled to supplement her scant earnings with tailoring, had sufficed, — never thought of taking a hat down for a customer for less than ten dollars; and she had her pockets and her drawers and several boxes full of the certificates. True, she owed heavily in Chicago, for goods. But what of that? She was paying no interest in Chicago; and the certificates were drawing ten per cent., if she held them six months.

And so she was well enough pleased to sell Mrs. Thurman, the blacksmith's wife, a hat for fifteen dollars, the poor woman not knowing which side of it went frontwise, as her experience in head-gear dated back to the day she was married. The fact of old Marvin coming into town one day with stockings on excited some feeble surprise; but that faded out when it was learned that he had sold the half of his farm for ten times what the whole had cost him two years before, and had the price — in savings-bank certificates — safely stored away at home, all made payable to his order, as a safeguard against thieves.

Old Bill Messenger had no sooner adopted the wearing of shoes, than he tired of the steady work of the farm, and determined to go into manufacturing; and, with the certificates he had in his hands, actually commenced the foundation for a woolen-factory, paying for the excavation in certificates. Mr. Burt smiled, and pointed to it as an evidence of the progress of the city, and as an earnest of the realization of the hopes of its founders.

Bartley Campbell, having by accident learned that there was an enormous profit on billiard-tables, announced his intention of establishing that branch of industry in New Canton, which Col. Peppernell encouraged.

"The game of billiards," said the Colonel, "is calculated to improve the intellek as well as the muscles. Relaxation is a necessity, and exercise is a necessity. There is no more cheerin' site than to see a blacksmith or a stun-mason, at the close of his day's labor, playin' billiards two or three hours for exercise. I prefer old-sledge or a gentlemanly game of draw, for exercise; but men is constitooted different. Billiards is also evidence of luxurious tastes, and proof of the means to gratify 'em. The time will come, Mr. Campbell, when every house in New Canton will hev its billiard-table; and therein you will reap yoor harvest. You cannot do better; and, by the way, Campbell, get diggin' the foundashen as soon as you kin. There will be demand enough by the time you are ready to fill it."

There was an enormous tendency on the part of the better class of citizens, to livery. In the old time, the landlord of the Eagle had kept a horse or two for the use of the infrequent traveler, — for funerals and such extraordinary occasions; but now there were not only livery-stables, but boarding-stables; and one who had been in Chicago christened his establishment " The New Canton Tattersalls."

Saloons — or " s'loons," as they were generally termed — multiplied like locusts. The Continental and Grand Central had bars gorgeous in magnificence; and, in addition, there sprang up the " Gem," the " Arcade *Restaurant*," and a dozen others, in which fancy drinks of elaborate composition took the place of the old-time whisky and tanzy. The Grand Central imported a bar-keeper from St. Louis, who parted his hair in the middle and wore a diamond solitaire; that is, it looked like a diamond, and was popularly supposed to be worth $15,000. He wore white cuffs and a brilliant scarf, and could pour a stream from a glass held over his head to another held in the other hand as low down as he could reach. The bloods of New Canton went wild when, one day, in mixing a sherry-cobbler, he jammed the glass into the tin shaker, and, after several artistic flourishes, tossed it high in the air, and caught it when it came down, with as much address as a prestidigatator. It was reported of him, that he had had control of the bar at the Planter's, in St. Louis, and had left there in consequence of a trouble one night, in which he shot several men — the number being stated variously from five to fifteen. When asked about it, he preserved a discreet silence, remarking that such things were not proper subjects for conversation in public, which convinced his auditors of the entire truth of the story.

But it was in barbers that the new condition of things came out the strongest. The word "barber" disappeared, and was known no more forever. The one little shop, where the citizens who could afford it had formerly had their flesh tortured with dull razors and their souls vexed with dull gabble, disappeared; and "tonsorial parlors," with carpets on the floors, upholstered chairs, "physiognomical artists," and "hair-dressing establishments" multiplied.

The spirit of improvement manifested itself in the churches possibly more than in any thing else. The little Presbyterian church, which was quite large enough for the congregation, was lengthened forty feet; the old-fashioned hencoop of a pulpit was taken down, and a modern platform erected; the church was carpeted, the pews changed, the venerable tenplate stoves taken out, and heaters substituted, which made the rooms as chilly and respectable as the most devout could desire. Innumerable church fairs, at which benevolence and thin tea were equally mixed, were resorted to, to pay for these improvements; and, as they kept the women of the town very generally on the move, saved the town much gossip, if it lightened the pockets of their husbands and fathers.

Poor Parson Latimer, who had been in the church from the beginning, was very zealous in these improvements; but, in the end, it was very bad for him. He was not the first man who has been hoisted with his own petard. With the bright carpet on the floors, the shining pews and the nickel-plated numbers thereon, — with the elegant Bible on the little carved desk, and the stained-glass windows, Parson Latimer did not fit. He was a little old man, devoted to his calling as any martyr that ever stood in fire; but he was plain. His hands were somewhat of the roughest; for he had been compelled all his life to eke out starving salaries, half paid, with work upon his little farm, and he was a rusty old fellow at best. He could help change other things in the church, which was now his pride; but he could not change himself. In all this grandeur he was a blot, as one cracked voice will spoil the effect of three good singers, and was as much out of place as the shoemaker's bench, on which the owner had once earned his living, would be in the drawing-room of the same man, when he had amassed a fortune.

As Mr. Latimer knew his people and his people knew him, it would have been well had they retained him. He was content with his small salary, for he had his fowling-piece and fishing-rod to fall back upon. No ragged boy in the village had more skill in enticing the wary sucker from the placid waters of Soggy Run, and his shot-gun brought more prairie-chickens to the pot than any one in the village. And he had patience. He could smile and smile and be the recipient of donation parties. He could be cordial, on such occasions, even to the Widow Scranton, who always attended with her four grown-up daughters, the joint contribution of the five being a flannel pen-wiper, and who always fasted a day to do justice to the bountiful supper the pastor always provided.

Nevertheless, a strong party was formed against the good old man. Mr. Gardiner and a number of the old citizens, who had sat under his ministrations many years, and loved the man who had buried their dead and married their living, who knew how to console them in their grief and sympathize with them in their prosperity, made a fight for him. They did not fight weakly; but they were few in numbers, and it was a weak fight.

The church-meeting at which the subject was considered was a stormy affair. The old man, always so meek and mild that no one supposed he would have the spirit to resist any thing put upon him, developed a degree of combativeness delightful to his friends as it was uncomfortable to those seeking to displace him. He stood up in the pulpit he had occupied so many years, and made a speech long remembered in New Canton. He repeated the reasons that had been given for his removal, and commented upon them briskly.

"It has been urged that I have not the manner for such a church, — that I have been seen carrying home a sack of flour on my shoulder. Brethren, I admit the heinous offense; but I assure you that I never wanted to. On a salary of four hundred dollars a year, a little over half paid — "

"But you had a donation every year," interrupted a brother.

"Yes," answered the Parson, with a sigh, "I had that additional expense. But, as I was saying, with four hundred a year, and a large family, and my house being the hotel for all the Presbyterians who ever visited New Canton, I was glad enough to get the flour, to say nothing of being willing to carry it home. I don't like to carry flour; but what are you going to do, if you haven't got the fifteen cents to pay a drayman? Then my hunting and fishing! I plead guilty to that also, and have the same excuse to offer. I like field sports. I should never have hunted or fished a quarter as much as I did, but Soggy Run and the prairies were my larder. I am not overly well up in flesh. I should have been leaner but for my shotgun and fishing-rod. Suckers and prairie-chickens have contributed a great deal more to the support of the Gospel in New Canton than the people who so sorely need it. I managed to live very well when you paid me enough in money to get powder and shot. I have no style! True, I used to dress better, and so did my family, but on four hundred a year! Religion isn't the cheapest thing in the world. I should dislike to guage your estimate of its value by the price you have been willing to pay for it."

The vote was taken, and poor Father Latimer was voted out, three to one. All the marriageable young ladies voted for a change; for the incoming man might be single! The same idea controlled the votes of mothers who had marriageable daughters; and this consideration, aside from a desire for something more genteel, carried all one way. Parson Latimer, thrown out of his charge, gave up the parsonage, sold his few goods at auction, and left for pastures fresh.

There was a quiet sarcasm in exposing for sale at the "vandoo" among the effects he did not wish to carry away with him, several boxes full of slippers, bookmarks, pen-wipers, tidies, and other entirely useless articles, which were described in the advertisement, as "the result of ten donation parties." Mrs. Scranton, who was present at the vendue, to pick up such bargains as might come to her notice — when she saw one lot of ten pen-wipers, warranted of the best flannel, remonstrated with the Parson for exposing her gifts for sale, and managed as to get them back again, thereby stocking herself for ten donations in the future.

The church was not long without a pastor. He was a young man from New England, just graduated from a theological seminary, and was, in all respects, a bargain satisfactory to the majority. He wore side-whiskers, long, soft, silky, and wavy ; a pale, thoughtful face, and beautiful high forehead, and such lovely hands! They were long, white, and the fingers were tapering. And he had the sweetest cough that ever was nursed by an interesting minister. He read the hymns delightfully, and had such rare taste in selecting them. He never suggested uncomfortable thoughts by howling out: —

"My thoughts on awful subjects roll,
Damnation and the dead."

But his selections were always about love and flowers and the delights of things in general. And when he put up those hands, and said, "Let us pray," Miss Perkins remarked, that to hear him was better than a lecture or an oratorio.

He never offended any one. He took Mrs. Burt's medicine, and smiled.

He could talk, not of horses and crops and sick

people, and such topics as old Mr. Latimer was wont to indulge in; but he had read Emerson, and knew personally the Boston celebrities, and was a walking library of literature and art. Mr. Calthrop was an eminently popular young man, and became more so when it was rumored, that, on the death of an uncle, he would become very rich indeed.

The Methodists did not go so far as the Presbyterians; but the spirit of certificates pervaded their society. They enlarged their church — chapel no longer; and, whereas before they had been glad to get anybody to preach for them, they now insisted on being promoted to the dignity of a station, and began to worry the presiding elders for just such a minister as they wanted. They put a steeple on their church, and in it the most discordant bell that could be cast.

A select few, the cream of New Canton society, organized an Episcopal church. It took them a long while to get used to rising in the right place, and it required much study to accustom themselves to the responses; but, as the Episcopal was well known to be the aristocratic church, they persevered, and in time got into the new customs very comfortably. They built a church, and, in conjunction with another town, supported a minister, and, in less than three months, got to be very High Church. They didn't know the difference, but they were opposed to any thing low.

And the man who had raised this whirlwind sat quietly in his office, pouring oil upon the fire, and fanning it with his never-ceasing breath to a brighter and more furious blaze.

CHAPTER XXI.

PLAYING AT LOVE.

THE last heavy-footed client had shambled out of the office, and the young lawyer leaned back with a delicious feeling of well-earned leisure. He put up his papers, docketed this abstract of title and that mortgage, scribbled off two or three letters, and shut and locked his desk like a man who knows he turns all his troubles under key, and leaves them there. His thoughts flew back to the warm, dark face and lighted smile they had come to know so well. He had made excuses to find himself at the Burt's as often as his audacity would allow, within the last two weeks, and a close watch of the Burt premises had so far befriended him that he was on the sidewalk lighting his cigar whenever Emeline ventured out for her evening walk in the fresh air. On such occasions he had always been going her way by accident, and strolled along in the friendly shade of the catalpas that lined the streets of the village, lounging by her side, without permission or excuse, till he bid her good-night at the door of the acquaintance where she made her evening call. He had been smoking in the moonlight near the post-office, where she must cross on her way home, and had caught up with her two or three blocks further on, as if on his natural way home. But, once at her side, he had fallen into a very slow walk, and ventured to propose to vary their way by strolling round a block or two, while he finished some college adventure, thrillingly interesting to her unused ears. How lovely her face looked in the moonrays between the boughs, — tired, but absorbed in his words! He noticed she was tired; and they two had taken leave to sit down on the steps of John Keeler's unfinished house, and talked in the moonlight, he caring most to look at her, as every motion or turn showed delightful. She did not say much, her part being to listen with pleased attention, while he searched his memory for what would please this untaught but nice taste. How keen her little sayings, and how sweet her voice and her laugh! He would give all his books to hear that laugh again; and with that he started up, resolved to see her at the Burt's by some means that very night.

When the only moments that separate a young man from the girl in whom his interest centers are those of the tea-hour, he makes those moments very short. Scant justice was done the baked pigeons, light muffins, and blackberry jam, which furnished forth the home table; and his answers to his mother, though sweet and courteous, were brief. When he vanished, in fresh array, out of the front door, that acute parent put two and two together in this way: —

"He goes out after supper, and comes back after twelve, but he is not dissipating. He must be after another girl." And the affectionate mother heaved a sigh of content. There are things which some women dread worse than daughters-in-law, for their sons. I think Mrs. Gardiner even loved her son so well that she would have seen him actually married to the plainest girl in New Canton, rather than have him return to his evil courses — a feeling which all high-minded mothers will properly repudiate.

James was wily enough to make good his welcome at the Burt's, as well as insure their winking at any philandering in which he might indulge with Emeline. To this end he made interest with old Goss, a country client, for some new celery roots, which he was now conveying to Mr. Burt's garden, together with a brace or two of pigeons for the female Burt, who, being an invalid, with delicate powers of digestion, was supplied by devoted neighbors with victual of a rich and savory sort, like mince-pie, black-cake, mango pickles, head-cheese, and doughnuts enough to suffice for the maintenance of an ordinary workingman. James had made a pleasant little programme for the evening, to be brought about somehow by his unequaled powers of management. The first steps were not clear in his mind, but it was to end with a stroll down the mill-road and a good-bye after midnight. A moment more, he said to himself, as he paced the road between the two houses, and he should be in that sunny, welcome presence, and those large, eloquent eyes would meet his in the innocent, happy look, the thought of which made him happy.

No form bent over its sewing on the sunny porch, no flutter of a light dress about the grass-plot in the back yard gave promise of what he came to seek at Burt's house.

Mrs. Burt was in the sitting-room, the windows tightly closed and the shades down, to keep out flies.

The heavy steps in dining-room and hall were not Emeline's; and, as moments wore on without sign of her, James began to fear his luck was changed. He ventured to ask for Emeline.

"She took it into her head," grumbled the amiable Mrs. Burt, "that she wanted a vacation, and she left the day before yesterday."

"Then she's gone home, I suppose," hazarded James.

"I don't know where she keeps herself, I'm sure," responded Mrs. Burt, with that supreme contempt with which the country mistress gives a visitor to understand she is above taking an interest in a hired girl.

James would hardly have believed it possible, as he trod the walk slowly back, that failure to meet any woman could have caused him such utter heart-sinking as he felt at not finding Emeline. That sweet, gracious presence had grown in such short time to be so much of a necessity to him that he rebelled against the idea of a day without seeing her.

Where had Emeline gone? Why had she left without giving him some hint that their pleasant acquaintance was to close? Close? He would see about that, spite of Mother Burt and all her kindness. But, like the strongest man when met by feminine wiles, he felt bewildered and helpless. He only knew Emeline was gone, and had left him no clew to find her. There were some less than five and twenty townships in the county, and he was equally at a loss to tell which particular one might be holding her at the present moment. The clew struck him, and he almost threw his hat up for joy. He had a horse, thank fortune; and could he spend the evening better than by going to her home, to get word of her? He must do it, or he felt that he could not sleep that night.

Imagine, in five minutes thereafter, an impetuous young fellow dashing round the back way into his own father's stables, harnessing and leading out his own horse, and driving out of town in a flash of glorified dust and wagon-spokes.

Tige, his dark Morgan, had never traveled the mill-road at such a gait before; and his owner never felt more kind to him than when he drove up to the gate of the Butterfield farm in seven minutes. James flung himself out of the wagon and to the door, it seemed to him, with one motion.

The dash through the fresh air had cooled and steadied his nerves; and he walked up to the low door of the Butterfield house with the air of a gentleman on business. Butter — that was the errand he made for himself. Mrs. Gardiner wanted to engage her summer supply, and, knowing of the excellence of Mrs. Butterfield's dairy, had sent him there to see about it.

While saying this, his eyes took in eagerly every object that might be some clue to the presence of Emeline. Was that a little black jacket lying on the lounge? He had seen her wear it a hundred times; and the fresh ruffle, scarcely bent, showed that it had been lately worn. She was there, then. He had found her, and his pulse grew glad and still in a moment. He was a self-possessed and gracious young gentleman again, ready to take the seat offered him under the vine-shaded window, and listen to the quiet discourse of an old woman who had lived all her life in the country. The extreme neatness and comfortable sort of poverty in the lowly home appealed to him. It seemed hard that he should have had things all his life so much better; and here was Emeline, whom he cared for as if she were a true and gentle-hearted man friend, who, with her woman's taste and delight in pretty things, had to be content with such a home as this. It was but an instant's thought; for the homely room, with its delicate order and simple comfort, would have won upon more exacting taste than his own. The sweet wind was as much at home in that room as among the mignonette and French clover and heart's-ease in the flower-borders, a faint, wholesome odor of new bread just drawn from the oven being the only sign of housekeeping about the house. The neat lounge, with its big ruffled pillows scented with sweet-clover, that Emeline loved to strew in her cushions, invited the young fellow to linger, and make much conversation, of an agreeable sort, with Hannah Butterfield, while he sat there taking in every trace of Emeline about. The workbasket, with its white spools marked with her initials in pencil, he had seen with her at Mrs. Burt's; and was not that her dress of pink and gray gingham, with pretty flounces, lying half-finished across a chair? Would she come in while he was there, or would he have to go home again without seeing her? To make time, he asked for a glass of water, and took the pail from old Hannah, as she was starting for the spring, too much of a gentleman to let a woman wait on him, especially if she was old and homely and unused to attention.

The spring flowed a few rods from the house; but

not a sign of Emeline did he find in garden, orchard, or lane. A turn took him along a grassy strip at the foot of the orchard, where the bank sloped a yard or two to the water, and wild fruit-trees screened it effectually from prying eyes. Why wasn't Emeline in this nook, of all others the place to meet him? He stooped to fill the pail, with a feeling of vexation, when far-off bursts of laughter, as if all the witches of the wood had gone mad with fun, caught his ear. Through the orchard he saw Emeline coming with her little brother, their hands full of wood-spoil and water-cresses.

A low, clear whistle made her look round in surprise that was delightful to the eyes keenly watching her. She knew the signal instantly; and the recognition was sweet flattery to the young man.

"You did not expect to see me?" he said, as she saw him, and came slowly forward.

Her hesitation might have been taken for want of pleasure at seeing him; but she was only embarrassed at seeing him in so poor a home. It vanished as she looked into his face, at what she read there. He was her friend of all the world, eager and glad to see her just as she was, face to face. He took her hand, and drew her toward him, recollecting himself just in time to prevent him from kissing her, as it seemed the natural thing for him to do. His eyes kissed her, and her eyelids fell, with the quick interpretation Nature gave her of this unspeakably slight and tender sign.

"How shall I keep from kissing her, she is so beautiful?" he was thinking, as he held her hand an instant.

"Does he think so much of me?" was her thought

the same moment. But this was not what he was saying or she answering.

"How could you go away, and not let me know where you were?" he asked, reproachfully.

"How did I know you would care?" she said, simply.

"Care! As if I could help caring," he said, gently, looking into her eyes, as if she were a child he was petting. "Oh! if you knew how glad I am to find you again!"

"Didn't Mrs. Burt tell you I was at home?" she asked innocently.

"Mrs. Burt didn't know where you were. I suspect she ought to be churched for telling a story. Have you left her?"

"Mrs. Burt knew I was coming home a fortnight to do some sewing," said Emeline, with a little natural indignation. "She probably didn't know whether I was in the south field or the back room when you spoke to her. But won't you come in the house?" she asked, mindful of decorum.

"Can't we as well stay out here?" he pleaded. "The air is so good, after being in the office all day; and I have so much to say to you. It's so long since we have been together! Would it cross anybody's ideas if you sit down on this little bench? Here is where you stole off to read your first novel, 'The Pirate,' you told me."

"Did I? I didn't know I ever told any one that. You make me tell you a good many foolish little things."

"That shows I'm a safe person to trust. I don't think any thing you could say would be foolish. It wouldn't be to me, you may be certain. How delightful this is to find you here, in that sunshine and this cool, grassy place! It's heavenly!"

She was sitting on a little seat fitted into the bank, in the shade of a wild-cherry tree; and James had found a place on the grass at her feet, where he could lean looking up into her face. There was a clear, warm bloom in the air, promise of a most beautiful day on the morrow. The little nook was lovely with deep, fresh grasses and enameling of fern and lichen and late spring flowers. A wild-rose set its burning cup in the hedge, and a pale primrose had already lighted its evening flame. Through the silence and sweetness, the clear water flowed; and the afternoon lights and freshness were Paradise come again.

He took in the delight, and turned to her with a sigh of content. "How I have missed you!"

"I shouldn't think you need to miss anybody," she said. "I wish I knew half as many people as you do."

"I'm glad you don't, for you'd have to find out how little they are worth knowing. Emeline," — calling her by her name for the first time, unconsciously, till he saw the blood dyed her cheeks at the freedom, and liked her for the sight, — "I ought to have asked you (oughtn't I?) first. But I couldn't help it. We understand each other so well I can't feel as if there ought to be any form between us. I've said it. Why should I ever call you any thing else but Emeline, now? Need I?" he pleaded, softly. Her look gave him assent, and he went on.

"I was going to ask if you knew why I followed you out here, on the chance of finding you at home.

It was because I couldn't find another single creature in that town to change a word with. You are the only one who understands me. We like the same books and the same things, and — we don't like the same people; and that's more of a bond than the other."

"Change words!" she said, in pure bluntness. "Why, I don't say one word to your twenty."

"I know it," he went on. "You're not a great talker, Emeline (how pleasant it is to be allowed to say your name); but your eyes say it all for you, and I am answered when I look into them. Emeline, you understand me now better than anybody in the world," he pronounced, with the air of a young man who thinks he pays a woman the highest compliment in the world when she understands his shallow and immature self.

"You pay New Canton people a great compliment in coming out so far to talk with me."

"Possibly I don't like New Canton people."

"Out of so many, you might find some to please you. Are there no young ladies there?"

"None for me."

She looked at him demurely. "I didn't know they had all gone out of town of a sudden."

"There was one I used to like and have good times with. She loved what I loved and had the same dislikes I had. She was a good girl, and I felt better when I had been with her. After the men I was compelled to associate with, an evening with her was like being in another country."

"Why didn't you stay with her?" — demurely.

"I meant to; but she ran away without letting me

know where she had gone, and a pretty ride I had to find her. She bid fair to become the light of my eyes; and she had to cut short all our delightful walks and talks as if they were no account to her. She might have had some care for my feelings. Don't you think so?"

"I never heard of a woman's acting so," Emeline declared, with deepest mock seriousness. "Probably she wasn't worth minding."

"You don't know her, or you wouldn't say so. She was the brightest, the wittiest, the prettiest girl I think I ever knew. And, when I found she was gone, the town was empty. When you have but one friend in the world, Emeline, it goes hard to lose that one."

She believed him, she said with sincere concern. She had never had a friend to call her own, but she could imagine it would be hard to lose one.

"Then what do you act so for?" he demanded, suddenly.

"I'm not in question? You're talking of some other girl."

"I never think of any other girl but you. I don't believe I'm decently civil to any other one. You're prettier than any girl in town, though that's a poor compliment. You have something to say for yourself instead of drawling, 'Mr. Gardiner, do you intend to attend the mite society next week?' or 'Mr. Gardiner, what do you think of the new novel?' Their only conversation is asking questions, as if a fellow was bound to carry round information for their emptiness. I don't really care much for any girl but you, Emeline, to be candid. You're frank and kind, and you help me to forget."

The last words came out unconsciously, with a half-sigh that moved his hearer's heart more than any priases could have done. Indeed, flattery was so novel that she heard it with a certain pain, as something not quite worthy for her to hear or another to say. She found things in the world to interest her more than herself.

"I suppose it would look very strange, my coming out here after you," he said; "but a sweet, clear-headed girl, I knew, would understand just the lonely feeling that made rush after you when I found you had deserted me. The fact is, Emeline, I've had some very sad times lately; and, if being with you helps me to be steady and forget trouble, why shouldn't I? I haven't anybody's leave to ask but yours, have I? You are not going to tell me I mustn't see you and walk and talk with you, when the world is so full of things we might enjoy together? If I should come up this way, and find you sitting out of doors to sew (I suppose you do sew out of doors, don't you?), and, if I should happen to have a book in my pocket, why couldn't I sit out with you, in this pretty place, and read and talk to you? I don't suppose, of course, you would like it as well as I should; but you might for my good. What are you looking so shocked for, Emeline?"

To her unsophisticated ears, his little affectation of doubt sounded just as if he had been telling falsehood; and her face, like water, betrayed her feelings. But it was only a moment; for was he not offering her the best gift that had ever come her way — his young, frank, honorable affection? She did not mistake one word. Implicitly she took his word at its face value, and did not count friendship for love, or even know that the leaves in her hand might turn to gold by the magic of daily nearness and woman's power. It was good to be sought and prized, ever so coolly; and she heard, and gave all her loyalty in return.

"I wish I had a sister like you, Emeline," the kind voice was saying. "If I had one, I should want her to be like you — so steady and sweet. Only you are too cool to suit me quite. I suppose you could love, if the right man came along. Couldn't you?" The full, dark eyes, lifted to his suddenly, told of a depth that would surprise him, if he had read it right. "Yes, you'll do. It's settled, then. You are to be my pet friend, and I'm to be your next best friend; and I want you to arrange so that I can see a good deal of you. I'm going to ask something of you some day, when you come to know me right well; but I won't now. I did think of you enough to bring you a novel." The truth was it had been lying under the seat in the wagon since his last drive; and it struck him at the moment that it might be a welcome thing for Emeline, out in the woods.

"Mind, it won't be all fair sailing with me," he added. "You will have to keep me steady, and I get the blues horribly sometimes; and I shall ask you to take an interest in things that I want to talk about, that you don't care for. But it won't be one-sided, for I shall be at your beck and call for what you want. Oh! I assure you I am ever so much better than a woman friend. I can choose patterns and match shades as well as a lady; and, if we were cast away on a desert island, I could do up hair. So, you can talk to me about your darning and knitting, and I will take an interest in trimmings. By the way, is that your new gown I saw in the house? It looked like your taste. And you can afford to hear my scandals about Driggs and the other lawyers; and I shouldn't wonder if I asked you to read my speeches, if I ever made them. I shall come to-morrow, with your permission. Good-night, Emeline. It will be a better night for me than it would have been without seeing you. Good-night."

The little dell lay in shadow. There was no one in sight. She was unspeakably fair and fresh, and James was no novice in lovemaking. He stooped, laid his lips respectfully, but, oh, how fondly! on her brow, and was gone.

"On a desert island," he said to himself, as he gathered up the lines in his wagon; "I wish we were on one, Emeline."

CHAPTER XXII.

MR. BURT BUYS A PIANO.

MR. BURT paced slowly home to his one-o'clock dinner, with his usual absorbed business air, under which he saw all that was going on. He saw Mrs. Holt's washing out on the line, Wednesday, too late for good housekeeping. He noticed Mrs. Graham's stand of house-plants in her bay-window, and wondered why those at his house grew so spindling and ran to leaves. He saw Mrs. Brown's children at play in the yard, in fresh pinafores, and wondered if it had been such a lucky thing, after all, that his wife had brought him no children. They would have been very inconvenient when he was poor and making his way. He heard young Lyddy Craven singing in her high, girlish voice at her lesson with the piano, and thought how pleasant it would be to have a pretty girl of thirteen, at home, and see her eyes brighten, and see her whirl round with delight, and feel her arms thrown round his neck at his return. He wanted some tangible result of his money, something besides the mere satisfaction of getting it. He was no such ascetic by nature as he had made himself for years, and he felt the spring of many tastes rising impatient in his heart.

He had touched a life of wider sweep and more lively hues than this small, behindhand, pretentious village existence. Some of the men he did business with cemented good feeling by introducing him to their families; and he saw women who wore their dresses and carried their good looks in a different way from any he had ever known — women whose eyes and lips knew how to smile with intelligence, who had a dozen ways to amuse a man and a dozen things to say to him where a New Canton woman had one. They made a man show the best that was in him, and he found himself more of a gentleman than he supposed in their society. He could admire pictures and fine women when they were pointed out to him, and give an opinion on them with a discrimination that was a discovery to himself. He wanted to bring into his home the refinements he saw in other men's houses, no better off than himself. A New Canton woman made her courtesies as she made her gingerbread — by receipt. She asked a male visitor to lay off his hat, and if his family was well, and inquired when his mother or his wife was going to call on her, and seemed relieved when the visit was over. He could not imagine his own wife saying or doing any thing that any mortal could reasonably find fault with, or that could make any mortal wish to stay near her an hour, if he could possibly get away. She was as positive and unsympathetic in her tastes as in her colors; and there she sat in her window, in a spot where the carpet was worn by the feet of herself and her gossips, watching whoever went up or down the street.

What ailed that unfortunate woman, that, spend as much as she might on her appearance, the dress she wore always seemed the last thing she ever ought to put on? She had heard that blue was the color for blondes, and drab went with blue. Accordingly, her favorite wear was a neutral "alpaca," which suited, as may be imagined, a sallow, pale complexion, relieved by a hard blue bow at the throat, and made still more ghastly by a pink rose and geranium leaves, which, with a fiction of making herself charming, she had stuck in her curls. Burt's eye fell on her, and a shudder ran through him, instantly put down with the facility of self-control which comes of long marital training. There was space in the entry to smooth his face to the regulation look, — the dutiful smile and kiss of welcome, that insignificant chirrup which the conjugal kiss becomes after a few years of matrimonial pretense. He was met with the original remark: "You're late to-day. Dinner's getting cold."

"All dressed up," he said, duly noticing the flower, like a model husband. "It is pretty."

"For my Chadie," was the affectionate response. "Does it look well?"

"I never saw the time when you didn't look well to me," was the dutiful answer.

When he came out, Emeline was at the table, in her neat working-dress of brown calico, with traces of wear, it is true, but entirely neat and becoming. What delightful curves filled the calico, with its lily-white collar inside the dark neck-ruffle. Her hair was knotted close, a little rough from her work, but sufficiently neat; and she looked fresh and wholesome as she would at threescore, if she lived so long. Burt glanced at her, and helped the soup in absent fashion.

"I thought I'd have soup to-day, to use up the rest

of that piece of beef." said Mrs. Burt, who felt quite equal to all the talking. "I want to get it all eaten up, so'st' we can begin on poultry. A man was round to-day with chickens, and I did want to get some; but I knew this beef would last a week."

"Couldn't you let the beef go, and get the chickens?" asked Burt. "We've had beef for two weeks."

"Why, you wouldn't have me waste five pounds of roast-beef, ready cooked?" said his helpmeet. "I wanted Em to get through with the light quilt she is doing over for the beds in summer, to save washing the Marseilles so often, it takes so much soap and hurts the quilts so to wring them so. I thought we'd have that beef cold for dinners this week, with hot gravy and potatoes, and you wouldn't mind."

"Of course not. You always do things right," was the admirable answer.

"Perhaps you'd like some horseradish with the cold meat," said his amiable wife, bent on being agreeable. "It's good to clear the head, and I think you've a touch of catarrh. It's good in spring, anyhow, when the blood's thick. Uncle Isaac used to say it was better than sarsaparilla. Em, I don't believe you took any sarsaparilla to-day."

"Mrs. Burt thinks I need something to stir me up, because I'm lazy and don't do enough on that quilt," Em laughed.

"Mrs. Burt sees you're falling away in flesh and spirits," said Mr. Burt, looking across at her with the joke in his eyes. It was good as a draught of spring water to hear Emeline's gay, sweet laugh, not loud, but running over, as a child's does when it is pleased.

Mrs. Burt looked over the gravy-tureen inquiringly. She did not always understand what Mr. Burt and Em were laughing at, at first. For her part, she thought laughing at table bad manners. Her mother, at least, never encouraged it. But it pleased Burt, as she phrased it to herself; and, for the sake of the successful man who was making so much money for her, a greater offense might be condoned.

"Celia Goodrich is up to-day, after her broken leg," said Mr. Burt, by way of more becoming conversation.

"Dr. Rice told me he thought it was doubtful if she ever got round again with it," said Mrs. Burt, in a tone of injured surprise, as if Miss Goodrich had given unpardonable offense by going against predictions. "I'm going round there after dinner to carry some of that tansy and horehound bitters Em steeped for me. We can spare some. Her mother will be glad of it, anyhow. How did you hear?"

"Miss Jane Ashton was speaking about it."

"How long since you took to harmonizing with Jane Ashton, I wonder!" asked his wife, in surprise.

"She was at the office to-day, to see about getting some lots."

"See here, Charles," said the devoted wife, with a peculiarly amiable smile; "I guess I shall have to go down town with you myself, if ladies take to doing business with you. I don't think it's right for women to go flirting round men's offices."

"I don't know that I'd care to do it, if I was a woman, myself," said Burt, suavely. "But, then, Miss Jane is so old and her looks and the style she dresses in are so much against her that she can go anywhere. I don't see what women want to be tall and raw-boned for, with color, like a watermelon," added Burt, letting his eyes wander over his wife's person in a way that she took for a compliment, as she certainly was the reverse of these obnoxious qualities.

"Well, I suppose the old lady can't see to business, she is getting so old," Mrs. Burt observed, in a molified tone. "Did she buy?"

"She didn't decide, and I don't know whether she will make out to invest at all. Parting with money to such a woman is worse than telling how old she is."

"But she couldn't do any thing better with her money than to put it in land. Did you tell her that, Charles? I'd bear down on her a little, if I were you. You can make that woman do whatever you tell her to, she has such confidence in you, Chadie," — looking at him with anxious eyes tempered with veneration for his business talent.

"Thank you, Mate. I may be able to urge her to buy, if she doesn't feel inclined of her own notion," said Mr. Burt, placidly, without the slightest trace of sarcasm.

"People need pressure brought to bear on them," said Mrs. Burt, placidly, cheerfully, and unblushingly, grinding a generous mouthful of the cold beef at the same time — Mrs. Burt being one of those persons who pride themselves on their ability to do two things at a time.

Her husband had come home that day with a purpose to carry out, as well as gossip to impart. Over the molifying dessert, he opened play for an indulgence he coveted and meant to have.

Mr. Burt was a man wise in his generation, and well aware that women like to feel the management of affairs in their own hands. He spoke of the improved style of living in town, and mentioned that a Chicago dealer had opened a music store in the village. Also, that a Chicago singer thought of establishing herself there to give lessons. Kingman and Pritchard and Newman had ordered pianos, and Mrs. Newman was going to take lessons.

"Take music lessons!" exclaimed Mrs. Burt, in a high key. "Better attend to her children. She's as old as I am."

"As young as you are, my dear," said Burt, suavely. "But" (in his softest voice), "do women never learn any thing after they are thirty?"

"A woman ought to be ashamed of learning anything after she is thirty," asserted Mrs. Burt, dogmatically.

Burt bowed, and resumed his topic. For his part, he thought nothing looked better in a house or gave it more refinement than a piano, as soon as a man could afford it. A house always looked lost without one, to him. Her own sister's husband had been in with the idea of buying a piano for his girls.

Mrs. Burt heard, and reflected. If Sophia was going to get her girls a piano, it was a step ahead which no younger sister, who was held not to have improved the family standing by marrying a farmer, ought to be encouraged in. What did Sophia want with a piano, when she, whose husband was able to buy hers up, farm and mortgages, owned a parlor without one? Still, pianos cost lots of money, and Sophia would be out of pocket so much. There was some comfort in that. She had a great deal better put it in town lots.

Burt cautiously added that the Lees were changing their piano for an upright one. A piano had been offered him in exchange for lots, but he had refused. "We shall never have any use for a piano."

Mrs. Burt thought he need not have decided without letting her know about it.

"A piano!" said Emeline, softly, with hands clasped and lips parted, a color and light rising in her face such as Burt had never seen there before.

"I should think you might have let me know about it," repeated his wife, "before you refused such an offer as that."

"What can we possibly want with a piano — plain people like us?" asked Mr. Burt, carelessly.

Mrs. Burt was roused. She considered she had as good a right to have things as anybody, and she wasn't going to sing second to anybody in that town, if she knew it. She might want a piano herself before she came to die.

"When you do," said her husband, scoffingly, "you shall have one."

Mrs. Burt, being thus judiciously approached, was taken with the idea of having a piano of her own. As she observed, meditatively, nothing furnished a room so much as a piano and a handsome stool. Was he *sure* Sophia was going to get a piano?

So it happened, that, after Mrs. Burt had argued the point for a week, Mr. Burt, out of pure desire to please her whims, found a piano, which a friend of his in Chicago, breaking up housekeeping, wanted stored; and Burt, though he thought it would take up a great deal of room in the parlor, was willing to take it, if she was sure it was what she wanted.

Mrs. Burt, overjoyed to furnish her parlor at so slight expense, wanted that piano brought right home, for fear somebody might get it who was willing to pay for it. And Mr. Burt carried out his own idea in his own house, and his wife had not the least suspicion of it.

The first piano! It brought a flow of delight to Burt's musings, which he was careful to mention to no one. It was the earnest of ease and refinement which were to follow. He said to himself, that he did not mean to be satisfied with a piano. He would have pictures and books and fine furniture, like other men; and then —

But there was nobody to play on the new toy. Mrs. Burt sat down before her own piano, and rambled her hands over the keys; but it did not sound talented, as she said. Burt tried to pick out " Hail Columbia " with one finger; but the result was melancholy. Behind them stood Emeline, her eyes like stars.

" Em," said Burt, peremptorily, " sit down, and see what you can make of it."

She sat down like a born musician, and her fingers trembled with delight as they touched the keys. " I can't do any thing," she said ; " but I believe I could play ' Bonnie Doon ' if I should try fifteen minutes."

" Try, then," said Mrs. Burt, impatient to hear music from her own piano. " Here, Burt, let's leave her alone awhile, and see if she can't play for us."

The pair withdrew, and Emeline felt as if the gates of bliss were opened to her. The halting, unaccustomed touch of the keys made such music to her ears as a mother finds in the cry of her first-born. Music was born in her, the kind that comes by ear and instinct; and she was hunting the melody, overjoyed when she found the right notes, and almost wild with joy when she fairly got them under her hand. She went over and over the melody again. It was only the air with a simple bass, and the fingering went wild; but she struck the notes with fearless touch, and was sitting rapt in her own music, and singing like a bird when Burt opened the door half an hour later. He came softly and stood behind her, without disturbing her.

"You seemed pleased with the piano," he said, at last.

She turned a face alive and glowing with happiness. "It's heaven!" she breathed, in a voice that echoed hidden music.

"Emeline, I didn't know you had such a love for music, though I thought you looked as if you loved it. I was not mistaken, it seems."

"Doesn't music rest you, sir? A book or a song always makes me feel as fresh as sleep."

"Emeline," said her employer, dropping into a chair with an expression of pleasant relief which she had never seen him wear before, "do you always mean to be a housekeeper, and spend your time in work that isn't the thing for you, when you might do so much better? I'm not speaking for my own interest, Emeline; for we could never have any one to take your place. But don't you want something better for yourself?"

"Yes, sir. I want it and mean to have it."

This was said with such firmness and simplicity as made Burt smile. In talking with this girl, his face grew softer and wore a friendlier look than usual on that visage of calm politeness.

"Indeed! You have your plans made up. May I ask how you intend to carry them out? You might find help where you least expect it."

"Only to work and make the best of my chances," was said, with a regretful cast of countenance, as if chances lessened when counted up.

Burt took a turn or two down the room, his hands behind him. Emeline sat with her eyes on her knitting, and he saw keen regret and patient longing shadowed on her face. She was so sensible, so brave, so gentle, he half forgot how pretty she was, in the genuine homage a man pays to womanly worth.

"Suppose you had a chance to go to boarding-school for two or three years, and fit yourself for something better than housework. There are such chances, you know, Emeline. What would you say if a friend could be found — a lady friend, perhaps — who would advance the money, and let you pay it when you came to making money? Tell me seriously."

The color grew under his gaze. The very idea brought such light and gladness that it did not seem the same face. The light faded, however, and left only the longing, as she said: "I don't know any thing else in the world I could wish for myself. But if there were such a chance, it wouldn't do for me to take it. It would be robbing the folks at home of all I might make while I was studying. If it wasn't for that, I should have been at school long ago."

"You are not in earnest, Em, in throwing away such a chance?" Burt spoke quickly.

"If my brother was old enough to do any thing for mother, I could go. But I can't think of leaving her alone," was the steady answer.

To all his pointed arguments, she gave but the one return. Her slender earnings were needed now at home, and after awhile it might be too late to help her mother.

"I should feel all the while I was taking my pleasure in studying, and being where it was nice to be, as if the rest were faring hard when I might have helped them. By and by I shall be able to study, when Tommy is old enough to work."

"Don't you ever expect to get married?" asked Burt, bluntly. "You don't seem to think of that way out of your troubles."

She flushed burning red an instant, but her steady voice was unchanged, as she said : "Yes, I suppose a good many girls would look to that. But I can't. I shouldn't want to marry the kind of man who would take me as I am; for he would have to make more allowance for me than would suit me."

"You should not talk so, Emeline," Burt interposed. "Are you sure that there are not men who would give up friends, position, and credit, and be proud to call you their own, just as you are? I tremble for fear some one utterly unworthy of you may carry you off before you know your own worth. You are too good for any one in New Canton."

He spoke with warmth, and there was a tone in his voice to which it was difficult to hear unmoved, from a man so calm and undemonstrative. Once more Emeline recognized the friendliness, the care, which had made the wedding party so pleasant for her. She was grateful for it; she warmed again in the sunbeam of unselfish interest, unlike the exacting heats of her April love. Never is friendship so welcome as when opposed to the aggressive, if infatuating, fervors of love. Then, his opinion was a sweet, sweet prophecy that the love she knew best might be more than a passing flame. She smiled at Burt the reflection of the joyous hopes that filled her heart. She hardly knew him, the face before her was so open and kind. In the blending of entire friendliness, discernment, and will the face before her was attracting, almost handsome.

He came up to her, and stood over her, as she sat. "You are a good girl, Emeline," he said, gently, and in a voice much moved. "I can't advise you to do any other way than you have chosen. I have only one thing to say — make the best of whatever opportunities there are in my house. I wish to heaven there were more to offer you. You *shall* have what you desire; but keep your intentions to yourself. Those about you would call them high-flown, and you would get no help anyhow. You will not speak of this on my part; for I have no such offers to make to any one else, and it would be thought that I might have exerted myself elsewhere."

"I should like to tell Mrs. Burt," said Emeline, gratefully. "I could thank her better than I can you."

"It would hardly be worth while," he said, gayly. "I do not care to have any one know that I ever get kind notions into my head, — it isn't good for a business man, — and you will hurt my feelings, Emeline, if you speak of this to a single soul. I do not love to have my left hand know what my right hand doeth. I am only a hard business man, and I don't believe in going about trying to pick up people's troubles for them. There is only one creature in the world worth helping, and I shall help her. Tell Mrs. Burt I shall not be home till late, and she need not sit up for me."

He went into the entry to the hat-rack, and Emeline thought him gone. She leaned back in Mrs. Burt's best easy-chair, and gave herself up to delicious dreams. He looked in the half-open door, as he passed, and the sight appeared too attractive to leave. He came back, his hat in hand.

"You look as if you belonged in this parlor, Emeline. You would be all that a man wished to make his home. I wish you *did* belong here. I—"

He waited a moment, words struggling with his breath. Emeline looked up.

"You were going to say something to me?"

"Take care of yourself, Emeline. Hold yourself high. Do all you can to fit yourself for the best position the world can offer you. It will be yours if you will take it. Only believe in it, and wait."

He stood once more close to her. Something indefinably suggested to Emeline that he was going to kiss her; but his glance was cool, as she looked up. He shook hands with her, and parted.

Emeline stood looking in the mirror in her low-roofed chamber that night, watching the warm-cheeked, rich-tressed image that met her eye. It was beautiful, gentle, even refined. She turned away with a little cry. "My dear, dear, dear! I shall be fit to be even yours!" was what she said in her heart.

CHAPTER XXIII.

THE CONSERVATIVES BEGIN TO BELIEVE IN NEW CANTON.

MR. GARDINER, Senior, had always believed in New Canton as much as Mr. Gardiner, Junior, had disbelieved in it. Whenever he had visited Jim's office and found lines derogatory of the great Burt on his desk, he had always called the young man to account, as one who was doing his best to depreciate and belittle the father of the greatest enterprise that the human mind had ever conceived.

There was no reason why Mr. Gardiner should not continue to take an interest in and have a full belief in the land company and the savings-bank; for he was one of the sponsors of the first, and the second was simply the outgrowth of it. He was committed to the whole scheme; and, no matter what others thought of it, he was bound, by interest, to stand by it.

But, to the surprise of Mr. Burt himself and Col. Peppernell, others, who had pooh-poohed the enterprise from the beginning, began to talk of the progress of the city, and to assert that it had a most solid and secure foundation. These were men who did not leave their own houses, and build new ones, or make additions, or put on wooden cornices, or plant plaster statuary in their front yards. They were men of the the class, who, in the Presbyterian Church, sustained Parson Latimer and opposed the organ, the extension, and the new minister; and the Methodists who voted Nay on all propositions to rebuild the church, and desired to be kept as a circuit for awhile longer. And the wives of these men still wore sun-bonnets, and did not insist upon carriages or put on any style whatever.

Peppernell rushed into the office one day in a glow of delight, and bursting with something too good to keep to himself. Good news was the only thing he ever shared with anybody.

"Burt, Masten — old Sam Masten — and Curry and Peterson have all bought property this morning of me. They have contracted for it, and will be in in an hour or two to have the deeds made."

Mr. Burt did not look pleased.

"And, what is better, they are talking New Canton just as lively as they used to abuse it; and they are as solid converts as we could want."

Mr. Burt still looked gloomy.

"Why, the news don't seem to please you! What would please you this morning?"

"Colonel, what do they pay in?"

"Why, our certificates, of course. They have stacks of 'em. I'm going out to help 'em talk. They are doing us a world of good."

"What have they contracted for?"

"Masten takes the Pollock Farm, at $100 an acre; Curry, the Bigler Farm; and Peterson, the Smith Place. They went dog cheap; but, as they only stand us in $50 an acre, I thought it better to take their offer and get their influence than to let 'em go. But I want to see 'em. They're in front of the post-office now."

And the enthusiastic Colonel scurried out to join the party that were talking so much of New Canton, and all recent converts.

Mr. Burt looked troubled. He sat for some minutes with his head buried in his hands, and, rising in a sort of wearied way, occupied an hour or more making figures. Finally, he put on his hat, and went out.

These were the thoughts that passed through the mind of Mr. Burt: This land was worth, a year ago, $20 an acre; and, but for the land company's work, it would be worth only that to-day. And yet three of the most conservative unbelievers in the town have paid $100 an acre for it. Not one of them believed it worth more than $20. Why had they done it? He did not believe, with Peppernell, that they were converts to the future of New Canton; he looked for their motive from another point of view. They had paid for this ground in certificates; and these certificates they had got, partly in the way of business and partly by the sale of ground when the flow of certificates was limited and there were fewer in circulation. For those they had taken for their wares, they sold goods at an advance of two to three hundred per cent., so that they could almost afford to pay four prices for land, and come out even; and those they had taken for land, of course they could afford to pay for land.

The point at which Mr. Burt took alarm was, that he saw in this movement a disposition on the part of these men to "unload," and get out from under the crash they saw was certain. Suppose others should do the same?

But Mr. Burt was a man not liable to be cast down. He joined Peppernell, and so managed the conversation, that the recent converts not only endorsed all that he had ever said of New Canton, but a great deal more; and he made them say it so that it was heard of men. They were harnessed to Mr. Burt's chariot, and they pulled as advantageously for him as though they had been in the team originally.

But Mr. Burt took his hint. He was a quick observer of indications in the financial sky, and he felt that his time had come to act.

He took a sudden fancy for horses; and, as he bought all he could exchange real estate for, it was noised abroad that he had a large contract for a Chicago dealer. The warehouse offered a still higher price for wheat; and the farmer, who sold his crop and got out without making an investment in real estate, had to run a very close gauntlet between Burt and Peppernell. And, no matter what kind of property is was that could be turned or twisted into honest money, Burt and Peppernell took it in exchange for land or the certificates.

It afforded Mr. Burt exquisite satisfaction to sell Masten a few lots, although he took his pay in refuse goods; and it was a glad day for him when he sold Curry a twenty-acre piece for a pair of very poor horses, which brought him only $150 in Chicago.

The indefatigable man did not confine his work to mere retail operations at home. There was not enough for him to do at home; for sellers were larger in number than the buyers. Everybody had land to sell, and the competition was too sharp. Besides, he did not want to break the market by entering into competition with his own neighbors. So, he made frequent visits to Chicago and Peoria and everywhere else; and whatever he could trade New Canton real estate for, he traded it. Western lands, railroad bonds, stocks of old goods were rather good property; and he was not above wagons, harness, guns, and watches, provided he got them in large enough lots and convenient to an auction store, where, without his appearing in it, they could be turned into cash. The price actually received was not a matter of moment. In the registered deeds, the consideration could be put at any thing that was deemed advisable.

The "Forum" and "Sentinel" were impelled to redouble their energies.

"On the occasion of a recent visit to the metropolis" (the editor had taken advantage of a pass obtained by two years of solicitation, and had been to New York just once in his life), "we met and conversed with both capitalists and merchants. The capitalist was eager to aid us. The merchant shivered whenever the name of New Canton was pronounced; that is, such as were intelligent and knew the progress of events. 'Another jobbing center,' they said. 'Another vast distributing point to cut our trade.' Time will bring it all about. The streets of New York may not grow grass; but what is now prairie about New Canton will be crowded with the busy marts of trade, and the rumble of vehicles will be heard where now the frog's melodious croak alone disturbs the stillness."

From the "Forum of the People."

"The uneasiness of the merchants of New York, at the development of Western trading points, strikes us as absurd; though it is, we are bound to say, an injury to us, inasmuch as it discourages investors. The jealousy manifested toward New Canton, in those cities, shows a short-sightedness, to say nothing of ignorance of the condition of the country, that astonishes us. Do not these men know that it is impossible that one city on the eastern coast shall forever be the distributing point for the continent? Do they suppose the boundless West, with all its wealth and all its strength, will forever depend upon the already decrepit East for business facilities?

"The jealousy is unfounded; for the growth of the West is only equal to the growth of the East. New Canton, for instance, the wonderful development of which has excited feeling in New York, will do the trade, we will say, of an area of 500 miles which heretofore paid tribute to New York. This is a loss to New York. Very good. The Eastern States are increasing with the same rapidity; and, by the time New Canton is firmly fixed in its trade, the states of New York, New Jersey, Connecticut, and the eastern part of Pennsylvania will have increased in population enough to make up the loss; and the volume of trade of New York will remain the same, though it will be confined to narrower limits. Its trade, so far as jobbing goods, will be merely local.

"While, as a matter of course, New York will not increase with the rapidity of former years, it will hold its own. It will always be the great importing center, and Wall Street will always be the controlling money center — the most sanguine New Cantoner does not deny that; but, as for supplying the West, that day has gone by, and the number of New Yorkers who are investing in real estate here shows that the more far-seeing have already read the handwriting on the wall. Still, we do not have it in our heart to blame those who are making a struggle to retain their trade, even for a time. It is the selfishness which is the common fault of our weak humanity.

"New Canton has no jealousy of New York. It will always take pride in its greatness; for New.York and New Canton belong to one country and one people."

From the "Sentinel."

"Of all the enterprises inaugurated by that Napolean of finance, Mr. Chas. Burt, the savings-bank has, probably, been of the most benefit to New Canton. The last statement shows the deposits to have reached the enormous sum of $225,000, all of which is securely invested. The certificates of the company pass on our streets as money, and are preferred to Government issues. At least, we infer so; for we see more of them than any other kind. We take them on subscription for the "Sentinel;" and, by the way, a few of them would not come amiss this week. The character of the managers, the soundness of the institution, commends it to our people. Mr. Burt informs us, that he has lent money already this season to build one hundred and sixty dwellings, besides enough to finish eighty-one that were commenced. The bank does this, and secures itself by mortgage on the premises. It has accomplished a vast amount of good, and is just in the beginning of its career."

Mr. Burt was busier than ever, and his management of those who came to him was sublime. He had one party out in his carriage looking at lots.

"These are desirable lots, sir. The ground is perfectly level, and the soil is easily taken out for cellars. It is a mistake to get into clay; for it adds to the cost of digging, and you have trouble to get rid of the earth. Here, the ground you take out is just enough to make the proper elevation for your house; and your cellar, when walled, is just right. And the ground lies so prettily it will make a splendid site."

This lot was sold. The next party was taken to another part of the town.

"There are no better lots than these in the city. It costs a trifle more to dig in the clay; but it leaves a cellar so beautiful. Many of our people who have lots in the clay soil did not consider it worth while to put in cellar-walls at all. It may be a prejudice, but I prefer clay ground to build upon."

The lot was sold, and another party took the vacant place in the carriage.

"These lots, my dear sir, are very desirable. You may object to the depression" (they were as ugly holes as were ever seen), "but you see you have your cellar ready made. All you want is to put in your wall, and there you are. Besides, you avoid the expense of having your dirt removed, which, in a growing city like this, is considerable. Labor is high here, there is such a demand for it."

The next purchaser was taken to some very high lots, which came very near being hills, Nature having changed her mind just in time to save them.

"These are very desirable lots, sir, very. High and dry — no water in your cellars. Some people might suppose that the grading to the level of the street would be an objection, but it is quite a mistake. There is so much level land here that needs filling up, that thousands, sir, will be glad to take off the earth and all that they can get out of the cellar, for the sake of having it to fill with. It is an advantage, sir, which ought not to be overlooked."

And then to the bank of the stream with another party, where the rock showed itself.

"These lots are extremely desirable. The cost of blasting out the rock for cellars is something; but the stone is worth a great deal here, sir, where it is so scarce. That taken out to make a cellar will go a long way toward paying for a house. And then your cellar is always dry. It is a mistake to get into the loam or clay, away from the creek."

And so he went on, selling lots and putting out certificates industriously to whomsoever he could. But he was also equally industrious in getting together all the money possible that was not of the savings-bank kind.

CHAPTER XXIV.

HIGH SCANDAL IN NEW CANTON.

AS I have said before, one of the good old customs of New Canton was that of back-door visiting. The old settlers thought a great deal of neighboring, as they called it. To live next door, was either a bond of sacred intimacy or a cause of bitter feud. Not the least of its privileges was that of running in from two to twenty times a day, by the family entrance, without ceremony — a cosy, hearty custom. One of the conditions of neighboring was to have a gate cut through the line-fence, for these visits; and the paths through the gardens were kept in good repair. When a woman had a dress to rip, a shirt-bosom to refresh, or six yards to hem for pleating, she "threw something over her head," and wended her way through the plum-trees, past the rhubarb-border, the grape-vine trellis, and cistern, to the side door, appearing with work in her arms and the latest gossip on her tongue, — always welcome.

Burt, who was a quiet observer of human nature outside of business, was wont to say, in a purely meditative way, that more lies were brought in at the back doors of New Canton that all the men and women could carry out at the front. By this means, Mrs.

Pettit came to tell Mrs. Morse that her husband was suspected of going to New York with another woman, which Mrs. Pettit thought Mrs. Morse ought to know, making a pretty kettle of fish for Morse when he came home full of worry about the notes his partner failed to pay. Then, it came out, that Morse had been guilty of meeting an old schoolmate, who was going home sick to her brother's house, and had been man enough to show her a little attention. Morse experienced the full truth of the saying, that mud will stick. There were several good people in New Canton who could never be brought to believe that there wasn't something in the report; "for somebody had said so," with the beautiful credulity with which people assure you that a thing must be true, for they have seen it in a newspaper.

There was something ill in the wind for Emeline. The doctor's wife had it from her husband, who had heard it in the drug-store while he was putting up his own medicines behind the screen. Mrs. Long was sewing at the doctor's house, and mentioned it next day at Mrs. Eaton's, who told it in the presence of two or three callers, who made a wider round than usual to give the matter a good talking over. It was "Oh, dear!" It couldn't be true! and they should like to know what New Canton was coming to. And, when the first shock of surprise was over and they had taken breath, they found space to reflect that that girl had been getting ahead too fast and needed less notice. And there always was something they didn't just like about her, — something too original and independent for one in her position; though there were not wanting others, who never could see what people found in her out of the common — a girl James Gardiner had been able to lead about as he wanted, and, they hoped, left her owing much to his mercy.

How glad those well-to-do women were of a chance to flout at her. Not one of them but had her count of petty disgrace to answer for, if it had been known, — her stinginess and acted untruths, and stones thrown with deadly aim, though they never happened to do much hurt. Among those sober matrons, who walked looking askant at Emeline, there was not one in whose record would have read as well as the patient, ardent unselfishness of the girl, whose desire life was to be loved and to make those, whose sole hope and dependence she was, happy. Those women had been dutiful daughters, in their time, to fathers and mothers whose pride was in their children, who left them comfortable plenishings and creditable names and the memory of indulgence and fondness, which was something to blame for their complete absorption in themselves. They had been good wives? Yes, to men who spent their lives in toil to give them and their children sure and good livings and handsome dress and well-furnished houses to compare with their neighbors', and to make provision for them against time of need, — men whose names gave them shelter and credit, whose strength supplemented their weakness and peevishness, — men who not seldom looked from their work to ask what satisfaction there was in this thankless labor, — men who went to the lounging-places and hotels, for want of the companionship these model wives failed to provide for them. These women had had their returns for every pennyworth of help or duty they ever rendered in their lives; and not one of them was above stabbing another woman or woman's child, if it would enhance their own consequence.

Emeline was neither saint nor heroine; yet it could be said of her, that she never stepped on a worm or mangled a spider, and left it without killing it, because it was too much trouble to end the creature's agony. She never was known to slight a thing she had to do, — she never believed a scandal or repeated one maliciously; and it was a part of her instinct and belief, that, to see a chance to do a fellow creature good and not do it, was a crime to rise up against her in her own need. An odd notion, by the way, which, if it were carried out by each of us, would make this world a place worth living in without further ado. She was pitilessly just; for, with her, justice was akin to mercy, and, with its aid, she held there would be no need to call on mercy, whose name men like so much better. It would be ill, if, in her future, that clear vision was warped or any case set in false colors before her; for her hand would be as swift and steady in carrying out her right or her vengeance as ever it was to carry kindness. Nature had given her such hidden weapons as she puts into the hands of many creatures — wit, fearlessness and endurance, foresight, and memory for a favor or a wrong; while to these she added special gifts without which the others come to nothing, as we see every day, when the race is not to the swift, but to the slow and unbaffled; and the battle is not to the strong, who disdain to guard their own right, but to the determined will which never abandons an advantage of which it becomes possessed. This was the woman whom feminine New Canton meant to put out of the way with hairpins.

Miss Ritchie met Miss Garnett, on the way to her German lesson, primed with the latest news, and aching to dispense it. As it happened, Miss Garnett had the latest new novel, and Miss Ritchie wanted to read it. Edith Garnett would be delighted to let her have it as soon as Emeline Butterfield was through with it. Immediately, Miss Ritchie's air grew cautious and her face so delicately non-committal, as to convey to Miss Garnett that her friend's sensibilities retreated from the mention of Emeline. Ants talk with their feelers. It is by such slight signs that women read each others deepest feelings.

"Do you see much of that girl?" asked Miss Ritchie, significantly.

"She is as bright and sweet as she can be," was the ready answer. "I see all I can of her. What of it?"

"Nothing, if you like her."

"What is the matter?" demanded the girl, who detested side-firing.

"Nothing at all," was the truthful reply. "I didn't know you were on such good terms with her, or I should not have spoken so. Is your muslin apron done yet?"

"My apron is much obliged for your interest. You've said too much, Virginia, to turn me off like this, without telling exactly what you mean. I don't think it's any way to treat a friend. If you have any thing against Emeline, say so. I don't know much of her, but she seems a very pleasant, pretty girl."

"James Gardiner seems to think so, too," was the mysterious answer.

"Well, is there any harm in that? I don't know that is any thing against Emeline. There are plenty girls in town who wouldn't mind having the same thing said about them."

"I'm glad to see Miss Butterfield can find people to get up such an interest in her on short notice. She has the gift of manœuvring them into very ardent friends."

"I'm not ardent. You are always chaffing me about being ardent, because I stand by people when I don't know any thing against them. I can judge people as well as you do, and I don't believe in saying any thing against them on a dislike that isn't founded."

"Well," with a lofty air, "Edith, I know you consider me prejudiced; but I can't alter my likes and dislikes at a word, even from you. I don't wish to say any thing against this girl. I'd rather you would form your opinion for yourself, and not ask for my impressions. You may find something to like in her very much. I cannot. But I am singular in my preferences, and I want to know more about people before I take them up as New Canton was taking up that girl. She looks too sensational to suit me. I don't think any young lady would go walking with a young gentleman, and meet him constantly on the street and in the grove, unless she was very careless of her reputation or had none to lose. That's all."

"She's not a bad girl," flashed the warm-hearted defender. "Look in her face, and say that, if you can. Besides, Mrs. Burt wouldn't have her in the family if she was like that."

"Perhaps Mrs. Burt don't know the way the girl

carries on evenings. Jane Ashley says they have been seen ever so many times on the road to the lower grove; and Peppernell heard James make an appointment with her one Sunday, when she was going home from church. The Colonel heard him say, 'This afternoon, in the old place.' If he means well, why don't he go and see her at the house? Would you let a gentleman make appointments with you like that, and set the whole town talking about you?"

"I don't care! I can't believe it. I've never seen a thing wrong in her, and she can't be such a fool as to throw herself away like that. I won't believe it."

"I don't ask you to," was the dry answer. "I'm not trying to get you to believe it. I don't want to do the girl any harm. What is she to me? You talk as if I had some *spite* against her. I must say you might have some charity for your friends, as long as you have so much for girls nobody knows. All New Canton is talking about her. I hope it may prove groundless, and James turn out all right, for his mother's sake. But you know he has been very wild of late. I thought, since you had taken Emeline up so ardently, it was just to let you know how she stood. I should dreadfully hate to get myself talked about with her, if I were you."

The thistledown was floating that would catch in every corner and bear evil for Emeline. She, unconscious, was finding life a great deal too pleasant, in thoughtless rambles and endless satisfying talks with the handsome young lawyer, whose manner of late conveyed very strong signs of being in love with his pretty friend.

In love with her! Not possible! In all her wildest dreams of her girlhood, she had not looked for this. Some well-to-do man might in time fall in love with her and marry her, she was sure; for the seven-by-nine mirror did not hang in her room for nothing, and she knew that naturally curly hair, small hands and feet, and big black eyes had a value in the world. But that James Gardiner, who held himself at such a magnificent pitch, should come to her night after night, and walk with her, hold her hand in his, and adjust her shawl, and say his brightest things to her, was as if the sun and seven stars had been left her as a legacy. The half-story bedroom at Burt's was as full of happiness as it could hold; and she lived and walked in such a brightness that it seemed as if the rest must see it and find out her secret. She went home after those precious walks thrilling with a nameless great delight, that kept her healthy eyes open till the moon looked in the southern window.

At first, there was no room in Emeline's heart for any thing but adoration of the man her beauty had won to her side. It was so strange to be loved, to be met with glad glances and the warmest, softest words. She had a sense of being contented and protected, as a young bird in the nest which its mother defends with her fierce, beating wings. She never thought that he was the banker's son, and she the poorest woman belonging to the lowest family in the county. It seemed right that he should love whom he chose; and, as he would lower himself willingly, it followed that she was as good as himself. Else how could there be love between them? She thought no further. The hunger of the soul for love goes so far beyond that of the body or of pride that it is long before either wakes if the divine craving is satisfied. Emeline was content to be loved. She could have walked all her life in her humble path, in the shadow of this love, and never asked for more. The cup of unselfish love is filled by a divine hand, and whosoever tastes of it shall thirst for nought besides.

How was it with James? A young man taught by the circle he moved in to think the wearing of good clothes and leading an agreeable life indispensable conditions of existence, he was naturally slower in forgetting his code. But he could as well try to be insensible to attar of roses as deny his heart to Emeline. He made few words of love suffice, but he could not deny himself its signs.

The summer fled too fast for one so happy. Emeline laughed at her past life of privation, the present was so rich in attention and love. She counted herself, and many others counted her, with her gifts and prospects, the most fortunate woman in New Canton. James had been her devoted companion those long, bright months, every hour that either could lawfully contrive to spend together. What strolls after dark down the mill-road, where the road led into the heart of the woods, and the stump under the landmark oak grew their regular resting-place, and two figures in light summer dresses flitted there every fair night. When Mrs. Burt was away, what earthly wrong was there in James making his appearance, book in hand, to sit with Emeline, while her swift fingers flew over the sewing. Mrs. Burt always knew when Emeline had company by the extra work she finished; and, finding her own account good in the matter, concluded, if Emeline chose to let Jim Gardiner come fooling round her, *she* had no cause to interfere. So, allowed to associate freely with her, he taught the girl unconsciously the refinement of thought and manner she was better fitted for by Nature than himself, a grace which she returned by as much loyalty as a woman could give to a man.

The year had taken its downward dip to autumn; but the days were still sunny and the wood-seat a pleasant tryst. Unconscious of the ill breath busy with her name, Emeline made ready one evening to meet her lover. The weariness of the brisk day's work left her healthy young frame at thought of his handsome figure, coming through the trees between her and the sunset. Out of her toiling in other people's houses and sitting in the lowest place at their tables, from her poor, ill-kept home, she was coming to love and honor. A man as brave to look at, and standing as well with his fellows as one could find in a summer day had chosen her and waited for her; and she would see him to-night, and his deep eyes would dwell on hers in less than an hour. She felt them now, so kind, so trusty, a heaven of ardent, enduring love to the hard-worked woman, who in all her life had known few such looks and longed for them with such a mortal hunger. How good she could be to him — better than ever woman had been to man since streams ran under the sky of Illinois; and unawares she trembled to think what a hold he had upon her.

All was bliss and tender, shaken hope in that low chamber under the roof at Burt's. The small mirror showed a face lovely in its flushing anticipation, set free from the composure in her position. There was room, now that she was by herself, for pride and pleasure in herself and the little nice touches she gave her toilet. Never was gay gingham so fresh and perfect as that she slipped on now, holding her breath as she drew it over her glossy curls, for fear it should disturb their ruffled gloss and glory. Her face smiled beautiful as Egeria looking up from a fern-shaped spring in the depths of a wood, — a face that small children fell passionately in love with and cried for, — a face of warmth and mirth and quickness, with its creamy skin under the shining, shadow-haunted disorder of her hair. She was the happiest creature in town as she crossed the little bridge and went down the road in the edge of the wood. The marshy flats were deep pile of velvet in greenest glow under the light that momently left it. Blue eyes of asters looked up from the tawny grass by the roadside; and a warm, brooding breath of softly fading things was abroad, pierced with the odor of late mint steeped in the sun. She had only time to snatch a tuft of blossoms as she went, and thrust them in her hair; for was she not going to see her lover, and could flowers make her wait on the way to him?

A shadow that was not of tree-trunks fell behind the screen of a birch, and she grew glad beyond speaking. He was looking away, moving restlessly, till at her step his face brightened kindly, and her two hands were in his.

"Why didn't you come sooner? Wouldn't the old cat let you?"

By such names Mr. James used to speak of Mrs. Burt.

"Would you want me here before you? No, she

didn't keep me. She's comfortable in vinegar and brown paper for the night, and won't think of any thing but the bad taste in her mouth for three days."

"How does Burt live with such an apothecary's pet? I smell rhubarb and senna two blocks off, when the wind is her way. How do you like being clerk in that drug-shop? I won't have you scented with her herbs; but you are sweet as a rose anyhow. Haven't you any thing pleasant to say to a fellow who's been half an hour looking for you?"

"Then I haven't been making myself agreeable to you? Why don't you set the example? Perhaps you don't know when you are well treated."

"I should never find you any thing but pleasant," his voice sinking to a delicious cadence. "My poor little, dear little girl. She doesn't like to have me call her poor even in petting her."

"I'm rather tired of being called poor, seeing I've been used to it all my life. I'd rather hear something else from you."

"Proud thing! I don't blame you. Well, there's one man to whom it don't make a straw's difference whether you have a dollar to your name or own all the scrip in the New Canton Savings-bank. How nicely you do cling to a person. Don't you want to put your head where it was the other night — on my shoulder? It rests me to hold it there. I've got the sweetest girl in the country here, just as I like to have her. Now talk to me."

"There is too much to say for talk."

"Then tell it some other way. Shall I say this, and this, — that you are the only girl I care to kiss alive, and I wouldn't take another world for her? You beauty!" (21)

"You don't mean me. You're thinking of some other girl."

"I never think of any girl but you. I don't want to see any girl but you. You are square and kind. Kiss me, pet, and help me to forget."

She was close within his arms, and his face was away from her; but a flood of pity came at his tone of hurt pride and mockery at the old remembrances. It was instinct with her to try to cheer him by every woman's wile; and in such art she was, unfortunately, skilled by Nature.

She was thinking of James, and feeling as if she would give her life to win him from his sorrow. He was hers to comfort for an hour, and he had given her liberty to caress him. She wound her arms about him, as she would around a hurt child, rocking him gently, touching his face here and there with the tenderest lips. "They should not use you so," she said to herself, in her deep tone of affection. "How could they? It never shall be again — never again! How *could* anybody turn against you when you had loved them?"

"You know, everybody knows about town, that I was to marry Mary Lewis; but her old mother broke it off. The girl I had loved as long as I could remember," he added, with pardonable embellishment; for, by long pondering, his attachment to Mary Lewis seemed to cover his whole life.

"Yes, I heard of it," she said, softly. "And I felt awfully sorry for you at the time."

"I suppose so," he said, with some of the old bitterness. "Everybody in town knew it, high and low. It's a comfort to know you've been in the town's mouth for six months."

"You mustn't mind it," Emeline said, gently. "Everybody said you had been badly used, and you lost a bad mother-in-law, at least. How could any woman make a girl leave you when she was promised to you?"

"You will be doing it some day. You'll see some other man you like better, and run off with him, and leave me to find it out," he said, looking at the first star just over her curls, as he sat enjoying very much the innocent, pitying tenderness she gave him. His idle speech touched her more than he could have believed. She put his arms away, and looked into his face with eyes of such intensity, that, whenever he thought of that moment, he seemed to see them before him.

"I shall never care for anybody as I have cared for you. I do not know how to go back on a friend; and, if you ever teach me to forget you, it will be better for me that I had never been born."

"When I lose you, the best, truest friend a man ever found in a woman," he said, seriously, sobered by her earnestness, "it may be as well for me that I had never lived."

"Come, Emeline," he said, a moment after, to regain the sportiveness they had lost, "this is quite like lovers. We agreed once to be nothing but good friends; but I don't know but we will end in love, spite of ourselves."

"We promised never to talk love to each other," she said, simply and seriously, "and I shall keep my word. I shall never fall in love with you; but I shall never cease to love you. It is your doing."

"Emeline, you are the coolest girl! Well, I don't

see any use in freezing a fellow with speeches that sound like so much and mean so little. Would you have the goodness to tell me what I am to you? Am I your friend or your lover or brother? Speak frankly, for once."

"Neither lover nor brother," she said, turning her eyes large and clear upon him, too true, too full of feeling to shrink. Then, with voice and gesture of incomparable tenderness and sincerity, "You are all I have in the world."

"Emeline, I will be all the world to you," he declared, carried out of himself with this sweet, ardent attachment.

Heaven help her!

CHAPTER XXV.

NEW CANTON ENTERS ON A HIGHER PLANE.

THE young ladies of New Canton had long been of the opinion that the place was dreadfully behind the times and hopelessly given over to money-grubbing. Young ladies everywhere, having neither occupation nor experience to prevent their forming opinions on every subject under the sun, stand ready to give the world the benefit of their accumulated wisdom, and to take its administration bodily on their own shoulders, and usher in a premature millennium at once. In New Canton they contented themselves with lamenting the dearth of public spirit and the sad fact, that their fathers and brothers had time to think of nothing but making money. They forget, that, till the money-making mania seized the place, there was very little means or chance for gratifying any one's tastes.

With the new order, new ambitions seized its inhabitants.

In old times, the men contented themselves with paying their taxes regularly, and the minister when it came convenient, and allowing their wives to get three or four dollars out of their pockets at a church fair once a year. As for home adornment, they put a new picket in the fence when it was needed; and, if they had a spare dollar when a fine-art peddler came round, indulged their women-folk with a big chromo text, a wall-pocket with a picture let in the front, or a similar article of "bigotry and virtue." But, when the dollars came to have company and the wives to know of it, naturally there was an easier state of living.

First came the carriage mania. Old Simon Wood, who lived a mile and a half out of town and had been saving for the purpose half a dozen years, bought a carriage for his wife to ride to meeting in; and its glossy sides and silver mountings, as he drove about town, were quite conspicuous. Next week, Sherwin, the express-agent; Dillingham, the shoe-man; and, of course, Fitzhugh, whose brother had just died and left him three hundred dollars, which he was aching to spend, were about town asking the prices of family carriages, — nothing high-priced, you know, but something substantial, that would look stylish enough to suit the times, — a sort of carriage a man would get his money out of. And, as that phrase included many specifications that agree in all respects with the ideas of buyers of family carriages, they are commended to the notice of the trade. They wanted a carriage that you could drive with one horse or two, with seats enough for the whole family and the mother-in-law, and one that a man could drive round in alone, without looking lost in it, — a carriage with top to let down and sides to roll up, — an open carriage for Fourth of July and a close carriage at Thanksgiving; low enough for the wife to get in easy, and high enough to look stylish when her husband drove alone, and genteel when the oldest son wanted to take his "girl" in it to county fair, — the ideal country carriage, which is expected to have as many excellencies as a country minister, to cost as little and last almost as long. When Fitzhugh and the rest heard the price of a new carriage of the very best description, of course came the hesitating inquiry what a second-hand one could be had for — one in first-rate order, that looked as well as ever, — a second-hand one that hadn't been used, that didn't cost more than a quarter as much as at first, and could be bought on a man's note, with two years or so to pay it in.

Probably, the wise carriage dealer had the exact model of that highly-desirable class of vehicle within his reach; for, in six weeks from the day old Simon Wood first drove down to the post-office with his shining bays and glossy carriage, not less than thirteen new carriages, buggies, and phaetons made their appearance in the streets. Those who had them to sell were ready to dispose of them on credit, as the only way of selling them at all; and a good many notes for six and ten months were in shrewd hands before the month was out.

The march of improvement was on foot. Burt told his wife and Emeline, one night when he came home, that neither could guess the latest addition to the list of gentry in town. Mrs. Burt wanted to know, in her matter-of-fact way, if Mrs. Paddleford had a baby.

Burt hoped not, if the child would ever have to live to know its father, which his wife thought a shockingly-unnatural speech.

"Has Mrs. Fitzhugh sent out cards for a party?" asked Emeline.

"No, nor Black Moses, either," Burt said; "but the Symmeses were building a new house."

"Why, it was only last winter Caroline Symmes wanted to do over your shirts to pay for the old rocking-chair for her mother; and Malinda Symmes took care of Sophia when she had that run of typhoid, and she was as glad as could be of one of Sophia's black dresses to make over for herself. Wore it to meeting Communion Sunday; for I saw it on her, at the altar," concluded Mrs. Burt, with this interesting bit of contemporaneous history.

"How ever such folks have the presumption to think of living in a good house passes me," said Burt, in one of those dry, matter-of-fact tones which his wife never suspected were not entirely in earnest.

"Well, I don't know but they may have as good a right to it, if they've earnt it," she said, in a calm, judicial tone. "They came of a good family — cousins of ex-Governor Symmes, out in New York State, brought up, and went to the same school after he left it."

"His leavings in the way of education were good enough for any of his relations, I suppose," said Burt, reflectively.

"I hope so, Mr. Burt," said his wife, with emphasis. "Of course, these Symmeses are not to be compared with the higher branch of the family; but I don't think it can be called presumption if they have been prospered according to their deserts."

"Meaning the deserts of their family," said Burt, piously. "Emeline, when are you going to put up your house, with a bay-window and a Mansard?"

"When I find my fortune in a hollow tree," said Emeline, lightly.

"Emeline has too much sense to have notions put

into her her head. She knows she comes of a different family, and her expectations are different."

Nobody but Mrs. Burt could make this pharisaic little speech. Burt looked at Emeline, apprehensive how the girl would take this. Apparently, the delicate and kindly nature of the remark had not reached her; for the smile on her face was perfect. No angry flame dyed her cheek; but a soft streak of rose shone through its whiteness, which perhaps was clearer than usual. Burt thought he had never seen her look better.

"You are right, Mrs. Burt," she said, with a quiet voice, which made itself heard and felt distinctly. "My expectations are wholly different from any thing in New Canton."

Mrs. Burt heard the humility of the speech, and approved.

"You were made for other things," Burt took up the parable. "Fix your mind on things outside of New Canton, Emeline. Keep to your own sphere."

"Burt's teaching that girl her proper place," thought Mrs. Burt, as she heard it. "It takes him to do it as it ought to be done."

But it was a fact, that the Symmeses, who had done odd jobs of carpentering and mending for the neighborhood, while the women had taken in sewing and gone out nursing, for years, had not saved and slaved for nothing. They had lived in a small way, and eaten mush and molasses for dinner many a time that nobody knew of; but they never forgot that they belonged to an old family. So, the one-story cottage, with its three rooms, was raised, and a front added, with bay-windows and a porch as fine as a child's skirt, with wooden frilling and openwork.

Old Browne, of Browne & Chapman, who had sold calicoes at three hundred per cent. profit most of his life, felt the time had come for him to let his neighbors see what he could afford. His house had the roof raised and plate-glass windows put in, besides two verandas and a Mansard, which, as nothing could be seen from where Browne's house stood, was considered a highly appropriate mark of taste.

Mrs. Fitzhugh was taken with dire heart-burnings when she saw the tower going up, and made disparaging allusions to the way Browne's calicoes ran in the wash, for three weeks.

The Lymans, Hartford people and connections of a celebrated missionary, felt that it would hardly credit the culture of New England if they did not join in the general renovation. In their improvements, they showed the calm correctness of people who received their ideas on taste, as on morals, politics, and education, at second hand from the very best society. No white houses with mahogany-colored doors for them. The house was painted a chocolate color, with bilious trimmings; and rustic seats, of the heaviest and most uncomfortable pattern, were placed in the dooryard, and remained there sacrifices to the duty of ornament; for nobody was ever known to sit in them, there being a current impression in New Canton, that sitting out of doors was showing off, and was immoral, and had a tendency to rheumatism at the same time.

The building fever set in in earnest. Simon Orr painted his whole house the most brilliant white, and the blinds Paris green, with cornice of the most elaborate pattern in the carpenter's book. Bliss, the lawyer, added a wing to his brick house, put up a summer-house, and laid out a garden with white iron urns and two rustic seats, and hung the canary out sunny days, to look ornamental. Mr. Cornelius's daughter gave him no rest till they had something to distinguish their place too ; and the comfortable two-story house had its bay-window added, to be kept hermetically sealed the year round, and an octagon porch, which Mrs. Cornelius found convenient to stand umbrellas in, wet days, to let them drip. In the poorest yard were to be seen attempts at decoration and improvement, such as trunks of cherry-trees sawed down and surmounted with tin pans of money-plant, or wandering-Jew as the imaginative called it; or else heaps of stones piled in the front yard, crowned with a cracked tureen from which straggled a vine somebody was coaxing to run over the rockwork. One of these heaps was quite a success in its way; for the loyal owner had trained a periwinkle over it, and kept a plaster bust of Lincoln on the top in the rain and sun. Such ornaments as tombstones, which nobody found time to put up, no longer lurked about front gates ; and it was considered very ungenteel to hang the blankets to air in sight of the sitting-room windows, as formerly.

Crockford, a successful speculator, projected a house, which was so magnificent that it was considered worthy of special mention in the " Forum : " —

" The magnificent mansion to be erected this season by our public-spirited fellow-townsman, Gen. Crockford, is destined to be one of the leading landmarks of our town. It is designed to be one of the handsomest houses, not only in New Canton, but in the entire West; and no pains or expense will be spared to make it fully equal to all that the taste of the owner and the resources of the country could suggest. It will be fifty feet on side street and forty on the main front, with a carriage-house and other outbuildings to correspond. The design is from Wait & See, who are rapidly taking their place as the leading architects of this section. The wood for the fittings, which, in the parlors and guest-chamber, will be entirely of walnut, is furnished by Dale & Petitt from the choicest stock they have on hand; while the doorknobs, bolts, and hinges are from Davitt & Pettis. The furniture is, we learn, being made to order, from Gen. Crockford's own designs; and will do credit to his means and artistic tastes. All will join with us in taking a cordial interest and pride in the building, and wish the fortunate and worthy owner many years of happiness in his new domain."

But it must not be supposed the daring spirit of innovation stopped at the outside of houses. It would be interesting to trace the development of art in a town like New Canton. Of course, none of our present readers can remember when the cheap colored lithograph was the popular form of art, or I would take pleasure in recalling the pictures of the slim-waisted lady, in side curls and a violent red dress; likewise, the lover, in blue coat and high, rolling collar, with an eminent expression of virtue and vacuity on his countenance, posing for models of " Happy Love " or " The Engagement." " Innocence," in side curls, low, blue velvet bodice, and short sleeves, was a favorite exponent of that charming quality to rural minds. Another embodiment of the genteel and highly affecting was " Parting for the Wars," in which a gallant hero in a tightly-fitting, bright blue coat, with yellow epaulettes, and long white trowsers, very full and pleated on the hips, with flowing sash and full side whiskers and exceedingly thin and square-toed boots, was embraced by domestic passion in the shape of a female, who wore her features regular and her hair in sympathetic curls, while a smaller image of affection, on her precise model, was half way up his left leg.

These *naive* and touching scenes, which used to be gazed upon with wet eyes by appreciative owners, were in time displaced by the annual steel engraving distributed to patrons of the art association, by which the country-side became familiar with the " Signing of the Death-Warrant of Lady Jane Gray," " Irving and his Friends," " The Jolly Flat-Boatman," Peale's " Court of Death," and kindred engravings, whose worn-out plates could be purchased easily.

The success of the land company worked a change in these things. Prize chromos and art-association engravings receded year by year, and left their places of honor for the spare room upstairs and the family sitting-room, while the shilling lithograph fled to the hired girl's bedroom and the playloft over the stable. There yet remained two schools of taste in New Canton. One believed nothing was too good for it, and went in for the best that money could buy — people who furnished in solid mahogany and walnut burl, marble-topped tables and broadly gilt mirrors for their best rooms. Nothing in design could be too bold or too complicated for their notions. Their front doors were gay with inlayings in red, brown, and yellow woods, real and imitation; their parlor wall-paper could not be too satiny or too thickly figured with gilt, at a dollar and a half a roll; nor could the headboards of their beds be too high or too elaborately carved, nor the center-pieces of their ceilings too ornate in plaster mouldings. A firm article of their creed was a belief in cornices; and, accordingly, the tops of their walls were cornices of plaster, fit in design for nothing short of the house of a Roman patrician. Their windows were brave in gilt and walnut "cornishes," as they were popularly called; mirrors, dressing-bureaus, and washstands were top-heavy with cornices, if they had nothing else to boast. Next to this was their fondness of having their "monogram," as they called the single initial of their name, on every thing, from the sugar-bowl to the slop-pail, so that a man could have the pleasure of seeing a visible mark of his ownership on every appurtenance of his household. He impressed his individuality on his property, old Browne said, thinking it out over his fancy borders, as he hoed and clipped and watched his new geraniums and white oleanders — the very last thing in the way of flowers heard of in New Canton.

The younger people, who had been to Chicago and studied the frescoes of their hotels, thought the body-Brussels and gilt wall-paper out of date; and were all for "interiors," with the wall-paper dark red one-third of the way up and sage-green the rest, with heavy, kaleidoscopic friezes in wall-paper cut out by hand, which were counted preferable — why, they could not understand, save that flowers on wall-paper had gone out. Young Doctor Mills and the retired Professor, who had been abroad, because it was cheap, furnished their parlors and sitting-rooms in sad-colored stuffs, with walls in cheerful contrast of chocolate and dark red with black trimmings, which might have been acceptable perhaps at Pompeii with the sun blazing everywhere, but, in little sixteen-foot parlors under a doubtful Illinois sky, were gloomy and trying to all beholders. Browne saw, and approved his own parlor, gorgeous in bronze reps puffed with cherry satin, with a big-figured, scarlet carpet and walls paneled with strips of gilt paper, like a saloon, — where wax flower-baskets and Californian chromos, slim gilt and genteel stands with fire-gilt chains, made things cheerful for each other. The Doctor's rooms and the Professor's looked like a perpetual church fair, with their nonsense of brackets and fretwork and little pictures and preparations of nobody and nothing in particular, but were rather forlorn with their artistic walls; and their wives swept and dusted with their own hands, and sat down to making night-clothes for their little ones without the least feeling like high-toned matrons or having one particle of art feeling penetrate their souls.

The second class of householders in New Canton were people who alluded to themselves as being "obliged to economize," as if any thing else was ever expected of them. They desired to make up for less expense by more taste, preferred simplicity to so much show, and hoped they could teach their children to lead a truly refined and intellectual life in a home where something was thought of besides fashion and display. "Editha, don't rub your buttery fingers on the whatnot! nasty little thing!" this being the way in which Mrs. Myra Mold was heard to wind up on the subject.

Mrs. Mold was the saddle-and-harnessmaker's wife — a prosaic connection, as she felt in her soul, but not without pretensions of a finer kind. Her uncle was editor of a denominational weekly; and she was allowed charge of a home department, which she filled with compilations, aspirations, and receipts, receiving the title-dignity of editress, without pay, as her relative said, because it pleased her and it didn't hurt the paper any.

As she said, Mrs. Mold believed in simplicity above all things; and she was fond of writing articles on home adornment, where pictures, flowers, a simple carpet, furniture, and curtains made up a home where a man might turn from the allurements of brilliant parlors to find "true rest and larger life." She was also fond of protesting against women who devoted themselves to the care of the merely physical wants of their families, such as getting up good dinners for their husbands and children and seeing that their households were clad in scarlet, as praiseworthy women have done, from Sarah down. Mrs. Mold disdained the drudgery, which pulled her down from her more congenial flights; and her table always had poor bread, her washing was irregular, her mending of the sketchiest description; and her husband had long ago resigned himself to limp collars and rusty shirt-bosoms. She believed in "living on a higher plane" and devoting one's self to the worship of "the good, the true, the beautiful;" and the meat and the buttons might take care of themselves. She had already been successful enough in cultivating the spiritual in her children to cultivate one of them off the face of earth, the doctor said, for want of nourishing food; and she was troubled with a neuralgia, which was directly traceable to generations of failure in breadmaking and a systematic preference for cold, tough meat to fresh steak, as being easier to get up. She was a delicate looking woman, who was only hindered from being pretty by a slight pinch in her aristocratic nose, a suspicious thinness toward the end of her nostril, and a habit of keeping her upper lip screwed down tight. She was the devotee of simplicity and its upholder in New Canton. Her mantel and her lace curtains were decorated with the beauties of Nature, in the form of autumn leaves, dried and glazed, which rustled and rattled every time the door opened, came off inconveniently, and looked like the falling sickness at any time of the year. Her windows were unavailable for looking out of, being full of plants, that grew spindling and ran mostly to leaf. In the sunniest corner was a Boston rocker, scratched and battered; for Mrs. Mold was not one of those housekeepers who are so particular about a scratch or a flaw as to go about with a bottle of furniture polish hunting up flaws. There were flowers on a very dusty mantel, besides a clock that did not go. The table, spread with papers and magazines, was in one corner; but a table so filled may be rather an uninviting object, when the magazines are dog-eared and soiled to a degree and the papers show a liberal allowance of fly-specks. The photographs and water-colored prints would have been seen to better advantage if they were hung exactly, and if a dead fly or two had not caught himself to a spider-web under the glass. A handsomely bound album, with verdigris on the clasps, lay on the little scratched writing-desk, over which a hanging bookshelf was sadly out of line. "If I was to go hunting about for dust and spiders," candidly avowed Mrs. Mold, "or putting every thing to rights, I never should have any time to myself; and so I never see any thing that would offend me."

Mrs. Mold loved the same simplicity in all her arrangements. If she had a friend to see her and found it more pleasant to talk with her than to look into the kitchen, she would invite her half-famished guest to a cabbage soup, with boiled rice and a watermelon, as complacently as if her bill of fare was the most stimulating to appetite. She plumed herself on once regaling a whole teachers' institute on mush and milk for dinner, with the supplement of ripe currants, which gave a few of her amiable guests a severe pain — not in the brains. Her simplicity of housekeeping led friends to be shy of her hospitality; as steady-going people, not used to living on boiled rice and intellect, found their health and spirits depressed by a longer sojourn than the first day. One look at the simplicity of her spare chamber, with its "simple" white bed piled with brown cotton comforters, the "simple" washstand garnished with chipped china, and the "simple" paper spattered and torn, was enough to make one homesick. She lived in an ideal world, constantly posing for her memoirs; and the record of her life as it shaped itself, from her interior view, would have been one of devotion to the noblest aims and sympathies. Old ladies of experience, who had brought up families, shook their heads over Mrs. Mold's goings-on; and exemplary housekeepers openly declared her feather-witted.

It happened that Mrs. Mold was a near neighbor of Mrs. Burt, and undertook to cultivate that lady, whom she was forced to drop as hopelessly common and wanting in sympathy and taste — meaning Mrs. Mold's taste. To see Emeline once or twice under James Gardiner's escort was enough for the fertile brain of this matron. She at once set to work to find in Emeline an uncommon character, — " absolutely a genius, you may say," — and to develop an ardent interest in her. Mrs. Mold announced to herself that she meant to " take that Butterfield girl up," to " bring her out ; " as, positively, she was a girl to do any one credit. Benevolent, seraphic impulse ! The only trouble being that Emeline was supremely unconscious of the attempts of Mrs. Mold to " take her up," and refused to read " Bitter Sweet " with enthusiasm ; and, after one afternoon visit, during which she hemmed pillow-cases, while Mrs. Mold, with her hairpins sticking out of her head, read scraps from her intimate friends' letters, and rummaged out Goethe, Swedenborg, and Miss Alcott, and discussed her own next editorial in the most flattering, genteel, and affable manner, Emeline could never be induced to come into the room again while her airy neighbor was there. Of which due notice was taken by Mrs. Mold, in return for her condescension, the results of which may be traced in a succeeding chapter.

CHAPTER XXVI.

THE CLOUD BIGGER THAN A MAN'S HAND.

THE growing intimacy of James Gardiner with Emeline Butterfield was commented on in all the circles of New Canton. It was discussed in the parlors, in the vestibules of the various churches, over kitchen stoves, and across fences. All the middle-aged ladies who had marriageable daughters pronounced it a shame. Mrs. Fitzhugh remarked to her husband, who was a cobbler no longer, that, " when sich girls as old 'Liph Butterfield's daughter could take in sich a man as Jim Gardiner, there was a chance for Luella Adelia ; " and Tom Paddleford remarked, that it was what he had always supposed would happen. Gardiner was nothing but a low fellow, any way, — this with a wicked glance at his wife. Mrs. Lewis said to Mary, after Tom had left the room, that she might congratulate herself in having escaped wretchedness with such a man.

Col. Peppernell was especially severe upon Gardiner, and more so upon the poor girl. He had attempted the girl himself; and, while she had not given him the cut direct, she had so skillfully avoided him that he wisely forbore pursuit of her.

No such man is ever content to see another happy

in the possession of that which he desired himself and could not attain. He hated Emeline and he hated Gardiner, and was willing to make almost any sacrifice to put gall in their cup.

He was standing at the bar of the Grand Central, — he was standing there a great deal of late, — when James and Emeline passed, intent upon each other.

"Jim Gardiner and that Butterfield girl are very thick," observed Simpson.

"Yes," said Peppernell, glancing out of the window at the pair, a redness spreading over his face as he spoke; "it's too bad for a man like Jim Gardiner, with a 'spectable father and mother, and with all sorts of a futur' afore him, to let himself be so eggerejusly picked up. It's a shame, and his friends ought to interfere."

"What's the matter with the girl?"

"Matter! Great Heavens! She's old 'Liph Butterfield's daughter. Kin any thing good come out of sich a family as that? Take another, Simpson. This likker is better than we hev got here lately."

And, while the artistic barkeeper was pouring out and mixing "another," the old sinner went on.

"She came here, and went into the Continental as a waiter-girl. You kin imagine what kind of a show she had for gittin' out of that safe."

"You boarded there at that time," said Simpson, poking him knowingly in the ribs.

Peppernell smiled a smile indicating that he knew more than prudence would allow him to tell, which was more damaging to the girl than if he had said all his look implied, and continued: —

"Then, she went into a milliner's shop, — Mrs.

Crosby's. Somehow, she didn't stay there. Mrs. Crosby is very particular about her girls. She won't hev any immoral or loose women about her. Then, she got around Mrs. Burt, and hez bin there ever since. Of course, Burt — but I won't say any thing about him. Only the girl is smarter than chain-lightnin', and Burt is — take another, Simpson. It's a pleasure to drink De Forest's cocktails."

Simpson, the next time he saw the two together, winked very wisely, and remarked that some of Gardiner's friends ought to interfere and save him. It was a shame that a young man of so good a family should be seen every day with a girl old Peppernell had cast off, and who was so common that even Mrs. Crosby couldn't have her about, and who, if she didn't make trouble in Burt's family, would be because Mrs. Burt was too much taken up with her medicine to see what was plain to everybody else.

And, as Peppernell and Simpson spent much of their time in bar-rooms, the entrapping of Gardiner by the Butterfield became the usual topic in these resorts. As Gardiner, before he cut the places, had generally paid for all the regular bystanders, he had been a popular man in the bars; and every member of the drinking fraternity felt that the Butterfield girl had defrauded him.

Pilkin especially did not like it, and he was very free in expressing himself to that end. When once a man got to coming regularly to his bar, he felt that he had a mortgage on him for life, or, what was the same to him, as long as he had any money; and he took it as a personal affront if a victim spent any of his means in any other way. He missed the pleasant sound of Jim's voice as he asked "the house up to take suthin';" and he missed sadly the careless way with which Jim threw down his money and the utter abandon with which he swept the change into his pocket, without counting, which topers who knew Pilkin better were always careful to do.

"I like a customer who hez money and who hez been crossed in love," said the philosophical Pilkin. "What do they keer about a quarter more or less? When a feller's lost his gal, w'at's money to him — till he get's another one?"

And Pilkin considered himself defrauded because James quit drinking before he had squandered what he thought himself entitled to.

"The critter hez gone to work!" he exclaimed. "Bah!"

When Mr. Pilkin discovered that James Gardiner was spending his time with Emeline Butterfield, and it became evident that that young lady was keeping him away from bad company, he laughed at the infatuation of the young man, and he threw all the mud at the girl he could lay his experienced hand on.

"Jim Gardiner, a young man with a respectable father, takin' up with that kind uv cattle! Sobriety develops the worst elements in a man. A waiter at the Continental! a daughter uv old Butterfield, who lay drunk — not that there's any harm in a man's takin' his tod," said Mr. Pilkin, with quick appreciation of the necessities of his own business. "The idee uv Jim Gardiner takin' up with her! I woodent beleeve it."

All this and much more to his regular customers, who hated Jim for leaving them to pay for their own liquor as viciously as Pilkin, and who hated the girl as the cause.

Each man who repeated the story added to it, till, within a week from the time the insinuation left Peppernell's lips and his eyes, it was an insinuation no longer, but stated and believed, that poor Emeline was a scheming, reckless girl; that she had flirted with Peppernell as long as that gay old gentleman desired; that Mrs. Crosby had actually "hustled her out" of her establishment; and that just now she was playing a double game, being Burt's for the time, but ready to throw him as soon as she could fasten Jim Gardiner, who could be married.

It is astonishing how long such stories can circulate before they come to the ears of those directly affected by them. Jim and Emeline, as innocent as doves, were enjoying each other's society, without knowing that he was the object of pity, and she of suspicion of every man, woman, and maid in the village.

But Gardiner was very soon made painfully aware of it. His old friends deserted him, and became distant and cold. The young ladies with whom he had always been a favorite, despite his engagement with Mary Lewis, drew away from him; and the matrons, who had always treated him as familiarly as their own sons, met him with a coldness that was appalling. Finally, his father and mother called him to account. The old gentleman reproached him for throwing himself away upon a "common girl," who was the talk of the town and whose reputation made her unfit for an alliance with any decent family.

Mrs. Gardiner, who was present, begged James to remember that he was an only child, and that any disgrace coming to him would kill her.

"Disgrace!" exclaimed the young man, indignantly. "The girl is as pure and as good —"

"James," answered the father, quickly, "I trust you are too good a man to pursue a girl simply for your own amusement. You must know that she is not a fit woman for you to marry. Ask Peppernell. Ask any one who keeps the run of these wretched matters. The daughter of a miserable, ignorant farmer, a waiter at the Continental, and a servant in Burt's family! She is common talk in every barroom in New Canton and a jest on the lips of every dissolute man in the place. James, you are either very much deceived, or you are —"

James did not wait to hear the end of the sentence; but he rushed out of the house, very angry, and more determined than ever to hold to Emeline, because she had been subjected to such injustice and cruelty.

He went to Sam Livingston, his particular friend, in a white heat.

"Sam, did you ever hear any thing against the character of Emeline Butterfield? Understand me, I want the exact truth."

Livingston looked up from his book, and slowly expelled a volume of smoke, regarding his friend as he would an escaped lunatic.

"What?"

"You heard my question."

"Jim, are you in earnest asking it?"

"Certainly I am, and a good deal depends upon the answer."

"Jim, are you really struck with that girl?"

"Answer me what I asked of you."

"I supposed, Jim, that you were amusing yourself with her, and several weeks ago I would have spoken to you about it; for I don't believe it pays to get mixed up with such people, only I thought you were of age. But I see it is something more serious. Did I ever hear any thing of her? Yes. I don't know whether it is true or not, — for any practical purpose it makes no difference, — but I have heard every thing of her. Old Peppernell is credited with knowing a great deal too much of her, and so are a great many other fellows here. Even the immaculate Burt has not escaped being linked with her; and you can — no, you can't, for they are too considerate to talk in your presence — but any one else can hear all the details any night in any bar-room in the city, with as much pity for yourself as you could desire. Jim, she is town talk. Now you know all about it. I wouldn't have told you, but you insisted on it."

Gardiner left his friend, and rushed back to his room, in a rage with himself and the world.

"We are the town talk, are we? I'll end that by marrying her to-morrow, and then we will see who dares to talk."

He went to see her, and stayed late with her; but she noticed that he was absent-minded. When they walked she noticed that he took streets that were lonely and not frequented, and looked nervous if he saw any one they were likely to meet.

He slept over it, and the next morning gave it another good hour of thought. Marry her! Of course he would. He wouldn't be so craven as to let the gabble of a lot of cocktail-drinkers and gossips stand between him and his happiness. But then —

How would it answer for him to have for a wife a woman who would go into his circle with a smirched name? How would it do to have a wife who had been charged with being the intimate of a man so thoroughly debased as Peppernell? How would it answer for him, with her hanging on his arm, to meet the old boarders of the Continental, who had been served by her when she was a waiter at that hostelry? In short, how could he meet the cruel snubs of the women and the covert sneers of the men with whom he must live.

Fight it out! Unfortunately for such cases, there is no enemy to fight that can be seen and met. You may resent a blow; but you can't quarrel with a woman who avoids your wife, if she does it politely enough. You can't quarrel with a man because his wife does not invite your wife to her teas, nor can you make trouble at gatherings where, though you can't help being admitted, your wife is left to herself.

Poor Emeline! While these thoughts were passing through the mind of a man you loved with all the singleness of a great, true nature, you were planning how best to please him. You were thinking which of your two dresses to wear to meet him that evening, and, having decided, were arranging your one hat in a more becoming way, and putting a bow on your dress here and there, to be more pleasant in his eyes. She re-read a passage from an author favorite with him, in which she thought she had found a new meaning, that might interest him.

She waited that night for him, but she waited in vain. In vain was the little ornamentation of the dress, the freshening of the hat, the reading of the favorite author, and the preparation for the delightful discussion to follow.

Eight, nine, and ten passed (he had sometimes been delayed and came as late as ten); but, when the weary hands crept on till eleven, and he did not come, she went to her bed, heartsick and frightened.

He had started to see her, and had gone nearly to the house, thinking all the way of what Sam Livingston had told him; and, as he neared the door and was ready to give the usual signal for her to come out and join him, he felt that to walk with her again and take the chances of meeting any one would be adding fuel to the flame of scandal that was burning into his very soul. "Peppernell's girl" hanging on his arm and looking up into his eyes! The "scullion" (he had heard that word used in connection with her name) of the Continental with him, and the whole town sneering at him!

To do him justice, he did not believe one word of the stories that were in circulation about her; for he knew her to be as pure and as devoted to him as a woman could be. He knew Peppernell was a bloated old liar — a Falstaff without Falstaff's humor,— that all his vaporing had come partly from malice and partly from his vanity to be considered a successful wicked man, and that all the other stories were merely offshoots from the accumulation of a lie, which certainly does gather as it rolls.

But, lies though they were, he knew they would stick like burrs, and that, even if he undertook to live them down, they would still be believed; and that all the credit she would get for years of a blameless life would be the credit either of a repentant woman, or an artful one who had no further necessity for sinning.

Could he afford all this? Should he go and throttle Peppernell, and cram the lie down his throat, and make him acknowledge that he had slandered her? That would do very well so far as silencing one liar. But would it stop the rest, or would it alter the opinion of the others? He could not answer all these questions satisfactorily; but he did not go and see her that night.

CHAPTER XXVII.

EMELINE AND JIM.

FOUR days passed, and James Gardiner did not come near Emeline Butterfield. Every night he intended to go to her, every night he had started; but every time he started, the terrible words "Peppernell's girl," "waiter at the Continental," came to him like disquieting ghosts, and drove him back. He was not in a comfortable frame of mind. He felt and knew that he was acting the coward. He felt and knew that the girl was as pure as a snow-flake, and that every word that had been said against her was a cruel slander. He knew that she was as much superior to the women who were hunting her down as strength is to weakness, as refinement is to vulgarity, and that she was the most fit woman for him he had ever met.

But there came into his mind the sneers of his fellows, the blind prejudice of his good old father and his dearly loved mother, and the sickening thought of the life of struggle he should have to force and hold a position for her in the little world where he lived, or (should he not make the fight) the utter and entire seclusion he would have to content himself with for her sake.

Nevertheless, the fifth evening he did go to see her. She had waited, night after night, with a cold fear of impending disaster, all the more terrible because she did not know from what direction trouble was coming, and could make no preparation to meet it. She waited, with the fear oppressing her; and her cheeks lost their roses, and her eye its brightness. She moved about the house mechanically, like one in a dream; and, though she did her duties, it was without the intelligence or readiness of former days.

Mrs. Burt noticed the change, and insisted on her taking taraxicum three times a day. Mr. Burt knew the reason, and knew it was a matter that no medicament could reach; and the sight of the girl's pale face and wearied, worried look hardly displeased him as it should have done.

James came, and how gladly she rushed to meet him! His presence, his kind, loving words, the pressure of his arm, and his lips against hers was all that was needed to bring the vanished roses to her cheeks and set the heart of the impulsive, loving girl at rest.

But very little comfort did she get of him that night. He kissed her with more tenderness than ever, and looked upon her so kindly and yet so pityingly that she drew away from him.

"Jim! dear Jim! what is the matter? Why do you look at me so? I can't understand you."

"Nothing, darling. Nothing."

And then he relapsed into silence, and they walked some distance before he spoke.

She said nothing, though a strange fear was tugging at her heart and she was dying to know what was before her. That never-erring instinct which every woman has, told her that there was something.

"Why have you kept away from me so long, Jim? I have waited for you four nights, and it made me sick, almost. I am so glad that you came to-night! I should have been sick in earnest if you had disappointed me again."

Should he tell her and break with her that night? Could he tear himself away from her, and go back to his old associates? On the one side was the sweet girl, who loved him to distraction and who was worthy of him or any man; and, on the other, were his ambitions and all that is first in most men's minds. He determined to tell her the truth, and tear himself away, never to see her again; but, just as the words came to his lips, the moon sailed out from under a cloud and baptized her lovely face in a glory. He looked down into her eyes, and read there truth, devotion, loyalty, every thing that a man should love and cling to in a woman. The cruel words that spoke a divorce between him and so much that was good froze on his lips. Instead of speaking them, he bent his face down to her's, and kissed her with an intensity that was all the more fervent because it had cost him something to do it.

From that moment he was himself again. He talked with her as he had before the cruel slanders had shaken his devotion to her. She quoted the passage from his author in which she thought she had discovered a new meaning, and was delighted beyond telling to find that, when she had made it clear to him, he saw it as she did. After an hour of most delightful converse, he had forgotten the terrors that had beset him and was himself again.

Happy souls! There was nothing but love between

them, and he was entranced as he had been an hundred times before. He felt that, for the sake of the love of such a girl, he could face all the gossiping cats of women and all the blackguard men in the world, and all the fathers and mothers too. Father! Let this delightful being get the right to be to his father what she was to him! Mother! Let but Emeline get the privilege to be near her! He had no fears. He felt a strange lightness of heart at being so well out of his troubles; that is, having his duty and his inclination jump so nearly together.

They walked on. He did not avoid the frequented streets that night; for the delight of having her so close to him and having so much faith in her gave him a courage which he had not felt since he had absented himself from her. He turned into the main street, and was passing with her on his arm, she leaning closely to him and both oblivious of where they were or whom they might expect to meet, when they came full upon a party issuing from the "Gem" saloon, and all more or less under the influence of liquor. Peppernell was in it; Tom Paddleford —who, since his marriage, could be found there every night — had the old reprobate's arm, and straggling along with them were a dozen of the most dissolute young and old men of the town.

Gardiner saw them, and would have shrunk away; but it was impossible, without showing that he did not want to meet them, and he was too much of a man to do that. He drew himself up to his full hight, instead of the bending position he had been walking in, and, with his face straight in front of him, walked past the crowd. The girl, who saw the party, understood his change and tried to avoid contact with them; but one or two of them brushed against her, as they passed on the narrow plank walk. She shuddered instinctively. They were her death, though she did not know it. As they passed, Gardiner heard a hoarse, mocking wheeze from Peppernell's whisky-scarred throat, and a jeering laugh which he recognized as coming from Paddleford, and thought he distinguished his own name and Emeline's in the jeers. Angry and in rage, had he been alone, he would have gone back and demanded the cause of the laughter; but, with the girl on his arm, what could he do? She had some idea of what it meant; but, frightened and afraid of, she knew not what, she clung close to him and said nothing.

She was not surprised, though she felt hurt, when, at the next corner, he left the main street, and turned down a street where they would not be likely to meet any one.

They came near to Mr. Burt's house, her home. He stopped suddenly, and, releasing her arm, turned his face full upon her.

The moon was shining at its full, and she could see that he was terribly agitated.

"James!" she spoke, in alarm at the agony which a less acute woman could see plainly in his face.

"Em, tell me and tell me the truth. Did you ever give those ruffians any cause to laugh as they did when they passed us? Did you ever—"

All was clear to the poor girl now. She knew the enemy she had to contend with, and exactly what the struggle meant. She knew that James Gardiner, the only son of the best man of New Canton and the most promising man in the village, had been jeered at and laughed at for taking up with one who had come from a questionable family, who had been a waiter in a hotel, and who was now a servant in a family.

Stunned, — for, in her pure love and her unselfish devotion to the man she loved, the idea that she was not fit for him had never occurred to her, — she choked, and could make no answer ; but tears came, and she leaned her head upon his broad shoulder, and, feeling the utter desolation, the utter helplessness of her position, sobbed as though her heart would break.

It was the worst answer she could have made.

"Emeline," he said, sternly, " answer me. Yes or no?"

"Never!" she replied, with a sob.

"Did that old brute, Peppernell, ever approach you?"

"He did."

"When?"

"When I was in the Con—"

The hot young man, drawn one way by his love for a girl and another by his pride, disengaged his arm from and stood facing her, angry with her, himself, and all the world.

"Ever since?"

"James, what do you mean? I have told you the truth. I was alone and helpless. I could not avoid these men. They made advances to me there, because I was there ; and Peppernell afterward, because I was Burt's servant, I suppose. Men feel that they have a right to insult a helpless, lone girl, who has no one to protect her. But, as God is my judge, never one of them —"

"I believe you, Emeline; but we won't talk of this any further to-night. Go in, darling. I am very much troubled. I do believe you, and —"

She did not hear him out; for, having regained her self-possession, her strength came to her, and, without a word, without even a good-night kiss, she threw herself inside the gate and into the house.

James Gardiner paused a moment, as the girl disappeared, and walked away ill at ease. He could not bring himself to part with the girl, for he loved her devotedly. But she was old 'Liph Butterfield's daughter, she had been a waiter-girl at the Continental, and she was Burt's servant. Disguise the position as " companion," it was all the same. She was Burt's servant, on a stipend payable weekly, — an upper servant, but a servant all the same; and, as 'Liph Butterfield's daughter, as a waiteress at the Continental, and as Burt's servant, every low fellow in the village had been privileged to speak to her familiarly, to make advances to her; and she had confessed that Peppernell, the most odious man in the town, had actually approached her. And no one knew better than Gardiner what that meant.

Then, came into his mind another ignoble thought. He hated Burt, as any open man hates one whom he believes to be a hypocrite and a sham; and he remembered how anxious he had been to take her out of Mrs. Crosby's into his own family. He knew how little there must be in common between a man like Burt and a woman like his wife; and he had seen enough of Emeline's influence in the house to know that she controlled it: and the sickening suspicion came into his mind, that perhaps Burt, the sanctimonious Burt, had his own end in view, and that he had been made a double fool of, — that Burt, after Peppernell, had tired of her, and that he was to take a girl who had been twice a cast-off.

He did not believe all this. But it all came into his mind as possibilities; and, dwelling on it in a jealous, frantic way, possibilities grew into probabilities, and, before he slept, the possibilities had with him become almost certainties. His dreams were terrible. He saw Emeline with the greasy Peppernell, he saw her with the equally odious Burt; and he waked half-crazed.

And this fact impressed him: innocent or guilty, good or bad, his people and the town would hold her guilty.

Emeline left him in that flush of indignation which any woman feels at being suspected, when she has given no cause for it. Was it for this that she had given this man all there was of her nature? Was it for this that she had loved him so unselfishly, and had compromised herself for him? For, in repulsing Peppernell, she felt herself acquitted and in a strong position; but, in loving one above her station and showing that love as unreservedly as she had done, she had given the gossips a right to trifle with her good name.

"I have sacrificed more than he has!" she cried, in agony. "He can afford it; I cannot."

She felt outraged that he should ask her such questions, or that he should let any doubt of her come into his mind. He knew before he approached her whose daughter she was, how she came to New Canton, and all about it. He knew that she had been at the Continental, that she had been at Mrs. Crosby's, that she was at Burt's, — before he had ever spoken to her. Why did he come to her, and — why did he throw himself in her way? Why did he make her love him, till he was her world, — all that was worth any thing in it, — if he did not intend to take her just as she was and precisely as he found her?

Worthy of him! She felt that she was the better of the two, and that, in the life-struggle that comes to every one, she could be of more help to him than he could be to her. She knew her strength; and she knew, what evidently he did not, her integrity.

And, with a feeling that she had been outraged, that the world was very cruel to one who was simply doing her best and who deserved better of it than she was likely to get, she fell into a troubled slumber.

What were her dreams? Not pleasant ones. She saw James before her, and reached out her hands imploringly to him. But there came between her and him the forms of Peppernell, with his coarse, brutal laugh; Paddleford, with his rat-like grin; Burt, with his smooth presence; and another shadow, not well enough defined to strike at and kill, but stronger than all the rest — public opinion.

She woke from her miserable sleep a changed woman. She had lost her love, and gained what did not become her so well — ambition. Gone was the softness and sweetness that sat so lovingly upon her: in its place there came a hard, stern determination that the qualities she knew she had should be used hereafter for herself and no one else. And, thus filled, she found she could remember her lover's weakness without despair and even without a pang. Life had something in it to her beside him.

The next morning, James Gardiner was walking toward his office, still troubled and worried. He could not make up his mind to leave Emeline; for he loved her, and without her life looked cheerless enough. Nor could he prevail upon himself to face what he knew he would be compelled to. If he married her, he could not take her and leave New Canton; for he could not leave his father and his mother in their old age, he being their only stay. Besides, he knew that change of place makes no difference in such cases. Emeline's misfortunes would follow her to the end of the earth.

Thus torn and troubled, he met Mary Paddleford, for the first time since her marriage. When he had seen her coming, he had always avoided her, as he would have done now had he seen her soon enough. But, wrapped in thought and walking with his head down, he did not notice her till she was too close to avoid recognition. He bowed, and passed without saying a word.

He knew, what all New Canton knew, that Mary Paddleford and her husband were not living happily together: he had heard it said that Tom so far indulged his natural tendency for meanness as to beat her; and, as he passed, she looked so sorrowful, so sad, so utterly miserable that he changed his mind, and turned to speak to her. She had also stopped, as if in hope that he would turn.

"Mary!"

It was the old tone, softened by grief, and kindly, but with the slightest tinge of reproach in it.

In a frightened way, as if to see if any one was observing them, she came back to him.

"What do you look so frightened for? Is any one watching you? Are you afraid to speak to me on the street?" was his exclamation.

"Oh! Jim, if Tom should see me speaking to you, or know that I had, he would kill me!"

"Kill you for speaking to an — old friend? Mary! What is this?"

He noticed a blue-black spot on her face just where the hair joined the skin over her temple.

"Don't ask me," she replied, shivering with terror; "and, Jim, don't talk to me any more. I am afraid. I — I — am very miserable. But, Jim, I wanted to say to you that it was not my fault that I married him. I could not help it. I did not dare to tell you why, and I had to let you go thinking I was heartless and cruel and fickle. But I was not. Ma forced me. Why, you will know some day. I did wrong in yielding to her. But, Jim, I am paying for it. I am thoroughly miserable; and, if I dared, I would kill myself, and end it. Don't speak to me any more. I just wanted to say this to you, and say that I care for you now as much as ever. But never speak to me again."

And, with the same frightened look, she hurried away.

Gardiner looked at the poor woman, as she moved away from him, and something of the old feeling for her came back to him.

The sad look on her face haunted him and stayed with him all the day. At every turn he saw her tearful eyes looking appealingly into his; and, loving Emeline Butterfield as he did, he felt half angry with himself that he had permitted his first love to be sacrificed without a struggle for her.

"I could have married her. Emeline, never!" he said to himself a hundred times. And, locking himself in his office, he undertook the hardest task man ever takes, that of obtaining control of himself.

CHAPTER XXVIII.

ONE NAIL DRIVES ANOTHER OUT.

THE sunny afternoon had been quenched in rain. Not a storm that smote the levels in wrath and sent the dying flowers to wreck and ruin ; but a mild, low-whispering, sighing rain, that melted out of the soft gray sky, and forebore to call notice to its grieving over the pale herbs and faded flowers. It was a time when stirring, ever-busy housekeepers sat snug at their endless sewing, with gossiping, bright-witted girls around them, — when farmer brothers found time to read newspapers up garret, as by stealth, reveling in speeches of " our member," which stirred their untouched enthusiasms to high flame ; or wrapped in romances, which taught them emotions they secretly resolved to test for themselves ere long, — afternoons when they paid attentions to the state of their front hair, and stole off by the back door to the next neighbor's, whose daughter happened to wear an interest for them, — days when the old farmers were graciously willing to harness the team, and go to town for a can of baking-powder, a stint of sugar, or such trifling errand as the weekly mail, which in better weather was an impertinent interruption. Long errands they made of those half-pint cans or those gallons of kerosene that detained them in the safe end of Paddleford's store, which had not modern impatience of its customers, till long past dinner time. It was a pleasant, neighborly rain, too wet to work in, but not enough to hinder crossing a field or so to sit an afternoon and sew a long seam.

The easy, half-humorous temper of the Burt household was overcast. Mrs. Burt did not understand it, but laid the blame comfortably on her husband and Emeline's ill-judged levity, which must have its downs to pay for running on such a high key. She had fidgeted round a day or two, and went off to her sister's one evening when it slacked up, Emeline thought, out of especial consideration for her. Now, she could have her funeral in her heart, and weep her grief out unrestrainedly.

She was not one of the sort to cry outwardly. She wept one fatal night three dreary hours, till the sluices of her grief were drained. After that her eyes were too tender, her frame too weary to cry any more. But the wound within began the intolerable ache which makes every day and hour full of pain. It bled inwardly, and the midnights passed with moans and hot fights with pain. It was too soon for grief to whiten the roses of her cheeks, or give her pale and sodden features, such as are worn by those with whom sorrow has become a habit; but a close observer could see that the roses on her cheek were whitened, the lines growing sharp, and the eye fixed and mournful at its best. She went about her tasks mechanically, like one whose body keeps a habit of activity, that releases the mind all the more to suffer. And all the time the woman was looking on the face of her dead happiness.

The stupid, gross materialism of the world had hold of her lover, which recognizes nothing of value unless the world has stamped it, — which can see nothing in spirit, keen-edged sense, or faithfulness worth more than a faint, sentimental approval, — which knows no selling all it has for the sake of a pearl of price, — which would not know such a pearl unless appraised by the jewellers, and in setting of gold in the latest fashion. He had been willing to play with this girl, and admire himself for his condescension in doing it, and elbow all considerations out of the way that might interfere with his sovereign pleasure in so doing. Like most, I might say, all young men, he knew how to respect women of his own class and circle; but, outside that circle, he had no more real conception of any regard and protection due them on account of sex than he had of worship for the Virgin Mary, nor half as much. Take a young man of the present day at hazard from any circle in city or country, and you will find him — a thin veneering of sentiment and fair manners scratched off — as worldly, cool, selfish, and calculating as any titled lackey of the great Louis's court. They have not even the grace of gracelessness which led a professed *roué* like Aaron Burr to reprove Pierrepont Edwards for kissing a servant girl, reminding him that a gentleman pursued his amours in his own rank. In these godless, chance-bred days there is little enough principle of any kind manifest in any relation, where one-half the world is led by interest and the other half by taste. There is no principle at all in love. How was a young fellow, brought up to consider wearing good clothes and living in good style essentials of life, and keeping his precious self amused and in good spirits the major and only and ultimate end of life, what was he to know or care about the pain he was inflicting or the loss he was entailing on himself in leaving the warm, intense nature he had taught to love him. Yes, the loss. Many a man throws away the success of his life in the love of some unformed woman, whom he has not learned to hold at her true value.

Emeline was alone in the sitting-room, absorbed in thought. She had gone through the bitter waters, and had her fill of disgrace and humiliation. Honest and true, faithful to the man she loved, and wrapt up in him, she had, for no fault of her own, been cast off, thrust out, and abandoned to the tender mercies of a set of harpies, not her equals in any sense, but who resented her taking possession of the most promising young man in town.

Would she stay in New Canton, and give up all the hopes she had cherished and all the expectations she had formed? Could she stay in Burt's house as a servant, — not as a companion, — and subside into the mere nothing which servants always are? Add to that the fact, which she recognized, that she was under a reputation which she did not deserve and which she never could outlive, and her heart failed her.

She looked up from her sewing, and saw Mr. Burt sitting in an easy-chair, reading his paper. He had come in so quietly she had not seen him, and had been observing her for some time. He knew what was passing in her mind.

"Emeline!"

"Emeline, I know what you are going through, and I came here to speak to you. You have loved a man not worthy of you — a man who did not understand you, or, if he did, had not the courage to stand by you, as he should have done. He did not dare to face the gossips of this miserable village. He has left you, as I thought he would months ago. Had I not been convinced of it, I should have interfered sooner. You cannot stay here."

"Where can I go?" asked the girl, her face flushing.

Mr. Burt sat in silence for a moment.

"Emeline, there will be changes here that will make this house no home for you, or for any of us perhaps. Put your own affairs aside one moment, if you can, while I speak of mine. The land company is on the point of failing. There will be trouble for Peppernell and his lot."

Burt spoke with indescribable triumph and dilating nostril.

"It will be best for me to be somewhere else. This is no new thing, Emeline. I have been looking for it, any minute, for a year. It is a wonder it did not come before. But you needn't look alarmed. I have something ahead. I thought I had a right to the pay for my services" (he spoke with a sneer); "for you know I have worked hard for New Canton and the company. My savings and investments elsewhere will leave me enough to live on away from here. I am sick of this wretched town and everybody in it; and, if I had not hated it before, I should, for the way it has treated you. I came of a family as poor as yours, though I took good care never to let a soul know it. My mother made vests for a living, and I swept the schoolhouse for my tuition, when I had to eat my lunch behind sheds, so that the boys and girls couldn't see it was bread without any butter. All that you have gone through I went through years ago; though, being a man, I could emancipate myself, which a woman can never do. What a man does doesn't count, if he succeeds; and that success I have achieved. I hate it all. I hate the life I lead, the men I am compelled to associate with, and the women. I have determined to quit it all, and find the life I want somewhere else."

"How will Mrs. Burt like going away from her friends and her home?"

"I have not asked her," Burt returned, grimly; "and I don't intend to. Have no fear for her. I am not a mean man. I shall leave her well provided for — with this house in her own name and rents to collect as it pleases her. And she will have them all without the encumbrance of a husband."

"You're not going to leave her?"

"Leave her!" exclaimed Burt, rising, and glaring about the room. "Leave her! Yes! I shall leave every thing that reminds me of the life I have been leading and the lie I have lived, and I hope never to see any of it again. I leave behind me fools and idiots who were an annoyance to me, and the rascals and thin frauds whom I despised. I shall go out to a life that holds something for me."

"Not alone?"

"No, no; not alone. Emeline, I shall go, and take somebody with me."

"Who?"

"You! I love you. You know I do, and I always have. I knew how your connection with that half-baked Gardiner would result, and I was willing to bide my time. But, when I was forming the inexperienced girl that came to my house, it was not for him but for myself. You are too good for him. You are good enough for me."

Burt did not look as though he expected an answer, but paced the floor like a man crazed. Emeline sank back, half fainting and half frightened at the vehemence of his words and his excited manner. The blood came and went, there was a film before her eyes, and, for a minute, she was incapable of speech or motion.

"Will you stay here and be the common drudge, to be sneered at by women and pointed at by men? Will you stay here to endure Peppernell's coarse jokes, and to be an object of pity, as the aspiring kitchen-girl whom Jim Gardiner wanted to marry, but dared not? Emeline, you are too good. You can have the freedom I shall have, and all that I have; and you will have a man, who, if he is not entirely worthy of you, can, at least, appreciate you."

The next morning, Emeline informed Mrs. Burt that she had determined to leave New Canton. Mrs. Burt complained bitterly, and objected strenuously. Who could give her medicine so well? It would take months to get another girl to understand her ailments and be so handy with her medicines. Was it wages she wanted? She didn't think it right to be made to continually raise wages; but she liked Emeline so much, that, if an additional half-dollar a week would satisfy her, she wouldn't object. She didn't like changes, and was willing to submit to what she considered extortion rather than to endure them.

"Will that be satisfactory, Emeline?"

"I prefer to go," was her answer.

"I think it would be better to let her have her own way," said Mr. Burt, quietly.

She went, and the women of New Canton felt relieved. Their scandal was removed, and their rival, as they hoped, forever.

CHAPTER XXIX.

SOMETHING HAPPENS.

IT was an unfortunate thing for Mr. Gardiner that he was not omniscient and not omnipresent. Had he been on the streets of New Canton one night, with good eyes, he would have seen a sight that would have made him uneasy. He would have seen Mr. Burt enter the bank, closing the doors behind him softly, and getting in with that quick movement which indicated a desire not to be seen entering; and, after getting in, he would have seen him in a quiet back office, closing all the blinds and drawing the curtain down very carefully. And, a few minutes later, he would have seen Col. Peppernell unlock the front door with his key (he had always insisted upon having a key of his own), and go straight to the same room. And he would have seen Mr. Burt start up with a half-frightened and half-annoyed look, as though some purpose was interrupted by the Colonel.

But, as Mr. Gardiner was quietly sleeping in his own room, and as Jim was walking the floor of his office, very wretched, no one in the Gardiner interest saw any thing of these movements.

Col. Peppernell had been growing uneasy; and the object of his visit to Burt in the back room of the office that night was to in some way, remove some of the doubts that were oppressing him.

Mr. Burt had been going to Chicago too frequently to suit that astute gentleman, and he felt it his duty to see what it was all about. So, one day, after giving it out freely that he was going to Peoria, Col. Peppernell went to Chicago. He knew something of Mr. Burt's haunts in the city; and, moreover, as a director in the land company and bank, he had a perfect right to make inquiries after the interests of that now somewhat famous corporation.

The Colonel did not find out much in Chicago; for Messrs. Price and Hawkins, and others with whom Burt did business, were very reticent as to any thing connected with it. They knew nothing; and they knew nothing so decidedly and with mouths so close, that Col. Peppernell knew there was something kept from him. The more he demanded, the further they were from telling any thing.

"If we have had any business with Mr. Burt,— understand me, I say 'if,' — it is necessarily a matter between Mr. Burt and ourselves. You can see for yourself — you are a man of business — that business is confidential, and that, whatever has transpired between us, — if any thing has, — we should be no more justified in revealing to you than we would in writing to him that you had been here making inquiries about him."

Thus Mr. Hawkins; and it is needless to say that Mr. Price agreed with him.

The Colonel left as wise as he came.

As he left the office, Mr. Price smiled at Mr. Hawkins and Mr. Hawkins smiled at Mr. Price.

"Burt don't want to waste any time," said Mr. Hawkins.

"He's got 'em, though, if he's quick enough about it," said Price.

"Don't worry about him," was Hawkins's answer. "He's smart enough for forty Peppernells." And they dismissed the subject.

Col. Peppernell took the first train for New Canton, and went directly to the bank, where he found Mr. Burt alone.

On one memorable occasion Mr. Burt closed the doors very carefully. This time Col. Peppernell did so, and he was as particular as Mr. Burt had been. Mr. Burt showed no surprise.

"Burt, I want to ask you a plain question."

"Being a plain man, I shall give you a plain answer."

"Bah! All that is wasted on me."

"My dear sir, you ought to control yourself. Suppose you don't believe what I say, is there any occasion for your telling me so bluntly? It is not the proper thing, Col. Peppernell."

"How much money have we got?"

"In the land company, perhaps two thousand dollars. I will tell you exactly, if you desire it."

"That's near enough. In the bank?"

"Perhaps thirty thousand in cash."

"And how much in securities?"

"The bank and land company are mixed, somewhat. The money received from depositors has been used very largely in improvements and in paying for lands purchased. We have property for which we have paid $267,000. We have bonds and mortgages for property sold for as much more — in all, say a round half-million."

"What could you sell the securities for, and how much money could you raise on mortgage? I mean out and out, for cash in hand!"

"I suppose about one hundred thousand dollars; that is, if anybody could be found to purchase them. But we would be very stupid to sell them, or undertake to. It is true that the mortgages are for an amount largely in excess of what the property would bring in cash, or even for what might be called, in the language of trade, negotiable paper. To make it entirely clear to you, a mortgage for $1,000 on a lot containing one-seventh of an acre of land, which no one would pay twenty dollars an acre for, cannot be considered very good security, unless the mortgager has some other assets than the land. I am happy to say that the most of those to whom we have sold have assets outside of the land, and that collections from them are not entirely hopeless. But, Colonel, this is the view to take of it to-day. To-morrow it may look different. We must discount the future. We must labor and work and wait till that lot is actually worth the thousand dollars. And — and why should we not? Look at our maps, Colonel! When Soggy Run is im — "

"Bah! You'll drive me crazy."

"When Soggy Run is improved, and the system of railroads which must make New Canton a central point are built; when the com — "

"Mr. Burt, could you, counting cash and what we

could realize from the sale of the securities we have, make up one hundred thousand dollars? I mean by this, could you do this and close up the whole thing suddenly?"

"I suppose we might. But what do you ask for? Have you any idea of throwing the company into bankruptcy? To close now, would leave us with a load of liabilities we couldn't work out in years. We have an immense volume of our certificates afloat. We must make these securities we hold worth what they represent. In short, why do you ask such questions?"

"Burt, there ain't no use of trying to humbug me. This kind of talk is well enough when we are sellin' lots outside; but it's all wasted on me here. I shel be what you never was — plain. My proposition, in two words, is this: You and I hev done this work. We hev made all there is of New Canton. We hev blowed up this bubble and we hev control of this property. I propose that yoo and I sell these securities for jest what they will fetch, quick, and light out. Ther's 'nuff to make us both comf'table in Europe. I'm tired of the whole thing, and want to quit."

Mr. Burt's look at this speech of the Colonel was an expression of astonishment, virtuous indignation, and pity.

"Col. Peppernell, I do not quite understand what you mean by "lighting" out. But I gather that your proposition is to embezzle the property of the company, of which you and I are the confidential officers, and abscond. Am I right?"

"That is about the size of it."

Seizing a ruler from the desk at which he was sitting, Mr. Burt assumed a posture of offense.

"What do you take me for, Col. Peppernell? Did you come here to insult me? Have I lived to have such a proposition made me? You infernal old fool, leave the office this minute; and, if I don't make this public to-morrow morning, you have my leniency to thank for it. You and I can never breathe the same air again. Go!"

The Colonel looked at him, but he did not blanch or change a particle. With a muttered curse, he left the office.

When he had gone, Mr. Burt drew a long breath and his face grew pale as death.

"He has been to Chicago, and tried to pump Hawkins and Price, as they telegraphed me to-day. He's too late. The train leaves Freedom in an hour, and I have just time to get over. This is my time. From Freedom south to Peoria, hiding in Peoria till they don't know where I am, then Europe."

Burt unlocked the safe, and took out some packages of bills, and put up with great care. "$5,000; $10,000; $20,000; $5,000. Not enough, not so much as I should have made out of this; but I can make it go. Peppernell wanted to share with me. He's got enough. He has $30,000 worth of secured property, and he never made a dollar of it."

Mr. Burt stowed the treasure in his inside pockets, and, taking a hand-valise, went out into the darkness.

His wagon stood convenient, and he rode out into the night. The vehicle was turned loose in the road; and, at a small station on the main line, closely muffled, he boarded a freight train, with a passenger car attached, and went twenty miles, to a cross-road, where he waited for another.

By devious routes, traveling on unfrequented trains, eking out the distances from one road to another by private conveyances, and walking miles along unfrequented roads, Charles Burt, the secretary and treasurer of the New Canton Land Company and president of the New Canton Savings-bank, now a felon and a fugitive, made his way to safety.

Many a time, as he was combating the terrors of the night and the more awful terrors of anticipated pursuit and capture, he wished he were back, a dentist, earning an honest, if an humble living. But it was too late; and, with wealth on his person, he made his way, like one walking among pitfalls, afraid and alarmed. He, whose pride it had been to manage men, became afraid of the sight of a man; he who had by sheer force of will managed every man with whom he came in contact, dodged to avoid a child, and ran in affright from the sight of a man. The Delilah of ambition had shorn his strength; and, from one of the strongest, he had become of the weakest of men. It was too late to go back. He had burned his bridge.

CHAPTER XXX.

THE EFFECT ON NEW CANTON OF MR. BURT'S DEPARTURE.

THE absence of Mr. Burt was not a matter that awakened any surprise. It was a very common thing for him to make long trips in the interest of the land company; and business went on at the office during his absences as usual. Col. Peppernell would happen in, and direct things; and the clerk knew as much about the property as Mr. Burt, though, of course, he had not that gentleman's winning way of entrapping investors.

Three days passed; and, as Mr. Burt did not put in an appearance, Mr. Gardiner began to be uneasy.

The day before Burt went away, he had come to Gardiner's bank, and borrowed ten thousand dollars — that is, he had exchanged cheques for that amount; and the cheque, certified by Mr. Gardiner, had come back from Chicago, and Mr. Burt had, singularly enough, neglected to provide for it.

Gardiner went, in some trouble, to James; but that young man had troubles of his own, and he put it off with the remark that Burt would be home in a day or two, and that, doubtless, it was all right. And James, who was playing a game of chess with Sam Livingston, went on studying the position of his king. The father went, feeling that it would be cruel to divert his son's mind for so trifling a matter as $10,000.

"Jim," said Livingston, "the old man's troubled. If I were you, I'd look this matter up a little. Your father's the most confiding man I know of, and they will beat him yet."

"Who are *they?*" asked Jim, not looking up from his game.

"Burt, Peppernell, and the rest of 'em. Burt is a smooth hypocrite, Peppernell is a blustering old scoundrel, and Peak and Sharp —"

"A pretty character to give leading citizens," was Jim's answer. "Sam, you've got me."

"Not as bad as those fellows have your father. Jim, you've no time to lose. The old man isn't the one to deal with them. Three days ago I saw a cheque in Burt's hand, as he came out of the bank. I saw the figures, and it was certified. How much do you suppose it was for?"

"I haven't the faintest idea," said James.

"Ten thousand dollars; and Burt has been gone three days, and the old man is worried. There's something wrong, depend upon it, and you can't look into it too soon."

"Some mistake, I suppose. Banks are always making mistakes, when they ought to be the most correct institutions in the world. I took the old man's place once, one day; and if had stayed there a week I'd have ruined him. Every cheque that came in for $10, I paid $100 for. It was a mercy for us that the people about here are or were tolerably honest. But I think this matter ought to be looked into, and I'll go down and do it."

On his way, his father met him, pale, agitated, and so nervous that he could scarcely keep his feet.

"Come with me to the bank, Jim, at once. I want you."

James went with his father to the little private office.

"Jim," said the old man, in a low, tremulous voice, "I ain't easy in my mind. Burt came in Monday, and got an accommodation cheque certified for $10,000."

"What did he want with that much money?"

"The land company, of course. I don't know what for. He has done it a hundred times before, and he has always met them promptly."

"Well?"

"The cheque was cashed at the First National Bank of Chicago, where I keep my account; and it has come back."

"What?" exclaimed Jim, springing to his feet. "This is serious. Stay in the bank, and say nothing. I will go and find out where he is."

The son now took the lead. He went to the Burt residence, and Mrs. Burt answered the bell in person.

"Mrs. Burt, can you tell me where Mr. Burt is?"

"I can't say. He left here Monday night. He packed his carpet-bag himself, and said he would be home in a few days."

James went to the station, and found there that Burt had purchased no ticket and had not gone by train. While he was making his inquiries, the station-agent at Freedom happened to be standing by.

"Burt?" said he. "He came to Freedom Monday night. I saw him, but he didn't go north from there.

He took the train south. Didn't get a ticket, for the office wasn't open."

Jim, the elder Gardiner, and Livingston went to the office of the land company, and, after questioning the clerk in charge as to Burt's whereabouts, demanded the books.

The clerk handed them over. There was no record of the cheque, but the cash balance for the land company and the savings-bank showed $50,000.

"Great heavens!" exclaimed Gardiner. "With this balance, what did he want of $10,000 from me?"

"I have my notion," said Jim. "Where is this cash?"

"In the sub-treasury," said the clerk.

"Give my father the keys."

"I haven't got them. Mr. Burt always keeps them. When he goes away, he leaves out enough cash for the business, and carries the keys with him."

"A cold-chisel will unlock it," muttered Jim. "I guess there ought to be one in the pocket of every stockholder."

Slocum, the blacksmith, was sent for; but he, not being a practical burglar, made slow work of it. He got it open, and the three men looked in. Gardiner fell to the floor. James cursed.

Empty! The money was gone that the books showed ought to be there. The valuable papers were gone — the mortgages, notes, and every thing else of value.

By this time, Sharp and Peake had heard of the extraordinary proceedings, and came in.

"I can't account for this," said Sharp. "We have always entrusted the detail of the business to Mr.

Burt. Col. Peppernell might know something about it, if he were here; but he is gone, and won't be back till morning."

"What did he want of $10,000 in Chicago?" moaned Gardiner, clinging to the idea that it was susceptible of explanation. "We owe nothing there, that I know of. I hope there is nothing wrong with the company."

"There can be nothing wrong with the company," replied Capt. Peak. "This cheque of which you speak, was it made to the order of the company or — "

"Burt said it was for the company; but it was made, as all such cheques were, to the order of Burt himself."

"Thank Heaven!" exclaimed Peak, quickly. "If any thing has gone wrong with Burt, the company will not be holden for that. But there can't be any thing wrong. Mr. Burt is — "

"Burt's a thief!" broke in Jim, impetuously; "and, if I am not mistaken, there are more of them."

"Sir!" exclaimed Peak, threateningly.

"Never mind. We shall find out. I leave for Chicago on the next train."

James came back next day. The Chicago capitalists made short work of his hopes. Every note given to the New Canton Land Company had been made payable to Charles Burt on order; and he had sold them in a lump for what he could get, and had not been seen since. He was *non est*, with all the available assets of the land company, with a great deal of Gardiner's money, and with every dollar that he could borrow in New Canton and Chicago.

Great and terrible was the rage of Col. Peppernell, who returned that night, when he heard of the absconding of the treasurer.

"He's gone, with all the funds of the company! Blast him!" he energetically remarked. "And left me as poor as a rat, after all I've done to develop the resources of the country. I shall never get any reward for my labor and capital. What I regret the most is, that, in consequence of this scoundrelism, our enterprises are for the time blocked.

To say there was consternation in New Canton when the flight of Burt became a certainty is to state it very mildly. It was not consternation, it was stupefaction. It was as though a man who had implicit faith in his wife had come to his home and found she had eloped with his coachman, — as if a man who had a million should go to his hoard and find it all gone, or as if the sun should go out at noon.

Every man, woman, and child in the village, with very few exceptions, had money on deposit at the bank. Everybody was interested, directly and indirectly, in the land company. The value of every foot of ground in the section depended on it; and its collapse was the bursting of many a bubble, whose existence the world never knew.

Poor old Basset, the Congregational parson, had his year's salary therein; and Mrs. Basset looked aghast when she realized that her hopes of a new dress for herself and some decent clothing for the children were baseless visions. The old man groaned in spirit, and confessed to his wife, that it was a special visitation to punish him for too much worldly elevation of spirit when his church raised his salary from three to four hundred a year. But, as philosophical and humble as he was, that evening he used unusual fervor in praying that the doings of the wicked might recoil upon their own heads; and he went the unusual length of banging the back of the chair at which he was kneeling, as if it were the heads on which wicked deeds were to recoil. Mrs. Basset became a Methodist to the extent of startling her children at this point with a very distinct " Amen ! "

Financially, New Canton looked like a field after a ten months' drought. Men gathered in knots, and talked and swore; and the bars of the hotels and of the groceries did a larger business than ever.

What was to become of New Canton? Who now could sell lots? Who could catch the Eastern fly? Who could bring capital to New Canton? Where was its growth to come from, now that Burt, the head, brains, and inspiration of the project, was gone? How were the innumerable speculators, who had " gone into real estate " at almost any price, knowing that, under the Burt forcing process, they could get out any day at an advance, to save themselves?

Lots dropped the first day ten per cent.; the second, twenty; the third, fifty; and, the fourth day, they could not be given away. The bottom had dropped out.

New Canton was doomed.

The Colonel, Peak, and Sharp called a meeting to "consider the state of affairs and to devise the best way of meeting the troubles; " and they appointed the great hall of the " Burt Institute " as the place of meeting. Sharp and Peak declined to attend; but Col. Peppernell, who was not afraid of his fellow-citizens, went alone, as the representative of the land company.

He displayed on the walls of the institute all the maps which he had taken from the land-office, with all the railroads branching: he showed New Canton as the center of an area of five hundred miles; and he had every thing to prove that nothing could come amiss to the great enterprise. He worked himself into a perspiration, and made a speech.

" Men of New Canton," he shouted, " what ef Burt hez run away! Did he take the town with him? Did he take the Midland, the Grand Pacific, and the Trans-Continental?"

" He wood hev took 'em ef they hed bin here," shouted a disgusted investor in those enterprises.

" I will not be interrupted!" shouted the Colonel, fiercely. " Did he take the additions the land company laid out?"

" I wish he had, and left the money!" shouted another.

" Above all, did he take with him the enterprise uv the citizens of Noo Canton? Did he take with him that indomitable energy, that far-seeing sagacity, that immense recooperative power which enables the man uv the West to rise superior to misfortune, and go upward and onward, confident in his strength and serene in his power? No! A thousand times no! And Noo Canton will go on. It will realize all the anticipations we hev hed uv it. All the hopes that hev bin raised will be fulfilled.

" But we must hev none uv this grumblin', — none uv this half-heartid layin' down over little troubles, — none uv this stumblin' over molehills. Our bank is

THE EFFECT ON NEW CANTON.

bustid. Very good: we must hev another bank. Our land company is embarrassed. Very good: it must be strengthened. Our citizens is short. Very good: they must be helped.

"I took stock in Noo Canton — not Burt. Is the runnin' away of one man to rooin us? I b'leave in Soggy Run, in the railroads, the slack-water, — not in any one man! Men of Noo Canton, let us be up and a-doin'! Times of darkness and distress is when the reel strength uv a man comes out. Yoor fair-weather man is no man for me. When the storms lour, when the litenin's flash and the thunders roll, the man I trust in is he who is on deck, with his hand on the hellum, his eye on the clouds, and his hart filled with the sense of the responsibility onto him. Instid uv mournin' Burt, let us remember that we hev other men left, and that we kin go on and repair the breaches in our Zion, instid uv sittin' down and hangin' our harps on the willows."

Time was when such a speech — a stirring speech, filled with all sorts of oratorical sage and onions — would have set New Canton wild; and, had its purpose been to levy a tax of fifteen per cent. on the valuation, it would have carried it. But it had no effect now. The people jeered and hooted at his allusions to the resources of New Canton; and, when he spoke of the railroads, he was compelled to dodge a quantity of missiles thrown at him, every one of which was unsavory. It took Mrs. Col. Peppernell, a most patient lady, exactly an hour to clean the clothes of the irate Colonel after he had pressed through the mob and reached his home.

He consoled himself by examining a packet in a little iron safe he had in his house. (25)

"One kin stand noomerous eggs and sich for w'at I hev," was his remark to himself. "They can't git at Mrs. Peppernell's property."

Stich, the tailor, went back to his board; and whoever said New Canton to him that afternoon got very short answers, albeit he took in several jobs of mending, which, a day before, he had turned up his nose at. As for Fitzhugh, the shoemaker, there was no job of cobbler work so desperate that he did not accept it; and as it was with these so it was with all.

CHAPTER XXXI.

THE TROUBLE THAT CAME UPON THE GARDINERS.

THE calamity bore down upon the Gardiners with terrible force. Their hope for months had been in the success of Mr. Burt's enterprise; and, now that Burt had carried away so much of the scant capital left, they were in a critical condition.

Could they keep their situation from the people?

The old man went to his home with the hope that, if his actual condition could be kept from the public knowledge, he could yet sail through, or, at least, keep in business till he could save something from the wreck. He still had the confidence of people, for he had done nothing to forfeit it. He did not know that his losses were as well known to his neighbors as they were to himself — that they were discussed before the butter had fairly melted on the buckwheats at their tables, and that, while sympathy with him might do something, there was no hope from concealment.

Long and anxious was the interview that he had with his son, before he retired to his sleepless pillow that night.

"How bad is it, father?" asked James.

"As bad as it can be. I can't do any thing with the land of the company; for the bottom is out of that, and lots can't be sold now for the acre price before Burt came. If the people would only give me time to go on, something could be made by using your mother's property and — "

"What grandmother left me," said Jim. "All right. I'll throw in all I have."

"But, Jim, what shall we do to-morrow? There is certain to be a run on me, and then it's all up."

"How much currency have you in the safe?"

"Ten thousand dollars."

"What securities have you?"

"Possibly fifteen thousand more."

Jim looked at his watch uneasily.

"Father, there is just one thing to do. If they make a run on you, you must meet it. If they come in the morning, we must be there, and pay out dollar for dollar till we have got to the end. Possibly, after the people have seen us pay a dozen with a good face, the rest will let us alone. But go down with me to the bank and give me those securities."

"What for?"

"This night I shall go to our friends, — if we have any, — and get cash advanced on them. Time is every thing. We can keep the crowd off till night with $25,000, and something may turn up."

The young man assumed the lead without a show of resistance on the part of the elder. The strength in James Gardiner, that had lain dormant so long, began to show itself.

The two left the house — it was yet early — and went to the bank. The securities were taken from the safe; and, before midnight, $15,000 were added to the ten already there, and James and his father went to their troubled rest. Before the minds of both, rose the ghost of murdered credit and hopeless bankruptcy. There were groans in plenty from the bed of the old man, which even the tender consolations of his old wife could not mitigate.

They had not calculated on the sleepless hatred of one man. This was Tom Paddleford's opportunity, and he improved it. No man living knew better how to do a mean thing, and no one more delighted in that kind of work.

While the Gardiners, father and son, were working to avert disaster, he had been very busy to assist it. The night of the closing of the land company's offices he followed a farmer out of his store, who lived twenty miles away, and, in a whisper, asked him if he had any money in Gardiner's.

"Money in Gardiner's? No. What do you want to know for?"

"Nothing. Only I don't want to see you lose. Old Gardiner lost $50,000 in New York and twice that in the land company. Don't say a word to anybody. I don't want to hurt them; but I wanted to put a flea in your ear, to save you if you had any thing there. Don't say a word to anybody; for Gardiner is a good man, and I wouldn't hurt him for the world."

This farmer lived twenty miles north. He said the same thing to one who lived south, to one who lived east, and to one who lived west. When he had done this, he went back into the store, with an infernal chuckle on his ugly countenance.

"The Gardiners will smell woolen before noon tomorrow," he said to himself.

What Mr. Thomas Paddleford intended happened exactly, which showed that he knew mean human nature to a dot.

Each one of these farmers rode home, full of a secret which would give them some consequence in their little worlds, as men who were posted in "town."

This conversation occurred everywhere on the road : —

"Simpson, did you know old Gardiner is in a bad way?"

"No. Is he?"

"He lost $75,000 in New York and over a hundred thousand in the land company. He's busted, shoor. I drawed what I hed in his bank this afternoon."

Mr. Paddleford did not stop here. For convenience, he had an account at Gardiner's; and, at precisely nine in the morning, he was seen very conspicuously on the street walking to the bank.

He was bareheaded and breathless; but he found time to stop and speak to everybody willing to talk with him.

He was going to Gardiner's, to draw out his balance. He hoped it was all right. The Gardiners were good men; but it was every man's duty to look out for himself. He was not such a fool as to leave money in the hands of men reckless enough to make such large losses. He didn't want to do any thing to hurt the Gardiners; but no man could stand up under such blows, and there wasn't any use of his taking other men down with him.

This kind of talk he peddled out from one end of the town to the other, to everybody who had a dollar in the bank and to those whom he knew would talk to depositors he couldn't see.

There is nothing so sensitive as credit; for there is nothing earthly so good as a dollar; and even those who were friendly to Gardiner became uneasy. Before ten o'clock, depositors were dropping in to draw money, for they all had pressing need of it; and it was a singular fact, that they had pressing need of just the amount of their balances.

Jim Gardiner was behind the counter with his father, and he smiled bitterly as Tom Paddleford drew his balance. He smiled another bitter smile as Lewis bustled in, with a half apology, and took out his.

"Father," said he, in a low tone, "there is no disguising it: there is going to be a run, and that little devil, Paddleford, has set it on foot. Pay out as slow as you can, delay all that is possible; but pay."

They came, first, single; then, by twos; then, by dozens. In an hour, the little bank was crowded with anxious people, hustling, crowding, pushing, and swearing. Men came from twenty miles, on horses foam-flecked and exhausted with hard riding, and elbowed their way through the crowd to the little window, with their books and their certificates, demanding their money.

The men outside, who could not force their way into the room, were howling like Comanche Indians, and elbowing and pushing backward to keep from being mashed into jelly.

It was a curious fact, that those who had no money in the bank howled the loudest; and those who never had a cent there, or anywhere else, where most furious in their denunciations of thieves who had robbed the people.

It could not last long. At noon every dollar was gone.

"It's all gone, Jim," said the old man, with a shiver. "What next?"

"This," said Jim, coming to the front, and shutting down the window. He waved his hand to the crowd.

"Hang them!" yelled an excited man near the door, who had been vainly endeavoring to force his way through the crowd. "Hang the swindlers!"

"You'd better not try it," said Jim, springing upon the counter and looking defiance at the angry mob. "Some of you would suffer before you got either my father or myself with a rope about our necks. We are not swindlers, and you know it. Tom Follett, my father set you up in business, and has carried you all these years. You owe him to-day more money than your carcass is worth; or would owe, if he made you pay a half that you should have paid. I've known you to come and beg like a dog for money to buy stock, when your note wasn't worth the paper it was written on and you couldn't give security for the price of a shoe-peg. You have in the bank here now twelve dollars and a half; and I'll do what you can't — borrow the money, and pay it. Get out, you hound! If my father hadn't been so generous to you and such as you, he would be able to-day to stand up under the frauds of the thieves who have plundered him.

"We have paid out every dollar in money that we

have in the world, and there are yet $30,000 to be provided for. My father's house and this building are worth half that amount, my mother has some stocks in her own right she inherited from her father, and I have the Oak Grove Farm my old grandfather left me — enough to pay off every dollar of our indebtedness. We have been unfortunate; but we are neither thieves nor scoundrels. Every man of you shall be paid; only those we owe must wait till we can turn ourselves."

The fickle crowd turned in their favor, and poor Follett and other advocates of hanging were very glad to get away with whole skins.

They gave the father and son three cheers; and those who had been foremost in demanding their money offered it back again, and urged the old gentleman to go into business again, or, rather, to go right along as though nothing had happened.

"Old Gardiner was always a good man," was the remark of scores of them; "and Jim is as good as his father."

"I shall never go into business again," was Gardiner's response. "I can find something to do that will take care of my wife and myself; and, as for Jim, he will have to shift for himself. I am too old to commence again. It's hard, at my age; but I shall either die or get used to it."

James Gardiner left the bank sadly and slowly, with the mien of a man who hereafter would be compelled to ask favor of the world instead of demanding it.

Mrs. Lewis was satisfied; for she had proved herself to be a prophet, and the consciousness was more to her than the ruin of those who had never injured her.

Tom Paddleford found his wife in tears, the cause of which she refused to tell him.

CHAPTER XXXII.

MORE FAILURES.

TOM PADDLEFORD was compelled to eat the dirt he prepared for others, sooner than he expected. The excitement of the two preceding catastrophes was mild compared with that which shook the little town when the fact became known, that Paddleford & Son were insolvent, and hopelessly so; and this was followed by the announcement that Mr. Lewis was also hopelessly involved.

New Canton had never had such wealth of excitement before; and, as the most of her prominent citizens had gone into that bourne of bankruptcy from which so few return, it was not likely to have it again for many years.

A dozen tea-parties were given to afford an opportunity of discussing the calamity — its causes and consequences; and it was astonishing how many people there were who never had any confidence in Paddleford & Son, and had always predicted they would fail. Equally astonishing was it to find how many sage men and wise matrons had noticed, for years, in their methods of doing business the seeds of inevitable ruin.

Mrs. Wheeler, the wife of the wagon-maker, got the

reputation of being a very Minerva by producing at her tea a bolt of muslin, which she declared she got yesterday. " Paddleford owed Wheeler $10 for work on his kerridge ; and I made up my mind, yesterday, that I hed better get it out in something we could use. I said to myself, ' We have lost enough by such people ; ' and I wasn't willing to lose any more."

The fact, that she had had the bolt of cloth a month and that she didn't get it of Paddleford at all, was not generally known ; and her guests remarked, as they left her house, " Mrs. Wheeler is a far-seeing woman, and can't be took in."

Scarcely was the sensation caused by the failure of Paddleford fairly at the hight, before the little town was again shaken — if, indeed, it could be said there was enough left of it to shake. It was officially announced, that the Lewises had lost every dollar they possessed.

New Canton stood aghast. The land company, Burt, Gardiner, Paddleford, Lewis! The three wealthiest of her citizens and the only institution she had, all gone ! It was too much.

Old Seth Martin, the worst drunkard of the old sort in the town and a man whose credit never had been able to compass a day's supply of tobacco, leaned against a post, when he heard it, and said, dolefully : " Great heavens ! who next ? After this, I ain't certain of *my* standing ! "

The citizens felt the town was like one of those fabled villages in New Jersey, which sink into caves overnight. No man was chidden for staying downtown nights, though he didn't put in an appearance till the unheard-of hour of half-past eleven. He might count upon his spouse being up and waiting for him, clad in her nightgown and nightcap, with a small woolen shawl over her shoulders, her countenance wreathed in an endearing smile, and a plate of doughnuts ready to munch in comfort, while he told her the news.

From early morn till late after midnight, knots of men gathered wherever a post made leaning comfortable, or a dry-goods box made sitting possible; and the topic was always the failures. Farmers came in from miles around, mechanics stopped their work; and failure was the one theme of talk. The wildest rumors got afloat, and embraced every possible cause of financial distress, from forgery to speculation. Finally, Truth, the slowest moving of all slow-moving things, got out of her well, and aired herself.

Paddleford & Son, who had always operated largely in produce, at the beginning of the land company had joined a Chicago party in an attempt to "corner" wheat, by buying all attainable and holding it for a rise, or, rather, compelling those who had sold wheat to deliver, to buy it of them at their own price. It was a beautiful scheme, and would have made them all rich. But every thing went against them, as every thing generally does against men who attempt to outbid Nature and control the elements. Another ring formed against them, which had more money and wider connections, who sold the Paddleford ring all the wheat it wanted, and had no difficulty whatever in finding the wheat to deliver. It's all very pleasant amusement hunting the tiger; but what if that sleek animal hunts you? Speculation would be very pleasant, if you could only have every thing your own way ; but were there ever a set of acute men who did not find another set just as acute ?

The Paddlefords were actually bankrupt long before Gardiner failed.

The prospect of the ultimate failure of Gardiner at the time of the New York loss gave Tom Paddleford the idea upon which he acted. He was still supposed to be rich, and he knew well enough that Mrs. Lewis would never consent to wedding her daughter with the son of a bankrupt banker ; for Mrs. Lewis loved money as few men do, and was ambitious as Lucifer for herself as well as her daughter. He artfully sowed the seeds of suspicion in her mind, and set her husband on the track to confirm his surmises. He intended to oust Gardiner, and, before the ugly fact of his own failure became known, marry the girl himself, and, with the capital of the Lewises, rebuild the fallen fortunes of his house. Should the Lewis family refuse to put their means into the firm, he would, at least, be sure of a very good living all his life. The position of son-in-law to a moderately wealthy man is not a hard thing for a young man who is fond of luxuries and does not like to work.

Why, then, the failure ?

The night before James Gardiner got Mary's note informing him so piteously that she must marry Tom Paddleford there was a scene in the Lewis house, which it would have been better if Tom Paddleford had witnessed.

Mary was called to the mother's bedroom, where Mrs. Lewis sat, gloomy as a graveyard and severe as the Fates. Then and there the demand was made, that she should at once dismiss all thoughts of marrying Jim Gardiner and prepare herself to receive the addresses of Tom Paddleford.

"Great heavens, mother! Why?"

Then Mary was informed, with much circumlocution, that, with the laudable purpose of doubling their fortune, her mother and father had invested, not only all the money they had, but all they could borrow, in bonds of the North Alaska Railway Company, at 33, which everybody supposed certain of going to par within a year. They were endorsed by the president of the company, the eminent financier, Magnus Plutus, Esq., who had successfully negotiated the bonds of the Government at a time when the bonds were a great deal better than the money the people paid for them, and had thus attained great distinction as a financier in the world of money, and might have failed for ten times the amount he finally did.

In consequence, anything he put his name to was considered perfectly good; and a great many people besides Mrs. Lewis bought North Alaska, in serene confidence that the bonds would go up in a short time to thrice their selling price. Then, they proposed to sell, invest in eighteen per cent. mortgages nearer home, like honest, contented people, and forever after be happy.

But, one day, Magnus Plutus exploded. It was discovered that *he* was the company and all there was of it. Not a mile of the road had ever been built, and the assets were limited. True, there was the land-grant; but, as the land wouldn't support a chipping-bird to the acre, besides the disadvantage of being under snow nine months in the year, that security was hardly desirable.

"But no one knows yet," continued Mrs. Lewis. "If I did not know that Gardiner *must* fail within a few months, I should prefer to have you marry James; for I like him better than Paddleford. But that's impossible. Paddleford is rich. He can redeem the homestead, and can easily support your father and me, not in the style I had hoped to live, but in comparative comfort. It is the best I can do, and it must be done."

Thus spoke Mrs. Lewis, as though the girl had no interest at all in the matter, but was merely the means of giving her father and mother a living.

"But, mother, I can't marry Tom Paddleford. I love Jim Gardiner."

"Would you turn your father and mother out into the streets, you ungrateful girl? What can Jim Gardiner do for you or us? Love, indeed! Bread and butter is the first consideration now."

"But, ma, if I marry Tom Paddleford, I must first tell him our condition."

The girl wanted an escape, and she knew Paddleford would never think of her without the expectation of the fortune.

"Never, child!" exclaimed Mrs. Lewis, in alarm. "Never! You would ruin every thing, you foolish girl. Leave every thing to me. Goodness! How much managing in does take to get on in this world!"

Possibly, Mrs. Lewis would have got on better if she had done less managing. Managing can be overdone.

And, so, after oceans of tears, and protests as vigorous as a girl without much will could make, she was driven to consent to marry the man she hated and jilt the man she loved.

And, womanlike, as she had to do it, she insisted upon its being done at once; for she wanted to put herself and the man she loved out of misery.

After the flight of Burt and the downfall of the Gardiners, when borrowing became impossible, Tom came to the house one morning, and wished to see Mrs. Lewis alone. Mr. Lewis was present; but Mrs. Lewis remarked graciously, that that would make no difference. In her presence, Mr. Lewis never did make any difference.

Thomas opened his business with a great deal of hesitation, for he had learned to fear as well as love his mother-in-law. She was a superior woman.

"Well, Thomas?" said she, encouragingly.

"What I have to say," spoke up Thomas, "concerns your daughter very closely."

"I hope she is in no way a disappointment to you?" queried Mrs. Lewis, wondering what was coming.

"Not at all," was Thomas's answer. "A more delightful girl never lived."

"Well, what is it?"

"Nothing but this," said Tom, determined to get at it at once. "I want you to lend us — that is, Paddleford & Son — $30,000; and, what is more, we must have it."

"In the name of Heaven," gasped Mrs. Lewis, "what do you want of so large an amount?"

"Simply this, mother," replied Tom, who had recovered his composure and some of his audacity (a rat will fight when driven into a corner). "Father and I lost more than we were worth, months ago, in Chicago wheat; and our paper is coming due every day. We have kept afloat by borrowing. If we can get $30,000, we can go on. If not, we go under to-morrow, sure. You don't want a bankrupt son-in-law, do you?"

Mrs. Lewis turned pale. Every thing looked black, and she sought to relieve herself by a series of groans. Mr. Lewis, not less a woman, sat and moaned and wrung his hands. Tom looked on in wonderment, not comprehending this excessive emotion, while Mary alone preserved her composure. In truth, she was rather glad of it; for she saw a distant prospect of an escape from her misery. Very quietly she occupied herself in reviving her mother.

The woman returned to consciousness, and sat in a half-dazed condition in her chair. Finally, she got herself together enough to speak.

"Thomas," she said, at last, regarding him with a stony glare, "we are the most unfortunate of people. You lost your all in Chicago wheat; we lost our all in North Alaska bonds. We've got to all starve together."

"What!" exclaimed Tom.

"We haven't got a dollar. The homestead is mortgaged, and every foot of land we have in the world. It all went in North Alaska bonds."

"What in the name of all that is insane induced you to go into North Alaska? *You*, of all other women! You deceived me cruelly."

"Thomas, what in the name of all that is reckless could have induced you to go into Chicago wheat? *You*, of all other men! — you, who refused to touch the land company! Thomas, you deceived *me* cruelly."

Tom put on his hat with a smash, and, with a smothered curse at everybody and every thing, rushed to the store, where he and his father had a conference, which lasted an hour and involved the looking-over of many books and papers.

There was a shifting of goods, a forced sale of some few lots, for cash only; and, in a few days, the sheriff was in possession.

Jim Gardiner smiled once more. " Now I know," said he to himself, "why Mrs. Lewis threw me, and compelled Mary to marry Paddleford. The old Jezebel! How she did lay down the moralities to me that morning! How pleasant it must be for Tom, who never cared a straw for the girl, when he looks at his bargain! Poor Mary!"

CHAPTER XXXIII.

THE CONDITION OF THE PRINCIPAL FAMILIES OF NEW CANTON.

THIS was the condition of things in the principal families of New Canton: —

They had all been playing for something, and most of them had won the game they had played for.

Those who had won were infinitely worse off than those who had lost.

Mrs. Lewis had lost her all in North Alaska, and had hedged by worrying Mary into marrying Tom Paddleford, that she might live upon his money.

Paddleford had lost his all in wheat, and had hedged by marrying Mary Lewis, that he might live upon her money.

Gardiner had lost his all by the failure of the New York bankers and the scoundrelism of Burt. And his son Jim had lost the girl he should have married.

Paddleford had got the girl, but not a dollar of money; and had a father and mother-in-law on his hands, the latter being especially objectionable.

Mrs. Lewis had sacrificed her daughter to the worst man in New Canton, but had not got the dollars she had expected.

CONDITION OF THE PRINCIPAL FAMILIES.

There was trouble, disappointment, wrong, and anxiety all around; and no one was where they ought to be or in the right place.

Tom Paddleford never loved Mary Lewis. His desire to possess her was merely desire; and, now that he was saddled with her, without money, he absolutely hated her. A woman may be the greatest delight or the greatest curse to a man. To Paddleford, without money, the best woman in the world would have been an insupportable burden. In marrying her by force and fraud, the rat had crawled through a noisome sewer; and what was his cheese worth, now that he had his teeth in it? To him it was an empty rind. Nothing more. The heart of it — the girl's love — he couldn't have appreciated if he had possessed it, and the money he wanted he had not got. For the first, he cared nothing; for the second, he mourned sincerely.

In his altered circumstances, he was compelled to take a situation as salesman in the very store where he had been proprietor.

What galled him was the thought, that he was burdened with a wife whom he hated, when, without her, he might have lived on his salary.

Gone were his enjoyments, his expensive drinks, his fragrant cigars, his glossy hats, his new pantaloons that reduced the curvature of his legs. And, when he paid the board of his wife in very cheap rooms at the Grand Central, and thought, that, were he alone and free, he could live in something like comfort, he cursed her with all the vehemence of a low, mean nature.

Then began a series of annoyances of a petty kind,

admirably calculated to kill the poor girl. Petty men, like Tom Paddleford, can worry and nag, and nag and worry, till the object of their little spite turns upon them. They make the other the aggressor and place themselves in the aggrieved position, which, with such people, is a strong point.

"Where is the hot water?" he growled, one morning. "I don't have so many comforts but I am, at least, entitled to a convenience now and then."

He was shaving, and stood before the glass, with one suspender hanging over his hips.

"There's the water, Tom, right beside you," was the meek answer.

"Hot? Do you suppose a man can shave with water that's lukewarm? What are you good for, anyhow?"

"Tom, I try to do every thing you want of me."

"Every thing! If I hadn't allowed you and your scheming old mother to trap me into marrying a whey-faced, helpless nothing, I shouldn't have to shave in such water. Ah!"

He had dipped his finger in the water, to test its heat, and the exclamation followed the touch.

"What did you have it brought up scalding for? Take that!"

And he threw the water full at her. By adroit dodging, the poor girl escaped being burnt except in a few spots. She had become expert in dodging. She had plenty of practice since she had left her mother's roof.

"Get me some paper!"

The paper was brought.

"Old newspaper! It does seem that you never can

learn any thing. Get me some soft paper, something that won't dull my razor. And — "

By this time, Mary was in tears; and, with the tears, came some little spirit.

" Tom, I won't bear this abuse. I am doing all I can to please you; but you won't be pleased. I'll do nothing more for you."

" You won't? You won't, eh!"

And he approached her, with a monkeyish, malicious glare in his little mean eyes.

" You won't do any thing more for me, will you, you daughter of a miserable fraud? You won't?"

And he approached her, waving the razor in one hand, near enough to frighten her to death, and took a long drink of whisky from a bottle on the bureau, to terrify her more; for she always feared him after one of those terrible draughts.

" Tom! Tom! What are you going to do? Don't, Tom! Don't!"

" Oh, I ain't a-goin' to kill you! I am goin' to administer needful correction. Take that for your impudence!"

And, with the flat of his big, cruel hand, he struck her, first on one side of her cheek and then on the other, till she shrieked with pain and terror.

" Stop that infernal howling," he hissed, in an undertone. " You will have the house up here."

His caution came none too soon; for the landlady, hearing the screams, came to the door to know what was the matter.

" Oh! nothing serious," said Tom, holding the door slightly ajar with one hand, while he delivered a series of admonitory shakings with the other to his wife, cowering in terror out of sight. " Nothing, only Mrs.

Paddleford has been taken with one of her spells. It's nothing."

And, shutting the door, he said to her, "Get up, and behave yourself!" aiding her to rise, with a most vicious kick.

One great trouble with these rat men is, they never know when to stop, unless a fist or a foot is interposed to bar their progress. Poor Mary did not resent his naggings and his beatings; and, as she was profoundly miserable under them, he doubled the dose. He was experimenting to see how wretched he could make her; and he pushed his investigations as far as he could this side of killing her.

It was a favorite method of making her miserable to ask her when she had seen Jim Gardiner last, implying in his tone and manner that it was his belief that she was in the habit of seeing him, and that the interviews were not altogether innocent.

"Gad!" he would remark, "how I wish he had married you. You and the old woman were too sharp for that. You figured his failure as certain, and you didn't want a poor man in the family. You had no notion we could fail, or you wouldn't have roped me in. Why don't you go to him, now, and take yourself off my hands? Why do you make me support you? He sees more of you than I do. Oh! you —"

The epithet he applied to her would not look well upon paper.

And the poor girl, who remembered how it was that she married the little beast and gave up every thing that made life of value, and how gladly she would go to the only man on earth that she ever did love, would go away, and sob as though her very heart was broken.

CHAPTER XXXIV.

WHAT MR. BURT FOUND IN CHICAGO.

HAGGARD and worn, sick at heart and exhausted with excitement, Charles Burt entered the obscure hotel, in the suburbs of the great city, to which he sent Emeline Butterfield three weeks before.

He came in the night. He waited in the outskirts till the darkness enshrouded him. He threaded alleys and dark streets, and skulked under the shadows of walls and dark buildings. It was as though he carried something on his face that he did not dare to expose to the light.

It was not the same Burt who had once presided over the destinies of the land company and the savings-bank. That Burt was a smoothly shaven, decororously dressed man, a man who feared nothing in the form of humanity, and who was noted for being able to look any one squarely in the eye without shrinking. That Burt was a cool, self-possessed man, whose hand never trembled, whose face never blanched, and to whom fear was unknown.

This Burt was quite another man. He was unshaven and unshorn. His clothes hung loosely and shabbily about him. His boots were muddy and broken, as if they had become acquainted with hard and unsavory ways. He was hollow-eyed and wasted; and there was a dodging, blinking, shrinking way about him as unlike the old Burt as daylight is from darkness. He had hardly need to disguise himself. His most intimate friend would scarcely have known him.

He asked for the room of " Mrs. Elwood;" and was shown to it by a hall-boy, who kept the professional eye upon him, as though he thought the shabby, sneaking man needed watching. Alas! that the impressive Burt, before whom clerks had quailed and hall-boys had bowed in the first hotels, should be watched in so small and miserable a tavern as this! He entered the room with an eagerness that was the first show of any thing like manhood he had shown for days. His head was raised, his eyes glittered, his wasted form seemed to dilate and resume something of its old proportions.

In the center of the room stood " Mrs. Elwood," in the person of Emeline Butterfield; and toward her he sprang, with arms extended and a look of intense delight upon his face.

" Emeline!" he exclaimed. " I am here at last and in no further danger. Dear girl!"

Emeline avoided his embrace, and retreated to the furthest extremity of the room.

" Emeline, is this the reception I had a right to expect? What do you mean?"

" Only this, Mr. Burt. I came here because I said I would; and I stayed here till you came because I thought it only right that you should hear from my own lips, rather than upon paper, what I am about to say."

"Don't say it, Emeline! Don't say it!" said Burt, feverishly, anticipating what was coming. "Wait, a day, or two days. Don't say it now."

"I shall say it, and say it now. I have looked for your coming anxiously, that I might say it and have done with it. I shall not leave the country with you, nor shall I go anywhere with you. There will, from this time forward, be nothing between us — nothing. You go your way and I shall go mine."

"But, Emeline," said Burt, fiercely, "you promised me, that night in New Canton, that you would accept my love, that you would go with me, and that, from this time henceforward, you would be to me that love I have longed for so long and found in you. You promised."

"True, I did. And, when I promised, I meant to keep my promise. I was crazy and desperate. The man I loved was too cowardly to stand by me; I had been hunted down by people not as good as myself; my good name had been taken from me; and I saw nothing before me but a life of privation and misery. Every hope I had in the world had been cut out from under me, and every aspiration had been crushed."

"I knew it. I loved you long before I told you so, and swore to do for you, myself, what others had left undone. I would do for you what Gardiner would have done had he been man enough to have appreciated you."

"Very true; and, when you came to me that night, and told me you loved me and would be to me what James Gardiner should have been, I was desperate enough to promise any thing to anybody that would enable me to take vengeance upon those who had persecuted me, and inflict pain upon those who had deserted me when they should have stood by me. I wanted to hurt Gardiner; for he loves me, notwithstanding he dared not marry me, and I knew that to elope with you would be the severest punishment I could inflict upon him. And so I consented, and did leave New Canton, and did come here, intending to carry out my promise, as we agreed; and here I have stayed."

"Then why not fulfill your promise? Gardiner is yet in New Canton; and, the moment the Paddlefords go down, — which they will, — he will take back the girl who, loving him, married Tom. Why not, Emeline?"

"I have had some days of rest and time for reflection. I will not throw myself away. I do not love you, and I never did. I did have a respect for you; for you are different from the other men I have known, and I have gratitude for the kindness you showed me, no matter what the motive was: but to carry out your purpose would be to make me miserable for life; and I am not the kind of a woman who would suffer alone. I am too good a woman for the purpose you desire, and it is impossible that our connection should ever be any thing else. I would not marry you were you free, and nothing less will do for me. We will end the matter here."

"Emeline, do you know what you are doing? Do you want to make me miserable for life? Do you want to wreck the dearest hope of my life and make me utterly miserable? No, Emeline, you cannot. You will go with me. You will try and love me. I will be every thing to you. I will —"

Emeline regarded him with a pitying look, that Burt took as a sign of relenting.

"You will not cast me off, Emeline. I beg you to relent. You do not know what you are doing."

"What I have said, I shall do. My decision is irrevocable and cannot be changed. You must go and leave me."

"But what will you do?"

"I do not know. I am here in a great city. have will and energy, and I shall make my way. Here I shall stay, and do what seems best for me. You will go abroad, as you designed, — alone. I have no wish for you that is not good; only our paths must be widely apart. I shall never see you after to-night."

Burt looked once more at the girl, as she stood before him, to see if he could not detect some sign of relenting, some possibility of a change. There was none. Cool and determined, he read his fate in her face. Then, as he looked at the queenly woman standing before him, and felt that the one hope of his life was leaving him, passion and rage filled him. He sprang toward her, and grasped her fiercely by the wrist.

"Emeline, you shall not leave me! you shall go with me! I have risked every thing for you — for you I have lost my good name and made myself a felon. I love you too much to let you go; and, if I did not, I would not be cheated in this way. You must go with me."

The grasp on her wrist tightened, as the passion that had supreme control of the man welled up into his face.

"Let me go," she said.

"I will not."

"Help! help!" she shrieked.

There were footsteps on the stairs, and Burt came to himself. Releasing his grasp upon Emeline, he sprang to the door. There were three or four men of the hotel on the stairs. Dashing through them, with a curse on his lips and an expression of fright on his face, he plunged out into the night again. Frightened — yes, frightened. This, the dearest of his hopes, the one great thing in his life, that for which he had waited and schemed, — that, without which he would scarcely have taken the great risk he had, had failed him. Would not the rest of his ambitions crumble the same way? Was not this failure the precursor of others? Was he to get any thing for his labor and his planning and plotting, after all?

Back again, through alleys and by-streets, hugging walls and enveloping himself in shadows, the miserable man went, until he had gained the open country. He was alone on the prairie. No, not alone. There was with him his crime and, what was more terrible to him, his disappointment. He was doomed never to be alone again; for, go where he might, there would always be with him the twin ghosts, Remorse and Disappointment. He had lost his standing in the world. He had, so far as his entity could ever do him any good, died; for there was henceforth to be no Charles Burt on the face of the earth.

His old mother, back in Connecticut, who had been so proud of him and who had hoped for such great things of him, would weep when she thought of him; and his brothers, poor and humble as they were, would thank Heaven that they were not like him. The curses that the poor of New Canton, whom he had robbed, had hurled after him found him in the night, as far away as he was and as dark as it was. No distance could prevent their following him. There could be no darkness so dense that they would not find him; and they struck in leaden showers upon his bruised heart, and turned him cold. The one thing that was nearest and closest to him had slipped away from him, beyond his grasp.

There was with him what he could not get rid of — a gnawing, hungering love which he could never enjoy. He had sold himself to the Devil, and had been cheated out of his price. All he had was the package of money in his bosom. And what was that to him, as he was? He could not use it for his ambitions, for there were none that a felon could pursue. It would simply give him the means to prolong a life, which had now become a burden to him, and for which his two hands had always been sufficient. On he went, through the night, like a second Cain, never to know peace and happiness again.

The girl, after his departure, drew a long sigh; and a happier expression than she had worn for weeks came to her face.

"Thank God that I had strength enough to do as I did. Now, my new life will commence; and I will make it one worthy of a woman. I will find my way; and, God helping me, I will yet have what I have always hoped for."

She left the hotel the next morning.

CHAPTER XXXV.

WHAT HAPPENED TO TOM PADDLEFORD.

TOM PADDLEFORD was going to the dogs at break-neck speed. His money gone, he had nothing to give him hold upon his old associations. He took to drink, finding in rum the only solace of his life.

Jim Gardiner saw Mary frequently, and his sharp eye took in the situation at once.

"The little rat is abusing her, is he?" he said to himself. "He is beating her. He tears her hair. I saw the bruises on her temple, and I saw where he had pulled her hair out by handfuls. Tom Paddleford, I did a foolish thing once, which you profited by. I will undo as much of it as possible. You shall never strike her again."

Tom was increasing his brutalities day by day. He would go out, and fill himself with the new whisky of the region, which seems to have been made expressly for wife-beaters, and come back, and nag and nag, till the little courage that was in his wife would assert itself, and extort some outburst that gave him an excuse for striking her.

One night he was more than usually vicious. His employer had reprimanded him, in the presence of his fellow clerks, and, while he was about it, had taken occasion to tell him, that, if he did not quit drinking and make himself less obnoxious to people generally and keep himself in better case and attend more strictly to his business, with all the other things that employers delight to say to poor devils who cannot get away from them, he would be obliged to discharge him.

Now this, said in the presence and hearing of the very men over whom he had once shaken his rod and to whom he had said the same thing a thousand times, galled him to the quick.

He came home that night in a fearfully ugly mood. If he had hated his wife before, he hated her now with ten-fold intensity. He was as full of venom as a rattlesnake, and as blind as to whom to visit it upon, provided the object was weak enough to make it safe.

So ugly was he that she did resist him with some little vigor. Desperation gave her strength; and, when he struck her, she flew at him, and, departing from her usual custom, screamed for help. Wise would he have been had he stopped then and there. But fate is always against a fool.

At that very moment, Jim Gardiner was walking through that corridor, from the room of a sick friend. He knew the cry and knew the cause of it.

Never was a cry for help more quickly answered. The door banged open, and Tom Paddleford went to the floor. When he sat up, he found Jim Gardiner standing over him, with his fists clenched and his eyes blazing.

Tom struggled to his feet.

"What business have you in my room?" he demanded, blue with rage.

In another instant, he was on his back again, and Jim Gardiner was on his knees, not exactly in the attitude of prayer. He had a knee outside of Paddleford's body, and in each hand he grasped one of his long ears, and bumped the head of the prostrate wretch with all the power he could command. Each bump was accompanied with appropriate remarks.

"Business in your room!" (bump). "I've heard you abuse that woman" (bump) "for a week, which is just long enough for any man, even if he didn't happen to care any thing for her. If I let you up alive now" (bump), "it will only be to have the pleasure of killing you at leisure" (bump, bump). "Get up, you dog, and remember what I say to you. I shall always be within ear-shot of this room, when you are in it; and, if I ever hear a word that is not kind to that woman, or ever know of your laying a finger on her, I'll kill you" (bump, bump). "Do you hear me? I'll kill you" (bump); "I'll kill you!"

And Jim, lifting Tom up, left him dazed and bewildered, not knowing which he hated most, his wife or her champion.

It was impossible that an event, which had in it all the elements of a scandal, should be kept quiet in a village like New Canton. The landlady of the hotel was discreet; but landladies are always in the vicinity of whatever scandals occur under their roof-trees. She was at the door while Gardiner was teaching Paddleford a lesson in decency, and heard the quarrel. Being a woman, and over forty-five, can it be wondered that she confided it to her sister, and that it was over the town in less than twenty-four hours? Paddleford's fellow clerks noticed the bruises on his face, and asked the cause; and his employer reprimanded him for appearing at the store in such a state.

That evening, in his cups, Paddleford cursed Gardiner, and made a threat against him, which was virtually a confession of the precise facts in the case. And, when he was drawn out by experienced drinkers like Peppernell, he inveighed against a man who could come into another man's room, and interfere between man and wife.

He found himself the butt of the town, and could not avoid it. Mischief-making men advised him every hour to wipe out the disgrace that Gardiner had put upon him, and, in his cups, he threatened to do it; but, in the morning, his courage evaporated, and, if any thing were necessary to finish the evaporation, it would be a sight of Gardiner's burly figure and a remembrance of the force of his blows, which he had twice felt.

He became more and more miserable every day. Those who had been his friends when he had money dropped away from him now that he had none; and the poorest and meanest of the loafers of the town jeered at him.

"It's nateral," said the philosophical Pilkin. "It's nateral. There are men whose conversation is worth their likker; but, ef a man like Tom Paddleford can't pay for yer rum, w'at does anybody want him about for? Every man must be good for suthin'. I am a-goin' to cultivate myself, so ez to have suthin' to fall back upon agin the time I go under."

Mr. Paddleford could not endure this kind of a life. To be a servant where he had been master was bad enough; but to be a complete outcast, shunned by everybody, was too much; and one night he managed to rob the safe of all the money there was in it, and left for parts unknown.

The robbery was large enough to have given him a term in the penitentiary, and Gardiner took the steps to have him properly indicted, the people said to make the procuring of a divorce more easy.

No careful pursuit was ever made; for, when he had got away and people remembered the peculiar circumstances under which he labored and the indignities put upon him, a little pity sprang up for him.

"Ef he never comes back," said Pilkin, " then we kin afford to lose the money. Four hundred dollars to git shet uv Tom Paddleford is cheap."

And he was heard no more of in New Canton.

CHAPTER XXXVI.

WHICH IS THE LAST.

PROCEEDINGS for a divorce between Thomas and Mary Paddleford were begun within a day of the flight of Thomas, James Gardiner, Esq., appearing for the plaintiff; and it is unnecessary to occupy paper in saying, that, within an hour after the decree was obtained, Mary Lewis and James Gardiner were united in the bonds of holy matrimony. Mrs. Lewis was averse to so much haste, for she still desired her daughter to marry more money than Jim Gardiner had or was likely to have for some time; but, to her surprise, she found that her daughter had some will of her own.

"I married once, mamma, to please you; I shall marry this time to please myself. And, besides, I don't see that you did any better in marrying me than I would have done."

So they were married; and James, having no rich father to bolster him up, and having a wife to care for as well as his father and mother, became at once a hard-working lawyer. There was no case that had a five-dollar fee in it he would not take hold of, and the day had not enough hours in it for him. Much to the disgust of the other lawyers in the town, he attended so closely to his business, that, in a year's time, he had the leading practice and was in a fair way to realize all the hopes that Mrs. Lewis originally had of him.

Was he happy? Yes, after a fashion. He could have wished at times,—though he never allowed it to dwell in his mind,—that his Mary had had some of the wit and some of the strong sense of his second love; but, as that was gone and hopeless, he was tolerably content. At times, the dark hair, the sweet eyes, the clear mind of the girl he had deserted came to him, and he sighed, "It might have been." He found, as he grew older, that public opinion was not such a giant as he once thought; and that, if he had married Emeline and made the success he was making, the world would have made up with them in three months. But, as that was all gone, as Emeline was no one knew where, and as he was the husband of Mary, he turned to his books and his cases and strove to forget, and succeeded tolerably well. There is no such Lethe as work, especially when it is successful.

Was Mary happy? Of course she was. She had for her husband the great, broad-shouldered man she had always loved, and he was kind and good to her; and, if he fell into fits of musing and drew long sighs, she ascribed it to his business cares. She was fortunate, in his discretion and kindness, that he never permitted her to know the reason. Her father and mother were nicely established in a pleasant cottage, and they were living very comfortably. Mrs. Lewis volunteered to come and live with them and take charge of their house; and the only difference they ever had was on that occasion. Mary was decidedly in favor of it; but James objected with such vehemence and vigor as to bring on tears. Mrs. Lewis said he was a brute, and flung herself indignantly out of the house, and vowed that she would never set foot in it again. James replied, that he had sufficient strength to endure even that desertion, and it ended. Mrs. Lewis predicts his failure, and ascribes whatever of success he has to her council and advice; but tells her friends, confidentially, that he is a close, selfish man, who does not appreciate the blessings Providence has showered upon him.

Peppernell! Gorgeous Peppernell! On a splendid farm, stocked with the choicest cattle and the finest horses, lives the great Peppernell. It is in his wife's name; and the creditors of the land company and savings-bank have tried to get at it, in vain. He passes his time at Pilkin's (the Grand Central and Continental are no more), and inveighs loudly against Burt, who he declares ruined him and the town as well. But the people declare that he was as deep in the mire as Burt was in the mud, and, if he did not get his full share of the swindle, it was because of Burt's superior shrewdness. He has friends, as any man may have who is willing to pay for unlimited rum; but, among the good people of New Canton, Col. Peppernell has lost caste. He ran for an office once, but was so ignominiously beaten that he gave up all idea of ever taking his old place again, and contented himself with what money he has and what it would bring him.

Mrs. Burt was left with a competency in her own name; and, as no one connected her in any way with her husband's transgressions, she lives as she always did. She never doubted the devotion of Charles to her, but believes that Peppernell, Sharp, and Peak inveigled him into speculations that ruined him, and that it so preyed upon his mind that it drove him away, even from her. She consumes more medicines than formerly, to keep her spirits in any thing like working order.

In Brussels — Belgium being a country which has no extradition treaty with the United States — there was seen for a time a wan, pale-faced man, known among the few who knew him at all as Mr. Elwood. He was a nervous man, who scanned very closely all the Americans he met in public places, and made no acquaintances with people from the Northwestern States. He was a full-bearded man, with luxuriant whiskers and moustaches, and dressed in the English style. He had a trick of starting uneasily when any one came into the room where he was sitting, as though perpetually on his guard against being surprised.

It so happened one day, that, in a public hall, an American observed him closely, and walked up to him, despite Mr. Elwood's desire to avoid him.

"Burt, is this you? Heavens! how you have changed! I should hardly have known you. What do you keep so close for? Don't you know me? Hawkins, Chicago. I am here for a little trouble I had. You needn't fight so shy. They can't take you back from here. I don't back down, as you do. I am here in my own name. Of course, the nice people know all about my trouble, and keep clear of me; but there are lots of good fellows who don't care a straw, so you have the ducats to pay your way. Why, Burt, we have a little club here, made up of gentlemen in trouble, who left their country for its good; and roaring times we have, I assure you. It's jolly."

The coarser thief slapped him upon the shoulder and rallied him upon his down-heartedness.

"Did my leaving make much stir?" asked Burt, tremulously.

"Of course it did. It was in all the papers as the cutest thing for years. You got out so easily and so neatly and got away with the plunder so nicely. And then the wonderful girl you carried away with you! By the way, is she here? She was pretty enough to make a sensation in this place. What do you keep her mewed up so closely for?"

Burt rushed away without the courtesy of a parting salute. He a fit man to be proposed as a member of a club of defaulters! He the associate of a low scoundrel like Hawkins! And the allusion to Emeline, for whom, more than for any thing else, he had brought this degradation upon himself; and she as far from him as though death had taken her. It was too much.

The next day, he found Hawkins had evidently made him known to the frequenters of the public places, and his identity was known. He was stared at everywhere; significant looks were cast at him, and eyeglasses were leveled, and the common courtesies that strangers pay each other were denied him.

He would not go among thieves, and he was barred from every one else. He left Brussels; and, assuming another disguise, went to Paris. He was allowed but little quiet there. Disguise himself as he would, he found plenty who knew him. London was no better, Berlin could not hide him, and he wandered from one city to another; but wherever he went his sin found him out. He could not go home, for there were indictments against him which he dare not face; and he wandered, an outcast and pariah. He lived, for he had invested his stealings well; but all that he desired to live for was gone. Existence of the loneliest and most miserable kind was all that was left him.

In a poor hotel in a small village in Germany, a wasted, faded man was lying sick. The physicians were puzzled to know the disease that was taking him to his grave, and they prescribed entirely at random. One night he had a long interview with an American who happened to be at the hotel, — there were some sort of medicinal springs there, — and many papers were drawn up and signed, with the array of witnesses that the law in all countries makes necessary. He died the next morning, and was buried, at his own request, without a tombstone to show what fragment of mortality was left in his grave. But, some weeks after, Mrs. Burt's attorney in New Canton, received letters from an American attorney in Germany, enclosing papers necessary to draw a large amount of money, with instructions to pay certain sums to a number of poor people in New Canton, who had lost their all in the failure of the savings-bank. This sum did not make them good, but it was a help to most of them; and, though the attorney kept the secret, it was generally understood that the defaulter, in his last moments, had done this act of justice to those whom he had defrauded. And so his memory came not to be universally execrated; for a death-bed repentance was accounted as better than none at all, and they could all recollect instances of generosity in him when he was among them and all-powerful. Had they known how great the price he paid for his sin, and how much he suffered, and in what bitterness he repented of it, they would have cherished still less feeling against him. The poorest woman he despoiled enjoyed more of life in her abjectest poverty than he did with all the money he carried away with him.

When the last events narrated in this history were well-nigh forgotten, Jim Gardiner, now a prosperous lawyer, had business in Chicago. He was walking one of the principal streets, when, turning a corner, he came full upon a lady, who started back, when her eyes met his, as though she would avoid him. It was too late; they recognized each other.

"Emeline!"

"James!"

He spoke in a tone that had in it much of the tenderness of old days. In her voice there was a perceptible quaver, as though her old love, half-forgotten, had at once sprung into life, as something that could not die.

"Emeline, you here in Chicago?"

"Yes, I am in Chicago, and have never been anywhere else since I left New Canton."

"May I ask —"

"How I am living and what I am doing?" she

said, with a lightness that was more than half assumed. "I was teacher in a primary school till I fitted myself for something better. Then I taught music, and I have had more success than I expected."

"Not more than you deserve, Emeline, I am sure."

There was increased tenderness in his tone.

"No; for I worked very hard. I had every thing to contend with. The people have been very kind to me, and I have worked through. My father died. My mother sold our little farm, and we have a little place here, and are very comfortable and happy. Tommy has a place in a wholesale house, and is doing well."

"*Are* you happy, Emeline?"

She turned upon him a quick, inquiring glance. Did he ask to have her say that his desertion of her had made her unhappy, and that she still mourned for him?

"Happy? I am contented. I owe no one for what I am and what I have. Those who might have helped me when I needed it most left me when it came near enough to killing me."

James winced under this; but Emeline affected not to notice it, and went on.

"I am contented; for I owe no one for what I have. I have my little ambitions to employ my time; my books, my music, my friends, my brother and mother; and, I suppose, I am happier than most people. I never injured any one, and never left any heart-aches behind me; and I am happy, as the world goes. I hope you can say as much."

"Yes," was the reply; but it was said very slowly, and in a tone that gave it the lie. He looked at the woman before him a moment, as though there was something on his lips that he would have said; but he restrained himself. Bidding her good-bye, with some incoherent words that he would call upon her when he had more time, he went hurriedly away.

"What a magnificent woman! And what a fool I was!" he said to himself.

Emeline looked after him as his figure faded out of her sight, and sighed as she walked to her home.

The right man does not always find the right woman; and, if he does, he does not always know it.

With the flight of Burt, New Canton evaporated into thin air. The houses built under his stimulating influence were either moved to a village which sprang up on the Branch, some miles distant, or silently and ingloriously rotted to the ground. The streets which had been laid out and graded were surrendered to prairie grass; though for years (locust lasting a long while) posts remained, with boards bearing the names of "Magnolia Avenue," "Poplar Street," and "Burt Street," monuments of the futility of human calculations and expectations. As Mr. Gardiner, Sr., passed by these posts when he took his walks abroad, his face would give way to a dry smile. "If I was a fool," he would say to himself, "I was in excellent company."

The organs were taken out of the churches and sold to pay their debts; the furnaces were removed, and the good old ten-plate stoves replaced, which, ugly as they were, had the merit of warming the auditorium; and, as the new clergyman, with white hands and the expansive forehead, took flight as soon as disaster struck the village, good old Parson Latimer was installed in his old place. He wanted the platform removed, and the old hencoop pulpit put back; but, as it would put a burden upon the overloaded people, he said he would get on as it was for awhile. He didn't ask much salary; but, as some one had given him a new breech-loading fowling-piece during his absence, and as fish were plenty in Soggy Run, he thought he could get on. The first time he went a-fishing, he remarked, as he showed, with rather more pride than becomes a clergyman, his string of shiners, that he believed the days of manna were not over, if you only know where to find it and how to get it.

In his first sermon, he dwelt perhaps unnecessarily upon the sin of being puffed up and the deceitfulness of appearances. But who could blame him? And the tea-parties he had at his house and at Gardiner's again with all "the old set" were as delightful as they were innocent. He professed that New Canton was quite large enough for him, and that there were more sinners there already than he could care for.

Society received a terrible back-set. Receptions, parties, and all that sort of thing went out as suddenly as they came in; and the old-fashioned teas, sewing-circles, choir-meetings, and church-sociables took their places. Singular as it may seem, the people enjoyed themselves once again, and, in their simple way, were happy.

Soggy Run is Soggy Run still. Its placid waters have never borne upon their bosom any craft more ambitious than the frail canoe of the youth who fish for mud-pouts, or the water-fowl at whom Jim Gardiner, when he can spare the time, and Parson Latimer, when he gives a tea-party, takes an occasional shot. Steamers bearing the wealth of the Farther Ind have never yet vexed its waters, and there is no prospect that they ever will.

The "Continental" and the "Grand Central" are deserted, and are gradually subsiding into the soft soil on which they were built. The doors have become askew, the cheap paint has worn off, and children wake the echoes in their deserted halls. Pilkin has reopened the little old tavern of ante-Burt times, and he finds it quite large enough for the trade of the town.

Gone are the milliners, the mantua-makers, the "artists," the "Tattersalls," the "depositories," the "pharmaceutical establishments," the "palaces," and the other things peculiar to small and ambitious cities; and in their places are a much smaller number of plain dressmakers, photographers, stores, and people and things of that description — less airy, but doubtless more useful. The "tonsorial parlors" have subsided into barber-shops, the "saloons" into groceries. The mighty are fallen indeed.

There was as sudden an exodus as there was an influx, and New Canton has got to be the exact place described in the first chapter of this history.

You may blow up a bubble, but it will be only a bubble. Soap and water will not harden into marble and granite.

THE END.

THE MUCKRAKERS

A series of American novels of Muckraking, Propaganda, and Social Protest

EDWARD BELLAMY
    Equality
ARTHUR BULLARD
    Comrade Yetta
CHARLES W. CHESNUTT
    The Colonel's Dream
WINSTON CHURCHILL
    Mr. Crewe's Career
JAMES FENIMORE COOPER
    The Ways of the Hour
ERNEST H. CROSBY
    Captain Jinks, Hero
REBECCA HARDING DAVIS
    Waiting for the Verdict
IGNATIUS DONNELLY
    The Golden Bottle
MARY EASTMAN
    Aunt Phillis's Cabin; or, Southern Life as It Is
HAMLIN GARLAND
    A Member of the Third House
ROBERT GRANT
    The Orchid
SARAH J. HALE
    Liberia: or Mr. Peyton's Experiments
ROBERT HERRICK
    The Common Lot
RICHARD HILDRETH
    The Slave; or Memoirs of Archy Moore
JOSIAH G. HOLLAND
    Sevenoaks
JAMES M. HOPPER & FRED R. BECHDOLT
    9009
FREDERIC C. HOWE
    Confessions of a Monopolist
SYLVESTER JUDD
    Margaret
REGINALD W. KAUFFMAN
    The House of Bondage